The Diver
and the Lover

The Diver
and the Lover

JEREMY VINE

CORONET

First published in Great Britain in 2020 by Coronet
An Imprint of Hodder & Stoughton
An Hachette UK company

I

Copyright © Jeremy Vine 2020

The right of Jeremy Vine to be identified as the
Author of the Work has been asserted by him in accordance
with the Copyright, Designs and Patents Act 1988.

This book is a work of fiction. Although some characters and events are real,
they have been used fictitiously by the author.

A CIP catalogue record for this title is available from the British Library

Hardback ISBN 9781529308433
Trade Paperback ISBN 9781529308440
eBook ISBN 9781529308464

Typeset in Stempel Garamond by Palimpsest Book Production Ltd,
Falkirk, Stirlingshire

Printed and bound in Great Britain by Clays Ltd, Elcograf S.p.A.

Hodder & Stoughton policy is to use papers that are natural, renewable
and recyclable products and made from wood grown in sustainable forests.
The logging and manufacturing processes are expected to conform to
the environmental regulations of the country of origin.

Hodder & Stoughton Ltd
Carmelite House
50 Victoria Embankment
London EC4Y 0DZ

www.hodder.co.uk

For Rachel, Martha and Anna

AUTHOR'S NOTE

This book is based on a real painting and real events. *Christ of Saint John of the Cross* was painted by Salvador Dali in 1951 in Port Lligat, Catalonia. Soon afterwards it was bought for £8,200 by Tom Honeyman and still hangs in Glasgow's Kelvingrove Art Gallery and Museum, where I have been to see it many times. Dali's masterpiece was inspired by a sketch by Saint John of the Cross, a sixteenth-century Spanish priest, who was accused of blasphemy for drawing the crucified Christ observed from a position above the cross. Because of the cost of the painting, Dr Honeyman's brave decision triggered protests in Scotland. He was forced out of the job he loved three years later.

It is very difficult to estimate the value of the painting today. In 1958 Sotheby's sold what was assumed to be a poor copy of a Leonardo da Vinci for £45. In November 2017, the very same painting, which experts had declared a genuine Leonardo after years of analysis, sold at Christie's in New York with the world watching. The value of that small piece of canvas – two feet high, eighteen inches across – had risen by a factor of ten million in sixty years. The image is called *Salvator Mundi* and it sold for $450,312,500.

How much would Dali's Christ sell for? Thankfully it is not going anywhere near an auction house. It will remain modestly displayed in the Kelvingrove, where a small label beside it says the American stuntman Russell Saunders was Dali's model. He was hung from a gantry in the studio so the artist could see the effects of the pull of gravity on his body.

In my story I have tried to make sure the details of Russell Saunders' life (1919–2001) and career are correct, although the events surrounding the painting are mainly fiction. Mr Saunders never married and had no children. I hope he might have enjoyed reading this story.

PROLOGUE

You Had One Job
Glasgow, 2001

He sat for a full hour, frozen. Each time his hand reached forward for the keys, Craig Maskell sniffed disconsolately and pulled it back again. Three cups of tea had been brewed and drunk while he stared at the vacant screen. At one point he forcibly struck the letter G and held his finger down on it, watching a long ggggggggggggggggggggggggg stretch before his eyes like a caterpillar. He jabbed the delete button and saw the caterpillar shrink to nothing. Frustrated and upset, he even found himself blinking back a tear.

Maskell was not a man at ease with outward displays. The museum guard had always been a single man with no wife or wider family, and was a little jealous of those who had such things. He had always seen emotion as self-harm. But now the grief and guilt would not leave him alone.

The Microsoft computer's clunky hard drive chattered away as if gossiping about him. *You had one job*, he thought. Since being sent home he had simply sat at this desk, hand hovering over the keyboard buttons, dreading the moment when the cursor blinked and the blank screen demanded the written explanation for his failure.

The cat sidled up to his trouser leg and brushed against his calf muscle as if out of concern. 'Food time is it, Jagger?' Maskell grunted without looking down. 'Let me just get this started first. Jesus, I have to get this started.'

His spectacles had slid to the end of his nose. He sighed loudly and wondered why he was bothering to write anything at all. Certainly they would blame him. He knew there would have to be – that phrase from old movies he watched as a child – a fall guy. He should have been aware that this kind of thing always ended up with an inquiry. The inquiry would reveal just how many warnings there had been. How much he, personally, had ignored. For God's sake, in two months she had made at least thirty visits! How many times had she been alone in the room with the painting? He should have turned down that bloody promotion in the spring.

For years Craig Maskell had been able to choose any moment to walk into that oblong room and stand opposite the most powerful painted image he had ever seen. Often he was alone and simply drank in the splendour. Experts be damned – Maskell, poorly educated as he was, with a pitiful collection of Scottish O-Grades sat in the eighties, knew every inch of that canvas. Every pock and groove in the oil. Not just every brushstroke but every hair on every stroke. And he knew what it all meant, because he knew what it meant to him.

Only now that it was too late did he understand that his most important role at the museum had been to protect it.

The words came fully formed as he stared miserably at the computer screen.

'You had one job.'

He added an obscenity under his breath.

The cat reacted by smudging itself on his leg again.

After five minutes spent clicking different icons to shut off the italics and open a blank page, Craig Maskell exhaled a belly-deep sigh and began to type one-fingered.

This statement has been written and signed on each page by Mr Craig F. Maskell, security guard (senior) at the Kelvingrove Art Gallery and Museum, Argyle Street, Glasgow, Scotland, about the outrage involving the painting Christ of Saint John of the Cross.

If he had to give a day when it started – a day and a date and a time and a place – he would have landed on the moment he first saw the old woman in the gallery. He knew now it was 18 June, because it was a Monday and it was the day he began training Tyra Gayle. The young black lady was a new recruit to the security detail. He was taking care to use the right language with her.

'Sometimes we need to be a bit, as it were, undercover,' he said. 'Plain clothes undercover.' Maskell had a large stomach which projected over his belt. He believed that if he let it expand a little inside his uniform while he spoke, the inflation made him more commanding. 'Obviously that may be difficult for you.'

Tyra was at least ten inches shorter, and twenty-five years younger. She was chewing gum, and at his remark her jaw clenched. She peered at him, eyes alight. 'In what sense would it be *difficult*, Mr Maskell?'

'In the sense of you standing out from the . . .' Here he paused, aware of the trap he was falling into. *Standing out from the crowd because of your colour* was the sort of phrase they had banned, and he was keen to ensure his first weeks as supervisor were incident-free. 'There are crowds,' was all he said.

They walked as he spoke. The Kelvingrove, he told her proudly, was by a country mile the best museum in Scotland. Two million visitors a year. Thousands of objects, large and small, artistic and scientific. Everything from a full suit of armour for a horse – a horse! – to the mechanical model of the solar system known as Fulton's Orrery, made by self-educated shoemaker John Fulton two centuries earlier. 'What other place in the world contains a church organ and a Spitfire? I'd like to know.' His job, he told the young woman importantly as he directed her towards the flight of stone steps on the east side, was to keep it all safe.

'Do you have a favourite thing here?' Tyra asked.

'Thing? I wouldnae call it a "thing". An exhibit? Aye, for sure. But I guess you'll reckon me a bit obvious if I tell you.'

A slight pause. 'Not at all.'

'Well, I will show you the piece now. Our most famous artwork. I like to spend at least an hour with it every day.' This made him sound unprofessional, so he added: 'For security.'

Her heels clicked on the steps as they went up. He wanted to tell her now, *You'll be wearing flats tomorrow please, those fancy things could chip the stone*, but he didn't want her fixing him again with that intense stare. Feeling a little pain in his hips as they climbed, Maskell paused with a hand on the heavy balustrade and looked left across the gaping space.

The vaulted interior was enormous, an aircraft hangar made of stone. Visitors milled below them. 'By the way, over there is the Spitfire,' he said, puffing slightly. He pointed as if there was more than one aircraft to choose from. A shaft of light from a leaded window above them caught him full in the face so he could not see her reaction.

His hip throbbed now. 'There, above the elephant. A Spitfire.' It was suspended from the ceiling above the tourists and school-children, invisible wires making it look frozen mid-flight. 'Built in '44 with a Rolls-Royce Griffon 61 engine and a five-blade propeller. It flew with the 602 City of Glasgow Squadron. Mark 21 Spitfire, LA198.'

Still she did not look.

'If you're not interested—'

'No, I was thinking, that could be a line of poetry.'

'What?'

'What you just said. "There, above the elephant, a Spitfire."
It had, I don't know, a rhythm.'

He put his hand up to shade his eyes, frowning at her. This
girl was crackers. 'I'm not aware it rhymed at all!'

A pause. 'So – you want to head on up?'

Maskell nodded reluctantly, disappointed at how long the
pain in his hip needed to settle down. 'I love the smell of a
gallery,' he said, moving up the stairs. 'Like a kind of natural
perfume. The objects breathing in and out, making me think
of a field of bluebells, bright flowers, alive and brimming with
energy. I see this as a living place. The smell is fresh, you know?
It comes to me like colours.' He hated words like 'musty'.
Fugitive specks of dust chased each other in the giant bowl of
light, driven from eight thousand exhibits by the early morning
cleaners, each carrying a signature of the object it had left. He
breathed them in like snuff.

The sun poured in through glass arches above the upper
balcony. White stone made each step echo. 'Every exhibit is a
marvel, Miss Gayle,' said Maskell. 'But chiefly I love just to
move around the space itself. Is it not a wonder? They say this
whole building was put up back to front, and when the architect realised his error he threw himself from the central tower.'
Destroying his own story, he added: 'I believe it is urban myth,
but even so . . .'

He led Tyra Gayle to the small room – higher than it was
wide – and, coming to attention like a soldier, indicated the
canvas Salvador Dali had painted fifty years before.

Fixing his gaze on the image, Maskell could have sworn the

room moved around it. The painting seemed to suck the air from his lungs.

Here it was, the greatest work of art he had ever seen. And here he was, giddy with responsibility, its guardian. He would almost say – *its owner*.

The image in front of him blurred. Snapped back into focus. He inhaled deeply, taking in the odour of the frame and the oil, heart banging.

Only two visitors were there, tall blond men wearing caps. One had his face in a gallery map and was yawning loudly. 'Finns,' whispered Maskell into Tyra's ear, calm again. She did not respond, so he clarified: 'I would say Finns or Swedes.'

'How can you tell?'

'No manners.'

At that moment Maskell's boss walked in. Stella Wlynarczyk was a powerfully built woman with shot-putter shoulders and legs too short for her body. Her dress was black with yellow-and-orange zig-zags below the waist which, Maskell thought, looked like road markings. Wlynarczyk had an unsettling way of flicking glances to the side as she spoke, as if surveying the room for danger.

'Found you, Ms Gayle! You'll remember me interviewing you, of course, in that rather airless room. So – congratulations on the job! I thought I might find you here. Craig showing you his baby?' A sudden glance left and right. 'Unfortunately we have taped off Roger. Have you told her about Roger, Craig?'

'Ah – yes – well . . .'

'Roger?' Tyra's question betrayed him.

Maskell explained, 'Downstairs. Our eleven-foot-tall Asian elephant.'

'Perhaps you didn't mention it after all, Craig.' Stella

Wlynarczyk's voice was pure schoolmarm. 'Sadly it looks like a child has tugged at one of the feet and torn the fabric.'

'Jesus,' said Tyra Gayle. Appalled to hear the blasphemy in this sacred space, Maskell wanted to say, *Not in front of the painting*, but stopped himself.

'I'm heading down to Roger presently.'

'Ha – well, you can tell Ms Gayle about this artwork first, I'm sure. We are very proud of it. You especially, Craig.'

Was she laughing at him? 'Aye. Well, I do spend a lot of time in this room. Professionally of course.'

'Protecting our Dali from danger.'

'I feel a closeness to it, yes,' Maskell said, blushing as if he was talking about a woman. 'Mainly because my—'

Wlynarczyk's phone vibrated loudly. She bustled out of the room, tapping away at the screen. Maskell raised his eyebrows at the rudeness. But at least the woman had given him the cue to say his piece.

He cleared his throat importantly, spoke slowly. 'The painting shows Jesus Christ hanging on the cross. It looks like a view from outer space. Jesus hangs in darkness above a beach and some boats. You only see the top of his head. I would describe his hair as rusty and tousled. Note that there are no nails driven into the hands or feet.'

Tyra Gayle fidgeted.

'The top of the head is the centre of the painting, Miss Gayle. Note there is no crown of thorns and no blood.' At this point Maskell chuckled knowingly. 'I once heard a guide come round and say, "See how the triangle points on the canvas are the left hand, the right hand and feet of Christ", and then add something like, "the triangle represents the Holy Trinity". Or whatever. Absolute barmpot, this fellow. He spent a long time on what sounded like geometry, and frankly I could see his group were bored. *It is not a bloody triangle. It is a picture of Jesus Christ . . .'* He became aware he had raised his voice.

Wincing, Tyra nodded. As she turned he noticed a bright red stud in her ear, a gem edged in fake gold. So he would be speaking to her about that, too – the museum did not approve of jewellery.

'I like the hair,' she said thoughtfully.

Her words cut in on his thought. Maskell grasped that this young thing knew very little, if anything, about art. 'Ah yes, the hair of Dali's Christ. It seems to change colour depending on who looks. To me, it's brown with some blond flecks. But I heard an American woman ask, "Why is the hair *purple*?" which made me look again. Purple! What we can say is that this is a modern haircut. Which makes it rather strange for the hair of Jesus. I wonder if the hair might be a –' he needed a word that made him sound educated – 'a placebo.'

She shot him a puzzled glance. He opted not to go further. Instead he told her how the painting had originally been purchased by the Kelvingrove's first director. The man had gone to see the artist in Spain, negotiating the price directly. Dr Honeyman was his name.

'There was a lot of haggling. Eventually he got Dali down to £8,200. It still caused a right lather in Scotland because people said the money should be spent on local art by students instead of a foreigner. There were protests.' Maskell gave a lopsided smile. 'I often wonder how much it's worth now – possibly as much as a million pounds.'

'A lot more than that,' Tyra said, with such authority that he was thrown. He ran the tip of his right thumb backwards across his forehead, dislodging his museum cap, trying to work out how to respond.

Just then a figure over Tyra's shoulder caught his eye. An

old woman in a patched-up overcoat had a handkerchief knotted around her forefinger. She was polishing a small white plaque on the opposite wall. The pensioner stood as if uninterested in anything but the back-and-forth movement of the handkerchief, her tiny feet placed inches apart, ankles slight and bony in frayed stockings.

'Well, here's a test for you, young Tyra,' whispered Craig. 'Do you think we should ask her to stop that?'

Tyra Gayle looked round. 'Is that the text that goes with this painting?'

'The gallery label, yes. Explains how a stuntman posed for it. Has a little picture of the same man waterskiing with a girl balanced above his head. I forget the name.'

'But it's strange, isn't it,' began Tyra, still chewing on the gum, 'that a surrealist should need a real human being to pose in front of him? I guess this postdates Dali's surreal period. I think it was 1951 this was painted.'

Before an astonished Maskell could reply, Stella Wlynarczyk arrived back in the room. 'You're both still here? Is he filling you in properly?' she asked. 'We do all love our Craig. Or are *you* helping *him* with the facts, Tyra?'

'She possibly is,' Maskell said stiffly. He braced his shoulders, as if his discomfort was more physical than social.

'Tyra has a degree in – was it History of Art?'

'I have always wanted to work in a gallery,' Tyra said.

'Strictly speaking, it's a museum,' Maskell started to say, but his eye was drawn back to the elderly lady behind them. Quickly, he turned away from his colleagues. '*Hey!*'

Two swift paces took him to where the pensioner was standing. 'What exactly are you doing, madam?'

'Nothing.'

'Were you trying to remove that plaque?'

'No! Get away from me!'

His boss and Tyra Gayle both stared at him for a moment, and under their gaze he felt acutely self-conscious. He was certain he had seen the old woman place the end of her finger beneath the plaque to prise it off the wall, but the small rectangle of plastic – no bigger than two playing cards – was firmly attached. He now wondered whether his eyesight had let him down. He started to move away.

When he rejoined Tyra, his boss had gone again.

'Your first task might be to keep an eye on this old lady,' he whispered. 'Keep a low profile and follow her around a bit.'

A week later Tyra Gayle approached me in my office. She had taken my instruction seriously. She told me she had been following the pensioner. As I expected, Tyra was unable to trail her around without it becoming extremely obvious. This was partly because the lady walked with two sticks at a shuffling pace. Tyra told me she had a number of people ask why she was moving so slowly herself. Her tactic in the end was to offer to help the woman when she saw her, and keep an eye on her that way.

Tyra discovered the woman was in the museum as often as three times a day. In the period between my first sighting of her and the crime, we know she attended the museum around thirty times.

At a routine meeting of security personnel, the following was noted.

(1) She was polite to staff.

(2) She always made her way directly to Christ of Saint John of the Cross *and never looked at anything else in the gallery.*

(3) She stood in front of the painting on her sticks, some-

times for more than an hour, and would not move for other people which caused two official complaints. After staring at the painting she would often sit drinking a small glass of wine in the canteen. Sometimes she told the cashier she wanted Spanish wine, having discovered it when she travelled there, during which time she 'met Salvador Dali' – on hearing this I concluded the woman is a fantasist.

(4) Someone saw her crying one day in the canteen.

(5) Each day, when she returned to the Dali room, she would take up a position in front of the painting and stare at it, occasionally making notes with a pencil stub. Staff had tried to see what she wrote but it was predominantly scribbles. Despite her sticks, she would never use the bench in the room.

The only additional thing I should mention is that the lady could get extremely upset when other visitors stood in front of her and blocked her view of the painting.

I stressed to my staff that we take no chances with the safety of the Dali painting. It has been slashed in the past, by a mentally unwell person in the 1960s (I mean no disrespect to people with mental challenges), and some years later another cretin fired an air rifle at the canvas, penetrating Jesus Christ with a pellet. Thus a number of colleagues discreetly watch for anyone who might be carrying a weapon or a knife. An air rifle can be folded. We also watch for spray tins, marker pens and suspicious bags. I would always be ready to wrestle someone to the ground.

Because the Dali is one of the most famous paintings in the world, people seem to 'light up' when they look at it. The exception to this is teenagers taken round by parents. They just look bored and angry. I see them thinking, 'I could paint that, what's the big deal?'

I used to watch those teenagers carefully. My worry was always that an angry youth would be the one who attacks a painting. But in 1999 I went on a course entitled 'Art Gallery Security and Supervision' and they had gathered a list of all the attacks on artworks in the last fifty years. When we were shown the stories of the attackers on the overhead projector, they were not who you might expect. Teenagers do not slash paintings because they are cross at being taken round a gallery. Art is always cut/shot/slashed/ sprayed by someone either (a) mad as a hatter, or (b) polit- ical. It is often academics, professional types, and they are nearly always male.

During the course we were all told about the case of the German maniac Hans-Joachim Bohlmann. He went on a spree lasting thirty years and he hit more than fifty paint- ings, usually with a hand pump containing sulphuric acid. What was worse was that he always aimed at the faces in the paintings. We are talking Rembrandt, Rubens, Dürer, etc. Security kept catching him and he kept coming back. So far Bohlmann has caused damage costing about £100m. So far as I know he still operates today, and as a result I carry a photograph of him in my wallet. I would take him out the second I saw him.

Then you might mention the Little Mermaid statue in Copenhagen. This was different. The Little Mermaid is a bronze statue showing a mermaid becoming human. She was decapitated by activists calling themselves situationists. The head was never found, so the government made another. That got taken too. Nobody really knows what a situationist is.

Also, in 1987 Mr Robert Cambridge entered the National Gallery in London with a sawn-off shotgun concealed under his coat. He blasted a Leonardo da Vinci sketch from up close. The sketch was shielded by thick glass, but the pellets broke the glass and the glass badly cut the image underneath. It was some sort of protest against what Mrs Thatcher was up to in Number Ten, though I couldn't for the life of me see a connection. Cambridge went into an asylum for a good long stretch.

So, I went back over my notes from this course and looked at the various motivations to see if I could work out where the elderly lady would fit in. I did not believe she was mad or political. At this point, I wrote the email to Stella W. saying our knowledge of vandals over fifty years suggested the elderly woman was not a threat to the exhibit and Tyra Gayle could stand down.

I deeply regret this email.

When the alarm was raised today and I raced to the Dali room, I was not sure what to expect, but I admit I sensed it might involve the old lady. What I saw was horrifying.

PART ONE

CHAPTER ONE

GINNY
Spain, 1951

She was, she knew for the first time, beautiful.

It came to her that day in 1951 like the opening line of a poem peered at for years but suddenly understood. It came to her without pride. It came without guesswork. It came as a fact.

There were other facts that day. The sun was a fact. Levelled at the two of them, a cannon firing light, the blank mouth roaring silence in a cloudless Spanish sky. The sun's rays were broken only in moments when they passed the trees. The sea on the other side of the trees was a fact. She felt the mottled morning shadows cross her face. Those shadows were a fact . . .

And so, she knew in the instant she saw him, was the troubled heart of the boy.

She called him 'the boy'. He might have been older than her, twenty even. Her sister had no idea he was there, of course. She was wound in, wrapped up like a reel of magnetic tape. Ginny would never blame her for that, not after all Meredith had been through. But Ginny . . . yes, it was Ginny who saw the boy. She saw her own beauty, and she saw the boy and his broken heart.

That first morning in Cadaqués had started with the routine Ginny and Meredith were falling into on their travels. They had asked for an early call. When the porter knocked rapidly on the door at six fifteen, the sisters rolled out of opposite sides of their double bed as if taking cover from gunfire. They began to dress in silence.

Ginny and Meredith had travelled from Hull, down through France to the north-eastern coast of Spain, with a map that gradually wore away through repeated poking and folding. Ginny had been happy to explore Spain, unbothered about precise locations. Yet Meredith seemed fascinated with *this* place from the moment they arrived in the country. She had pointed at Cadaqués on the map without speaking, focusing intently, scouring the roads that led to it as if this was a promised land, a place of secrets. She never told Ginny why she had chosen this small town near the coast.

On the room door, as was the way in 1950s Catalonia, small squares of card identifying the guests were slotted into narrow wooden frames –

MEREDITH CAIRNS
GINE MORANHUGH

– the younger girl's name spelled entirely wrong, of course. Had she known more about this part of Spain, she might have seen the error as a token expression of individuality – a small rebellion against the ruling regime in Madrid. Dissent was Catalan. But General Francisco Franco was a man you did not argue with. In his Spain every name was correctly spelled, especially on the death warrants that had done for tens of thousands. He would not have been the chosen leader in this corner of his country, no matter how many victories he had won on other battlefields. Here in rural Catalonia, Franco's Guardia Civil patrolled nervously if they appeared at all. To Ginny, who understood none of the politics, there was something bracing about searching for local sights amid an air of tension. She sensed it as soon as they arrived. Even the tapping of the porter's knuckle was like a secret signal.

Their hotel room was a sight in itself, a bungled attempt at Art Deco. The furnishings seemed too heavy for the space. Lopsided candleholders sprang in threes from thick brass brackets on the walls. Between the two largest windows was a full-length mirror. The glass was gilt-edged with flame shapes bursting from the sides. The floor was bare timber, pockmarked by the shoes of all the guests who had stayed before. In the middle of the floorboards was a faded rug whose pattern was, on close inspection, Arabic script. Their bedside tables were as wide as wardrobes – hefty shellac-finished rosewood blocks, rounded at the corners, with enough space inside for a child to hide in.

Ginny turned slowly, taking in her surroundings. Her gaze came to rest on her sister. Meredith's puddled skin moved around her like a diving outfit full of water. Ginny minded the cruelty of the thought even before she had it – the other woman took up twice as much of the room as she did. Hair grown wild in the night, Meredith silently wrestled off her nightdress and dropped it on the floor. While Ginny's skin was white as bathroom porcelain, her sister's was olive, puckered with lines and folds like a military map; Meredith herself had been the warzone.

Beside the bed was the older sister's white cane. The wooden floor complained every time she shifted her weight. If Meredith had been a painting, the artist would have apologised for rushing the detail. Her eyes were black dots below thick eyebrows, her mouth as thin as spite. But she was never unkind herself. She was cruelty's victim, its prize. Meredith was twice Ginny's age. Thirty-six! A crazy age gap for sisters, almost unnatural. She had been born in the middle of the Great War, Ginny much later.

There were other differences between them. Unless her mind was racing dangerously, Meredith kept her own counsel. She could be guarded to the point of silence. The younger sister was the opposite – open, confident, a happy chatterer. Just occasionally on this trip, Ginny had seen her older sister's frown lines uncrease as Meredith reached out to her like a trusted confidante. And Ginny had to remind herself of the miracle: *For years my sister, seeing nothing, never said a word.* She realised how much she loved Meredith. How she could never bear to see her hurt. And those thoughts gave the younger girl a pang – when she finally told Meredith why she had sought her out, would the older woman ever trust her again?

They had decided that early waking was best. So it was early on that first morning in Cadaqués when Ginny caught herself in the full-length mirror and finally understood.

Could beauty – her beauty – be a fact?

It really was.

Somehow, seeing it as a fact, seeing it as *information*, made the thought less outrageous. It was not headstrong or boastful to know that she was beautiful. Anyway, there was only an instant – just this precise instant, just a second, or maybe two – when she admired herself. She had never done it before. She could be forgiven.

Her own naked body that morning was a revelation. It occurred to Ginny that she had only glanced in pocket mirrors at home and taken in a jigsaw of parts that barely fitted. Small feet, skinny ankles, breasts too large, shoulders sloped. Neck a long line that slid away to nothing. Lips too heavy. She had once tipped a hand mirror at an angle to see what lay between her legs and was immediately remorseful at the intrusion into her own privacy.

Finally she had a full-length image of herself. Hotel Maravillas del Mar was not expensive but the mirror was a luxury. For the first time Ginny saw harmony in her own height and skin and shape, as her sister's struggle with pantyhose turned into a catastrophic ballet behind her.

Even at eighteen, she was taller than Meredith. In a single year Ginny must have shot up half a dozen inches. White legs that had been squat were silken pins now, calves narrow like you saw on the swimsuit ladies in *Illustrated*, the colour magazine her mother had every week for fourpence. The walking she did every morning with her sister had given her waist and thighs tone. She rolled her hips tentatively now, stepping on the spot to move her pelvis left and right. A line of muscle formed in her stomach and she wondered what it was there for, how she had earned it. Now she turned full-on to the mirror like an actress entering a scene, conscious of her every inch.

The triangle of black hair between her legs looked stray. She wondered what a man would do, or would become, were she ever naked in front of him like this. Would he become breathless, latch his mouth onto her breast? What would her skin, her freckled skin, taste like in his mouth?

When she had these thoughts, it was always an older man. She imagined a gentle swish across her belly, separate fingertips, a gossamer touch. A hum in her ears, her mouth becoming wetter.

She looked enquiringly into her own face and tried a knowing smile. Could she convince a man she had the confidence she saw in adults? The experience, the self-assurance? Her blond bob sat, in the modern style, high above her neck. When she shook her hair for effect, it disappointed her by moving only a little. That smile, though – her smile was not the smile of a child any more. Her green eyes glistened, and when she moved her chin up and parted her lips, even without the lipstick she had begun to apply on this trip, she looked incandescently feminine.

Ginny shifted to the right. The sun was now directly behind her, shining into the mirror, a great torrent of light across her shoulders like a waterfall. The body she saw was reduced to silhouette, framed like a shop window dummy. Enjoying the effect, she moved her hips and rolled her head. But there was suddenly a crash behind her and a theft of light as the blind snapped down . . .

'I can't see it!'

Meredith.

CHAPTER TWO

THE BOY

They were at the top of the outcrop, a few feet from the path that led from the grounds at the back of the hotel, the route having wound and climbed for nearly a mile. The path had started at the place where the hotel lawn stopped and nature took over. The sisters had little knowledge of what they were passing, and now stopped to stare at a copse of freshly harvested cork trees.

'Look, Meredith, the trunks are narrow where the men cut the bark away, I guess,' said Ginny. 'They use the cork for – wine, and . . .' She tailed off, feeling silly. She would not have passed for an expert in anything. The pair walked up to the trees, put their hands on the cork innards and breathed in.

'It smells like warm bread,' said Meredith. They gazed around them in silence. There were yucca plants here too – a cactus in all but name, hostile-looking. The leaves were narrow, pointed, sawlike. Most flowered at ground level. A few rose from the soil like dwarf palm trees that never moved in the wind. Their trunks were gnarled, armoured. The spike from a yucca had already ripped a hole in Ginny's socks, and now she knew to stay clear.

As patiently as she could, the younger girl was saying: 'Your book is in the hotel safe, yes?'

Meredith paused. She looked as if she was thinking hard.

'Yes?' Ginny prompted. 'Remember I took it there? So it couldn't be lost?'

'I'm sorry. I must have just forgot.'

'I know how precious it is to you –'

'Yes, it is.'

'– but Merry, when you suddenly say, "I can't see!"–'

'I didn't. I said, I can't see *it*.'

'It worried me, that's all.'

'I know.'

'When you panic,' Ginny went on, 'when you feel the world closing in, just stay calm if you can, okay? Until you've thought it through.'

'I count to five.'

'Whatever works for you.'

'Perhaps a million. I could count to a million.'

Ginny saw her sister's faint smile and relaxed. 'I care for you, Merry, that's all.'

'I'm getting better. It's just that a lot happened.'

'I know it did, sweetheart, I know.'

Ginny also knew Meredith would panic again over the whereabouts of her only valued possession, a battered green scrapbook full of mysterious cut-outs and sketches. Slashes of crayon and pencil alongside pictures pasted from magazines. Meredith kept the scrapbook close and Ginny could never ask about its history. The best tonic for Meredith was sisterly love, patience and calm. Not questions. Certainly not challenges. Calm was the medicine. Time was the measure.

'Why don't we have these plants in England?' Meredith suddenly asked.

'Why would we want them? They're vicious,' said Ginny.

'Yes. My leg is bleeding.'

Ginny looked down. The cut across Meredith's calf was

precise enough to have been made by a shaving razor. Small droplets of blood bulged from the wound. 'Oh, Meredith, come here.' Ginny took her handkerchief and knelt, wrapping the material around her sister's leg. Around her own it might have gone twice; with Meredith's she only just managed to get the ends to meet. 'There.' She tied a knot. The blood was stopped.

She had believed this landscape would help her sister. In the dining room the night before, Ginny had heard a podgy Englishman with a loud voice and a shrunken wife speaking like a college lecturer: 'The crops here are olives, almonds, rice and potatoes. Fruit farms have sprung up to cater for the demands of cities growing quickly since the war. Wherever we look,' he announced pompously, 'we will observe vineyards stretching into the distance.' But here by the sea Ginny did not see a landscape that matched the self-regarding man's description. The coastline was not fertile. The ground was parched, almost lunar. Bright greens had given way to dirty browns and rocks as black as charcoal. Now, on their first morning walk behind the hotel, they found strange combinations of dark crags and vivid blooms. Wind and wave had created spectacular geological outcrops that froze hulks of rock in the shape of spray. It was an otherworldly place.

Ginny remembered a strange moment in the journey. The sisters had boarded a bus, only to discover it had broken down and been sitting in the same spot for an hour, the passengers cooking behind the dirty glass. An old Spaniard, stripped to his vest and glistening with sweat, got up in the seat in front of them and passed Ginny a guidebook in English. He gave them a shrug and a toothy smile, his gestures indicating it had been abandoned on the seat beside him and he had no use for it. So, as they waited and Meredith dozed, Ginny read about

Catalonian history and tried to be interested – the Goths, the Moors, Charlemagne. A passage about the marriage of Barcelona's Count Ramon Berenguer IV to Queen Petronila of Aragon in 1137 sent her straight to sleep as the dates and names all blurred, defeating her attempts to take them in. Then a single line jumped into her dream and she woke: 'From the seventeenth century, Catalonia was the centre of a separatist movement.' Separatist? She opened the book to find the reference, flipping the pages back a century to try to work out where it had started, this desire to be a nation apart from the rest of Spain. Why would any group of people want to mark out a new border through fields and roads, and frisk their compatriots when they came to visit? It was unfathomable to her. But she got lost in the guidebook looking for answers, and turned to a sleeping Meredith to talk about it. As Ginny poked her older sister, the bus started with a roar and she woke. The windows rattled and the passengers cheered. 'Separatist,' said Ginny above the noise. 'What is that exactly?'

Before Meredith could reply, the man in the vest suddenly stood and turned again, his eyes alight. He snatched back the book and tossed it onto the seat beside him. For a second he froze, as if worrying he had overreacted, and then pointed to his ears and clapped his hands over them. He moved a single finger to his lips, vibrating the finger to shush the sisters, his eyes bulging in alarm. The bus took a corner and he was thrown back into his seat. Ginny giggled, but when she looked at Meredith she saw her sister was not laughing.

Even now, as they walked in the sun, the older woman's face was set into an expression of grim determination. 'I remember the name of those plants now. They're yuccas,' said Meredith as they walked. 'They're incredibly tough.'

'A kind of cactus?'

'I suppose so. They grow in cemeteries for some reason. They're hardy. They smell – sour. Like bad fruit.'

The pair moved on. The breeze circling them was like the air from a fire. They must have gone a mile, the hotel a long way behind them now. But Ginny was sure the climate, and the walking, were good for Meredith. The path took them right, and it was then she saw him, through a line of eucalyptus trees.

It was the merest movement at first. She thought it was perhaps the bright blue plumage of a bird. Meredith walked on as Ginny stopped.

'I'll catch you up in a minute.'

'What is it?'

She lowered her voice to a murmur and made a shooing gesture with her hand. 'Walk slowly, Merry. I'll catch you up.'

Meredith looked at her quizzically with those button-black eyes, but could not find the words to object. Ginny took ten steps and peered through the eucalyptus.

She saw his sadness before she saw his face. She could do that, she thought – see a mood. Ginny knew he was broken-hearted from the way his shoulders sloped. In a single movement he tore off a large blue shirt. His skin was bronzed, his arms and neck muscular. He reached down and she realised he was taking off his underpants.

Now he was naked.

Ginny shot a furtive glance at Meredith. She was fifty yards away, peering at insects on a pond.

Ginny looked back at the boy, squinting through the sun at him and blinking away a bead of sweat. He turned towards her, unclothed, contoured, the body of an athlete. Breathing quicker, she drew closer to see what was going on. Her way was blocked by thick shrubs, full-bloomed corema and santolina. Carefully she edged around the grey-green leaves and yellow buds into the shade, not wanting him to hear or see her moving closer. Ferns clawed at the fabric around her waist. She felt her skin glide against its own sweat.

The boy's body was broken into squares that opened and closed in the shifting gaps of light between leaves and branches, each an imperfect snatch of a whole she could not see. He was local, Spanish or Portuguese for sure. His thick waves of brown hair shone in the sun. Different sections of his frame were displayed as she shifted against the greenery.

There was a moment when he seemed to bow his head, breathing deeply, shoulders moving. Suddenly he shouted – the voice more like a yelp.

She could no longer see him.

Where had he gone?

Oh, God! Over the edge!

Ginny sprang forward, kicking at the bushes in her path and eventually bursting from the tangle, tripping and almost falling upon the spot where the boy had stood only seconds before.

His clothes were in a pile at her feet. Chest heaving, on her hands and knees, she gulped as if drowning in light. Ginny got back to her feet. She stepped towards the cliff edge.

Where is he?

No . . . this could not be . . . the boy had gone over the precipice. The rocks must have been a hundred feet down. He had been dashed to pieces. Ginny felt sick as she tiptoed further towards the cliff edge. The dry grass scraped her ankles. She was gorged with the brutality of what the boy had done. *He took his own life.* Surely no one would survive that plunge. And what a cry! Could she have saved him if only she had shouted, if only she had not got tangled in those bushes?

Ginny tiptoed forward, inch by inch, looking for his body on the rocks or in the sea.

Far out she saw a vessel large enough to be a battleship. It sat low and long in the shimmering water. She wondered if the boat might be American. The thought distracted her for a second. Then vertigo – a spinning of the mind she had never felt before – made her lean back and reach for something to hold. But there was nothing, and a gust of wind ten times more powerful than any she had felt that morning took her forwards. The earth under her feet at the edge of the cliff gave way.

Ginny fell. She opened her mouth to scream.

Before any sound emerged, the girl's drop was harshly broken as she landed on a lower ledge below the outcrop. The small patch of level ground now supporting her was no more than five feet below the clifftop. Fear engulfed her. If the ground crumbled beneath her, she would fall like the boy, fall to her death on the rocks below.

She found her voice and, without thinking, screamed.

'Merry! Meredith! *Meredith!*'

Nothing. The sun was fierce, the hot wind whipped around her. Nature would snatch and claim her. Rip her on the rocks, toss her body into the gaping sea. But she wanted to live.

'It's *Ginny!*' she screamed at the sky. And although the sun and wind were burning, she felt a shiver pass from her shoulders to her legs.

A head appeared above her, framed by the bright blue above them, silhouetted by the sun.

'Ginny? Ginny!'

'Meredith! I saw something, I went to the edge, the edge gave way. Help!' She was trying desperately to sound calm.

'Ginn—'

The word disappeared down Meredith's throat. Dazzled,

Ginny could only see the outline of her body. She heard her sister speak again.

'Ginny,' said Meredith, standing on the clifftop, 'I can't see.'

'Do you mean it?'

The moment seemed to stretch. There was no answer from Meredith, just a sob.

'Don't move another inch, Meredith,' Ginny said as reassuringly as she could. 'Don't come towards me. Please. There's a big drop.'

Ginny's heart banged. Above her Meredith froze. She counted, 'One, two, three . . .'

'Sit down where you are,' Ginny called. 'I'm fine. Just don't move forwards, whatever you do. Do your count and sit down.'

She saw Meredith move back a little then crouch down onto the grass, disappearing from Ginny's view.

A minute passed. Ginny did her best to stay calm. 'Can you still not see?' she called.

She heard Meredith's voice. 'I heard you screaming. I looked for you. And then . . . no, I can't.'

'Oh, it's my fault, I know it is! I panicked you! Meredith, I am so sorry, I didn't think. I cried for help . . .' Ginny turned to the sea, weeping silently like a child, wondering for how long this small ledge of cracked mud would hold her weight. 'Just relax for as long as you need. Let's both of us . . . please, Meredith, just relax.'

Ginny knew she must not burden her sister by shouting any more. But then she saw Meredith leaning over the cliff edge, stretching blindly for her.

'Pull on my arm, it doesn't matter if it breaks.' The older woman's voice was muffled. Her face was in the soil, her entire body flat against the ground.

'Merry, I don't want to pull you over the edge.'

'Just take my arm, it doesn't matter.'

Vertigo hit her again. She gripped Meredith's arm.

'This'll hurt, Meredith.'

She yanked the arm, praying her sister would not slide forwards. She kicked a foot up to find a knot of branch in the face of the rocks.

Her foot slipped. Meredith screamed. 'Don't let go, Ginny! It doesn't matter about me!'

Ginny kicked up again, this time with her left foot. It found a protruding knuckle of rock that felt no bigger than a tennis ball.

'Pull, Meredith!'

Face down in the grass, trying not to be pulled forwards, Meredith screamed again. Her arm seemed to crack as Ginny lunged for the grass on the clifftop with her free hand, still gripping her sister, using her left foot to push herself up by inches. She grabbed at Meredith's shirt and felt it rip in her hands. Meredith screamed even louder.

'Nearly there,' Ginny panted as her right knee cleared the top edge of the cliff. She scrambled forwards, feeling one hand shred Meredith's shirt, ripping the material all the way up her back.

Meredith stayed lying down, breathing hard, legs spread, star-shaped in the grass. Ginny was on her haunches, feet tucked underneath her bottom, chest heaving. 'Oh, Merry.' She started to cry with shock and relief. 'Oh my goodness me.'

'Are you safe?' Meredith asked, her face still buried in the grass.

'Yes. Yes. But you . . .' Ginny crawled to Meredith, brushed the hair away from the side of her face. 'Lift your head, Meredith.'

She did.

'Anything?'

'Some light,' said Meredith.

Ginny softly moved more hair away from her sister's face. 'It's coming back? Please God that—'

'No. Yes. The light, a bit, and – slowly the shapes are coming.' She turned over onto her back, blinking rapidly. 'What happened?'

'The ground gave way. I walked too close to the edge.'

'Why?'

Ginny stared at where it had happened, the edge of the cliff now missing a scoop of soil, the sea beyond sparkling like foil. The scene looked so undramatic now, just a divot in the cliff edge.

Then she remembered the heaving shoulders of the boy and his agonised cry. 'Oh, but Merry, I saw something terrible.' Ginny had not meant to tell her sister for fear of upsetting her. But now she blurted out the story.

As Meredith stood, Ginny saw what a mess she was. Mud on her face, blouse shredded. Rubbing her eyes as if she could massage her sight back, the older woman was tearful too. 'Jumped?'

'A huge way down. So far I can't see where he landed.'

Meredith repeated, 'The young man jumped?' She shivered.

They walked to the edge, stood there, held each other, backed off. The women were both crying freely now, hugging each other. Meredith's upper body was exposed and pulling the fragments of ripped blouse together did not cover her. Ginny pointed at the garments on the ground.

'Look there. Wear the boy's shirt.'

'I can't.' She was almost hysterical.

'It's big. Put it on.'

'I don't feel I should, Ginny. Not if he's gone.'

'They're just clothes, darling sis. They're not him.'

Meredith reluctantly picked up the blue shirt. 'We must tell someone.' She removed her ripped blouse to try the shirt on. Ginny felt dizzy with the strangeness of it all. Her sister, naked from the waist up in the sun; the clifftop both open to the ocean and blocked off from the land by the thicket behind them; and the blue shirt, voluminous on the boy but now clothing Meredith as tightly as a glove.

Ginny knelt and arranged the remaining clothes in respectful silence. 'Shoes, socks.' Meredith tucked the socks into each other and her sister knew, from that small moment attending to detail, that her sight had returned. Ginny slid the white underpants into the middle of the pile without naming them. There was a blue piece of cord he must have used as a belt. She wrapped it around her hand and placed it on the socks. The boy's red sports shoes sat neatly on top, toes pointing at the sun, a memorial. She reached a decision. 'You and I will bury them, Meredith.'

'Oh.'

'As he's dead—'

'Yes, we must.'

'Are you okay now?'

'I think so. It just scares me, when I can't see,' said Meredith flatly. 'What happens?'

Ginny stared at her.

'When I go blind,' Meredith elaborated. 'What happens?'

'I can only tell you what the doctors said. You remember. A link between the brain and the body, some sort of physical shutdown, "expressed in the nervous connection to the retina", wasn't that the phrase? Because of what happened to you.'

'It scares me,' she repeated.

'A prisoner went blind when the verdict came back in his trial. He was accused of a murder he didn't commit. He knew he would get the death penalty if he was convicted. When the jury foreman said the word "guilty", he went blind.'

Ginny wondered if she should have told such a morbid story, so she added: 'I'm just saying it so you know you're not alone.'

'Will it always happen?'

'Not if we get you better, lovely sister. That's what we came away for.' Again, that pang, deep in Ginny's stomach, at the untruth that came so easily to her lips.

Carefully, the sisters picked up the boy's clothes from the ground. Their faces grim and heads bowed, they walked slowly back towards the hotel, a funeral procession.

Two hours later, the sisters were sitting on a banquette in one of the two front bay windows of the hotel as guests came and went in ones and twos through the main doors. At the reception desk on the far side of the room, a radio crackled with news in Spanish. Bloated flies travelled with the new arrivals, almost big enough to demand rooms of their own. Above their heads a fan whirred uselessly.

Ginny looked around her. The walls and floors of the hotel were dark wood, almost black. The lack of colour meant the daylight behind them was stolen as soon as it passed into the room. Long rugs lay ruckled as if abandoned. Ginny glanced down. Beneath her feet were red roses stitched into a washed-out yellow background – and that Arabic script again. The ceiling was low, and the sound of guests arriving and leaving set up vibrations in the space that seemed to radiate their own energy. Behind the reception a visitor could go in one of three directions: upstairs to the bedrooms; straight on towards the gardens and the sea; or right, into a room marked BIBLIOTECA. 'Have you seen our famous library?' the sisters had been asked on arrival, and then at breakfast too – the question becoming tiresome, for Ginny had no interest in a room full of old Spanish books.

At that instant, two police officers came through the door and the sisters froze. The men were unshaven, faces hot below angular hats. Their jet-black uniforms made the noise of sandpaper as they arrived, then paused. They moved again and halted, starting and stopping at precisely the same instant like two clockwork soldiers. One wiped the heel of his hand against the stubble on his chin and the sound, again, was of sanding. Ginny felt her gaze drop to the gun at the waist of the first one, a young man with uneven eyes who looked suddenly at her.

'Shouldn't we go to—' Meredith began, but Ginny hushed her, trapped in the man's gaze.

Now both police officers were looking at the sisters. Ginny's blood ran cold. As if driven by an impulse to speak, she started to rise from the banquette. But in that instant the hotel manager strode in behind the officers. He greeted the pair loudly and they turned away.

Ginny commented, 'Those two looked nervous. They looked ready to shoot.'

Meredith was trembling, still in shock. 'Are they here to talk to us?'

'I hope not.'

'Someone must miss the boy. His mother. Maybe we should tell them what you saw.'

'But Merry, I don't know how the police work here. You saw them. They're on edge. They look very stern, military. I don't want you questioned by men with guns. I don't want the stress of all that on you. You've come so far on this trip. I see you coming out of yourself.'

'I went blind again.'

'No! You lost your sight for a moment. It's just a loose connection inside you. The doctors—'

'I don't want to have to take that white stick everywhere.'

'Then let's throw it away. Come on. Have courage, darling.' It was easy for Ginny to say, not having been through even a single day of Meredith's life. 'It was a loss of sight, only –' Ginny inhaled, wanting to find the right words – 'only for a few minutes, yes? So it was an interruption. And *now*,' she went on, 'I don't want us to get involved in something that starts all the stress up again, something this—'

'Strange,' prompted Meredith.

'Tragic,' Ginny said softly. 'How bad would it have to be to take your own life like the young man did?'

'When your own brain attacks you,' said Meredith quietly.

Ginny jumped to reclaim the words. 'I'm sorry, I wasn't thinking.' She added quietly, 'Let's say I went over and spoke to those two police. What would I tell them?'

'Say you saw a person take his life. Describe him. It's been a few hours now. *Someone* must be missing him. *Someone.*'

Ginny reflected on Meredith's insistence. She wondered if it was born out of her sister's own experience – of disappearing, for years, and no one seeming to care.

'Say you saw him take his life.' Meredith often repeated herself when she was under pressure. It reminded Ginny to tread carefully.

'When your sight goes, Merry darling, what do you feel?'

Meredith rubbed her eyes. 'It suddenly happens. I don't know. A panic.'

'Does the panic come first, or does it cause the panic?'

'It's like someone brought a curtain down.'

'Think of it as a safety curtain at the theatre. It's protecting you, stopping a fire spreading.'

'But the curtain is worse than the fire.'

Ginny tilted her head compassionately. 'And it's over after a few minutes?'

'The worst time was five years.'

The answer was so shocking that Ginny had no response. She felt her pulse quicken, but did not want to show her alarm. Five *years*?

'I wish I had known that.'

'I couldn't tell you everything, Ginny.'

'If we go to the police,' Ginny said eventually, 'we'll have to show them the clothes.'

'But they're buried.'

'We'll have to dig them up.'

'We shouldn't have buried them,' said Meredith with sudden decisiveness. She put her hand on her forehead and rubbed it, as if to drive the thought away. 'We could show them this.' The boy's shirt hugged Meredith's stomach tightly, but she pulled impatiently at a loose fold of material to make her point. 'They could identify him from this.'

Earlier they had clawed a hole in the forest floor with their hands, fifty yards off the path back to the hotel. Meredith worked with only one arm as the other still hurt from the desperate grip Ginny had taken on it. No one disturbed them. The soil was loose and dry. It came away easily. Ginny and Meredith had dropped the clothes into the hole and filled it back in, kicking the loose soil and leaves with their feet. Then they had stood and said a simple prayer.

'We need to wash our hands before lunch,' said Meredith.

Ginny looked at the black threads of earth in the grooves of her fingertips and sighed. The image of the naked youth flashed in her head. 'We have to put it out of our minds.' She cleared her throat. 'Meredith, there's something important I have to tell you. It's been on my conscience since the—'

Meredith looked suddenly across the room. 'The skinny man over there. Oh, my!'

She was staring at some guests near the reception desk.

'What is it?'

'Him – *there* – I know him – but – no, surely not—'

'What?'

Her hands were shaking as Meredith pointed. 'I know who that one is. The very thin one in the white suit and the straw hat, the one with his back to us. He's actually *here*, oh my heavens above. I never thought—'

Meredith suddenly fell silent as a woman standing beside the man turned briskly. She might have been six inches taller than him, and she was now walking straight towards them. Red-cheeked and freckled, with long legs and narrow hips that rolled as she walked, the woman reached their banquette in four or five light steps and sat neatly beside them, dress billowing. She made to light a cigarette. The match flared and she dropped it. 'God – oh, for God's sake—'

'I'll get it,' said Ginny.

'No – Jesus. Just leave it, okay? No point. It's only carpet. The skivs will sweep it up later.' She had said *curr-put. Jay-sus.* The woman crossed her legs, which was like watching a beach chair being snapped into its storage position. The supported leg trembled in apparent frustration. Her red hair, streaked with black, was tied messily in a bun and the front of her blouse dropped lower than was respectable. Pearls of sweat gathered above her sunburnt cleavage. She blew her nose and dragged at the cigarette. Any air of serenity, or even beauty, was dismantled by the trembling hands and rapid blinking.

'How can I have a chest cold in this murderous heat? Jesus Christ alive.'

The woman breathed in and leant back on the banquette. In front of them was a bright red ashtray shaped like a fish, the gills and scales drawn with wavy black lines in the Picasso style. She stabbed her cigarette into the eye. Then she started up again, head shaking, eyelids narrowed. 'This hellish weather, right – and this godawful man! Both of them together. How did I get into this?'

A second match flared in the woman's hand. She lit another cigarette and drew deep on it. This time she dropped the match on the floor deliberately and sank back in the seat, spreading her legs in a way Ginny found unbecoming.

The next words came quietly, like private thoughts. Softer, but through gritted teeth. 'It's not going to work. Chalk and cheese.' The woman gave a sudden rasping laugh. 'Ach, I don't mean to intrude on your restful day, ladies, turning the air blue.' The accent was strong, the words throaty. 'It's just my way. You're on a leisure trip? I'm on business. So I guess I feel the need to be the boss. Barking orders. That's just me, call a spade a . . .' She swept her hand over her face as if conjuring a smile from behind it. 'Shovel.' Her smile was more of a grimace, lopsided and fake. 'Truth is, I'm under pressure.'

Meredith asked, 'Is that man —?'

'You recognised him?' said the woman, brightening. 'Oh, thank God! My day is made, the hour is come!' The throaty laugh again.

'I knew him from the moustache, of course.'

'Moustache?'

'Wait,' said Meredith quietly, fearing another explosion. 'I meant the other man.'

'Who are we talking about?' asked Ginny.

'Ginny, can you see the two at the reception desk?' asked Meredith. 'The one in the white jacket, with the straw hat and the thick scarf, with his back to us – that one. The moustache. You'll see it when he turns.' She was being more precise than she needed to be. That was her way. 'That one. Oh, I do know him!'

The Irishwoman bridled. 'Okay. Let's go back to square one here. Two men at the desk. You see them? You do. Okay, now – the hat, the scarf, the moustache – *not* that one. The other one. Electric blue sports jacket. That one there.' The Irish accent made it *dat wan dare*. 'And I told him not to kick up, and he kicked up. Stupid men, right?' *Roight*.

The sisters were silent.

'My name is Siobhan Lynch.' She took another deep drag on her cigarette. 'I work with Mr Russell Saunders. There. Blue jacket. You'll know him, right. *Surely* you'll know Mr Saunders. God. Someone must! He's *so* famous, at least in his own mind.' The last phrase was muttered, almost bitterly.

Meredith and Ginny showed no recognition. 'Come, come,' pressed Siobhan Lynch. 'You will have seen Mr Saunders in movies. A Hollywood stuntman. The best. He is pretty much the most famous in the world. I work as his personal assistant outside the USA, and that's a big thing, right. His personal assistant.'

Fearing another explosion, Ginny tried to bluff recognition. Then the electric blue sports jacket turned suddenly.

They were presented with a blond man, well clear of his twenties, whose eyebrows arched in a way that suggested determination rather than intelligence. His nose ran unevenly to a point, but his cheekbones, thought Ginny, were a wonder – they could have been chiselled in marble. Saunders had the look of a film star, for sure. Yet she had never seen his face before.

He advanced on the three woman with a swagger, and Ginny imagined taut muscles in his legs rippling under his trousers.

'Hey, Siobhan.' He pronounced it *Syo-ban*. The voice was a gravelly Californian drawl.

'Sir.'

'How are you, honey?'

'Flaking in the heat slightly.'

'And who have we here?' The muscles in his neck flinched as he spoke. The Irishwoman stood and half turned dismissively. 'Don't even bother, Mr Saunders. They're the only ones in the hotel who haven't heard of you. British, I think.'

Saunders ignored her and reached out a hand to the sisters. 'Hi, ladies! Glad you've met my fixer.'

Fixer? Had Siobhan Lynch exaggerated her job title? The man smiled warmly. 'Hey, don't worry if you hadn't heard of me. There's still time for me to do something useful with my life, right?' He winked at them both. 'I don't mind that. What I mind is this heat. And not having a schedule. This man is so damn eccentric, I can't even begin to tell you.'

'Has he told you what he wants?' asked Lynch, standing at his shoulder and speaking as if she needed to ensure Ginny and Meredith did not hear.

'Listen. I thought it was a portrait. You said it was a portrait. I'm doing a portrait. I don't need to know any more. I need a drink, I need some food, and I need ice on my chest in a room in the shade. Dammit, I need—'

Ginny suddenly had the thought he was going to make a lewd remark – and she got ready to giggle indignantly. But Saunders must have looked at the sisters on the banquette and judged that they were not ready to hear his next line, because the sentence stalled. He shrugged. His cheeks flushed, as if he was expecting he would not get the drink or the ice or the girls, and his face was forecasting the indignation he was about to feel.

Ginny and Meredith looked up at Siobhan Lynch. It was

hard not to enjoy her discomfort. She had pulled a notepad from her bag and was shaking a pen to get the ink to flow.

'Watch the ink and this jacket, young lady, okay?' Saunders said. 'The guy is asking for something over there, a special table I think, and he's kicking up because they say the table is taken, and he just keeps saying, "I am Darley, I am Darley." It's embarrassing. I mean, who the hell is he?'

Saunders pulled off his jacket, revealing shirtsleeves. His forearms were muscled like a shipbuilder's. *The physique of a bull*, thought Ginny, staring at the flesh. A single tattoo on the left arm displayed an eagle with an arrow in its beak. Saunders' waist was narrow and rose in a V to the shoulders. Five foot nine, she estimated, a compact eleven stone. His body was interesting, but his eyes did not sparkle.

Meredith was looking at the man in the white jacket. 'I knew it was him.'

'Did he say "Darling"?' asked Ginny.

'*Dali.* Salvador Dali. Look.'

Saunders and Lynch were now walking back to the reception desk. The man in the straw hat and white jacket placed a hand on the surface of the desk and turned. He had a long waxed moustache, upturned at the ends, and was unsmiling. His chin jutted towards Saunders and Lynch and he said something. He waved an arm imperiously, eyes bulging. Then he hooted with laughter, but the laughter did not break across the top half of his face. The women saw that the scarf around his neck was actually a dead snake, or perhaps a rubber one.

'The great artist,' whispered Meredith, clutching her sides as if she was suddenly out of breath. 'Oh, my Lord. My sweet Lord.'

As they stared at Salvador Dali, their view was suddenly blocked.

One of the waitresses. Speaking in Spanish.

'*Robaste su ropa.*'

The sisters shook their heads.

'*Robaste su ropa!*'

'We can't speak Spanish,' Ginny said. 'I'm so sorry.'

The waitress turned to someone standing behind her. '*Inglese!*'

A figure stepped forward. The familiar face stared down at Ginny. Bronzed skin. A mop of tousled hair. His eyes blazed. He said something to the waitress. Then he turned back to the two women on the banquette and spoke clearly with an American accent.

'You stole my clothes.'

CHAPTER THREE

MEREDITH
Hull, 1914

Where does madness start?

Does it start in the moment, during adolescence or adulthood, when a person is torn – torn by events, torn by the world? Or is it there at the earliest time, in the moment they rip themselves away from their mother's womb? In that very first second of air and light? Is the madness already there inside the screaming baby, born as they are born, the world only a watcher?

When Meredith's mother Dorothy gave birth, the man of the home was away fighting. Before the war, Rex Luke Moran-Hughes worked in an ironmonger's in Hull. Below his apron he wore the same thing every day. Flannel trousers, pressed and grey . . . pressed and grey, just like his life. White shirt, sleeves rolled up. Lavender blue tie. He was a stiff and studious twenty-four-year-old with broad shoulders, a bony waist and not much flesh anywhere else. Rex had been mediocre in school, good with his hands unless they held a pen. He had no family connections to make up for failed exams. The marriage to Dorothy had been forced by her pregnancy, but they were devoted all the same.

They said goodbye under the new five-span roof of Hull's Paragon Station. The army train stood waiting at what was still termed the fish platform. As the young couple headed there, Rex took a slight detour to show Dorothy the new signalling system and explained it was electro-pneumatic, with 143 levers.

With time short, she wondered how on earth he could think such detail remotely important. They embraced by the train and he produced a brown parcel for her 'to open later'. She allowed him to touch her stomach under her coat, and felt her eyes mist when he did it. 'It is a right wonder,' he said. Then they kissed, his left boot already on the ledge below the carriage door. A minute later, the train whistled and puffed and was gone.

Like most volunteer soldiers in 1914, Rex expected a series of swift confrontations. A rifleman, he first saw action with the British Expeditionary Force at Mons. A Lee–Enfield could be shot and reloaded twelve times in a minute by a skilled marksman. Those dozen bullets could pepper a man-sized target three hundred yards away. Rex discovered he had skill with a gun. He could load and fire eighteen shots in a minute – no one in his unit could place so much accurate fire in the same grouping on a target. He let so many bullets fly that his weapon sounded like a machine gun.

At Mons the British had been outnumbered by the Germans, then let down by the sudden retreat of the French Fifth Army. Yet the British riflemen were so skilled their enemy thought they were facing automatic weapons. Rex screamed as he fired. Perhaps that should have been a sign. He saw men die around him and kept firing. After the withdrawal at Mons he fought at Marne. Again his rifle snicker-snacked like a circus whip. Again he screamed. He was at the First Battle of Ypres and Passchendaele. In the British offensive at Artois, a bullet tore into the tree beside him and a flying dagger of bark sliced a line across his forehead. Still he fired and fired, yelling curses as his vision filled with blood and he wondered if he was dying. That day he learnt from a telegram that he had a daughter.

Promoted to sergeant after the left side of his commanding

officer's face was blown away by a German sniper who had sat for hours with his sights set on a two-inch gap between sand-bags, Rex fought in two more battles before his eventual journey home in 1918.

In a book, Sergeant Moran-Hughes would be returning from war with his head in bloody bandages, limping, staring at his calloused feet. The reality was the opposite. He had left for war a modest man, an assistant ironmonger, a fellow neither academic nor sporty, just one of thousands of manual workers doing what they thought was their duty. Pressed and grey, like his flannel trousers. He returned with his head held high, weathered, laughing, a handsome hero.

Or so it seemed. Late at night his wife would watch him sleeping. The scar on his forehead was a perfect horizontal. One night Dorothy looked at that scar for a full minute, searching for even the slightest deviation in the line. It was almost surgical in its execution. God, if he existed, must not be an artist but an engineer, lacking the imagination even to leave a signature in a war wound.

Dorothy wondered why she had ever believed in a God who could preside over such chaos without intervening. She asked herself who her husband had become. How had his brain processed so much blood and bone when many others were in hospital wards? Even veterans without a scratch on them would leap out of bed every time a janitor dropped his bucket. There was a sorry soul in Hessle, it was said, whose war trauma was so great that he vomited every time he saw anything that looked like a trench, even spilling his guts over the award-winning flowerbed in a council garden.

Dorothy's own mother, who came from Caribbean stock, had told her quietly: 'Say your husband emerges from this war with his body intact. A man who nearly dies comes back with two lives. Will he not want something *grander* for himself?'

The question troubled Dorothy. So she had tried to improve herself while Rex was away. After his departure she had opened the parcel he handed over at the railway station and found a green scrapbook, with the note: 'For your dreams. Rex.' Despite a lack of self-confidence, she found an interest in paintings. The second decade of the 1900s was the moment modernism flourished in Europe. She would not have been able to explain to any of the other young mothers in Hull why they appealed, but she devoured news of Picasso, Kandinsky, Duchamp, Mondrian, Klee. Quarterlies would sometimes print the work of these pioneers surrounded by the sniffiest text, arguing that the new artists were illustrating how war had caused all order to disintegrate, even the simple business of applying paint to canvas.

But Dorothy saw something more uplifting in those grotesque splashes of colour, the zig-zags and insane shapes. She saw a new world, a world beyond the existing margins, a place that she and Meredith and Rex could make their own when this 'War to End All Wars' was finally over. Despite a crushing sense that people would think a mixed-race woman who scrimped for loose change in a terraced house in Hull could never have a valuable opinion on a painting, her interest became a fascination. Diligently she cut those precious pictures from magazines and, where that was not possible, sketched copies in the small green scrapbook with coloured pencils.

The green scrapbook went everywhere with her – until Rex's return. Dorothy baulked at telling her husband about the art, about how those painters set her heart racing. Although she had initially reached towards the artists because she worried Rex would find her dull without them, now she worried he might take her enthusiasm as a sign that she was tired of the real world around her. That the straight lines and charcoal smudges of their terraced existence in Hull were not enough.

There was, in any case, a lick of modernist colour in that house now. Meredith was a happy toddler, frantic and furious at times but always full of life. She was young enough not to register her father's absence or be puzzled at the man who returned.

Dorothy doted on her newborn. Back in Hull, Rex threw himself into fatherhood and played with her wildly . . . in a way that might have aroused concern in watchful adults. His manner was breathless, his laughter too loud. He tossed her high into the air. He screamed louder than the child.

Soon after he resumed work at the ironmonger's – discovering most similar shops were being rebranded 'hardware stores' – Rex was criticised for a cataloguing error and, eyes suddenly alight, punched a colleague in the shoulder so hard the man fell into a newly installed electric lamp. The shade broke. The bulb shattered as the lamp fell from its stand with a crash. There was darkness and panic. Electricity was new. Could it leak and poison them all? Into the gloom Rex shouted at the customers and staff: 'Quiet, everyone! I have come back from the war and am not yet myself. I must beg your patience.' He was immediately forgiven.

Back at home with his wife and young daughter, he never spoke of the battles he had fought. Instead he was animated on strange subjects: bird migration, throat cancer, dry-stone walls, nurses' uniforms. He spoke quickly, a blur of words. One night Dorothy dressed beautifully for him in a bell-shaped skirt of war crinoline and an extravagant slope-shouldered mauve tunic. Many people had boxed up and shelved such items in wartime because the consensus was that they used too much valuable cloth.

The lighting in their home was fuelled by gas pumped around the house, and a burner sat behind a stencilled glass shade above Dorothy's head, hissing gently as the flame flickered. She asked Rex with unusual intensity to be still for a moment, to concentrate. 'You know I will always love you, Rex,' she said, 'and this country owes you a debt for what you and so many others gave.'

He sat in silence, his fingers entangled.

She tried again. 'I need to know that you have your – health. That you have your mind. I need to know your mind.'

Rex breathed. Quickly, deeply.

And then the words came.

'In that war – I saw so much death – I believe I may have died myself. I killed many, *many*. I do not know their names. I fired and fired. Bullets passed close, and sometimes the jagged metal meant for me killed others. I am a sergeant only because my sergeant lost half his head to a sniper. I picked up his face, the cheek and the chin, where it fell. I picked up his mouth like a mask. I could have worn it – could have worn the mouth.'

He registered the disgust she was trying to hide, and changed tack.

'Dorothy, that person, your husband – myself – oh, my darling Dorothy – the quiet worker in the ironmongery, the lad who went up the ladder, down to the basement, who helped customers choose rakes and spades and nails – who spent his lunches deep in books – that quiet young man . . .'

She swallowed. The light flickered across her black hair and olive skin.

'That person is dead. And I am not sure who has replaced him. But,' he added, 'I promise you I am not unhappy.'

He said one more thing. 'I love you more than life itself.'

She replied: 'And I you.'

'I am sorry if my manner lately has been – queer.'

'Darling Rex, my worry –' she struggled to complete the sentence as the gaslight flickered above her – 'is that sometimes you seem almost *too* elated.'

'That's it!' he cried. 'Or – inspired! You see, that is how I feel! Elated! Some mornings I wake with so much joy in my heart I want to run, hug strangers on the street, take you out of this tidy little house and buy a mansion, with carpets, where Meredith can run with her brothers and sisters – a boat – and they can – we can – run in the bright sunshine, run in safety—'

At that moment, as if the urgent mention of her name had reached the child upstairs, Meredith cried.

'I do not really understand it,' he confessed, and tears sprang in his own eyes. 'My feelings seem – so intense.'

She paused, listening to their daughter. Crying husband, crying child. The light from the gas flickered. Above them, Meredith settled.

Dorothy removed the tunic, the undergarments. The warm glow fell across her naked breasts. Rex leant forwards to plant his mouth on the flesh, desiring her in that instant so much that he was trembling. She rose, drawing his mouth with her so that his body followed.

'Those brothers and sisters,' she said, backing towards the door, 'do you remember how we make them?'

So on that final night they made love. He was not the frantic, distracted veteran now. For once he was the attentive husband. What he had said had not calmed his wife's concerns. Rex had changed. Inside him a crevasse had yawned, and she could not be sure of its depth and danger. But that night at least, she had the undivided attention of her husband, the hero with the battlefield gash on his forehead.

Her war crinoline was in a heap by the bed when she awoke to Meredith's crying in the morning. It was a Sunday in March. Their thick curtains kept out the cold but only veiled the dawn. She needed to walk. To clear her head and think. Quietly, Dorothy crept from the covers to leave Rex sleeping. Guiltily she fished the undergarments off the floor, fetched Meredith from her room, went to the bathroom to change, and lifted the child from her bed. She carried the still sleepy Meredith downstairs. There she put her daughter into the pushchair she would soon outgrow and, conscious that Rex should not wake, quietly opened the front door.

Her last thought was the precious green scrapbook. Dorothy pulled it from the lowest drawer in the hallway dresser, and felt pleased to have it in her hand for the first time in a while. She slipped it into a side pocket of the pram.

Dorothy walked down their narrow garden path. She opened the iron gate, tipped the pushchair backwards to get it into the street, heard the springs squeak above the wheels and thought Rex could oil them later. A chill morning air burnt her cheeks. As she bent down to adjust the blanket on Meredith, who was waking and starting to look around, she did not register the unfamiliar roar of the new Albert motor car behind her, nor the fact that its young driver had lost control.

The vehicle mounted the pavement and killed Dorothy instantly.

Five years after the accident, on 8 May 1925, two police constables broke down the front door of a terraced home in Hull.

A father and child, it was rumoured, had become recluses in the house. Local police had been told more than once the little girl was absent from school. But in those days the authorities were reluctant to go beyond a front door, especially with so many traumatised men desperately trying to live normal lives on the other side.

In the case of Rex Moran-Hughes and little Meredith, the police took action only when a local woman reported the theft of some bread by a neighbour's child. The police learnt that the child had stolen the bread on behalf of 'a lonely girl who feeds it to her sick father'. The two children had been at school together.

The address was ascertained, the road discreetly visited. Neighbours confirmed they never saw the door open or the curtains part. Getting no answer to their banging at the front of the house, the two policemen smashed down the door with a discarded table leg they found in the overgrown front garden.

What the officers discovered as they fell into the hallway shocked them. The house stank. The policemen held their helmets over their faces as they climbed the stairs. The house became darker the higher they went. They listened for noise. A movement of sheets in a bedroom?

Rex, bearded and dirty, was lying in a soiled bed. The curtains were closed, the lamps off. The child was sitting on the floor beside her father, face aglow in the narrow line of daylight which passed through the gap between the curtains. Neither was able to respond to questions. One officer ran to the bathroom, gagging at the smell, and emptied his stomach into a bathtub full of dirty clothes.

They later discovered that the young girl had crept out through the back door in the evenings. Collecting small amounts of food from the homes of friends at her school, she begged them for secrecy. She would bring the food to her father and urge him to eat. Rex Moran-Hughes had barely taken any of the stolen food and was skin and bone. Both had scurvy.

'Look at his face, it's like a dead man,' whispered the officer whose stomach had turned.

The other policeman gave the girl a perfunctory cuddle. 'You'll be fine.' He produced a notepad. 'Want to make this easy and tell us how old you are?'

'Go easy,' said the kinder policeman, the nauseous one. 'What do you think she is, seven? — Are you six or seven, luvvie?'

'She'll be stunted. She could be ten,' replied the unfeeling one, glancing around briskly. He added, 'Touch of the tarbrush in the girl. Look at the skin and the hair. Foreigner. Watch for lice.'

Meredith, with the dusty face and wide eyes, did not cry. She looked into the air with a fixed expression, as if she was waiting for a signal to move. The kinder policeman noticed something and swished his hand in front of her face.

He moved to one side of the room, then the other.

'What are you doing?'

'She's blind.'

The unfeeling officer came closer and stared into those black eyes, frowning. He moved his face in an orbit around hers. The child flinched only when his sour breath wafted directly into her nose. He said 'Boo!' suddenly, and Meredith burst into tears. 'She's blind all right,' he confirmed.

Local people rallied round once the story was known. The man's heart had been broken by his wife's death in an automobile crash, following directly from trauma suffered in the trenches. His little girl had kept him alive with begged bread and cake and sips of water. She had lost her sight but no one knew how.

Initially, Rex was hospitalised and Meredith taken in by the local vicar. She was malnourished but responded quickly to a fattening diet, lard spread thickly on bread and sweet milky puddings. She said barely a word. The couple had been ready for a blind child but after a month they noticed something about her movement – a confidence that came from knowing where obstacles were. Her sight was returning.

Slowly, a personality emerged. After six months the child was still quiet, but would smile if indulged. Speech came, and with it a steady flow of questions about her father. The vicar and his wife told her as much of the story as they knew. 'Your mother was sadly killed in a motor car accident. Your father is no longer himself. He has a fever of the brain. A kind of – disordered thinking. It's – an illness, we are told. He has gone to a place of healing.' The phrase 'lunatic asylum' would have been too much for a child of ten.

Meredith was uncomprehending. She only ever replied with one question: 'Can I see my daddy?'

But every time she asked, the vicar and his wife returned such sorrowful expressions and smothering hugs that she felt she must have caused them pain. She was still too young to understand pity, and she had never felt it for herself.

Meredith was moved to a church family. They saw it as their duty to change the world, starting with her. Robert Cairns was a serious-faced banker who had moved to Hull with his family from Edinburgh. He had a Lord Kitchener moustache and drank a lot in the evenings. Moira, his wife, was a burly woman who seemed to cook and clean all day, constantly blowing her long fringe out of her eyes. Their three sons were nearly teenaged.

Robert and Moira Cairns had thought this little girl would be good company for their boys. They would often tell friends at the church how 'the poor wee lass we have taken in' was now back at school and gradually catching up on two years of missed studies. 'She is a young lady of few words,' Moira would say. 'She looks through you. She has these black eyes. Her blindness was healed, praise be to God.'

Robert Cairns always added the same observation: 'There's no joke in the world funny enough to make that little girl laugh.'

She took their surname. They were kind enough, although Mr Cairns showed flashes of terrible temper when he was in drink. Moira only appeared to care for her out of duty, as one of many jobs, and gradually Mr Cairns became a drunk in the mornings too. Meredith deeply missed her father. Was he not safer being looked after by his own daughter than by strangers? She had heard the word 'asylum'. What exactly was that? Had he been taken to that place because she had failed in her care for him?

Above all, though, she missed her mother. This gap inside her was confusing, for she could barely remember any moment of Dorothy's life. She only knew that she had been loved. Meredith wondered what it was like to have a real mother. What was it like to be truly loved?

Back at school, she was picked on by the other children who knew her story from the newspapers and thought her peculiar. The bullying went on for years, driving Meredith back into herself. The only trace of her mother was the green scrapbook full of irregular sketches and vivid pictures Dorothy Moran-Hughes had cut from magazines. The young girl would stare at them without understanding what she was looking at.

People said her mother's last action had been to throw the pushchair clear of the car. Meredith believed that one day she would understand that scrapbook, that it would show her who her mother was. Even if she did not yet know what those pictures and sketches meant, the green scrapbook was still the most precious thing in her possession.

CHAPTER FOUR

The Girl in the Gallery
Liverpool, 1940

At first the visitors came in ones and twos. Then four families arrived as one huge huddle, shaking snow-drenched coats below the high entrance pillars before moving under the portico and through the vaulted doorway. By noon, the building was full. Staff at the front desk had to ask the public to queue at the door.

The exhibition of modern paintings was the last before the Walker Art Gallery closed. It had been an early government decision. Public artworks all over Britain would be put into safe storage until the threat of air attack was at an end. Meanwhile, the building itself would be commandeered by the Ministry of Food.

Another war? It was January. Snow and ice were everywhere – on the ground and in people's souls. Across Europe, citizens who had recovered from the Great War, then barricaded themselves against the crushing economic depression of the late twenties and thirties, faced an uncertain future.

The garish paintings on display were an antidote for a few hours at least. Seven years earlier, the gallery had reopened after a two-year refurbishment. A modest display of Picassos and Gauguins drew international attention, and the board were pleased. With reports that Adolf Hitler's jackbooted crackpots were against all modern art, many outside Germany felt they should look again with more open minds. The painter who was your enemy's enemy was worth the price of a ticket at least.

Since 1933 the Nazi regime had acted with increasing aggression against the artists Hitler hated. An exhibition of 'Degenerate Art' in Munich in 1937 featured painters like Metzinger and Gleizes, whose work was subsequently destroyed. Picasso was denounced. Beckmann and Ernst fled after seeing themselves featured in the Munich display.

So now the Walker Art Gallery's posters carried a message about something more than painting.

SEEING THE FUTURE:
THE BRIGHTEST COLOURS
THE BRIGHTEST MINDS

This was about freedom: freedom to enjoy a spree of chaotic red and blue and yellow, freedom to enjoy even without understanding. For what in the current world could be understood anyway? The news that 'Seeing the Future' was the last display before the government closed the Walker Gallery only added to the buzz in Liverpool and beyond.

The best-known names in the exhibition were Bonnard, Mondrian, Klee, Vuillard, Dali, Kandinsky and Ernst. An early version of Kirchner's *Straßenbild vor dem Friseurladen* (*Street Scene in Front of the Hair Salon*) drew particular attention because the completed painting had been personally denounced for its lack of natural colour by a screaming Goebbels, who had been photographed in a hysterical rant while standing in front of it. Kirchner fled to Switzerland. Watching the annexation of Austria and fearing Switzerland was next, in 1938 the artist shot himself in front of his house.

Yet the art on display in the Walker Gallery was life-affirming.

Put all those canvases together and the gallery was a torrent of colour in a world submerged in funeral grey.

One of the couples came with a young child.

The man was tall with an almost hairless head, a blotchy tan and a careful gait. He was slender. Between his shoulder blades the upper section of his spine was starting to show a stoop. The man was around fifty, so an old father. He smiled a lot. His wife looked two decades younger. She stood out in that wartime crowd in her fierce bright colours that matched the canvases.

Their child walked confidently ahead of them, a fair-haired girl of seven or eight. Her knee-length skirt was the same shade of bright green as her mother's jacket. They might have been two halves of the same outfit. Sometimes the girl ran, turning sideways so her small shoes would take her skidding across the marble floor, and the mother would tell her to calm down. Occasionally she would call the girl back haughtily: 'Jan – don't run off! Stay where we can see you.'

The husband and wife spoke intently. 'A lot of the men around us won't come back, Nancy. I've thought about this a lot. It's not fair that I should be—'

'You think about everything too much. Think about it less! Don't harp on! Just enjoy this outing. Enjoy today.' Her voice was clipped.

'But I feel I can offer something.'

'Offer your life? No. They would *take* your life. They would take the life of Janine's father, of my husband, and what right have you got to offer that?'

'I—'

'It's not "I" any more, it's "we". Her father's life –' she pointed at the girl – 'is not yours to offer. At this rate there will be a new war every twenty years and you can afford to miss one. You made a sacrifice before.'

'I didn't give everything in the Great War, Nancy. That's why I am here walking with you and Janine. I don't want to be the person who – fled.'

'Jan! Not so close!' called the mother, seeing their girl reach up to a framed swirl of oil on the wall. She turned back to her husband, eyes following the narrow horizontal scar across his forehead so she did not need to meet his gaze. 'Look. If you want to make a sacrifice, give your all to her. And you still have something to offer at the factory. Aircraft windscreens, tank portholes . . .'

They passed into a room with a sign that read: FAUVIST ART. Underneath was an obscure list of painters: Vlaminck, Manguin, Derain. A female gallery attendant, her hair a mass of black curls, sat in the corner. She was plump, in her early twenties, and wore a black skirt and peaked cap with a gold museum badge front and centre. Moonfaced, she fidgeted nervously as she watched the visitors, only rarely standing up to ask someone politely to move back from a painting or help with directions.

The young woman was used to the electrical shocks that sometimes seemed to pass through her brain, the zap of current from a wire she could never trace back to a generator. A spark, a tingle, a hum. A flash behind the left eye. She could never find the right word for what she felt. Were the feelings thoughts, or the thoughts feelings?

But modern paintings calmed her. Pictures that were feelings, only feelings, where you did not need to stare and stare to find a meaning; or know a religious text or ancient myth to understand.

When the couple and their daughter walked into the room, the young woman's attention was on three teenage boys guffawing in front of a Georges Braque. She wondered if she should tell them to pipe down out of consideration for the group behind them straining to see the canvas. She was briefly tempted by the line, *Hitler scoffs at that painting, just like you.* That would have shut the boys up, but she did not have the courage.

Then her eyes fell on the family of three who had entered.

Her brain crackled.

The man walked a yard behind the bustling young mother and their daughter. His gaze swept the room, clearly not taking her in. But in that instant she glimpsed his face.

Her eyes moved to the forehead.

There was a frown line that looked unnatural. It did not move. It was perfectly straight.

She lifted her right hand, index finger pointing upwards, and with a trembling fingertip pushed the peak of her cap an inch higher. Underneath it the black eyes narrowed. Now the girl moved the cap back down and stood. No one could see how her legs shook.

That indent – on the man's face – was not a frown line. It was a scar.

The family moved through the crowd and out of sight. The crowd in the room had its own energy. It spiralled outwards from the inside, then twisted and became a wheel within a wheel. The visitors formed a figure of eight, turning outside-in and inside-out. By each door people were coming and going.

The girl left her empty chair in the corner – a sackable offence, she knew – and edged towards the exit so she did not lose them.

He was standing alone, outside the room. Meredith almost bumped into him. She stopped and drew back.

'Sorry—' She almost said 'father'. 'Sorry, sir.'

He smiled vaguely. Paused. Meredith felt dizzy. She believed her father would know her instantly. She saw his scar and knew it was him. Why did he not know her?

'Ah – sorry – am I in the way here?' he asked uncertainly, his voice instantly recognisable, bringing back memories of that dark house and the stolen bread.

Meredith frowned.

This, she knew, was the moment.

She opened her mouth to say who she was.

Who they both were.

But her nerve failed. 'Not in the way at all.' She smiled and moved away, her heart pounding so hard she thought it might break through her chest. In all her imaginings she had never expected to see her father so alive, so alert, so *recovered* . . . and with a new family in tow. She wondered if she had misrecognised him but there was no doubting that scar on his forehead. Ruler-straight, the most unnaturally perfect horizontal.

Back in her chair she tried not to cry. A buzz in her head came and went. She could not remain sitting. She set off around the gallery, desperate to tell him who she was and hug her father for the first time in fifteen years. Surely she had not been mistaken about him?

She crept up on the three of them in a crowded room with a painting outside the door labelled *Landscape at Cadaqués*. The Salvador Dali canvas seemed to show concentric allotments, each a different shade of brown; houses as boxes and sculpted trees. Inside the room were obscure German artworks whose erotic images were chaotically drenched in colour. Feeling light-headed, Meredith pulled off her cap and shook loose her hair so she could blend in with the visitors.

She followed the family, keeping the back of Rex's head in sight, conscious of the knock of her hard shoes on the floor.

They approached another attendant at a desk in the first-floor lobby. *Now*, she thought. *Now.*

They were having a conversation. Meredith wanted desperately to hear it. She moved closer. Rex and his wife and child had their backs to her.

'How many do you have?' asked the attendant, a boyish-looking middle-aged man with ruddy cheeks who never left his chair. Rex had to crane down to hear him.

'I only have the one,' said Rex. 'You're looking at her.'

'It's obviously not suitable,' said his wife.

The sign by the room said: NOT FOR CHILDREN.

'I just wondered – as she's young, maybe she wouldn't—'

'*It's – not – suitable*,' his wife repeated.

'You could try, I suppose, and take her out of the room straight away if she gets upset,' said the attendant. 'Ah! Let me ask my colleague here – a lady attendant might know better than me. I say, hello there – Meredith—'

The family turned sharply, but the attendant who had been standing behind them was gone.

Where does madness start?

Fifteen years after the two constables had broken down the front door of their home in Hull and found a blind child looking after a broken father, Meredith might have expected to feel the void left by both parents less keenly. But fresh grief now enveloped her like the snow and scree of an avalanche. She sat silently in her wooden chair in the corner of the room. The art that once had been her only comfort, reminding her of a mother she was sure had loved her, now just drove her deeper into sadness.

Had her father recovered his sanity and cast not a single glance over his shoulder? Was she nothing to him now, this man with the new wife and new daughter? His casual phrase rang in her head: *I only have the one.*

She imagined a conversation with him. 'Do I owe you an explanation?' he would have asked.

'Yes, yes, yes!' she would have cried back at him.

Would he have been puzzled, disconcerted by how anguished his oldest daughter was? Would he have asked her why she had never sought him out, and would she have told the truth – that she feared the impact of finding him, picturing him as lost and broken as he had been when they were both found in that house? Might he have been angry that she was even alive? What would his story have been? How would he have explained that he had recovered his sanity without ever searching for the daughter who saved him from death with stolen food?

She could have talked about her life. How she had studied in secretarial college. How she had taken a job in the gallery because she could not see a piece of modern art without thinking of her mother. How sitting in rooms filled with art was like being wrapped in her loving arms.

But he might not even have been interested. *I only have the one.*

As she sat in the gallery chair, Meredith reached inside her jacket to feel the green scrapbook she was never without. A mother had loved her once. She must cling to that.

As hundreds of visitors trooped through the Walker Gallery during the week that followed, some noticed that in the room marked FAUVIST ART the attendant seemed not to be alert. Often the young woman had her head down. A manager who reproached her saw, when she raised her chin to look at him, cheeks swollen and streaked with tears. At the end of that week, a dozen members of the public stood around the body of the staff member, curled up on the floor. A lady in a grey hat screamed. 'Is she dead?'

'Let me handle this,' said the manager, forcing his way through. 'Here! Cairns! CAIRNS!' He called her like a dog.

Meredith was not dead. Four attendants helped lift her into a private area of the gallery. They tried twice to place her on a chair. Both times she toppled to the floor. An hour later a doctor diagnosed 'severe idiopathic catatonia' and suggested, as he shone a thin light into the blank, unseeing eyes, that the problem was likely to be psychological. The best short-term solution was home care.

So Meredith was returned to the Cairns' house in Hull, where she found more acceptance than she might ever have expected. Mr Cairns was retired and the boys were heading off to war, so in that large empty house Meredith was their project again.

Nothing worked. All day she sat in a blue-painted bedroom. Some days she faced the wall for hours. Moira Cairns eventually gave up on conversation because Meredith never responded. The old lady turned to mumbled prayer. Meredith became overweight. Her twenty-sixth birthday was celebrated with only the merest nod of her head and a blink of tears. One day she ran out of the house into the fields at the back. It took an hour to find her. Sometimes there would be screaming in the night, and the couple would find her pacing in rapid circles. Mud on her legs in the morning meant she had escaped the house in the dark hours again. She spoke no sense, and eventually stopped speaking altogether. Finally, Mr and Mrs Cairns had to accept the girl was completely deranged – dumb and totally blind – and would not get better in their home. Moira Cairns, always a suspicious soul, began to wonder if Meredith's presence was a bad omen for the family. She contacted the authorities.

When the three sons came back from war in 1945, Meredith

was moved to the same institution in Hull her father had been committed to. They no longer called it a lunatic asylum, but the De La Pole Mental Hospital. The nurses took her to a locked room, their gloved hands gripping her armpits as if Meredith might suddenly break free. But to their surprise, as they locked the door they heard her thank them from inside the room.

Those were Meredith's last words for nearly five years.

Eventually a conference of senior consultants at the hospital reviewed the typed file of Miss M. Cairns with the intention of moving the young woman's case forwards. *Born 1915*, it noted. *Age: 35. Severe depression, rare episodes of mania. Mutism. Histrionic sight loss.* A debate ensued over whether her blindness was caused by physical or emotional illness. She had shown no improvement. 'Loss of vision, loss of speech, severe depressive retardation. That's a bundle of joy,' said one medic at the long table, a man in a stained tie with a habit of flashing his tongue from the corner of his mouth between every phrase. He shook his head wearily. 'I think I might prefer death.'

At the far end of the table another doctor, an older woman with thick lipstick and smoker's creases in her face, said: 'Her father was here, of course.'

A few others registered astonishment.

'Yes, in this very institution, when it was the lunatic asylum.'

'Oh yes, she's right,' said the first medic, leafing through his notes and shifting his body so his chair groaned. 'Her father was quite mad.' His tongue flickered across his lip again.

The creases tightened around the nose of the woman at the table. There was kindness and insight in the expression. From nowhere, she produced and lit a cigarette in a single movement, and now pushed it at the air like a magician's wand. 'Gentlemen, what do we think causes madness? The inheritance or the insult?' Before anyone could answer, she continued: 'If the first, if she has the same condition as her father, then her illness may alleviate spontaneously.'

'But,' said a young consultant whose accent and skin tone suggested India, 'it has been years! A radical solution is needed.'

'I have misgivings about any "radical solution" involving the brain,' said the woman.

'Typical of a woman – too soft!' said one voice, and the table exploded with laughter.

Another consultant, who until now had been staring out of the window, turned towards his colleagues. He shifted his chair towards the table. The doctor was a portly man with a grey-streaked beard which sprouted from his face like an abandoned shrub. His nose was large and veined.

Quietly he asked, 'Have we heard of a man called Walter Freeman?'

Their heads shook in response. He reminded them that a neurologist in Portugal, António Egas Moniz, had shared the Nobel Prize that year for a surgical technique known as the leucotomy. 'Well, an American neurosurgeon I know personally has been rather inspired by the early reports of swift or instant recovery among Moniz's distressed patients. He developed an instrument called an "orbitoclast" to perform leucotomies himself. Mr Freeman and I studied together several years ago. I now happen to have a copy of the very same instrument.'

Everyone on the table leant forwards. He produced from his jacket two metal objects. One, a miniature hammer. The other a narrow iron spike with a T-shaped grip at one end. The doctor puffed himself up and continued. 'Mr Freeman's work has been prodigious. He has used this simple device on more than two thousand people, some children, charging twenty-five dollars each time. It is essentially a modified ice pick driven carefully into both eye sockets of a patient with this small hammer. By moving the orbitoclast slowly left and right, the frontal lobe of the brain can be peeled away from the thalamus, which relays input from the senses.'

The table was silent as he concluded. The orbitoclast served to prevent a disorder of the mind from taking root in the body; to stop thoughts becoming feelings. It could even eliminate violent outbursts. 'And the technique is becoming so well known it is getting its own nickname – the frontal lobotomy.'

After a brief discussion, during which the woman consultant fell into a dissatisfied silence and vigorously stubbed out her cigarette, the date of Meredith's operation was set for 30 August, when all the staff were back from their summer holidays and could watch.

CHAPTER FIVE

THE FIRST DAY

Meredith offered only minimal resistance as the nurses led her from the room. They seemed to assume she had little understanding of what was happening. Her body went stiff as they strapped her to the trolley, then relaxed as methylparafynol and a barbiturate were fed into a vein in her arm. She never said a word.

As the trolley jolted, Meredith blinked. She felt the sudden shock of sight returning in snatches: a glow, a blur, and then a blinding clarity even the drugs could not obscure. Darkness again, then light. She wanted to fight, to resist the chemicals in her veins and the staff in their gowns. She wanted to plant her bare feet on the tiled floor and declare that she was capable of recovery and only needed time. But the trolley wheels trundled on.

Clearly thinking her deaf, as if not speaking or seeing meant not hearing, a group of medics had come to her small hospital room twice in the past week and described the operation in knowing ways to each other. One seemed to be named Professor Scott. Meredith sensed the hulk of a large man when he sat on the edge of her bed, and thought she could hear a beard in front of his mouth as he spoke. One day his stomach rumbled so loudly as he spoke that a nurse said he must ensure he lunched before the operation. He proudly told the others that he had studied the use of the orbitoclast through textbooks. When

Meredith groaned, they appeared to assume the blind girl was deep inside her own grief. But actually it was fear of what she could hear them saying.

Prostrate now, she saw the dirty white of the hospital ceiling suddenly come into focus. She watched her life played out in scenes framed by the fibreglass ceiling tiles above her, moving like celluloid as the trolley rolled. There, flickering in black and white, was the overturned pram at the roadside next to her mother's body, and Meredith inside it bawling. She was the child again on that hospital trolley, the little girl in the pram. No mother to push her clear.

More celluloid frames, black shapes shimmering on the hard white of the ceiling, ghostly shadows passing through them. The modern art of Duchamp, Magritte, Rothko, Pollock, Dali. A sudden image of Kirchner, standing in front of his house in Switzerland, putting a pistol to his temple. Then her father in bed, sick . . . she squeezed her eyes shut and, with superhuman effort, wrenched at the binding on her right arm. Immediately she felt hands grip her forearm, pushing it back, jarring the bone on the metal rail of the trolley. She was pinned down.

All she could do now was wait for the tap of cold metal on her eye socket. The orbitoclast. The operation, she had heard them say, took less than ten seconds for each eye.

But instead there was a clattering further down the corridor.

Was she conscious? She tried to focus. More shouting in the corridor. A woman's voice, young and unfamiliar. '*I demand it!*'

There was a stamp of hard shoe on cold tile. The trolley stopped.

'Holy Mother of Christ,' whispered a nurse beside her. She moved out of Meredith's peripheral vision with a bustle of white skirt. The patient did everything she could to look up, but she could not raise her head from the trolley even by an inch. The main strap was secured across her chest.

By moving her left hand, Meredith managed to the catch the intravenous tube and pull it from her other arm. The pain was like a hornet sting.

Meredith heard steps echoing off the whitewashed walls. A doctor was saying, 'No, no, come on, no.' It sounded like Professor Scott.

'What the *hell*?' shouted the voice, close now, and there was a gasp of astonishment at the language. 'Don't you "no, no" at me. I will scream the place down. Get that mask off your face now. You look like a bank robber.'

Someone had gripped the trolley in the chaos and was trying to steer it, but there was a collision and a scream. Maybe the young woman had grabbed the trolley and was pushing it at the surgeons. Suddenly, for the first time in years, despite all the medication and the terror of the imminent operation, despite everything that had brought her to this place, despite years of silence and darkness, Meredith felt the tiniest flutter of excitement.

And then, from above her head, the young voice screamed two sentences she would never forget.

'Let her go! This is my sister!'

Meredith was aware of a scuffle, of Professor Scott tumbling. Something clattered as it fell to the ground, and Professor Scott shouted: 'My orbitoclast!' There was more scuffling and the doctor said, 'It's bent. For God's sake, look at this. I will have to improvise or operate with a malformed instrument.' He hesitated. 'Oh God,' he groaned, but the sound was more anger than pain. 'I am bleeding, I have stabbed myself.'

'We cannot do the operation,' Meredith heard a nurse say.

The girl who had invaded the hospital corridor put in: 'You *will not* do the operation.'

'I am not being told what to do by a posse of washerwomen!' Professor Scott retorted. 'We have a schedule.'

'Washerwomen?' challenged the nurse. 'Sir, with that instrument broken – and look, her intravenous tube—'

'The orbitoclast is *not* broken, you damned fool!'

'Where are the guards?' someone said. 'The hospital commissionaires? Are they coming?'

'Listen up,' said the young voice, the military phrase suddenly commanding the space. 'You will not do it. My name is Janine Moran-Hughes. I am a lawyer.' The voice was breathless but the undertone unwavering. 'The woman on the trolley is my sister and I am her carer now. I want you to listen to me or there will be serious legal consequences. *Personal* legal consequences. As her closest family, I do not give consent. I am perfectly able to look after my sister. You will not cut her brain open, not today or any day.'

And for the first time since the corridor came alive with noise, there was silence.

Meredith desperately tried to move her mouth. She felt as if her lips were being pressed shut by a column of air above her.

She managed one word. 'My—'

A nurse's face appeared above her head, upside down, the nose and mouth masked.

'Look! Oh, God! She's speaking. She hasn't spoken for years.'

The air moved. Meredith felt two words emerge. 'My – sister.'

'This is irrelevant,' the doctor said, but his voice was distant, and had changed, as if the fight had gone out of him.

Slowly, Meredith was wheeled back to her room. The nurses unstrapped her and helped her from the trolley. She heard one say to the other through clenched teeth, 'That damned man,' and assumed the target was Professor Scott. Meredith immediately fell asleep in the armchair. When she woke, her slumber so deep it had been like falling to the bottom of an ocean, she could see – could see! – it was dark outside. Past midnight? And there, in the gloom, a young woman – much younger than she had expected from the voice, possibly just a teenager – came into focus, just staring at her, sitting at the far end of Meredith's bed.

'There's hardly any light in here. This lamp of yours seems to be on strike,' the young woman said.

Meredith watched her lean across to the bedside light and shake it by the shade. Dust fizzed from the dirty material. The lamp glowed brighter, but only briefly. The light bloomed for an instant on the face of the girl. 'Confession. I'm not a lawyer. I'm not even really an adult yet. I'm basically just an idiot. I was coming with my cousin, and he was going to pretend to be a lawyer – well, he *is* one – but then he thought it was all too serious, professional misconduct blah blah blah, and he chickened out. He just told me to use the words "personal legal consequences" as often as possible.' She chuckled to herself and shook her head. 'So I did.'

There were too many words for Meredith to take in. She raised her head a little and stared at the young woman. Blond hair, skin as white as paper, green eyes. The features dainty, the ears elfin. The face seemed composed of perfect lines, the jaw square, as if she had been sketched out with a sharp pencil. She was pretty, thought Meredith. But still a child.

Perhaps the girl had read her mind. 'Okay, I'm sixteen, well, nearly seventeen. Okay, not even half your age, Meredith. But I'm tall and I can act serious. And hey, we *are* sisters. Have you heard of me? I'm Ginny. Janine, I was christened. Same dad. You understand that? Rex Moran-Hughes. Maybe just nod if you understand?' Her voice was suddenly gentle, deeply compassionate.

In the armchair Meredith nodded sleepily. 'I understand,' she said, pleased to be testing her new voice. She smiled. In her heart Meredith felt a tiny bud open like a buttercup reflecting the sun. Was this what joy felt like?

Eyes closed, she asked: 'Why did you come, Ginny?'

The teenager swallowed, as if the question was difficult. 'There's no "why"! You are my family, and I don't have any other brothers or sisters. Meredith, listen. Our father came out of this place and set up as a gardener with the skills he learnt in the grounds here. He looked after the garden at a house where my mother lived on her own. Her parents had died. She was young. They'd left her a business and Mother was struggling. Our father found he was good at it. Glass manufacture. They married and had me. That's the whole story, pretty much. Well, give or take.'

'I'm glad,' Meredith whispered. She was taking in the objects around her. The scruffy dresser, positioned awkwardly by the window. A broken shoe-tree leant against the wall. The carpet was dark green, the wallpaper a sickly yellow. She had only ever bumped into these objects by accident, and now she felt her heart jump at the sheer certainty of it – she could see.

'What about you, Meredith?'

'I don't know what to say.'

'How – are you?' The simplest question.

'I can see. I can see and I can speak.'

Ginny looked puzzled, but did not ask what she meant. 'So now my father – our father – had a new family and he was, you know, set up in the world. But I didn't know about you, Meredith,' Ginny stressed with sudden outrage. 'No one told me. Not until – oh, wait, I mustn't give you too much to think about all at once.'

Ginny stood. There was an energy about her, a vulnerability too. The lamp made her shadow jump all over the room. Meredith shuffled upright in the chair. She took in her younger sister's grace and height. Ginny was tall, no longer a child. She could pass for someone in her twenties. She was also, to Meredith, unutterably beautiful, fragrant with the world beyond the hospital.

'As soon as I heard I had a sister,' Ginny continued, pacing the room, 'I had to find you. You see, something happened to change everything. Oh God, I don't know how to say this.'

There was a knock, cutting off the story. A man appeared, half opening the door and moving carefully around it.

'Sorry,' he said. 'I heard the voices.' He was holding a small torch. 'It certainly is a tonic to hear yours especially, Meredith.' The man was angular. Between sentences he took a pair of glasses out of his grey suit pocket, breathed on the lenses, replaced them, took them out again.

'We need more light in here,' Meredith heard Ginny say.

'Right,' he said, and held the torch upwards at his chin, which made his face look demonic.

The man spoke to the younger woman but kept his eyes on Meredith.

'Miss—'

'Call me Janine or Ginny.'

'I am one of the hospital administrators.' The torch shifted and the shadows above his eyebrows lengthened. 'Janine, if you are able to house our patient –'

'My sister,' stressed Ginny.

'– we will of course release . . .' The man tailed off as if reconsidering the word. 'We would expedite that. I feel we have done all we can for her.'

'At least you decided not to stab her in the eyes today.'

Meredith felt glee at the cheeky remark bubble inside her, an entirely new sensation. The manager turned to her. 'Well. It is very good to hear this young lady laugh.' She had not even been aware of laughing out loud. 'Miss Cairns, we haven't heard you laugh or –' he turned to Ginny again – 'or even speak much. For some time. Meredith had a traumatic breakdown. Blindness, mutism. I am a psychologist by training.'

'Blindness?' repeated Ginny.

'I don't want to talk about that,' said Meredith, her black eyes showing nothing.

The manager seemed not to hear. 'And somehow you have recovered your sight, have you? You see me?'

'She doesn't want to talk about it!' Ginny exclaimed.

The man hesitated. 'There was a breach of – procedure here. You will understand this as a – um, a lawyer.' It sounded like a word he could hardly bear to say.

'I should confess that I'm not actually—'

As if he cared little whether Ginny was a lawyer or not, the manager swished his hand and ploughed on. 'We do *not* allow surgical procedures to be undertaken in the circumstances that obtained early today. I mean lack of hygiene and lack of a collaborative approach and a — a slack attitude to an untested type of surgery.' He sounded like he was about to choke on the words. 'Professor Scott has been reminded of his duties.'

'The one with the beard and the nose?'

'The surgeon.' The manager was talking to his shoes now.

'The clown,' Ginny retorted bitterly. 'All he was missing was the striped trousers.' She pressed, 'Could my sister really not *see*?'

'There is some psychological chain of causation in her sight loss. The old model of medicine, the so-called Cartesian model, told us mind and body were completely separate. Descartes, thus Cartesian, are you with me? Your sister proves that distress can result in a catastrophic physiological response.'

'I don't know what that means, sir, but you're not doing any more experiments on her. I'm going to get her out of here.'

'We have responsibilities to our patients. Some of the staff failed to understand that no one is imprisoned here – no one is a criminal, people are allowed to leave if they have a safe home to go to.' After that sentence, a continuous apology in a single breath, the man appeared exhausted. He looked at his watch. 'Past midnight. Would you like a bed in the asylum, Miss Moran-Hughes?'

Ginny widened her eyes in mock horror. 'For how many years?'

'Overnight.' He gazed at her seriously.

'I'll sleep in the chair, thank you. Meredith, you get into your warm bed, darling.'

'Are we leaving tomorrow?' asked Meredith. She felt breathless. Was it true that this might not be the last day, as she had believed, but the first?

'Yes,' said the administrator, 'if you wish, in the morning. I should add –' he turned to Ginny, and there was an urgency as he lowered his voice – 'that if you are to be your sister's carer, you should understand that her illness has been pervasive. The events of today may have jolted her into a different brain state. Well and good. But we can't be sure. The disordered mind is fragile. There is so much we don't know about the pathology of Meredith's condition, whether it is melancholia, whether it is endogenous depression, whether she will exhibit features of mania and psychosis as your father did. Her blindness and mutism are physical expressions of mental trauma, her body speaking. She will need peace and rest and a lot of it. The mood of a person, you see, is controlled by what we call the limbic system, and – possibly I am being too technical?'

'No,' said Ginny, 'I understand what peace and rest are. I'll write it all down so I don't forget.'

'Perhaps travel would be good?'

They both looked over at Meredith. 'I don't think I realised the situation,' said Ginny. 'She needs love.'

'I am sure you can provide it.' The manager glanced over at a thick green scrapbook sitting on a table by the window. 'I think she does have an interest in paintings.'

At that moment Meredith lifted herself unsteadily out of the armchair and shuffled two yards to the bed. She sank down across it, lying diagonally on the covers.

'The sedatives,' she heard the manager say, 'were very powerful. They won't wear off for twelve, fourteen hours.'

Meredith stretched her arms out where she lay and said only one word.

'Sister.'

The manager left. Meredith sensed Ginny looking at her for a long time. Then she felt her sister climb carefully onto the mattress, roll around and slide into her embrace. Meredith closed her arms around Ginny so tightly that she could feel her heart beating between them, as big as a bull's.

Ginny saw her cousin Lawrence before he saw her. Standing outside the hospital the next morning, he looked cross. Ginny regarded him with affectionate annoyance as she approached with her newly discovered sister. 'You were about as much use as a chocolate saucepan!'

'Well, I did bring my car. You don't look like sisters.'

'Why are men such fools?' Ginny asked Meredith with a laugh. 'We were born a long time apart,' she told Lawrence.

'We had different mummies. Do you want me to draw you a diagram?'

They climbed into his grey Standard Vanguard. The hump-backed saloon body sank six inches closer to the tarmac. Next to Ginny on the back seat, Meredith said quietly: 'The first time I saw you, it was in an art gallery. You were just a child.'

Ginny was silent. Lawrence was searching for something in the glovebox, huffing and puffing.

Meredith went on, 'I was working in an art gallery and you came with your mother and father.'

For another moment, Ginny said nothing. There was so much she wanted to tell Meredith, and so little she could say.

'It pains me,' the younger sister said finally, 'to tell you that I did know that.'

Meredith's eyes widened.

'Not at the time, of course not at the time,' Ginny reassured her.

'You were a little girl.'

'Yes, and probably quite annoying. The "only child" thing.'

'But you aren't an only child.'

'I know that now.'

'So – how did—'

'Because, Merry, our father realised it was you. Not until a few days had passed. He woke one morning and everything slotted into place. He told me this years later.'

Meredith stared.

'Yes. It all suddenly made sense. You, your name, you in the gallery. When he realised, he went back to find you. But my mother did not know you existed. So he was careful about it. The staff said you had left your job. When he told me this I was much older.'

Meredith had her hand over her mouth.

'He came back for me?'

'Yes. He came back for you. Please, please, Meredith – don't cry.'

'I never knew he came back for me.' Trying to change the focus, Ginny called at her cousin: 'Hey, Lawrence, I passed myself off as a lawyer in there. Can you believe it?' The women were arm in arm on the back seat as he fished in his jacket for his keys.

He was unfolding a map. 'If you were a lawyer, a girl of sixteen a lawyer, you'd be pretty much the most famous one in the country.' Now he fished a pen out of his jacket pocket and held it up. 'Time for this, Ginny?'

She snatched it away with the speed of a cat pouncing. 'Later.'

'Later? Hey, my—'

'Just drive, please.' Before he could protest, Ginny continued, 'And I'll have you know I am nearly seventeen. Things are changing, Lawrence, you'll see. Are you ever going to start this thing?' She turned back to Meredith. 'Did that doctor give you some medications as you left? I saw him hand you something.'

Before Meredith could reply, Lawrence exploded in frustration. 'Oh, dammit! I need to turn her. Bear with.' He tossed the map aside, shoved the driver's door open and found the hand crank. As his head bobbed below the bonnet, an elbow occasionally appearing, Ginny pinched Meredith's arm affectionately. 'He's an old stick-in-the-mud, this one. The clue is the beard.'

'I can't wait to meet your family.'

A pause.

'Oh, Merry. I'm going to look after you.'

Ginny's tone seemed to worry Meredith. 'Is something wrong, Ginny?'

The car suddenly started, the engine thumping and whirring,

the exhaust banging underneath them. Lawrence bustled back into the driver's seat and looked at Ginny in the rear-view mirror.

'Is she okay?' Lawrence gestured at Meredith.

Ginny looked, her heart hurting for her sister. 'She's been so ill. God, so ill. But we are going to get you better, Merry, aren't we?'

'Slowly, yes.'

'That's Ginny for you!' said Lawrence. They were at speed now. He wore tweed with the elbows patched, and the patches swept up and down as he dragged at the steering wheel and the wheel fought back at him. 'Always saving the world. Meredith, you tell her if you don't want her calling you Merry.'

'I like it,' said the older woman.

They tore into the centre of Hull, taking lefts and rights so fast the two women were thrown into each other on the back seat. Meredith wound the window down a little to feel the breeze on her face, and Ginny even heard her giggle. How she loved the sound.

The day was a blur. They arrived at the house, where Ginny showed Meredith all six bedrooms and watched her gulp at the size of the dining room. The garden stretched back two hundred yards at least, and Ginny mentioned that her mother owned some land beyond it. They were not rich, she protested at one point, just comfortable. Meredith became dizzy looking at the chequered floor lino in the kitchen, and sat on the set of black plastic chairs one at a time.

'And these are new,' said Ginny.

Meredith had a feeling inside her of a flower opening, a bud. Was it excitement, or anxiety?

'Where is your mother?'

'Away until tomorrow,' Ginny replied.

'Does she know I'm here?'

'No.'

'You didn't tell her?'

'How could I know I would find you?'

'Will she mind me being here? And what will my father say?'

Ginny was silent.

Meredith repeated, 'My father?'

They moved outside. Ginny used a tea towel to wipe down the two garden chairs. She moved them parallel to each other, facing away from the house. They sat. Carefully, the younger sister started to speak.

'I don't think our father ever told my mother he had been married and had a daughter already. I remember when it came out. I was a child still. There was a huge row. He was crying. He was always such a sensitive man. He just kept apologising. I remember it because I always wanted a sister, and now I knew I had one. He told my mother about – was it Dorothy –'

'Yes, Dorothy,' confirmed Meredith.

'– your mother Dorothy, and you, and he explained that he had never wanted to talk about her or you, because of his past. But I think my mother felt he must have lied to her. He kept saying he never lied, but the time in the asylum just wiped it all out, the whole of his past, even the war. And I think – I am guessing – but I think he felt his problems might come back, he felt his illness might be triggered again if he acknowledged it all. He wanted his life with us to be a new start.'

'What is your mother's name?'

'Nancy.'

'If she does mind me being here, at least my father will be pleased to have me.'

'Meredith. Our father is dead.'

Meredith was silent for a full minute, then let out a howl of pain.

Ginny whispered, 'I just can't avoid saying it for a second longer.'

Eight months ago, during a storm, Rex Luke Moran-Hughes, brave veteran of the First World War, father of two girls born some years apart, latterly managing director of Albemarle Glass Limited, had fallen into the Barmston Drain, the land drainage system to the west of the River Hull.

Ginny listened to Meredith crying. She watched as the garden seemed to narrow, the colours drain from the perimeter, until all she could see was a single beech at the furthest end and a small wooden gate beside it. She wanted to run to the gate and escape.

The two women cried together. They hugged each other, shoulders shaking, and as their cheeks touched the saltwater mingled. It was not an exchange of blood but something more. The tears were a grief shared for a father lost. Their lives were joined now; they were sisters. Some might have called them half-sisters, but now those two halves were one.

PART TWO

CHAPTER SIX

The Dive
Cadaqués, 1951

'You stole – my shirt.'

He said it twice. The second time more quietly, with a gulp in the middle, as if the sentence was too much for him. He was looking straight at Meredith. 'I can see the red flash. There.'

He pointed.

It was a miniature mark in the stitching, just above the breast pocket. Lines of thread in the shape of a tiny Z.

It seemed to Ginny that the reception area had fallen silent. She was briefly conscious of Salvador Dali's head at the other end of the room appearing over the shoulder of the waitress, and the animated conversation he was having with the receptionist being stilled. Even the flies seemed to pause in the air.

The girls were so shocked their mouths hung open. Ginny had seen the boy die – how was he now standing in front of them? Her breath came quick. It was not possible. What could Ginny say? That they had thought the boy dead, so she and her sister had buried his clothes but kept the shirt to remember him?

She opened her mouth. But the sound came from beside her. It was Meredith, seated deep in the banquette cushions, cupping her face in her hands and groaning.

'No, no, this is my fault, Meredith,' insisted Ginny, hugging her. 'Please stay calm. I did this. I'll pay.' But Meredith broke free and stood up, her face still buried in her hands. She howled as the cushions around her fell to the floor.

'Hey, is she okay?' It was Russell Saunders. The stuntman, body full of transatlantic ease, approached as if he had seen this many times before.

The boy in front of Ginny seemed instantly to change posture. He smiled. 'Oh, it's fine. Honestly.'

Meredith was still groaning. Ginny stood and whispered into her ear. 'Meredith, Merry, I'll deal with it, I will. Go to our room, take his shirt off, you'll feel better. Let me do the explaining.'

As if suddenly conscious of the attention, Meredith lifted her face from her hands. There were red blotches on her cheeks and forehead. Her eyes were wet with tears. She breathed deeply and turned to Russell Saunders. 'Please apologise to Mr Dali if I've disturbed him.'

Saunders broke the tension. 'Holy hell, I think he likes this kind of thing! He's over there having an argument about why the hotel needs to put four tables together when it's only two of us eating. I guess so he can send the salt cellar skimming half a mile towards me like he's in a stately home . . .' He rolled his eyes and wandered off.

There was distant laughter. A tray falling somewhere. The reception area grew busy again. Meredith looked at the floor. 'I'm truly sorry,' she said, and Ginny felt her heart break, hearing her sister in pain. At the reception desk, Saunders rejoined the conversation and was beckoned towards the dining room by Salvador Dali, who still had the rubber snake around his neck and walked with his head and chin jutting upwards, as if trying to be the tallest person in the room. He looked ridiculous, thought Ginny.

The waitress, standing at the shoulder of the young American, shrugged impatiently. She looked disappointed that the show was over and no one was going to forcibly remove the shirt from Meredith. She stalked off. Meredith left too, in the direction of their room.

Now it was just Ginny facing the young American.

'Please – don't judge us until I explain.'

He had the slightest stammer as he responded. 'Of c-c-course I won't.' Somehow the speech impediment put her a little more at ease. 'I can't find any of my clothes.'

'I know,' said Ginny. 'I feel awful.'

'You took them?'

Ginny felt she should give him the whole truth, get it out of the way.

'We buried them because you were dead.'

It was quiet outside. The boy seemed to be possessed by a range of emotions. There had been fury at first, for sure. But Meredith's reaction in the reception area, her mortification at the realisation that she was being accused of wearing a stolen shirt, had made him stop, clearly confused.

Walking across the hotel garden, almost in step with him, Ginny dared shoot the American a glance. He was really not a boy, in the same way that she was no longer a girl. They must be about the same age. She wondered if he had looked in the mirror this morning like she had, and realised what he had become – a creature of power and agency. She decided probably not.

Discreetly darting her gaze left to take him in, she noted his height and the depth of the tan which had misled her into thinking he was local. The youth was lean and muscled, and strode with a rangy, loping gait, rolling his shoulders as he moved. His physique looked faintly familiar.

Hesitantly he asked, 'Um, is your sister okay? She ran off with that book.'

'You noticed that? It's her most treasured possession, her mother's scrapbook with all her favourite paintings in. She keeps worrying she's lost it.'

'That's quite intense. She – she l-l-looked upset.'

There was a painful lack of confidence in his speech which stopped her thinking of him as a Roman god and helped her understand that this person she had upset might well be adrift in the world, someone she could help.

'It's a long story. My sister will be all right but she upsets easily. She has had a period in an –' she wondered if she should say it – 'in an asylum, and I need her to be fully rested to get better.' Her voice broke. 'Oh, this is all my fault. I thought you had killed yourself. All we had were the clothes. We said a prayer and buried them. I am mortified. Honestly. Mortified.'

They walked a few paces in silence.

'I thought you had thrown yourself from the top of that cliff.'

'I did.'

'Deliberately?'

'Hey, I'm a diver! I do it every day. Early in the morning. Five thirty if I can. Before I come on shift at the hotel. Diving is the opposite of killing yourself, if you do it right. Diving is living. You breathe in such clean sea air. It fills your lungs as you go down. You burn with it, you feel alight.' His first smile. He seemed to lose his flow and added, 'The m-m-mechanics of it, incredible.'

'Maybe you can understand this. I have a sister who wanted her life to end for a long time. So – because of her, I guess – I worry about suicide. So I jumped to the wrong conclusion.'

'We both jumped.'

'Yes.'

'She wanted to die?'

'It's a long story.'

'Was she insane?'

Ginny paused. She did not know this young man at all. And now she felt she was sharing too much. She was about to tell him more, even, than her sister herself knew.

'Meredith was a tortured soul, for sure. And I found her in an asylum and we became sisters like we always should have been. She came out of the asylum and she came to stay in our home – with me and my mother, because our father died. But my mother made it quite difficult for Meredith.'

'Why?'

'She's someone else's daughter.'

'Oh.'

'And our father had died. And – there's something else I won't trouble you with.' She stared at the ground, skeletal leaves on the hard earth. 'When Meredith was in the house, Mother challenged me once, "What is she actually doing in my home?" And I just burst into tears. Why would she not see that Meredith needed us, needed a family? But the doctors had said travel would be good for Meredith, so I took her away.'

'Not just away. Far away.'

'Yes.'

'Why here?'

'I don't really know. I just wish I could find a way of breaking her out of herself. I'm saying too much. I haven't had anyone to talk to about it.'

'You are doing a very good thing.'

'I'm really not.'

'Sweet Jesus, was I naked?' He had suddenly realised what must have happened when Ginny saw him dive.

'I couldn't see because of the bushes,' she lied. 'Then I started looking for you, couldn't see you, and nearly fell off the cliff myself.'

'I feel bad that I accused your sister,' he went on, 'especially if she's ill. I feel very bad about that. P-p-please would you apologise to her for me?'

Nodding, Ginny aired a thought that had only just struck her. 'Do you know, when she saw that artist man, that's the first time I've seen her eyes light up, just before you arrived.'

'So I stole your moment too.'

Ginny did not want this to end with the young American being the guilty one. 'Hey, you're the victim of serious clothes theft, so don't go blaming yourself.'

'Let's shake on it,' he said. They were entering the woodland just as he reached out his hand, and he nearly tripped. In the shade, the air was cooling, like his anger. 'I don't have many friends here in Spain. I can't be doing with enemies.'

'Why are *you* here?'

'My father's business, but it's a bit of a secret.'

'Do I ask?'

'No, because I don't tell.' The line made him sound immature. 'Sorry. That was a bit pompous, wasn't it?'

'By the way, I would never be your enemy.'

'Really? I get the feeling that if I upset your sister, you would never forgive me.'

She paused. 'Yes. That is true, I think.'

They shook hands, just the two of them, standing straight-backed in the soil and leaves of the forest, a canopy of stone pines overhead. She thought he looked like a child impersonating an adult. Probably they both did.

'I should have told you my name earlier. Ginny. I was christened Janine but I'm Ginny.'

'Adam Bannerman.'

He said his name precisely, as if filling out a form. Her head swam with the Ms and the Ns. *Adam Bannerman.* Why would a parent inflict that number of matching consonants on a child?

'I'll show you where I dive in a minute if you want. But is this the right place?'

Ginny's promise to take him to where his clothes were buried seemed rash now. Every inch of forest floor looked the same. As they moved deeper into the shade she urgently searched the surface for disturbance, for missing leaves, for the footprints she and Meredith had left. In her mind she tried to calculate the distance the two sisters had gone from the path – coming in the opposite direction, of course – but it was pointless because everywhere looked the same. She could not even tell if she was within fifty yards of the original spot.

He was starting to laugh, and she hated that.

'You don't know, do you? Don't worry.'

'Not exactly.' She scratched her forehead with a finger. 'I'm working it out.' It was infuriating that he was laughing and she could not even smile.

He bit his lip and grew serious. 'It's not life or death. I suppose I'd like to see the red sports shoes again. My mother gave me them. They were so perfect, the fit and the shape.' He saw Ginny's distress. 'But she'll never know they're gone.'

Ginny reached for conversation. 'What does the "Zed" stand for?'

'Huh?'

'On your shirt. The letter.'

'Oh, we say "Zee". That was from my dad. He got the shirt. He likes – fancy things. The shirt and shoes were from my birthday last month. Alexander, so Zander. It's his initial.'

'He gave you a shirt with his *own* initial?'

'Yes. Is that strange?'

'It was like a tent on you.'

'It fitted your sister.'

'Well—'

'I'm sorry. That sounded cruel. It wasn't meant to.'

'It is true, though. Tight on Merry, big on you.'

'My mother would have got the size right, but she can't get to stores herself.'

Ginny resisted asking why, because there was a sadness in the way he had said it. But she felt she was storing up questions – about his father and his mother.

'Maybe your sister should keep it,' Adam went on. 'She might find a use for the "Zee". Perhaps marry a guy called Zac.'

'Or Zorro. I love those movies. The shirt doesn't work with our father's name. An "X" not a "Zed", my dad.'

'What is he, Xavier? Xerxes?'

'Rex.'

'Ah, the "X" at the end. That's fiendish. I can't think of many words like that.'

'Box, fox, cox.' She was enjoying this. 'Crucifix.'

'*Eaux.*'

'Oh?' she repeated.

'*E-A-U-X,*' he spelled it. 'It means "waters" in French.'

He had beaten her.

'Listen, I can buy you a shirt that fits properly, to make amends.' She added carefully: 'We have . . . some . . . money.' Ginny shook her head at the words she had used. They hinted at a secret she held so close that she barely allowed herself to think of it. Her phrase 'we have some money' was halfway between the truth and a terrible lie.

Adam appeared not to notice the conflict that played across Ginny's face for an instant, and smiled. His mouth lifted unevenly and two circles of unequal size emerged in his cheeks, like spots painted on. Those circles were so well drawn she figured he must smile a lot, and for a second resented how much of her time in the last two years had been spent only with Meredith's misery. Adam's asymmetrical face included a gouge where the cleft of his chin should have been, a dent deep enough to look like a historic injury, and she wondered if something he had done to himself had affected his speech.

On the clifftop he had looked to her like a god. Now he was mortal. He was gesturing at his hotel clothes, the black slacks and white shirt. 'I just want to get out of this awful stuff,' Adam said. The shirt certainly did not fit him as it should, hanging loose about the shoulders. Ginny saw each shirt button was fastened in the hole above the correct one. She felt an urge to reach out and make it right. Then she had the thought that reaching out and trying to make something right was precisely what had caused all the trouble in the first place.

She gazed around the forest floor, trying not to appear desperate. She heard herself asking him the question before she could stop it. 'So your father's job is secret?'

'Um – I guess you would call it naval,' he replied.

'And he lives in Spain?'

'You've heard of the SNS?'

She shook her head.

'Spanish Naval Station, seventy miles down the coast. Built with dollars. Basically a post-war thing.' He paused, as if he wanted to say more, but could not.

'My sister and I saw a battleship yesterday, sitting in the water a long way out. I thought it might have been American.'

Adam smiled awkwardly, but did not contradict her. 'You know about Franco?'

'Of course! He runs the whole country,' she replied keenly.

'But you know what he did in the war?'

'Not really.'

'Franco supported Hitler. Even let Spanish soldiers fight with the Nazis. But after what happened to the Germans in Russia in 1942 he saw Hitler could lose, which would destroy them both, so Franco went cold on his pals' act with the Führer. After that, Spain was neutral.'

'Sounds like a good move.' She kicked some dried leaves left and right, hoping he would not notice her continued search.

'It's why my father is here, in a way.'

'I don't understand.' Now Ginny was paying attention.

'I have to be careful saying this. After the war, countries like France and Britain were furious about Franco. I mean, his soldiers fighting alongside the Nazis! But Franco portrayed himself as this mega anti-communist. Nowadays it's the Soviets who worry us. The big enemy is Moscow. So Franco and his goons in Madrid turn out to be our best buddies.'

'Our?'

'Well, America's. And Britain's. Our president is Truman, you've got Mr Attlee, yes? They prop up Franco to get in the way of the Soviets.' He lowered his voice still further, and Ginny wondered how dangerous this kind of conversation was. 'Luckily I was born in Canada,' he said, 'so I don't have to keep apologising for American behaviour.'

'It sounds terrible.'

'The police here use British Land Rovers, so I guess your lot are to blame too.'

'Oh, probably.'

'Politics is dirty, Ginny.'

'I'm just enjoying the sun here. Keeping it simple, yes? Which is easy if you ignore the guns. I'm going to help my sister find some peace. I don't want to think about the other stuff. If you gloss over it, this place is heaven.'

'Can you ignore it?'

She sensed the challenge. 'I ignore it by not knowing.'

'Or not seeing.'

'I suppose so.' She needed a change of subject. 'What does your dad do, exactly?'

He bit the inside of his cheek. 'I can't say. But you can guess that in a place like this, the General needs some help dealing with a number of awkward customers.'

'Rebels.'

'Ssshhhh! God!' His eyes widened as he put his finger to his mouth. 'I've said too much.'

'I know a bit about it,' she bluffed.

'So you know we need to keep our voices down. These people don't mess about. Some of the Spanish troublemakers have just disappeared.'

She whispered, 'Do you love your history?'

'Wars, I guess. Is that a boy thing? I don't know all your kings and q-q-q-queens.' The return of his stammer appeared to make Adam self-conscious. He looked sad as he said, 'I would love my dad to tell me more about what he does. But he's quite a tough figure. He is like a statue made out of rock. A Rushmore face.'

'A what face?'

'Oh, I just mean he doesn't like giving way. He's a commander type, and he wants me to know some stuff and not other stuff. So right now he's got me studying French Indochina because of what's going on there. But if I ask about what's going on here—'

'He won't tell?'

'I think he actively lies. He told me he was an army engineer. Fixing their networks, vehicles and the like. I don't think that's what it is. I've never even seen him with a spanner. He's something higher up for sure.'

'I'd heard Mr Franco isn't popular round here.'

'Mmm. They've a pretty fiery resistance thing going on in Catalonia. Separatists, they call them.'

Ginny remembered the old man who leapt from his seat on the bus when she foolishly said the word too loudly.

'I thought the police looked scared,' she said.

Adam was suddenly animated. 'Scared? They are d-d-d-damn terrified. I see them trembling.'

To Ginny, he seemed too enthusiastic saying this, maybe even a little juvenile. But she was caught up in the excitement that the two of them were confiding. 'I wouldn't give someone a gun if they were shaking.'

He laughed. 'Quite.' Then grew serious. 'But let's keep our voices down. They are young and scared and trigger-happy, the GC. For them, the hills have eyes, you know? This is enemy territory, Catalonia.'

'I would panic if I were them.'

'They wouldn't say "panicking". They would use the phrase "highly alert".' The correction was unintentionally amusing to Ginny, but she stifled a giggle. She could see Adam felt he was in too deep, and now he changed the subject briskly. 'Hey, did you see that guy in reception today?'

'My sister was very interested in him.'

'He is one of the greatest, you know? He is actually amazing.'

Ginny tried not to mind that she had failed to recognise or even know who the artist was. 'My sister loves his paintings. That's all I can say. I'm not sure that if I was a great painter, I would be arriving in hotels with a rubber snake round my neck.'

He looked puzzled. 'That man? That was Salvador Dali, wasn't it? Oh, I'm not interested in him. His stuff is just super-monsterish.' The word made him sound less grown-up than he was. 'I mean the other guy. His friend. He is amazing. He's the artist – for a person like me.'

'Robert Saunders?'

'Yes! That's the one. *Russell* Saunders,' he corrected her. 'What he does – really, you have to see it – in the movies – it's honestly incredible. For someone like me, wanting to dive, you watch a genius like Saunders. He's my hero, I guess you could say.'

They moved through the woodland. The ground was softer, the trees evergreen – stone pine and juniper, caked with salt where their trunks faced the sea. Overhead, the canopy was so thick it blocked the light. They heard gulls above them, nesting in the branches. The place smelt like sawdust. As they moved into the light a breeze shifted the greenery behind them, as if it was registering their departure.

Without even discussing it, she knew where they were heading. To the leaning, lunar outcrop from which he had dived. From which she had nearly fallen. And as they walked, Adam Bannerman breathlessly told her all he knew about Russell Saunders.

In 1925 a small boy jumped off the roof of a barn in Canada. The barn was part of a farm in Manitoba. Among the farm animals were chickens. The boy had two of them under his arms when he jumped.

The child thought the chickens would sense they were in the air and begin flying as he dropped, carrying him skywards. Unfortunately the birds did not react at all. He and the chickens crashed twenty feet to the ground. One bird died. His parents were furious.

Possibly looking for a safer hobby, the boy started hanging around the local movie house in Winnipeg. His older sister, who worked as the cinema cashier, let him in to watch films free of charge. He was entranced. Although his jump from the roof of a barn had ended in disaster, he wondered if he could combine the thrill of barn-jumping with the glamour of movies. It took a while for him to work out how. Meanwhile, he learnt acrobatics at a summer camp.

In 1939, fourteen years since the jump with the chickens, Russell Saunders became the Canadian National Diving and Gymnastics Champion. He moved south to Los Angeles, thinking of finding an American university that might offer a diving scholarship. But then he discovered Muscle Beach in Santa Monica. A place where great acrobats went to show off. The boardwalk across the sand was already legendary. Hundreds came to watch strapping acrobats form pyramids and hurl the prettiest women into the air. The young Russell quickly became a star. He never repeated the jump with the chickens, but one day he persuaded fourteen people to stand side-by-side and bend over at the waist – then somersaulted the entire line.

A small break in movies came. In 1940 Saunders had a minor part in *The Great Profile*. But he was playing the part of an acrobat, which he did not really want to do. There were not many parts in movies for acrobats. His real aim was stunt work. The perfect job came in 1942. Chosen by Alfred Hitchcock for the movie *Saboteur*, Saunders stood in for the actor Robert Cummings. Pursued by both police and fifth columnists, his character had to jump out of a car, spring off a sixty-foot bridge and swim a hundred yards in handcuffs. He needed only one take to give Hitchcock the perfect sequence.

After war service in Europe, Saunders featured in a slew of movies – *Joan of Arc*, *Adventures of Don Juan*, *The Thing from Another World*. Most famously he doubled for the arrogant Gene Kelly as D'Artagnan in *The Three Musketeers*, jumping from rooftops and swinging into an open window by clinging to the threads of a ripped flag. He was furious when Gene Kelly put it around that he had done all his own stunts.

'And now he's in our hotel,' said Adam. 'Russell Saunders! What's he doing here?'

Ginny was impressed. Not so much with the history of Mr Saunders, but with Adam's admiration of him. As she looked at him she made the same calculation as she had made with Saunders. Five foot nine, one hundred and sixty pounds. That was why the boy had looked faintly familiar. It was not his face but his body. He had the exact same build as the stuntman.

'His assistant told us he is going to have his portrait done by Dali,' she said.

'I would really like to speak to him. Show him a dive, get him to help my technique.' As Adam spoke they came to the cliff edge. Ginny felt nervous, remembering the gust of wind that almost took her life.

'I don't think I'm cut out to be a waiter,' Adam continued. 'It's like being a prisoner. The staff are given rooms downstairs. Each door is a different colour, mine is green. Like I'm being filed in a box.'

'Green door boy.'

'That's me.'

'At least you can get out here and feel free.'

'And it's safe. Really, Ginny. Even in this wind. You just have to dive when it drops. You wait for the precise instant. The wind can take a person, toss them against the rocks, you know? The really big cliffs are at the Cap de Creus further down the coast. Everyone knows them. This outcrop is small, more private. But just as high. I can tell you don't believe me but honestly, it's safe. I know the sea is deep enough down there. I'll show you, shall I?'

'This minute?' Her heart was banging in her chest. 'You want to put me through that again?'

He laughed. 'I was a, um –' here he waited for modesty to stop him, but it did not –'gymnast myself. Not like Mr Saunders, of course, just at school. I did win some medals. But no . . . actually, wait.' He rubbed his chin, his finger in the gouge, as though something had just occurred to him. 'I shouldn't do it now.'

'Why not?'

He looked embarrassed.

'You're scared!' she said playfully. 'Well, I would be.'

'I'm not.'

'How many feet down is it?'

'Eighty.'

'I'd definitely be scared!'

'I'm not scared, Ginny. I just – there's a reason.'

She looked at him through her sunglasses. His use of her name made her feel alive, and she hoped he could not see.

'Okay,' he said with sudden determination. 'I will. Just don't be angry.'

'Why would I be angry?'

He took off his shirt, tossed it onto the ground and kicked off his black working shoes. 'Because,' he said slowly, unbuttoning his trousers, 'I should dive in my underpants, with you here. But I *can't* dive in my underpants because somebody buried them. So. Look away, please.'

The trousers came off. He kicked them onto the shirt and her gaze fell with the clothes to avoid his naked body.

'No, Ginny, I'm really not scared.'

She tilted her head up, looking out to sea, anywhere to avoid the shape between his legs.

'*You're* not scared, are you?' He laughed beside her, completely calm now.

'Of what?'

'Some stranger stripping off!'

'These glasses are so dark I can't see anything.'

'And you'll guard my clothes while I run back up?'

'I won't bury anything this time.'

'I will be ten minutes, okay? Fifteen max. The first three seconds is the easy bit. Just me in the air.'

She did not want him to go. Her heart pounded. Her mouth dried, and she swallowed. 'Just concentrate and do it right for me,' she said, turning to him. No sooner had her gaze locked on his face than he moved as if snatched away.

Adam span, ran and jumped into the air, rolling sideways with his legs crossed at the ankles.

She started to scream but it turned into a yell of delight. Jumping forwards, she sank to her knees, lying flat so she could safely see over the cliff edge. She was just in time to see the flash of his body as it turned, tucked and stretched into the water. The splash was small and so distant that she did not hear it.

Ginny rolled onto her back and giggled. A feeling of joy deeper than she had ever known swept into every corner of her body as she lay beneath the blinding sun.

CHAPTER SEVEN

THE FIRE

Siobhan Lynch stood upwind as the dining-room window belched smoke. She looked over her shoulder at the sea, then back to the Hotel Maravillas del Mar. She made a shape with her mouth that could have been a reaction to sour fruit juice, and scratched the mole above her top lip. The garden was painted with shadow now, but her clothes still clung with sweat. The evacuated guests came out in ones and twos as, inside, hotel staff sloshed buckets of water. A lady who took the lowest stone step too quickly, in a mild panic, managed to go flying. She caught her leg in holly, yelped, and was assisted by a male admirer who pretended not to see the flash of petticoat. Most guests trod more carefully, with thinly disguised impatience, as if this sort of nonsense was beneath them.

The fire had been started by the artist. Having got his wish to have four tables aligned in the restaurant so that he and Russell Saunders could discuss their project while sitting at far ends like lords in a stately home, the two men had talked in loud voices about Dali's plans. Guests sitting at nearby tables had no choice but to listen. The fame of Salvador Dali – at least among the kind of people who visited Cadaqués in the summer – was such that no one complained.

Then Dali said something that annoyed Saunders.

The stuntman complained: 'I am an artist too, you know.'

At that point Dali had said: 'Watch. This table is the world. This is Russell Saunders and his brilliance.'

He took a napkin and folded it into a bird shape, which he moved with his hand as if it was flying – and then launched it, so it floated gently back to the table.

Russell Saunders had laughed uneasily at the compliment. 'You are too kind.'

'And *this*,' said the artist, 'is Dali.'

He rolled a second paper napkin into a tube, stood it on one end and jumped up, striking a match in a single movement. Dali let the match flare at his face, casting shadows from the tips of his long, waxed moustache all the way back to his ears. Guests were turning. He lit the rolled napkin. The flames ate it instantly, but as the material became ashes, its weightlessness caused it to lift off from the table towards the ceiling while still burning.

'Aaaaah!' one of the female guests cooed.

'*The artist is the one who flies!*' he called to the room. '*Salvador Dali flies!*'

'The fan is on fire,' said a large Frenchman at one of the tables, as if he was simply stating mathematical fact.

Everyone looked up. Sure enough, it was. The burning napkin had trailed flame into the linen apron on a ceiling fan and set the thick layer of dust on the material alight. The dust was as combustible as petrol. The flames caught the paint on the ceiling – cracked and hopelessly flammable – and, as shocked guests began moving out of the way, part of the fan had fallen to the floor. The large Frenchman got up and stamped on the fan, but a burning fragment was displaced under a table where no one could get to it.

And so the fire had started. Saunders was furious. Dali left the room. The waiters arrived with buckets. A manual fire bell was cranked to empty the hotel. An idiotic valet soaked a guest by throwing water at the ceiling and she slapped his shoulder in fury. Siobhan had watched as Salvador Dali, his fire still burning, was ushered respectfully to the front door and found a car with not-to-worry signals from obsequious staff. Now, near her feet, a large spider scurried across the ground. Seized with fury, she picked up a rock and crushed it. When she lifted the rock and saw the insect turned to mush on the underside, a single leg still twitching, she said, 'Everyone has to suffer a little for their art, buddy.'

Siobhan hated the ego-tripping Spanish show-off. How she wished she could crush *him* with a rock. But then there might be no payday. She balled her hands into fists and dug her nails into the palms.

She was trying to deal with a developing situation with Russell Saunders that made her want to lay him out with her fists, too. At that moment, considering it, she saw the silly English girl come into view at the far end of the hotel garden. The preposterous Ginny, or whatever her name was, seemed to be alone and deep in thought. Siobhan watched as she noticed the smoke, then quickly realised there was a fire and broke into a sprint up the lawn.

'I don't think it's serious,' said Siobhan as Ginny approached, putting out her cigarette on the same stone that killed the spider. The ash fizzed. 'They're mainly worried about the hotel library. Apparently it has thousands of rare books.'

'Is my sister in there?'

'I haven't seen her. Don't worry, it will have been quick.'

Ginny gave Siobhan a quizzical stare, wondering if she had just heard an attempt at a sick joke. She ran straight towards the hotel. The reception area was full of smoke, yet the staff seemed unbothered by her appearance. Ginny shot a glance at the dining room and could see a haze of grey but no flames. By the door marked BIBLIOTECA she saw two staff standing guard, as if fire could be verbally persuaded to turn back. She took the stairs in half a dozen rapid leaps and found the corridor which led to their bedroom. She banged on the door. At least there was no smoke at this level. Ginny found her room key and opened the door.

Meredith was sitting on the bed. The blue shirt was ironed and folded beside her. She was shivering, legs folded into her chest. Her eyes looked frantic.

'What's wrong?' Ginny asked her, not waiting for an answer. 'There's a fire in the hotel. You need to come, Meredith.'

'I didn't care when I heard them calling. I just wanted to burn.'

'Burn? What, Meredith, why—'

'I just didn't care, Ginny, I'm in such a mess, such a state.'

'Hey.' Ginny sat next to her as calmly as she was able to. 'That's why we came on this trip, right? To get you better. Now—'

'I've packed our cases.' Meredith jumped free of her sister as if scalded. She was shivering and sweating at the same time. Even under her blouse, Ginny could see Meredith's injured arm was still swollen. The younger sister noticed their suitcases, placed neatly by the wardrobe.

'I want to go home,' said Meredith. She started pacing the room.

'When?'

'Tonight.'

'But we—'

'*I want to leave tonight.*'

Ginny drew a sharp breath. 'Okay, okay.' A single picture

appeared in her mind: Adam diving, legs stretched, ankles inter-
locked, half piking in the air.

Meredith was standing, swaying, staring at the floor, breathing
hard.

'We can leave if you want to,' Ginny said, losing patience.
'But at this precise moment there is a fire in the hotel, started
by your painter fellow, and I can't let you just stay up here
and breathe in poisonous smoke.' Then she saw the box on the
bedside table. 'What's that?'

'Medicines.'

'I didn't know you had those.' Ginny prised open the lid of
the thin cardboard box with the first and second fingers of her
right hand, half expecting Meredith to jump on her. There were
twenty or more small tubes in there, each the size of a shotgun
cartridge.

The tubes were coated in silver paper, bearing the label:
BENZEDRINE INHALER.

'Do you have asthma? I didn't know.'

'Not really.'

'Bronchitis? These are inhalers, yes? For your lungs, or . . . ?'

Meredith was staring into the distance. 'I guess you'd call
them – mood drugs,' she said finally. 'From the hospital. They
gave them to me if things got difficult. The man you saw. Gave
them to me. As I was leaving.' She gasped at the air, chest
heaving. 'You breathe them in. For a lift.'

Ginny looked at the inhalers. The tops of four of them
had been torn off and they were empty. 'What did they have
inside?'

'A paper strip covered in Benzedrine.'

'But that's a serious drug, isn't it? Where are the strips?'

'I ate them.'

'You *ate* – come on, we must go downstairs.'

'I don't know if I can walk.'

Ginny could smell smoke coming from the corridor. 'My God,' she cried, crossing herself. She took Meredith's arm. It was hot to the touch. They stumbled out of the room to the top of the stairs.

'When I was a girl,' Meredith was saying, 'your father was very ill.'

'He was *our* father, Meredith.'

'Our father was very ill. He wasted away. I had to steal bread for him. When the police came I thought I was going to jail. No one ever told me I wasn't. No one has ever told me I don't belong in jail. I always expected someone to say the bread was stolen and I would have to go to prison. I was just a little girl, you know?' She sounded distraught, the words tumbling out. 'I was a blind little girl.'

'Turn left down the stairs,' Ginny prompted, wondering why the story had to be told now. 'Please, darling, focus.'

Meredith spoke as if from a dream. 'When the police came to the house I knew it was all my fault. The stolen bread and cakes. I knew they had come for me. Then today . . .' She started shivering again.

'You were accused.'

'Of stealing—'

'The shirt, of course, I see.' Ginny hurried her. 'Come this way. Quickly. Meredith, listen. I spent the last couple of hours with the boy. Adam. He doesn't mind. He showed me his dive. He's a lovely boy.' She corrected herself. 'Man.' There was that memory again, of the body and the light and the sea, flickering in her mind like the image from a Victorian zoetrope. 'He knows you didn't steal it. You wore it because your shirt got ripped. He understands. He's . . .' She needed a word. 'He's – fun.'

'And you gave him back his shoes, his other clothes?'

'We couldn't find them.'

Meredith groaned.

'We need to go downstairs. Don't worry, Merry. He was laughing about it. He's a beautiful young man. He wants to be a famous diver.'

At the bottom of the stairs, Ginny saw that the fire had been extinguished. Outside, three Spanish police officers were just arriving, climbing out of a Land Rover. The vehicle reminded Ginny of her conversation with Adam. The police officers, with their distinctive black hats like sailboats made from folded cardboard, carried their rifles in full view and looked thoroughly uninterested in helping anyone. One of them suddenly shouted, ran fifty yards to the bushes that bordered a path that ran to the front of the hotel, pointed his rifle into the greenery, and froze in that position as he swept the gun barrel across the space in front of him. Then he relaxed, snapped to attention, shouldered his gun and jogged back to his colleagues. Guests were huddled around the hotel's rear entrance, wanting to come back in. Their annoyance was obvious. A woman used a newspaper to fan the smell of burning from her face. Ginny caught sight of Adam, bending over an old lady who was sitting on the grass. He had placed his arms on her shoulders and appeared to be comforting her. The American was kind, she was sure of it.

The guests queueing to re-enter the hotel looked puzzled when Meredith and Ginny came out, Meredith unsteady on her feet. The sisters squeezed through the crowd and into the garden without saying a word. Ginny inhaled deeply and found a bench for them overlooking the sea.

'Meredith, darling, I am here for you. I will always be here for you. Whatever you have taken has overwhelmed you a bit—'

'I think we both smell of smoke,' said Meredith, sniffing at the sleeves of her blouse as she sat down uneasily on the bench.

'Probably.'

'We are leaving tonight.'

'Yes, yes, but let me just put you here in the warm for a little while so you can rest and breathe some clean air, while I work out what we do.'

Meredith suddenly asked, 'He understands, does he? The young man?'

'Understands what?'

'That we have to leave. He will understand?'

'Who, Adam? Oh, it won't make any odds as far as he's concerned.'

But it might, thought Ginny. *It just might matter to him.*

And then Meredith's eyes blazed.

'We have to leave, Ginny. Something terrible is about to happen.'

As Ginny walked back to the hotel building, she passed a eucalyptus tree and heard someone splutter on their cigarette. She stopped and brushed back the branches. Of course. Siobhan, still crouched under the thick foliage, concealed beside the trunk of the tree.

'Oh!' said Ginny, stooping. 'Are you still hiding?'

'I can't be hiding if someone sees you standing there.' Siobhan took another long drag of her cigarette and closed her eyes. Ginny took the comment as an invitation. Bending down, she crept under the eucalyptus leaves. Now the two women were close, the space filled with the combined odour of burning tobacco and burning hotel.

'Who started the fire?' whispered Ginny.

'The artist, of course.' Siobhan shrugged, eyes closed. 'After an argument, I think. How is your sister? Not dead, I hope.'

Ginny forgave the thoughtless joke, and in this moment decided a friendship with Siobhan was possible. After all, she needed to speak to someone. If she had thought about it more carefully, she might have chosen anyone but the Irishwoman. But in this confined space the need to share overwhelmed her. 'Meredith has a lot of difficulties. She was insane. I thought I could rescue her, but . . .'

'You got her out of the fire.'

'I wonder if that was the easy part.'

Siobhan shrugged. She looked up at Ginny, who took it as a cue to say more.

'My mother and father had quite a lot of assets. An industrial glass manufacturer's, a big house, a lot of money saved up. When my father died, my mother assumed everything would pass back to her. But for some reason he split nearly everything between me and my sister.'

'Nice.'

'Not really, because of Meredith's situation. Sure, my mum has her half of course. But if someone in an asylum owns twenty-five per cent of your company, believe me, the banks start asking all sorts of questions.'

Siobhan took another drag on her cigarette, saying nothing.

'My mother told me to find her. To go and get Meredith from the hospital and ask her to sign back her share.' Ginny remembered Lawrence holding up his pen in the car the morning they both emerged, grotesquely tactless. But then she had also thought the conversation would be easy ('a misunderstanding . . . I am sorry . . . of course my mother will compensate you in any way you want'), as if her lawyer cousin could simply deal with it on the way back from the hospital. 'My mother said we would take Meredith in, and she just thought I'd easily get the legacy resolved. But there's no way I could. As soon as I found

Meredith I realised how stupid I'd been. The emotions of that first day were incredible. And for me, the key is to get her better.'

'And the money doesn't matter?'

Ginny picked up a stick and poked it at the ground, which was so hard the stick immediately broke. 'My mother is still expecting me to get her to agree. That's why we're travelling, because it was getting too intense at home. My mother constantly asking me, constantly resenting her.'

Siobhan contemplated the bright lipstick smudge on the filter of her cigarette. 'There is nothing so wonderful as money.'

'So destructive.'

'I guess it depends.'

Ginny protested, 'With Meredith, it really isn't about money any more.'

'My dear, I really think it is.'

The space under the tree was small. The confidence shared, Ginny stopped, full of misgivings. It felt strange, being this close to Siobhan. She could see every pore in her face. The way the lipstick seemed to have been applied rapidly, maybe even angrily. The knots and tangles in her red hair.

'I'm dealing with a complete lunatic too,' Siobhan said. 'The artist. Both of them. Mad as hatters.'

'Setting fire to the hotel?'

'Dali did that. In fairness, they're different levels of madness. Dali tops the scale. Completely. Saunders is just a thick idiot. A farmer's son who jumps off roofs. What sort of skill is that, being afraid of nothing? I mean . . .' She sighed, the Irish accent permeating even the breaths she took. 'Salvador Bighead, setting fire to a hotel while wearing a snake around his neck.'

'The rubber snake – I saw that.'

Siobhan snorted and lit another cigarette. 'Rubber? That damn thing was real.' She made shapes with her hands, as if trying and failing to get a grip on the reptile's underside. 'I think he had drugged it or the reptile would have strangled him. I turn thirty this year, and all I've got to show for it is experience with a roof-jumping farmboy and a snake-wearing painter.' She smiled to herself. 'Never had enough excitement between the sheets, neither, not for a woman my age . . .' Siobhan laughed hoarsely and tailed off.

Ginny was astonished at the last outburst. She giggled out of pure embarrassment. Worried Meredith might hear, she crawled back through the eucalyptus leaves, poking her head out from under the tree, feeling the cool air on her face. Fifty yards away, facing the sea, her sister sat motionless like a large stone Buddha, shapeless in the sun.

Now she moved back into their private space, on hands and knees. Siobhan sat watching her with the cigarette in her mouth and an amused expression on her face.

'She all right?'

'I hope so. I don't know. She's – erratic.'

'The perfect time to broach your legacy proposition? While she's distracted.'

Disgusted by Siobhan's cynicism, Ginny was desperate to change the subject. 'Why were Dali and Saunders arguing?'

The cruel line of Siobhan Lynch's mouth was accentuated by her bright red lipstick, and the cigarette did not help. 'Working with those two is like translating for Japan and Italy in the war. Not a word either of them says makes sense to the other. Dali has his head in a cloud somewhere. It's all paintbrushes and cosmic dreams. He's "had a vision", he says. Here.' She pulled a ball of crumpled paper from her handbag, smoothed it out on the earth and peered at the scrawl on it. '"I have had a cosmic dream in which I saw this image in colour which in my dream represented the nucleus of the atom, and this nucleus later took on a metaphysical sense in which I considered it to be" . . .' She paused. 'I can't even read this nonsense, it's just words.' Again she flattened the paper with her hand, which Ginny noticed was shaking. '"I considered my dream of the nucleus to be the very unity of the universe, Christ himself!" Can you believe he dictated that gibberish to me? Got me to write it down for him?'

Ginny stared at her.

'A vision,' Siobhan repeated contemptuously. 'Now Saunders – there's a guy who wanders around in his swimming trunks looking for a bridge to jump off. He understands one thing, and that's how to land on his feet without breaking an ankle. And Dali is coming out with this crazy stuff about cosmic atoms, getting me to write it down, and Saunders is just staring politely –' here Siobhan laughed, the guttural noise catching in her throat – 'as if there's a smell in the room he can't quite identify, but he fears the worst.'

Ginny laughed too. She could imagine the scene perfectly. 'The visionary and the—'

'The vaulter!' Siobhan looked excited, completing the phrase. She blew cigarette smoke upwards as she looked into the branches directly above her. 'But hey – if I wanted to follow the money, I think I'd go where Dali is. They call him "Salvador Dollars", you know. I can't stand him, but the money – God, that camp bastard smells of it. He showers in money, he walks in it, he breathes it. And yes, I would very much like a piece of that particular action.'

Ginny almost felt like she was interrupting a conversation Siobhan was having with herself, looking into the Irishwoman's soul and seeing something corrupted there. 'So why is Mr Saunders working with Mr Dali?'

Siobhan shook her head. 'The instructions were so simple. "Accompany Saunders to Port Lligat for portrait with Salvador Dali." That's it, right? There's a payment. My assignment is a cinch from their point of view. Turn up here with Saunders – sorry, *Mister Saunders*, forgetting my manners – make him feel important, hook him up with Dali.'

She spat at the ground, stuck her tongue out, picked a stray piece of tobacco off it and grimaced.

'I have a boss in London. He has big dreams. The Dali account for the whole of Europe. I'd love to steal it myself, but I don't think that's a runner now.'

'Steal it?'

'Just go off with Dali as his personal operator, assistant, whatever. Do the deals for him. Right? So much money. All mine. Well, a cut.'

'Is Saunders paying Dali for the portrait?'

'No, you're joking!' said Siobhan contemptuously. 'It's the other way round. Dali has showered *our* side with money. Saunders gets the hotel room, rental car of the finest quality, and my room paid for too. Plus the great theory is, at the end of it you get this new thing they call Public Relations. It's a story for everyone to talk about – "Crazy Artist Paints Stuntman with Perfect Body". The newspapers can do stuff, columnists get by-lines and vendors get pennies, and everyone gets a little bit more famous.'

'So what's wrong with that? If Dali wants to do it and Saunders wants to do it?'

'Jeez.' Siobhan shook her head.

Ginny thought she seemed angry but couldn't understand why. She doubled her stake. 'To me, your assignment sounds wonderful.'

'I wouldn't have come from Dublin to this sweatpit if it didn't.'

'So?'

'They met today. In the hotel. You saw them. Dali and Saunders. There's a lunch. Dali explains the painting. It's not what you understand a portrait to be. Not at all. And now I'm about to tell you I can feel my stomach turning.'

'Why?'

'Dali wants Mr Saunders to be Jesus Christ, just wearing a flannel.'

Ginny stared at Siobhan, then burst out laughing.

'Ssshhh, fool. They'll know we're hiding here!' The Irishwoman inhaled, as if calming her anger. 'A fecking flannel.' She dusted earth off her knees and continued. 'I'm chronically Catholic. Know all the verses. Brought up that way. Fire and wine. Like Saunders – *Mister* Saunders. So it's not top of his list of wishes, to be a half-naked Jesus on a Wednesday afternoon, you know?'

'But then again,' began Ginny more seriously, trying to see the positive, 'all he has to do is sit there.'

'You see!' hissed Siobhan triumphantly. 'That's exactly what I said! Just sit there! I told him. But apparently Dali said something to him about the pose that didn't go down at all well. Something about the way he has to stand. Saunders was so furious he could barely speak.'

'He has to stand a certain way?'

'I don't know, I don't honestly know what Dali said, right? First he pulled the naked Christ thing, then he said something about the pose – there was a row, and the thing with the napkins happened, then the fire, the hotel nearly burns down, and it's gone to hell.' She stubbed her cigarette out on a flower and said, 'I wish it had burnt down.'

'And I thought *I'd* had a strange day,' said Ginny, realising she had not been asked a single question by Siobhan yet.

'When Dali left the hotel, he gave one of the valets an envelope for Mr Saunders. I have it here.'

'Have you shown Mr Saunders?'

'No, I opened it myself.'

'Can you do that?'

Siobhan gave Ginny a withering stare.

'Don't! Don't be trying to show me up like that! I opened
it and I read it.' She flashed the paper in front of Ginny's face.
'There, now you've read it too. So don't start preaching at me.
This tells Saunders to come to Dali's studio tomorrow at eleven.
But Saunders is so furious I know he won't go. He's locked
himself in his room.'

Ginny was stung by the aggression, and could only say:
'Problem.'

'Problem. Might be the end of the line for me. If my client
breaks his contract, and Dali complains, I'm finished.' She
blinked.

'My sister says we have to leave tonight,' Ginny said quietly.
'We are going to have to, but I don't want to.' From deep within
her the sentence completed itself: *Because I want to see Adam
again.* She told Siobhan, 'There's a waiter in the hotel who
wants to meet your man, you know.'

'Meet Saunders? He won't be in the mood now, that's for
sure. He's stormed off. Locked in his room, whisky, probably
reading the Bible and searching for the commandment that
forbids the wearing of flannels.'

'The waiter idolises him. He knows Russell Saunders' whole
life story. He is desperate to say hello.'

'What's his name?'

'I'm not sure,' Ginny lied, wishing she had never mentioned
it. 'I think he's American. Born in Canada, like Mr Saunders.'

Siobhan was quiet for a moment. 'I've been trying to think,' she said finally. 'This art studio of Dali's is nearby. A walk. Place called Port Lligat. Maybe two miles. Saunders is supposed to go there tomorrow. He won't, so I'll have to go alone. I know nothing about art. I can't give Dali flattery because he'll see straight through it. Without Saunders the whole deal falls through, right? There's a contract. Saunders gets nothing so we get nothing. In fact we get less than nothing, because Saunders is just staying in bed and whistling for his breakfast. So that would trigger a financial penalty, under the "unfulfilled obligations" clause. You need a proper reason to cancel. Serious illness, injury. So for the pleasure of working with this goofball, we actually end up with a bill.'

It was not clear to Ginny whether the goofball was the stuntman or the artist, but she said nothing.

'The only way we can break the contract without a penalty is if Russell Saunders is incapacitated somehow.'

'Incapacitated?'

'If he broke a leg, let's say. Or had a heart attack. Or accidentally got, I don't know . . . hurt.'

'Which isn't likely.'

'You think not?' She looked Ginny straight in the eye in a way that chilled her. 'There's stuff that would trigger a heart attack, or mimic one. It's just a question of how I get hold of it.'

Ginny stared. Was this woman for real? 'You don't mean it?'

'There is a substance. It's called methyl iodide. A friend in Ireland told me about it. He's a pharmacist. It can induce a stroke. That would do it.'

Ginny needed time away from this woman's voice, her foul ideas. 'You wouldn't do something like that, would you?'

'What?'

'What you just said about – hurting someone.'

'I was joking!' Siobhan said. She clearly had no idea how her words were taken. 'But I can't let this whole thing just fall apart on me. What would that say about me, if I let that happen?' She looked sharply at Ginny. 'You won't mention this to anyone, will you?'

'If you don't mention what I told you.'

'About what?'

'The – my father's legacy. That stuff.'

'I'd already forgotten it.'

Ginny hesitated. Could she really leave, with this awful woman planning to hurt the stuntman? But she had to leave, because of Meredith. And leaving meant she would never see Adam Bannerman again.

Suddenly it came to her: the solution. A single stroke she could pull off that would solve every problem at once. She looked straight at Siobhan.

'I have an idea for you,' she said.

CHAPTER EIGHT

The House

She opened her eyes at the faintest light. Reached left, fumbling, finding her sister's thigh. Got her bearings. Carefully withdrew her hand in case Meredith woke. Stared at the ceiling.

Then, tightening her stomach muscles, Ginny sat up silently in the dark room. She breathed in deeply, shifted the bedclothes across her legs, swung her feet out of bed and walked over to the window. Tweaked the curtain an inch and saw the first signs of dawn in the dark hotel garden. What was it, not even five thirty? She sat in the chair and stared out of the window, waiting.

Sure enough, fifteen minutes later, just as Ginny's head was starting to loll, she saw the long outline cut left from the back entrance of the hotel. It was him. Adam walked onto the lawn. Ginny felt adrenaline, her eyes now wide open. The sun was so low it cast his shadow thirty feet. Below her, the boy made his way across the grass, barefoot.

The boy. Her heart quickened. She looked back to the double bed to check her sister had not been disturbed. To her surprise, Meredith was sitting up in the gloom. The older woman blinked – dazed, unfocused.

'I'm heading outside for a while,' said Ginny. Her sister lay back down, as if responding to a circus hypnotist.

Ginny tiptoed down the darkened stairs and found the back entrance, noticing through the glass how the dawn light made a million crystals of the garden dew. Adam had disappeared into the woods at the far end. She gathered up the hem of her nightgown and jogged towards where she knew he would be, scattering the crystals as she ran.

The glade she had seen on that first walk with Meredith seemed to sparkle in the distance. Night was retreating across the sea. She covered the mile quickly. In the black-blue light she saw him. This time she did not hang back and watch.

'Adam—'

He turned. She broke through the undergrowth and stood there.

'How did y-you know I was here?' The American accent, the trace of a stutter, almost a shiver, sent a warm rush through her body. She studied him. His blue shirt, the same one Meredith had worn, was off and on the ground. The chill morning air brushed her shoulders.

'Please,' she said. 'I need your help with something later.'

'What do you need, Ginny?'

That question, with her own name attached! Her mind went immediately to what she really wanted to say, that she needed his arms around her, his strong body next to hers. She hesitated.

'Come on, tell me,' he repeated. 'If I get cold my muscles get stiff.'

He had pulled something out of a small washbag and was rubbing it in his hair.

'What's that?'

'Someone told me it stops the salt drying you out. Just a piece of beetroot.'

'Beetroot? I never knew that.'

'Well, I tried lemon and that just bleached me.' He rubbed his hair, the beetroot-half invisible in the palm of his hand. 'Is it vain to do this?'

'It might be quite purple.'

'Really? Can you see the colour in it?'

'A hint maybe, now you mention it,' she said gently. 'Look, I don't want to mess up your jump.'

'Dive,' he corrected softly. 'Not jump. A jump is when you go feet first.' He turned towards the sea.

Which is what I'm doing now, she thought. The wind howled at them for a brief second, making her suddenly conscious of the height and the danger. The air settled. She explained what she wanted Adam to do. The place was so silent that even though they spoke in whispers, Ginny feared the words might float on the morning air back to the hotel.

But she told him, and he agreed.

His agreement came with an air of puzzlement. 'I know you probably think I'm a stupid American. And I don't understand paintings or art history or whatever. But what I love, Ginny, is this. To spin in the air on my way down, because if I get the line of my body right, if it's smooth, I feel like I'm – creating something. So maybe that's like a spray of paint across the scenery. Maybe I can pretend that's art.'

'It is, it is.' She was almost pleading.

He shrugged. She sat on the dewy grass to watch, not caring about the way the wet seeped into her underwear. Adam took off his trousers. The clothes lay folded as he turned away from her in only his briefs.

Slowly, Adam revolved his body. He stood with his legs tight together and arms stretched out sideways, hands level with his shoulders. Then, in a blur of movement, the young man jumped. She leapt in the same instant so she did not lose sight of him as he dropped, piking and twisting down to the water below. He span in a gulp of air and hit the surface of the sea with barely a splash as she perched on tiptoe to keep him in view.

In her mind she saw what he had imagined – a puff of paint

behind him, coloured spray still hanging in the air seconds after he was in the water, pinks and greens and blues. She believed she understood him, understood the boy and his most private self.

Then Ginny pulled off her nightgown and stood naked on the clifftop, arms outstretched as if to gather him in with the dawn.

It rained gently outside for the first time since the sisters had arrived in Cadaqués. At half past nine, Ginny and Meredith were by the double doors to the hotel dining room. Meredith was clutching her green scrapbook. 'We need you for this,' Ginny said. 'Just for today. You'll see the artist.'

'And then we leave? I said last night . . .'

'I know what you said last night.' Ginny contemplated her sister, worried her voice had shown a trace of annoyance. 'But we can leave later today. If you still want to.' Meredith's determination to quit the hotel had softened the instant a visit to Dali's house was mentioned. Ginny's plan might be crazy, but it was working.

'It's why I came here, after all,' Meredith said.

Ginny stared. 'Really?'

'It's why I chose the place, because he's done so many paintings here.'

Ginny stared at Meredith. The older woman looked shattered. 'How's your head, Merry?' The Benzedrine had given her sister a migraine.

'Better.'

'Have you had breakfast?'

'I came down early when I saw you weren't there.'

To Ginny, even this was a revelation. Her sister had managed to find the breakfast area on her own, get served, eat something, drink coffee. She could imagine Meredith chomping messily on toast layered with jam and butter, staring intensely at the far wall from under that mess of jet-black hair, never acknowledging the greetings of other guests who passed her table. But two years earlier she had been completely unseeing and unspeaking in an asylum. The food brought to Meredith's locked hospital room in Hull had come – she remembered her saying this – on a metal tray.

And there were other signs of slow improvement. The focus on detail, for example. Meredith's ability to enjoy a walk in the morning or afternoon, exploring the grounds lopsidedly in her black shirt and dress, ignoring the scratch of the hard grass against her bare calves, pausing to take an interest in the long-legged insects skating across the hotel pond or the shape of a lone cloud. She was large and ungainly, and clearly unhealthy for her age, and perhaps that sad expression would never change. But despite all that, Meredith was slowly coming out of herself. She had even laughed once or twice – imagine it! – as if, despite the misery in her past, she could briefly be distracted by the present.

It made Ginny more and more reluctant to raise the subject of their father's will. She could not take the risk of unsettling her sister's recovery. If Meredith thought her sister had only rescued her on her mother's orders, for money . . .

'Did you drink water for your head?'

'It still hurts.'

'Oh.'

'I was sad this morning.'

Even this was a revelation, thought Ginny, a different way of talking.

'Why sad?'

'My past. My father.'

'Our father.'

'Feeling I'd lost everyone.'

'But I found you,' said Ginny.

'Maybe I'm not very good at accepting your kindness.'

'No, you are,' said Ginny. 'But there – you've just described Siobhan. "Not very good at accepting kindness." We are helping her but I don't think she realises.'

'Isn't she horrible?'

Ginny was silent.

'No?' asked Meredith.

'Okay,' conceded Ginny, 'she is quite horrible. Either that or she's just acting horrible, which is even worse. But that's not the point.'

'What is the point?'

'She's given us a chance to go to Salvador Dali's house.'

'So we really are going to see Mr Dali?'

'There's a letter. At eleven, it says.'

As Ginny spoke, Siobhan approached, the redhead breathing fire. 'The same bloody issue with Saunders, utter bloody horror show, he won't come unless he knows what he's getting into. *Jesus.* Sitting there in bed in his dressing gown, lodged underneath his breakfast tray, pretending he can't move, asking me to slide the toast towards him – slide the damn toast, dammit! At least he's unlocked his door now. That man doesn't give a pellet about me, right.'

'I don't know if you have properly met my sister,' said Ginny.

'The one who cried? The other day?'

Meredith tossed her head slightly, as if shaking the words away.

Ginny said, 'Don't—' and then swallowed her anger, touching Siobhan's arm. 'Don't always say what you're thinking. We all need kindness before truth.' Ginny was surprised at how adult the words sounded. Siobhan rolled her eyes.

'Meredith is here because—'

'She is an expert in modern art,' Ginny said with sudden firmness, 'which is what you need for this. You cannot just turn up without Mr Saunders and try to get on the right side of Mr Dali with a bluff. You need Meredith with you. Trust me.'

'Okay, well, let's give it a go. Anything that doesn't result in me having to call London and tell them the contract is broken.' Siobhan turned to Meredith. 'There's money riding on this. And I was telling your sister – ideally I could handle Dali's account, see. He is getting quite big in Europe now. I could actually be Personal Public Relations for the freak. Ha.' Siobhan eyed Meredith suspiciously. 'You don't say much.'

'There's not much to say.' Meredith's answer made Siobhan snort. Ginny wondered if her sister did not like hearing the artist insulted.

The last guests were leaving the breakfast room, some of them seemingly unimpressed that these three young women were blocking their way. 'What's that?' Siobhan asked, pointing at Meredith's green scrapbook. 'Let me see.'

Meredith lifted the scrapbook defensively. 'My journal of artists. Modern art. Surrealism. Especially Salvador Dali.' She opened the pages and a swirl of colours jumped out like unbottled genies – sketches, cuttings, words jotted in thick smudged ink, verticals and diagonals, anything but horizontal.

'What a mess,' said Siobhan.

'It's very precious to me.' Meredith hardly needed to say it. 'I'm bringing it today. It might help.' Siobhan peered at the book. She made to touch the corner, and Meredith pulled away.

'It doesn't look precious. But fair enough. You've come prepared. Meredith, you can do the talking when we get there. From what I've seen, the man needs worshipping. Obviously

I have some knowledge of paintings too, quite a lot, but I'll leave it to you out of courtesy.'

Ginny's jaw fell. The cheek of it! Siobhan had told her the previous day that she had no knowledge of art. Before she could say anything, Meredith was speaking. 'The whole panorama, as far as the Bay of Roses, seemed to depend upon my glance.' Siobhan and Ginny stared quickly at her. 'That's what the eight-year-old Dali said when his family moved to an apartment with a balcony looking onto the sea,' explained Meredith. 'He thought he could move the surroundings just by looking at them.'

'Bloody freak,' Siobhan muttered. 'Loon with a snake around his scraggy neck. Talentless too. Oh God, spare me from fools.'

Adam walked up to them. He wore his ill-fitting waiter's clothes, the black jacket and trousers. Siobhan's expression changed instantly. Her face lit up. 'Hello! I've seen you in the restaurant, right!'

Ginny stepped between them, placing herself in Siobhan's way. 'This might not work, Adam,' she said.

'Why not just stand in front of me?' Siobhan barked, a snipe at Ginny which everyone chose to ignore.

The American was saying, 'I'll try. They gave me lunch off, Ginny, if I work tonight.'

'It's so generous of you,' called Siobhan over Ginny's shoulder.

'I'm really kinda interested. I don't know art, however. You are aware of that, Ginny? No paintings for me. I'm a j-j-jock. I guess that makes me one-dimensional to you.'

Ginny shook her head. 'None of us knows about Dali.' She knew that sounded lame, a waste of breath. 'And you have all your history,' she added quietly, 'your wars.'

'But I really will get to m-m-meet Mr Saunders?'

Siobhan poked her head over Ginny's shoulder. 'Later. I promise. He promises.'

'We all promise,' said Meredith, as if they were conjugating a verb in class together. It was so well timed they all laughed. Ginny looked at her sister. The promise of meeting Dali had stopped Meredith insisting they leave the hotel, at least for a day. The promise of meeting Saunders had brought Adam to her. This was working . . .

This was the very scene she had pictured.

This, now. The four of them walking. From the west of Cadaqués to Port Lligat. Two miles. Two umbrellas between them as it rained. They passed a pair of Guardia Civil officers, who stared at them a little too hard and clutched their rifles a little too tightly, as if they were themselves afraid. This, now – Meredith alongside her, and Ginny glancing back frequently at Siobhan and Adam to check on their discussion. She hated the idea that Siobhan might be taken with him. That Siobhan might be claiming the credit for all this. Or that she might want to – the thought slammed into her – *seduce* him.

'How's your head?' she whispered to her sister, desperate to distract herself.

'Aching, but only a little now,' said Meredith. 'So . . . you want me to look around his studio and make conversation?'

'Siobhan was panicking. I know she's obnoxious, but I thought you could make it easier for her. Just show him how much you love his work.' She suddenly felt as though she was manipulating her sister. She added, to make herself feel better: 'I just want you to enjoy it.'

'Okay.' Meredith did that thing again, rubbing her forehead vigorously with the first knuckle of her thumb as if she was trying to remove a stain. 'I don't know what I think of actually meeting the artist. I'm nervous. I mean, I wanted to come here because of him, just to see some of the scenery he's painted, but I didn't think he was actually here. I thought he would be in New York or . . .'

Ginny was excited by how alive her sister seemed, in sharp contrast to the psychosis of yesterday. At last she understood why their journey had brought them here. But Meredith was prey to her moods. They controlled her and they could turn in an instant. Perhaps small pleasures were the key to getting her better. A little excitement here and there. Something like this, a trip to see her hero. Then she remembered the previous day, her sister's hollowed-out face and the warning: *Something terrible is about to happen.*

'My mother loved the modern artists,' Meredith said suddenly. Ginny was so startled to hear the sentence she stopped in her tracks, and the two walking close behind almost bumped into her. Siobhan rolled her eyes. Adam laughed. Ginny jogged to catch up with Meredith, who had not broken her stride.

'Yes, my mother made this book.' Meredith let a corner of the green sketchbook peek from her bag as she said it.

The four passed a white stone building with a bell framed by an arch above the entrance. A faded sign said: ERMITA DE SANT BALDIRI. As she moved past and the angle changed, Ginny saw a small cemetery behind the hermitage, and shivered.

'What was your mother like, Merry?'

'Oh, a lovely lady. The most beautiful, gorgeous lady, like a painting in my mind. I can't even describe – her skin, her face. She loved me so much. I know that. I just had one photo. It was lost in the asylum.'

Tears sprang in Ginny's eyes. 'I never wanted to ask. I know things go so deep for you.'

'She was killed in an accident.' As if not conscious of the power of what she had said, she continued quickly: 'Salvador

Dali was born in . . . hmm . . . I think, maybe 1905. He must be about fifty now. He was the first artist to show people you could take reality and bend it. If you want to call me mad, I suppose that's what madness is.'

'I would never call you mad.'

'I was mad. I think I'm getting better.'

'You were upset last night.'

'I was upset last night.' Meredith's repetition made Ginny wince. The older woman continued, 'Dali's paintings are the same as madness. I think my mother loved the modern artists because she was on her own in Hull, and she was an unusual person—'

'Unusual?'

'She was Caribbean.'

'Oh? Your skin, darker than mine—'

'And my hair.'

'I think I knew she was foreign. You told me she was. But I didn't realise how foreign.' Ginny felt she was putting Meredith's story together slowly, like a jigsaw built from the outside edge.

Meredith was saying, 'I know so little about her. I heard my grandmother came from a place called Cornwall, Jamaica. Dad told me this. She was brought over to work for a British family. Not slavery but something like it. My grandfather left her. My mother grew up trying to be British but no one would let her. When she married, I think it was suddenly like she was home, she belonged. But he went to war and she died so young.'

'Oh Merry, it's so sad, and you were so alone.' She watched her feet on the grass, each step seeming to move in slow motion. 'It's almost as if our father had two lives, one after the other.'

'Mother wanted to touch another – world. Reach out to

something different. So it was Georges Braque, André Derain, Raoul Dufy, Jean Metzinger, Maurice de Vlaminck—'

'Vincent van Gogh?'

'No. The impressionists were earlier.'

Ginny was out of her depth.

'Vincent was too basic for Mummy, I think.' Meredith tugged at the corner of the scrapbook. 'So no Van Gogh in this book. No Cézanne, Gauguin, Georges Seurat. No Toulouse-Lautrec. They started it, though. They gave birth to modern painting, to the crazy ones like Dali – the lunatics.'

Ginny laughed at the word.

'Who is the greatest.'

'Sorry?'

'Dali, who is the greatest.'

'You think so?'

'The greatest artist in the history of the world.'

'Really?'

'Okay, no, he *was* the greatest. He had some trouble and it made him unpopular. He ran away from the Spanish civil war carrying two flags, one from each side. He went to America for the Second World War. So if he's back in this village, well, that's quite a journey. Look, here it is!'

Port Lligat appeared below them as they rounded the bend. They were at the top of a sharply sloping knoll. The wet grass at their feet was the colour of fresh straw, bleached by sun and sea spray. The village below was a huddle of houses which lay like discarded cereal boxes. In the middle, facing the sea, they saw a collection of five fishermen's homes, their roofs a red terracotta. They were surrounded by a single wall, with a long outdoor pool in the shared courtyard.

'Is that his place?' said Ginny. 'Must be. I just want you to enjoy this, Meredith.' She bit the inside of her mouth, thinking she had lied again. They waited for the other two to catch up, the rain pitter-pattering on their umbrellas. Ginny realised furiously that Siobhan had slipped her arm inside Adam's and was laughing at some joke he had made. 'Hey, you two,' she said. 'Before we go on, listen to my sister.'

'The art expert,' said Siobhan. 'We need you now. Keep your voice down in case the artist is lurking near that open window.' The perimeter wall of the property, painted bright white, was directly below them, and a blue-framed window faced in their direction. 'God, I could do without this damned rain.'

'Meredith, go on. What you were saying to me.'

'Go on, Meredith,' Adam said, his voice encouraging. 'Help us.'

'Hmm.' Meredith made a little noise. 'Too much pressure, speaking to you all.'

They were crowded together under the two umbrellas.

'Meredith was just telling me that he is a surrealist—'

'A what?' Adam asked. 'Okay, I need to understand this.'

'Painting surreal scenes,' said Ginny.

Siobhan laughed. 'He's a show-off. A complete and utter homosexual show-off.'

They were silent.

'Merry?' prompted Ginny.

'I don't think I can,' she said, her eyes glassing with tears.

'Come on, please,' Siobhan urged. 'We won't be able to do what we're planning without you. Imagine we're with him, and he wants to hear how great he is. Brief us.'

Meredith stared at the grass as Ginny held the umbrella above her. Then she began, each syllable an effort, each word clipped.

'He is married, firstly.'

'A lot of them are.' Siobhan clearly couldn't resist offering a commentary.

Meredith continued carefully. 'He loves this coast, the Cap de Creus. He painted the rocks and made them look human. He once threw a child off a cliff. He said his only joy was receiving presents. He is a narcissist. The family had their holidays here. He hates his parents. He loves film. He wants to be in Hollywood. His wife is Gala, never Gala Dali, just Gala.' She was speeding up, the words coming faster. 'They hate him here in this village because, when General Franco took power, he mocked them for being poor and ignorant, and said they'd brought all their troubles on themselves. He was expelled from college because he said his teachers were unfit to examine him. He painted *Figure at a Window* here. He paints dreams. Melting clocks. Burning giraffes. He paints blood. Ripped-off arms, heads cut off. Some say he has run out of ideas.'

'Run out of ideas?' repeated Siobhan.

'He threw a child off a cliff?' Adam said.

'He says he did,' replied Meredith. 'He wrote about—'

'Holy sweet mother of—' Siobhan cut in. She seemed suddenly enraged and swivelled towards Ginny, coming out from under her umbrella. '*Run out of ideas?* Is she the diplomat of the year, your sister, or what? I thought she was going to praise him!'

'Hey,' said Ginny fiercely, 'she's helping us!'

Adam tried to calm Siobhan. 'Isn't that just Meredith's, er, critique? She won't say any of that to Mr Dali, will you?'

'I didn't mean to be insulting,' Meredith blurted out. 'I got confused. I just said everything in my head.'

But Siobhan had lost control. 'And the Franco stuff? Are you trying to get us killed?' She turned on Ginny. 'So we've brought your big hot air balloon of a sister, your crazy sister here to make things worse, have we? To rile the artist, to completely derail the whole thing? Did she actually say—'

'Hey, don't you be rude to her! She's helping us!' Ginny said again.

'Is she now, or is she just helping you?'

'What do you mean?'

'Well, you've done nothing but use her!'

'How dare you!'

'I—' started Meredith, but Siobhan cut in.

'Use her for money, use her for this, it's all you do! You just—'

Siobhan did not finish the sentence. Ginny flew at her. Eyes blazing, she ditched the umbrella and grabbed Siobhan by the shoulders, but the Irishwoman had shifted her weight minutely, so Ginny stumbled. The front of her skirt got caught under her leading foot and she tripped past Siobhan, still clutching her blouse.

'*No!*' Meredith shouted.

Siobhan and Ginny started to tumble down the slope. Meredith, who had been hanging on to her sister to stop her falling, hit the grass with a thud and slid. The green scrapbook fell out of her bag as they collided at the foot of the slope, a mangle of legs and arms beneath the blue-framed window. Ginny groaned. Siobhan swore. Meredith, her chest heaving, reached out for the scrapbook, the pages face down on the sodden grass a yard away. At the top of the knoll, Adam started to move towards the tangle of three bodies. Ginny saw him sit, ready to slide down to them and help. Then he stopped and looked over their heads. A woman's face had appeared in the window above them.

Her face was aged by the sun and her bright eyes seemed angled in a Y towards the nose. She blinked like a bird. The neck was long, the jaw fine. The mouth, even at this hour, was lipsticked.

The lips moved.

'I am Gala.'

In that expanse of white wall, behind the blue, weathered wooden frame, she looked like a portrait in a gallery. Perhaps she knew it, because having spoken, she became utterly motionless in the window as she stared down at them.

'Which one of you is the stuntman?' she asked.

'Why did you do that?' Adam asked Ginny. 'Try to hit her, I mean.'

They were following Gala's instructions to the front door. Siobhan and Meredith had grass marks streaked up their backs. Ginny sensed they were all seething. She herself was too angry even to answer Adam.

'I mean, I know *why* you did it. But why not a-a-apologise before we go in?'

'To hell with that,' said Ginny. She turned to Meredith and touched her arm. 'Sis?'

They had taken a gravel track to the seafront and turned left. To the right was a coastal path that ran along a slate wall. The wall and path both looked newly built – by the Dali couple, Ginny guessed, who were clearly establishing some sort of kingdom-on-sea here. The group followed the whitewashed perimeter wall to a low door painted green and sporting a pair of bulbous red metal lips.

Siobhan touched the lips with her fingertips as if she could part the mouth. The lips turned out to be hinged at the top. But before Siobhan could use them to knock, the front door opened inwards. Gala stood on the other side.

'Come in, he is waiting.' Even in the simple act of opening a front door, Gala made Ginny think of an actress.

'Sis?' Ginny tried again, more insistently.

Behind her, Adam said, '*Espero no llegar tarde.*'

Ginny looked back. She had not realised Adam spoke Spanish. Gala clapped with delight and responded: '*Dali siempre llega pronto.*'

They followed her into the grounds. 'What did you say?' Ginny asked Adam.

'I hope we're not late,' he replied.

'And what did she say?'

'I replied, "Dali is always ahead of time!"' said Gala. Ginny saw Siobhan roll her eyes in response. She threw a concerned glance at her sister, still silent. What a group this was, broken already, shuffling like schoolchildren called to the headmaster's office.

The inside of the house was bright, but – although they were now passing a stuffed polar bear wearing necklaces and holding several jewelled canes – in places the decor was more restrained than Ginny expected. The walls were mainly white. As they passed down narrow passageways, all the colour was in the materials below their feet. There were so many different rugs, all luridly patterned, piled on top of each other and rucked, that they had to step carefully to avoid tripping. Above them the ceiling was vaulted, with stone ribs leading to the highest point of the arch. Then, just as Ginny became used to the style, it would break and she would see above their heads the underside of half-round terracotta tiles.

The internal layout was a maze. Gala appeared deliberately to lead them down a corridor that came to a dead end. She laughed as if she was questioning her own sanity, but Ginny had no doubt she had done it for effect. Out of the window she glimpsed what looked like two enormous white eggs balanced on the rooftops and wondered how she had not noticed them as they approached the house. From several exterior walls, tree branches sprouted – cast in metal, she assumed – as if the tree were trapped inside the building and trying to escape. Ginny thought she could smell fresh paint. Suddenly she felt dizzy. She heard Adam talk more Spanish, fluent and confident, yet without any sense that he was performing. Siobhan laughed as if she could understand, which infuriated Ginny. The malice Siobhan had displayed even a few minutes ago was gone, and now she was trying to pass as a normal human being. Gala responded to Adam in short sentences and sometimes just a jerk of the head, leaving the onus on her guest to continue the conversation.

Eventually Gala led them into the open courtyard they had seen from the rear of the house. Ginny now saw the swimming pool was shaped like a phallus with balls at the end. She gasped at the sight and looked around to make sure no one had registered her shock. The pool was lined with jagged Cap de Creus stones and sea urchin figurines. The rain had stopped. The sun slowly appeared from behind a white cloud.

'The olive trees we planted in 1948,' said Gala, and Ginny noticed that the plants stood in enormous coffee cups. Seeing the shape of the pool, Meredith smiled and tilted her head. Ginny saw the smile and relaxed a little. Maybe she had not registered what had come out of Siobhan's mouth . . .

Adam and Gala were still speaking to each other in Spanish. He seemed to be explaining something. Gala frowned, sighed and tutted. He spoke some more. Ginny was impressed watching him, and frustrated that the events of the last ten minutes had put distance between them. He had been humble about his lack of art knowledge and modest about his language skills – wouldn't most boys have bluffed the art and puffed up the language? Gala pointed at a pink sofa by the pool. Adam nodded. Gala said 'Mae West', clicking her teeth as if she disapproved of her husband's fascination with the famed actress.

Ginny saw that the sofa was shaped as another pair of lips, just like the front door-knocker, and wondered how she could possibly have missed that at first glance.

Adam stood tall, and suddenly Dali's wife smiled, rolled her eyes and clapped Adam on the shoulders with both hands. Ginny sensed that she and Siobhan were both trying to understand what they were saying. They turned to each other. Then, clearly both remembering the scuffle at the back of the house and seized by their mutual loathing, they turned back to Adam and Gala.

'Okay.' He coughed nervously. 'This good lady says Dali may not see us if Mr Saunders is absent.'

'So what did you tell her?' asked Siobhan, evidently forgetting Gala's fluent English. 'Why did she laugh like that?'

'I *laughed*, young lady, because this beautiful and tender young man with the perfect Spanish says he has come in the place of Mr Saunders. Is that correct?'

Silence.

Siobhan said, too forcefully, 'Yes, that is correct.'

'He has the same physique as the stuntman,' Ginny added.

'Exactly the same,' said Siobhan. 'Same height and weight, just younger.'

'But he is not the stuntman,' said Gala, 'and the stuntman does not have streaks of purple in his hair, and this is not a game. Your young man is a—' She was interrupted by a gasp. Meredith ran to the other side of the blue water and looked through a window in a white wall, which ran perpendicular to the pool's edge at a level a few feet lower than the concrete they were standing on.

Meredith pressed her face to the glass. 'I know that picture!' She turned back towards the group, then pressed her face to the window again. 'Two of them!'

'Watch out for the brambles over there!' Gala said. 'And they are *paintings*! Not *pictures*, my dear! If you tell me what they are called, I will bring you to see my husband.'

Silence. Ginny nervously shifted her weight from one foot to the other.

Her sister breathed deeply.

'The one on the left is *The Madonna of Port Lligat*,' Meredith said. 'That's easy. The other one . . .' She stopped, as if drawing a blank. 'Oh.'

Ginny swallowed.

'The honeycomb shape,' said Meredith. 'But that's not the title.'

'It is the title that I need,' said Gala.

Silence.

Siobhan whispered, 'Jesus, this is embarrassing.'

Ginny couldn't bear it. Her sister was about to crumple. She wanted to run to her, hug her, and agree to leave this horrible place.

Gala giggled cruelly, as if she knew Meredith would never get the name of the painting, because nobody ever did, as if looking forward to escorting the humiliated group back to the front door and sending them on their way.

But then Meredith turned away from the window. She opened her green scrapbook and started flicking through the pages. 'It's not in here.'

Ginny's heart sank.

'But I know it. Of course I do. It's – it's *The Enigma of Desire*.'

'Full name, please.'

Without missing a beat, Meredith said: '*The Enigma of Desire, or My Mother, My Mother, My Mother*.'

Even Gala clapped. The others cheered. Meredith laughed

freely. Her whole body swayed with it. In that moment, Ginny felt as if the tussle had been forgotten.

And as they clapped and cheered, a man walked through the door nearest to Meredith, clapping as well. He wore yellow trousers and a red jacket and waistcoat.

'My darling!' exclaimed Gala.

'My dear Gala, you nearly had to send our group away,' said Salvador Dali. 'But now we are complete. We are complete without the stuntman, Mr Saunders, but why did our circus ever need the clown? All of you, come with me.' He turned to Meredith. 'Especially you,' he said.

Below Dali's cluster of fishermen's cottages, a void had been scooped out. Ginny guessed the excavation had been done when the pool was built. The artist offered no explanation as he waved them down a slatted wooden staircase into the darkness. The wide stairs had none of the polish of the decor above them. Dali went last.

Ginny had expected perhaps a dozen steps, but counted more than thirty. She had no sense of the space they were entering and found herself losing confidence in the dark. When they reached the foot of the stairs, they stopped abruptly. Dali said, 'Move on a little, children! The floor is clear!'

'It's bloody dark, right!' protested Siobhan. The only light came from the hatch above the stairs.

Though it was dark, Ginny sensed that Gala was no longer with them. As Dali reached the final step, she turned and looked at him. He was barely an arm's length away. The light from the hatch above made him luminous. He was nearing fifty, Ginny reckoned. His features were weathered. Cigarette smoke had favoured the left side of his face, which was craggier than the right, or maybe that was just the effect of the Port Lligat sun.

Dali was unshaven, but his moustache still pointed aggressively upwards and she thought she saw a gloop of gel glistening at one end. Looking at the receding black hair, which was unruly, Ginny wondered if the only thing Dali had done after rising this morning was shape his moustache. She imagined him sleeping late, the surrealist inhabiting his dreams – did surrealists have very dull dreams? – then being woken by their visit and Gala opening the front door . . . clank, clank, hello . . . hearing their distant conversation as they moved through the house . . . remembering the appointment (maybe) and throwing on his yellow trousers, red jacket and waistcoat . . . his head clearing slowly after sleep . . . then delicately teasing the moustache into shape and walking towards the scene just as Gala chided them for the absence of Russell Saunders.

'Stay here, please,' said Dali. He produced a candle and touched the wick with a match. Ginny noticed more of his features. An impatient, almost frantic look. Eyes bulging slightly in their sockets. The effect was disconcerting, because the rest of the features hung slack. Dali had a slight paunch, but she imagined stick-insect legs below his yellow trousers. He seemed both energetic and exhausted. Fascinated by everything but completely bored. Thrilling to be around, but tired of himself.

The hatch above them slammed shut. Now the candle in Dali's hand was the only light, the only sound the distant crashing of the sea. The artist stalked deeper into the gloom with his strange, loping gait. The yellow trousers and red jacket disappeared into the shadows. The darkness around them did not surrender to the candlelight, which licked ineffectually at the black shapes on the walls.

As Dali moved he held himself unnaturally upright. Arthritis? Ginny wondered. An attempt to make himself taller? For a second the group stood there, waiting for something to happen.

Ginny saw Adam's shoulder touch Siobhan's. Her hatred of the Irishwoman returned. What right did she have to start a friendship with him?

The four of them were completely silent, wondering what Dali was about to do in the darkness. Ginny heard Meredith breathing deeply behind her. 'You okay?' she asked.

Meredith sneezed. Adam said, 'Bless you,' just as Dali's voice boomed from the other side of the room:

'*Silence!*'

Then there was a sound of metal against metal, an object being slid across the floor, the snap of a circuit connecting. With a static hum the room was suddenly filled with a light so bright that Ginny was momentarily blinded.

They squinted back at the bulbs that were the source of the light.

And gradually they began to see where they were.

CHAPTER NINE

The Artist in his Studio

'Wait!' said Dali. 'The light is too—'

In each hand he had an old-style film set spotlight, which he was apparently trying to slide into different positions. Ginny clamped her eyes shut and shaded her face with her hands. She wondered if Dali had deliberately blasted them with the light, and was now only pretending he had put the lamps in the wrong place. As he turned the bulbs away, she uncovered her eyes. The room gradually came into focus.

The space in which they were standing was huge. The floor looked unfinished, poorly laid cement with sand strewn in places, like seed thrown on a barren field. A basin was attached in the corner, the pipes leading from the plughole askew, the white enamel spotted with colour. Next to the basin was a long narrow worktop cluttered with brushes, cloths and paint tins. The walls were unpointed brick. The jagged edges of the stone took the harsh light and angled it down, up and sideways. Two heavy iron pillars, box-shaped with rusted rivets, reached up at least fifteen feet to support the ceiling. There was a pair of easels, each the size of a billiards table. One had the beginnings of a painting on it. Rolls of canvas sat in one corner, maybe discarded, maybe containing works that would be sold for however many hundreds of thousands. High above their heads was a single overhead bulb with no shade. It was dead. Looking up, Ginny saw a spider on it, its long legs shaped around the glass, looking like a spatter of black paint flicked from a brush.

Everyone, including the artist, slowly looked upwards. There, in the ceiling, was a metal cross-girder bolted at right-angles to the huge wooden joists that held the walls of the basement in place.

The atmosphere was unsettling. Ginny sensed it. But Dali looked more nervous than the rest of them. Now the lamps were where he wanted them, he had straightened up. If the visitors expected a torrent of arrogance and contempt from the world-famous surrealist, it did not come. He looked slightly dishevelled and a little puzzled. He rolled his lower lip over his teeth and bit down on it, as if sizing up a violent gang in front of him and wondering if he could make a dash for safety. He flexed his shoulders under the red jacket, as if easing a pain deep in the bone.

Siobhan stepped forward. 'I feel I owe you an explanation, sir.'

Dali's eyes narrowed.

'For Mr Saunders, for whom I work. As PR. For the fact that he is not here. He is not here because—'

Dali waved his hand. 'The man is a cunt.'

The word dropped to the floor like a lump of cement. The shock of it was so great that even one of the powerful lamps seemed to flicker. Behind Ginny, Meredith gasped. Siobhan made the mistake of trying to find a less offensive description for her client. 'Well, he is . . . unconventional.'

Dali spluttered at the word.

'Not unconventional like you, sir, I don't mean that. I mean he doesn't always understand a *schedule*. And as I say, he is terribly unwell.'

'Let me speak to the other one,' said Dali. His accent was

Spanish, but the occasional word – like 'one', pronounced *warrrn* – emerged sounding as if it had been on a bus tour of North America. 'The one at the back.' The mixed accent made his English sound at once exotic and familiar.

Eventually Meredith ventured out from behind Ginny. 'Yes, sir?'

'Is she telling the truth? Your Irish friend here?'

Ginny spoke up. 'Sir, my sister can't answer that.'

'Why not? Is she your puppet?'

'She knows nothing about Mr Saunders.'

'But she knows about truth, don't you?' His voice had softened, his gaze tempered as he looked at Meredith. 'You know about truth because you are the one who sees into my paintings, who sees what they mean.'

The room was silent.

'Yes, Mr Dali.'

'Just Dali.'

'Yes.'

'And so, Dali asks whether the Irish lady is telling the truth.'

Ginny began, 'I don't think—'

But Meredith interrupted. 'No. Saunders is not ill. He is eating toast.'

Dali shook his head. 'Sweet Lord above. So, my darling, the one who understands, the one who sees, why have you come with this group of bandits and imposters on their desperate mission?'

Another silence.

'Because you are the greatest artist in the world,' said Meredith.

Salvador Dali stared around the cavernous basement, nodding forcefully, as if waiting for the brick walls to agree.

'I wanted to help them,' Meredith added, and Ginny felt so proud of her sister she could cry.

'Ah.' Dali spoke as if he was noting every word down. 'The person in the group who knows nothing is the person who knows everything.'

Siobhan looked as though she was about to say something, but Adam cut her off by touching her shoulder. He then put his hands on his hips and breathed in, inflating his chest. 'I am Canadian, sir. Well, naturalised American. So I don't understand art. Or your art. The surreal. Or – well, I won't even try. I just don't.'

Dali raised his eyebrows and shook his head. 'The Dream Ball was in New York on January 18, 1935. My ball. My idea. It took place at the Coq restaurant. Do you know it?' Meredith was nodding. He turned to her. 'You know it?'

'The music played from six gramophones inside a dead ox,' she said. 'But I wasn't there. I only read about it.'

'A bath was suspended above the guests, full of water. People dressed up as their own dreams. I am afraid,' he added ruefully, almost as an aside, 'that Gala's problems in America began with her costume that night. People thought she had placed a doll in her hair to make a joke about the kidnapping of the Lindbergh baby. But the evening was a huge success. The costumes were extraordinary. The waiters wore tiaras from Woolworths. We became famous in the United States. It was a success, you see, because the life of an American is a perpetual engagement with the surreal. So, Mr –'

'Bannerman.'

'– Mr Naturalised American-Bannerman, being transatlantic does not excuse you from great art. It *qualifies* you. Americans are themselves pieces of art, each a unique slice of the preposterous, in a country which is itself a vast surrealist gallery.'

That seemed to go over Siobhan's head, for she tried again. 'I hope I have not caused offence. I confess that I – I exaggerated the illness of Mr Saunders because I was embarrassed by his selfish behaviour and I didn't want you to construe that as an insult.'

'I construe it as a breach of contract.'

'I am hoping not,' said Siobhan, obsequious now. Dali merely stared at her. She continued, her words moving faster and faster. 'The problem, as I understand it, was a miscommunication between Baltimore, where Mr Saunders has his primary home, and Spain. Because the message came via London and Dublin, where my office is, although I don't think the failure was—'

Dali circled his right hand around the wrist, indicating impatience.

She ploughed on. 'Mr Saunders wanted us to coordinate global publicity because he was told you would be painting a portrait of him. When he found out you just wanted him to be a model for someone else—'

'Someone else!' Dali exploded, his words echoing off the cavernous stone walls of the basement. 'Jesus Christ! Our Lord and Saviour! Not *someone else*!'

Adam stepped forward.

'Sir, I will model the painting for you.' The American spoke as if he had just made a decision. In fact, this was exactly what Ginny had asked him to do that morning at dawn. 'They asked m-me to come because they said that if you required a m-m-model, I am the same size as Mr Saunders.'

'Take off your shirt,' the artist said. Dali was suddenly focusing so intently on the young man that he seemed to have gone into a jaguar's crouch. Adam pulled off both his shirt and trousers as the three women instinctively moved back from him.

'Do not shift even a single inch, Mr Bannerman.' Dali picked up one of the spotlights and moved it to within a yard of Adam.

The lamp was at eye level. 'Close your eyes,' the artist instructed. 'Do not let the light blind you.'

Humming with current, the lamp was so close to Adam that Ginny thought his skin might burn. Dali fetched the second light. Adam stood there, no trousers or shirt, the bulbs drawing pearls of sweat onto his tanned chest. The brown skin was as smooth as a baby's, but still Ginny thought she could smell hair burning.

Dali crossed the room and threw a switch which turned off all the other lights. The ceiling disappeared into darkness. 'Wait . . . wait . . .' the artist mumbled. He sank to his haunches in front of Adam and released the catches on the lampstands. The lamp casings dropped. The source of the light fell closer to the floor, meaning Adam was now lit from below. As a result his shadow flew upwards into the rafters.

'Here, wait.'

The spotlights were now just below the level of Adam's thighs. Dali angled and lifted them, tightening the nuts on each side and snapping the hatches fully open. He brought the lamps closer to each other so the shadow of Adam on the ceiling lost its blurred edges. From the worktop he brought two pieces of card and taped them to the lowest edge of the lights, sharpening the shadow still further.

Then he fiddled with the catch on one of the lampstands and moved it to the level of Adam's stomach. As Ginny stared at the ceiling she saw what the artist was doing. Adam's shadow was projected against the rafters, where the metal girder was bolted to the joists.

'Spread your arms, young man,' said Dali, now moving the lamps by inches only, on his knees before Adam, staring up and past him at the bare rafters twenty feet above. 'Stretch your arms out to the sides.'

Ginny saw it. The arms spread, the lamps moved, the light fled the complicated corners of Adam's shadow. Dali shouted: '*Tú eres el Cristo, el Hijo del Dios Viviente!*' . . . and there on the ceiling, floating above them, was Christ on the cross.

CHAPTER TEN

Saint John of the Cross

They all gasped. Dali killed the light by slamming closed the hatches on the spotlights. Ginny smelt burning hair, or maybe it was Adam's skin. In the dark, she heard Dali move away.

She longed to reach out to Adam. She was responsible for bringing him here, and responsible if he was hurt. The hatch at the top of the stairs opened with a creak. Sunlight flooded in and they blinked. She heard Siobhan whisper something to Adam: 'Why do people with no talent become painters?' But Meredith was breathless, wiping away a tear.

From above, Gala cried: 'Come up! Your work is done for the day. Meredith, you come first!'

Siobhan pushed ahead of her. Meredith followed. Ginny watched Adam's body language as he pulled his shirt back on and buttoned it. He looked shaken. Siobhan turned back from higher up the stairs, forcing Meredith to stop. 'Come on, Adam,' she called, voice booming. 'You were amazing!'

Ginny tugged on his sleeve and whispered, 'Take your time.'

He smiled unevenly. 'That was a revelation.'

Ginny thought it was a strange word to use. She felt her arm brush his and was desperate to reach out and embrace him. 'Are you okay? It was a bit crazy.' She looked downwards into the dark of the studio, but Dali had disappeared.

'He is crazy. He's fucking mad,' whispered Adam.

'He is fucking mad, for sure,' she murmured back, hearing the word on her tongue for the first time, shocked at how it sounded. 'Your chest is burnt.'

Adam had his back to her now, and seemed not to hear.

She watched the muscle in his legs move inside the hotel-issued trousers as the group headed back up the staircase. Adam had the physique of an athlete, just like Russell Saunders. The thought reminded her that Adam had come out with them today because she had got Siobhan to promise him a meeting with Saunders. Half of her hoped Siobhan would remember, half of her hoped it would slip her mind. Ginny did not want Adam spending a minute more than was necessary in the company of the other girl. She felt she could not compete with Siobhan's volcanic ability to erupt, her willingness to lash out at a rival's most tender spot: why, why had Ginny told her in that weak moment under the tree about her mother's scheme? She had an extra decade on Ginny, not to mention a great gift: the inability to be embarrassed or see herself as others saw her. Ginny, on the other hand, was constantly fretting over imaginary hurts she might have inflicted or careless words chosen. She was not to blame for the tumble they all took down the grass. But she would blame herself for that and everything else too. Yes, Ginny cared too much.

She cared too much for Adam, that was for sure.

At the top of the stairs, Siobhan reached out for him. 'Big fella,' she said, 'I thought you were red hot in there.'

'I don't understand what art is,' he replied, 'so I figured I should just stand there to find out. Turns out it hurts a bit.'

'Doesn't the word "passion" mean "suffer" in Greek? Or is that Latin?'

Wanting no talk of passion, Ginny interrupted: 'He is fine.'

But that seemed possessive, so she added: 'I'm hoping, anyway.'

'I am fine now,' Adam said softly, gripping the front of his shirt and flapping it to ventilate his scalded skin. 'When I was down there I just thought I m-mustn't move.'

She looked at him tenderly and asked quietly, so only he could hear: 'Why is your speech like that sometimes?'

'My speech?'

'You have a slight – forgive me – a slight stammer, not noticeable at all really, but it comes and goes, and I wondered.'

Adam did a peculiar thing. Raised his right hand and placed a finger along the deep gouge in his chin. 'See this rut?' he whispered. 'I annoyed my dad and he struck out. And since that day – my stutter came.'

'Really? He did that?'

'Hit me with a kettle.'

'How old were you?'

'Ten.'

Ginny's heart raced with the outrage she felt, the sheer fury, but Siobhan cut in before she could say anything.

'Did you see what your shadow did, Adam?'

'No, I couldn't look up.'

'He made you fly into the roof with your arms out.'

'Yes!' cried Gala. 'And do you know what he shouted?' Her shrewish face examined each of them in turn.

'Possibly a Bible verse?' Adam said.

'*Tú eres el Cristo, el Hijo del Dios Viviente,*' Gala said. '"You are the Christ, the Son of the Living God." He shouted it so loudly I could hear it up here.'

Ginny looked at Meredith again. Again, she was wiping a tear away. 'Are you okay?'

'I'm emotional,' she said.

'It's understandable.'

'Ginny, what did Siobhan mean – about the money?'

Ginny's heart sank. But as she opened her mouth to answer, Siobhan took over. She turned to Gala, suddenly businesslike, the tone all wrong. 'Right. Do you mind if I ask a couple of questions? Now we've done this for you, is Sir Salvador going to proceed with his painting?'

Gala slid past them and shouted down the stairs in Spanish. They heard no answer from below, but she straightened up as if the artist had responded in some detail.

'He is prepared to accept the young man as a substitute for Mr Saunders. He insists that you say nothing of this to anyone. The role of the famous stuntman, despicable as that man is, matters to Salvador.'

'For publicity, I understand,' Siobhan jumped in.

'No, no, for art! For Dali's art! Dali does nothing for publicity, only for art. The interest around Saunders doing this . . .' Gala shrugged as if she could not understand it herself. 'You will know about Dali's fascination with movies. He wishes to bring a movie star into a painting. So it shall be a *total secret* that your young man was his substitute. You will say nothing of this.'

'It will be our total secret,' said Siobhan. 'Obviously Mr Saunders will have to know.'

'Saunders will stay in the hotel, our prisoner,' Gala told Siobhan, 'and at the end we will announce that he is the one in the painting and nobody will know he never came near this house.'

'He will agree to that, I'm sure. I may not use the exact word "prisoner", though.'

Gala's eyes blazed. 'If he does not agree, I shall seek him out with wolves. Each of them will take a bite from the wrinkled and lotioned back of the preposterous stuntman, and Dali will paint a series of pictures of his flesh as we fry the lumps, season them, and cast them from a cliff to the swooping gulls.'

In the awkward silence that followed, Ginny was itching to speak. What about Adam? Did he have the time for this? Was he being forced into it? On the one hand she selfishly wanted Siobhan's project to fall apart. On the other, she could only see Adam again if they kept this connection.

And she had seen elation in Meredith's face for the first time. She said nothing as Gala led them into a small, pebbled court-yard on the first floor of Dali's property. She looked up, over her shoulder, and saw the shape of the property above her, how the group of white houses Dali had attached to each other looked like they were part of a slow landslide towards the sea. There was nothing but a wrought-iron fence between the visi-tors and the ocean beyond. 'Wait here while I bring us some water,' Gala said. 'I have one more question for our clever one here.' Siobhan puffed herself up, but Ginny was sure Gala was referring to her sister.

There were no chairs so they stood in silence. The sun was blinding, as if making up for its absence earlier. Siobhan pulled a notepad out and started writing. Seeing her, Meredith took the green scrapbook from her bag and opened it. Ginny thought she saw that some of the ink was streaked by the rain earlier. But if Meredith had seen the damage, she appeared unbothered. She brought the book to Adam and Ginny.

'My mother's book.'

'She kept a scrapbook of modern art? What an interesting lady she must be!' Adam turned to Ginny, who did not offer a correction, but was hoping he would not go further. She looked at the open page and changed the subject.

'What was the painting you identified earlier, Merry, the second one? Is that in your book?'

'No,' she said, closing it. 'That one shows a giant honeycomb in the desert.'

Adam asked, 'And it's called *My Mother*?'

'The big yellow honeycomb is a depiction of the rocks near us now,' said Meredith. 'The painting also shows a statue, maybe Dali, embracing his father, with certain symbols. A fish, a grasshopper, a dagger. But I don't know what they mean.'

'Maybe you should ask him,' whispered Adam.

'I'd be scared.'

'This is your chance.'

Ginny was immediately protective. 'You know so much, Meredith. You don't need to know any more. Leave it as a mystery.'

'Without you, Meredith,' said Adam, 'we wouldn't even have seen Mr Dali.'

Meredith moved away. 'Thanks for being so kind to my sister,' Ginny spoke softly, not wanting Siobhan to hear, 'but I don't know if that whole episode was healthy for you.'

'Why?'

'He burnt you.'

'No, he didn't!'

'I saw it. I smelt it.'

'I was just a little incinerated.'

She laughed. 'A little? I was worried you might be a little dead if he carried on with that.'

Siobhan shot them a suspicious glance.

'I don't want today to end,' said Ginny quietly.

'It would have been even better without the fighting.'

'True. I was trying to forget that.'

'But I was just thinking, if he wants me to be Jesus Christ

in a painting, how is that going to work? Do I have to grow a beard and look forgiving? Am I going to be with the disciples? Do I need to know m-more about the Bible?'

'Maybe you should pretend you thought it was a portrait, like Saunders did.'

'And storm out on the first day!'

As they giggled, Gala approached with four glasses of water on a tray. Siobhan and Meredith joined the circle as it widened. Gala spoke, the metal tray flashing the sun into the faces of her guests in a way Ginny could not be sure was accidental.

'I shall speak English, no?'

'Thank you,' said Siobhan.

'Who knows of the Christ of Saint John of the Cross?'

'Yes,' Siobhan responded immediately. 'Catholic upbringing for me, so lots of Saint John.'

'I have been speaking to Dali,' continued Gala. 'He wishes you to return tomorrow with information about Saint John of the Cross, and if you bring that information, the painting schedule will be set down and extra money will be paid.'

'Extra money?' Siobhan's eyes lit up. 'How much?'

'We have to continue to pay Mr Saunders because he must not leave Cadaqués during the project, or speak about this. And we must pay you for your time,' she told Adam firmly, 'you, beautiful young man with the tousled hair.'

'Well, he is being paid already, in a way, with diving lessons from Mr Saunders,' put in Siobhan. Seeing everyone look at her, she added quickly: 'But yes, certainly you should pay Adam.'

Gala inhaled deeply. 'The man's name, his title, is Saint John of the Cross. You see, young people? This man is long dead. My husband reveres him. Reveres his Christ. Come back tomorrow and make sure you know the story.'

'We can do it now!' Siobhan clamoured. 'I can do this!'

'*Tomorrow!*' cried Gala.

'Siobhan, wait,' Ginny began. 'My sister wants to say something about this.' Beside her, Meredith was opening her mouth and raising a finger like the shyest child in class.

'What's there to say?' responded Siobhan rudely, her tone indicating that Meredith could not possibly produce even a single word worth listening to.

'And when you return,' Gala said, as if halfway through a sentence, 'we will have the contract waiting for Mr Bannerman.' They all turned to Adam. Surely now he must speak. If he had concerns about the project, now was the time. Even Gala stopped to look at him, the sun forcing her to shade her eyes. Adam was no longer the passenger. Now everything depended on him. He had the power to stop it.

He only got three words out.

'So long as—'

Siobhan moved forwards. She tipped her glass of water down Adam's front. His white shirt immediately creased around the curve of his chest. His nipples became visible under the fabric. She looked playful. 'That'll cool you down, wonderful man,' said Siobhan. Gala and Ginny stared in astonishment. 'Well, he was burnt. Weren't you, Adam?'

'Yeah. I guess so.' He closed his eyes, breathed in, held his hand across the wet shirt. 'Wow, I n-n-needed that,' he said, opening his eyes and laughing, but Ginny thought he was just reacting in the way Siobhan wanted him to. 'What a tremendous feeling.'

She was completely in control, thought Ginny.

Afterwards a car arrived to pick up Siobhan. She pulled the young American into the back seat with her and made some excuse about space being limited because of boxes . . . boxes which Ginny could not actually see. She and Meredith waved goodbye to the car and started to walk back to Cadaqués. Meredith was silent. Ginny felt herself shaking. At first she thought it was the breeze coming in off the open sea. Then she realised she was not cold. For the first time in her life, Ginny was shaking with anger.

CHAPTER ELEVEN

SAUNDERS

He sat alone at the dinner table thinking of Muscle Beach.

In Santa Monica they respected him. Young girls would queue for lessons from the very best. He had never taken advantage. He strode the bleached boards, flexing, grinning like a champ. His skin burnt straight to brown, his back rippled shiny like a racehorse on a final furlong, and he knew it. Respect was not so much to ask for. He would show them a simple roll first. He never started till he could see his face reflected in their pupils, the black of the eye dilated into a mirror. The key was to tuck the chin tight to the chest the instant you moved. *Remember, the sand looks soft but it feels damned hard if you land wrong. So be aware of the space around you. I call that 'space awareness'. Sure, that's actually my phrase. 'Mine' as in – I invented it. Be aware of every millimetre of your body and where it is in the air, so you and the space work together. Space awareness, understand? Now, stand and launch into a soft roll. That's it. Now flip yourself in the air before you land. Yes, turn your body in the air. Trust your body. Watch me.*

When Saunders was thinking, as he was now, he liked to keep ideas separate. It helped him make a decision. Counting out the pros and cons of leaving Canada for California, he had used sugar cubes piled high on the counter of a Winnipeg diner. Then Hollywood – well, that was not so much a decision as a twist of fate. Hollywood was never a choice. Hollywood happened to you.

He had just done another movie, *Singin' in the Rain*. Due for release next year. He could not imagine working with Gene Kelly again. The man was a star, for sure, but he was also a beast. After the shoot Kelly gave interviews saying the film would be one of the greatest in history, and he never used a stuntman. To Saunders' mind, that was not just wrong but wicked. Morally wicked. What if a man died in a stunt for Gene? Would he still not even get his name in the credits? The tyrant had pulled the same trick with him in 1948 on *The Three Musketeers*, and Saunders should have been more wary.

The set of *Singin'* was the craziest he had been on. Chaos. They had to stop the 'Broadway Ballet' sequence when the costume designer Walter Plunkett realised you could see Cyd Charisse's pubic hair through her costume. After Plunkett fixed it he came out with the line, 'Okay, we've got Cyd's crotch licked,' and Saunders spat his tea out. That sprint up the wall into a backflip – Donald O'Connor nearly broke his back doing it. Great guy. Kelly bullied him. No question. The tapes had a fault and they shot the backflips a second time. They should have asked Saunders to take Don's place because he was dead on his feet by then, but there was continuity to consider. In the end, Saunders had not been used for anything spectacular in *Singin'*. They broke the news to him that he wouldn't be credited. Kelly's insistence, apparently. Hollywood could do that – make a sketch of a man, then rub it out.

Now the stuntman's mind was on a different movie. He glanced around the hotel restaurant. Most of the diners were locals from Cap de Creus. Upmarket Spanish ladies with dark red bows in their hair and shoes. Husbands stuffed into woollen jackets. Staff had cleaned the place up after the fire, but there was a scorch mark on the ceiling where the fan had caught. The melted fan paddles had been taken down. If Saunders had been quicker, he would have smacked that fool painter in the face before he could start the performance with the match and the napkin. But no, that would have been a bad idea. Spanish artist, Spanish hotel, Spanish police. He would have been carted off to the Cadaqués jail, no matter how much of a joker Dali was, no matter how many fires he had started. Only in Europe, degraded post-Hitler Europe, would a barking fop like that be held up as a genius. In Santa Monica the Salvadors swept the garbage off the roads.

Respect. Saunders rolled the word around his head as he rolled the wine around his mouth. He moved the salt cellar and the pepperpot close to each other so the porcelain clinked. Let's say the pepper was the artist – one shake and he's empty. The salt was the stuntman – raw, gritty, persistent. Okay, so move the pepper and salt together and ask yourself if that's how you want this. Stay in Spain so no one can accuse you of reneging.

Not that he ever wanted to set eyes on Salvador Dali again. Maybe he had to leave.

He stared at the salt and pepper as they slowly moved apart. Then Saunders took his hands away and lifted the wine glass to his lips. Two gulps was all he allowed himself. Two starters – today it was a mackerel salad and then some chicken liver pâté. No dessert. No sweet buns on the side, no steak. That gave him a lady's waist and a midriff like a wall, muscle stacked on muscle like unpointed brick.

In front of him was the document they had mailed. He guessed it had been dictated by a secretary in California to someone in London and posted from there. A movie with Richard Widmark. *Hell and High Water* was the working title. He moved the salt and pepper back together, and now the ashtray was involved too. The ashtray was Widmark. He liked Richard. They had worked together before, and he got complimented on the way he mannerised Widmark's jerky walking style. 'Mannerised' was his word, yep, Russell Saunders' own invention, and the stuntman had flushed with pride when the director said he was full of ideas.

Looking at the name of the movie, Saunders guessed some kind of cliff jump. His experience gave him that level of insight. And sure enough, there it was in the summary they enclosed. The fee would be $45,000 plus agency charges. If he broke his arm he would never earn another cent, so it was good money for a good reason.

He moved the ashtray, salt and pepper in circles around each other as he tried to work out what to do.

Savouring his last sip of wine, Saunders glimpsed two women at the table on the other side of the room. The larger of the two had a mound of jet-black hair and her back to him. He would not judge her from the unflattering outline of her blouse. Perhaps she was a mother of five, and ballooned just like his own mother after her seven, and then him making it eight. Facing her – and glancing at him now, he realised – was the younger girl whom he recognised from the previous day. Had they not been introduced to him as sisters? It seemed impossible. The young one had the most beautiful face. Flawless skin like bone china. A body without an inch of extra flesh, but the chest full. Virgin for sure. She looked upset. Agitated. Her delicate hands weaved in front of her mouth. The other girl, the obese one, seemed to be talking. Saunders allowed his gaze to rest on the dame facing him. He wished he was fractionally more intelligent and could impress a lady like that, set her mind at rest. He imagined teaching her to spring into a vault on Muscle Beach, taking her hand on the boardwalk and showing her what he could do. But that kind of lady would never be seen in that kind of place, half undressed in the Santa Monica sun . . .

He stopped himself. By God, the thing was barely out of her teens and he was making himself feel like a pervert.

Saunders smiled at the thought, and it accidentally became a smile at the young woman. She must have been looking at him directly, because her hands stopped their weaving motion and she froze for a second. Then there was an unexpected arrival. Siobhan Lynch walked into the room, waved half-heartedly at him without smiling, and sat down with the sisters.

Russell Saunders smarted, feeling something like a slap.

And there was that word again. *Respect.*

Ginny was surprised when Siobhan sat at their table. The PR girl plumped herself down as if expecting a welcome, as if they were all buddies. Ginny had been trying to hide the way her tears kept welling up as she sat opposite her sister. She knew Merry would not notice, deep in her thoughts as she always was, but was fearful that the grin from the American stuntman, four tables away, had been triggered by something obvious in her distress.

What did she have to be upset about? This part of the trip had actually been a huge success. Meredith had been transformed by the visit to Dali's house. She had spent the last ten minutes chattering gaily about the paintings she had seen in that peculiar residence in Port Lligat, and the Mae West sofa, and what might have been hidden on those canvas rolls in the basement, and the shape of Dali's swimming pool: 'Was it really . . . ?'

Ginny thought the morning's adventure had been unhinged from start to finish. If there was a single word to sum up her first impression of the artist, it was the one her mother had always aimed at her as a child – silly. Yet her sister saw him differently. Meredith seemed to find something profound in that house by the sea. Meredith, in her madness, had connected effortlessly with the master of the surreal. And now Ginny put it like that, the events of the morning made perfect sense. The deranged communicating with the disturbed. She, Ginny, was the disabled one. Her own sanity made her blind.

Deranged the artist surely was. A show-off. *Silly.* But how wonderful it was that Dali had singled out Meredith as his favourite. Like Christ choosing the cripple. 'Let him through the crowd!' Ginny had at least grasped Dali's sheer fanatical creative intensity. The way his eyes burnt. He must have the fingertip precision of a watchmaker when a brush was in his hand, yet the perfectionism was wedded to a need to draw constant attention to himself. To set fires. *Strange combination*, she thought. The watchmaker and the arsonist. Sad, in a way.

The setting sun sprayed rusted light across the room. Their salads had just arrived, Mediterranean peppers in oil and thick squid on bread. Meredith was clearly hungry and happy. So why was Ginny trying to stop herself blinking tears down her face?

The answer had just sat down beside them.

'Just to say, you know, thanks from me,' Siobhan said. 'I know we got into a bit of a fight back there but you sure as hell saved my bacon today.'

'How?' asked Meredith, always needing it to be spelled out.

'Well, you especially, with your art knowledge, showing him we weren't dunces. And you, I know you look like a child –' she was talking to Ginny now – 'but you saved me with that young man you found. The exact same damned V-shape as –' she lowered her voice – '*the bastard*. My God. Your young man has frankly blown my mind with that body.' With her Irish accent it came out as *moind*.

It was almost more than Ginny could take. She hated the way Siobhan switched between friendliness and menace, and would not tread carefully around anyone's feelings. She hated that Siobhan had whisked Adam off in a car from Port Lligat, leaving her with the angry walk back. Couldn't Siobhan at least pretend she had not seen his beauty, pretend it was obscure, known only to Ginny?

'He was burnt a little in the studio,' Siobhan went on, 'but we found some cream.'

My God, thought Ginny, *how much more of this?*

'Where is Adam?' Meredith asked.

'Coming down soon,' said Siobhan. 'Now I need to go and make sure Mr Saunders' – she shot the stuntman a smile so fake it looked like it was drawn on her face in felt-tip – 'is happy to talk to Adam about his diving, maybe give him some advice. That was the deal, wasn't it?'

'Yes,' answered Ginny firmly.

'We can probably take it from here,' said Siobhan pleasantly, reaching out and taking a slug of Meredith's wine. 'Ugh – what's that?'

'She dilutes it,' said Ginny.

'Because of your mental issues? Of course, yes. Like I say, grateful and all that, but you can leave the artist to us now.'

Meredith suddenly spoke: 'You don't need us?'

'No.'

'What about the question?'

'What question?'

Ginny carefully watched the exchange between Siobhan and her sister. 'About Saint John of the Cross?' said Meredith.

'Oh, that! Not a problem.' She waved it away. 'Believe me,

when you've been dragged to chapel forty thousand times like I have, you know every single thing there is to know about Saint John. Yes. Matthew, Mark, Luke and that lad. I could probably quote chunks.'

'But—'

'Chunks of it! "The disciple Jesus loved." Honest, I could take a quiz on those verses. Every bloody thing the disciples did, every one of them, inked on my brain. Still, I've found an English Bible. I'll bring it in case he asks something obscure.'

Ginny asked Meredith softly, 'What was Dali's question again?'

'Gala told us to return tomorrow with information about Saint John of the Cross, and I was just—'

'It's all sorted, right?' Siobhan butted in. 'Mr Dali will be so bored of Saint John by the time I've finished he'll wish he'd never asked!' She looked up. 'Ah! Mr Bannerman!'

Ginny could bear it no longer. She jumped up, smiled politely as Adam arrived, and left the dining room before her tears made it impossible to see anything at all.

Saunders watched. He was irritated. No, he was angry. It took a lot to get a man like him, a champ, angry. That incompetent woman, Lynch, had virtually barged into his bedroom that morning. Now she was jabbering away at the two sisters. Even he could see the younger one he had been admiring was distracted. Maybe even distressed?

Yes, he thought as she jumped up and left the room. *Definitely distressed.*

Meanwhile he was dealing with this pig's ear of a situation, booked for a job with the painter that was so far below his skill set it was unsavoury even to think about it. Okay, publicity had been promised for them both. Millions of inches in newspapers across Europe and America, no doubt. 'Dali Uses Famous Stuntman', all that crap. But it turned out that 'uses' was the operative word. Saunders did not want or need to be used. How desperate was he for publicity when Bob Yerkes had called him 'the best all-around stuntman I've known'? When he had Richard Widmark chasing after him from the other side of the world? A man like Widmark would not be impressed to learn his stuntman had surfaced in Spain wearing only a flannel.

Lynch was approaching with one of the waiters. Saunders looked angrily down at the table. The salt was sitting in the ashtray and the pepper was knocked over. That was his decision. Scrap the deal. Get out of here.

He was about to tell Lynch that Dali could forget his damn scheme when, to his surprise, she deftly angled her body to let the young waiter step in front of her. 'Mr Saunders,' he said in an American accent, 'my name is Adam Bannerman. I have followed your career and your work in the movies, and I admire every one. I was also born Canadian, like yourself. I did not want to approach you until I had been given permission.'

Saunders suddenly found his anger abating in the face of such deference.

'That's kind of you,' he said grumpily. 'Canadian, huh?'

The waiter was about to say more when the Lynch woman sprang forward. 'Mr Saunders, I know this has *not* gone to plan. Not at *all*. And I am *furious* about the way you have been treated.'

'So am I. For God's sake, a flannel?' He felt himself getting angry again.

'Relax, we have a Plan B.'

He hated her superior tone, he hated being told to relax. 'Widmark wants me,' he said. He meant to push the typed pages he had been reading across the table, but the waiter's unexpected praise had thrown him. Absentmindedly he slid his decision-making ashtray-salt tower towards Lynch and the waiter as if it settled everything. They stared but did not comment.

He said, 'What this comes down to, folks, is that I'm leaving town.'

'Can you please let me – just, Russell, please.' Lynch's Irish voice had a desperate tone. It was softer and she had used his first name. Saunders had her down as a top-class manipulator, the sort Hollywood was full of. She and the waiter pulled back the two chairs opposite him and sat down in such perfect unison that they might have rehearsed the move for a year.

'*Please* let me suggest an alternative, Mr Saunders.'

Silence, for the barest moment. The room coming together in front of him, everything in sharp detail, just like you want it before the clapperboard snaps, the cameraman pulls focus and the director calls for the stunt. Saunders could leave now with a leap onto the chair and then a flip to the neighbouring table, swing one-armed from the fan . . . no. There was no fan.

'I'm not doing the painting. I'm not going anywhere near that Spanish bastard with the box of matches. Look at the damn fan up there, he melted it.'

Lynch tightened her lips. 'You don't have to go near him again, Mr Saunders. You don't need to smile at him or even see him. You won't have to be in the same room as him. Adam here will pose for the painting. This young man admires you so much—'

'It would be an honour, sir.'

'You?'

'Yes. Me. I'll do it. I don't mind.'

Saunders paused. 'Have you got the muscle tone to be me?'

'I hope so, sir.'

'Show me.'

The waiter rapidly rolled up his sleeve and made his bicep bulge like an egg. The vein popped into an S-shape under the skin. But it was not enough for Saunders. 'Your solar plexus.'

Adam raised his eyebrows, then stood. He untucked his white shirt from his trousers and carefully rolled the material up. Saunders caught Lynch's sideways glance at the ribbed flesh not six inches from her face and saw her run her tongue across her lips. Immediately he understood what it meant. What it all meant. He threw a fake punch at the boy's stomach. Instead of jumping back, Adam leant in towards the fist and tightened the muscles. He would have sprained his wrist if his hand had connected, thought Saunders. This boy was built like he had been ten years ago.

'Mr Bannerman, your toning is certainly impressive – yes, please, son, do sit back down – but Miss Lynch, I am afraid I've already decided to break the contract.'

'This is a better way, Mr Saunders.'

'Explain.'

'So – you stay in the hotel. Prepare for your next big project. Dali still pays you. He'll pay some extra money to Mr Bannerman, too. We get an agreement with Dali whereby, so long as you are credited as the model—'

'*I don't need to be damn well credited as a model!*' Saunders roared suddenly, all of his anger exploding through his face. He tried to get up from his chair, but the table trapped him and he ended up in a semi-crouch, banging his fist twice on the table.

The restaurant fell silent. He knew he had gone too far, and he sat back down and put his face in his hands. 'I'm sorry,' he said. 'The frustration is . . .'

The sentence tailed off and was followed by an awkward

silence. An observer might have wondered how many frustrations Saunders was plagued by – this simple, single man who threw himself off bridges and buildings in view of a dozen cameras as if attempting a hundred public suicides, only being paid when they failed. Now the stuntman was motionless, face hidden by his hands, the acrobat who had messed up his big spring.

Gradually, the sound in the restaurant started up again.

Lowering his hands, he saw Bannerman take out his waiter's pencil, draw the long waiter's notepad from his breast pocket and flip it open to the first blank page. He drew an upside-down L with a swirling arrow beside it, what looked like a stick man with his body bent double, and another coiled arrow below. He tore the page from the pad, flattened out the crease, and pushed the sketch slowly across the table. It sat between the stuntman's elbows.

'I can do this,' Bannerman said. 'I jump forwards, somersault and bend double. That bit –' he pointed at the lower arrow – 'is a roll into the water. But I don't always hit the water how I want to.'

Saunders looked at Bannerman, frowned and stared back down at the drawing. 'You don't always hit the water how you want to?' he whispered.

'No.'

'What height are we talking, young man?'

'The cliff at Cap de Creus. And the one out back here, behind the hotel.'

'Wait. The second cliff at De Creus?' Saunders' eyes narrowed.

'The highest one.'

'I've seen it. I went to look. My God. What are you diving?' He looked at the page again.

'I'm not sure. What *am* I diving?'

'Front, back, pike open or closed? Jameson Twist?'

'I don't know the names.'

'You have people in the water, right?'

'People?'

'Don't tell me you do it on your own.'

Bannerman pursed his lips. 'I just found the highest point and dived off it, I guess.'

'You do it on your own? Have you seen what the surface of the sea will do to a watermelon?'

Adam shook his head.

'At the speed you're hitting the water, the melon explodes like a bag of blood. That's your head if you get this one millimetre wrong. You gotta have people in the sea, at least one, to help you out if you rip the water wrong. You break your back, you'll drown, and I saw a man do that once. You'll be doing fifty miles an hour coming down from that height, faster than a Pontiac. Sonny, you could break your neck. Easily.'

'That's why we hoped you would teach him, in exchange for him doing the painting,' said Lynch, her voice patronising.

'This man doesn't need a teacher, he needs an undertaker.' Saunders turned the sketch 180 degrees. 'So what does this mean? The top arrow. A forward roll?'

'Double somersault.'

'Jesus. Out of that into a pike?'

'I don't know what—'

'A pike. Legs straight, toes pointing at the sky, chin on your knees. Butt down first.'

'Butt first, yes.'

'Open or closed?'

'I don't know what that means.'

'Wait,' broke in Saunders. 'You've done this without anyone

helping? You don't even know what you're doing? You don't know the names of stuff? A body roll, a Jameson Twist, a full Cooper, an open pike?'

'No. I wanted you to teach me how to go off backwards.'

Saunders laughed quietly, shaking his head. 'Backwards, with all this,' he said.

'That's why we—' Lynch started to say, but she was cut off.

'I want to learn, sir,' said Adam.

'Sure I'll take you out,' said Saunders, biting his lip. 'I don't really have a choice.' He slid the piece of paper back to Adam. 'That would make a good design on a gravestone.'

'Thank you, sir.'

'I'm not praising you. I'm just thinking I'm watching a young man who could have died a dozen times, and somehow you've ended up here offering to take my place with Salvador Dali – which, by the way, I accept. You must have a charmed life, just like me. Because you've managed to do that jump without taking your head off your shoulders, and maybe it's a miracle that you had the luck to find someone who can save you while there's still breath in your body.'

'We go back to Mr Dali's tomorrow,' Siobhan said. 'He wants us to answer some sort of quiz before he goes ahead.'

'Quiz!' exclaimed Saunders, as if this final piece of information was the straw on the camel's back.

'About Saint John.'

'Quiz about Saint John!' the stuntman repeated. 'My oh my. Well, I've heard everything now.'

'I guess he wants to know we'll be properly engaged with what he's painting,' Lynch said.

'Glad I won't be there,' said Saunders. 'A goddamn quiz now. That guy is one lightbulb short of a . . .' He could not find the noun he wanted in time.

'It'll just be me and Adam going,' Lynch said. 'We don't need the other two. The intense sisters.'

Adam frowned.

'And that's okay with you, young man?' Saunders asked. 'To be me in the painting? In exchange for some lessons from the very best?' He was suddenly back to his old self. Easy and agreeable.

The young waiter reached out wordlessly. He shook the stuntman's hand. Russell Saunders realised he was winning here.

On the clifftop, Ginny felt exposed. To the sun, and the sea, and the truth.

The truth that her love for Adam was not rational. It was, in fact, ridiculous. It angered her that she should feel this way. These feelings had flowered after barely half a dozen encounters. If they'd had a hundred meetings, maybe she could have justified what she felt. She could have compiled a list of qualities that explained this uncontrollable flow of emotion. Was it just infatuation? Wasn't that supposed to pass quickly, like a bout of sickness? But she felt consumed by the desire to be with him and him alone. To explore him, and for him to explore her.

She cursed her childish heart. Her foolishness. These stupid thoughts. Was it looking in the mirror that morning that set her off? She had seen herself naked and been awakened. She had admired herself and been corrupted. That mirror! She would turn it to the wall when she got back to their room.

But maybe she would not go back to the room. If she could not have Adam, maybe she could die where he had lived for diving. Maybe she could throw herself off the edge of the cliff.

She turned the thought over. To die where he had lived. The drama of it exhilarated her. But of course she would not do it. She did not have the cold heart it required. Nor the precision she imagined was necessary for a successful suicide, the careful scoring of all the reasons for and against. She did not have the bravery.

She wondered about her father. They had all pretended it was an accident. High winds, they said, had pulled him into an industrial drain.

The very thought of plunging off the cliff seemed ridiculous now. She sat on the grass, unhappy with herself. The sun was setting. She thought of Adam again, of his flesh, his voice, his arms, his legs. His modesty, alloyed with a surprising self-confidence, as if he already knew who he would become. Did he even want another person?

Yes, she thought, he wanted Siobhan Lynch. And if he did not know he wanted her, Lynch would make sure he did. She was older, she had experience.

There was a sound behind her, and she half turned. It was Meredith. Her sister came and sat beside Ginny. 'There was shouting in the restaurant,' she said.

'Oh, who?'

'Mr Saunders got angry. I'm not sure why. I didn't like it.'

'Well,' said Ginny, facing the sea now, and letting the light bathe her, 'it doesn't matter now. I think you were right, Meredith. We should go. Let's continue our travels. I want to see Rome. We can get to Rome from Barcelona, by boat. It's ten hours on the ferry. We don't need to be here and it was selfish of me to persuade you to stay.'

'But I enjoyed it! Meeting the artist!'

'I got you to stay because I wanted to stay myself. It wasn't fair. And it's not just that. There was another reason. I don't know how to say this.'

'It doesn't matter.'

'My mother—'

'It doesn't matter.' But Meredith's voice was smaller, as if she was dreading what was coming.

Ginny changed track. 'Look, our adventure here is over now. You heard Siobhan. She doesn't need us any more. She and Adam can do it together.' She wished she had phrased it differently – her own phrase wounded her.

They sat listening to the wind and the sea.

Meredith put her arm around her younger sister. 'It's not over. She can't do it without us.'

'Yes, she can. Siobhan is such a bloody tyrant. She can do it without anyone. All she cares about is herself.'

'I don't mean that. She can't do it without us. She just can't. I've found something out.'

Ginny waited for an explanation, but it did not come.

'Can't you say?'

Meredith looked at her, as if affronted to be asked direct. 'No.'

'No? It sounds important.'

But there it was again – Meredith's anxiety, hands clasped to her knees, the fingers wound around each other. Ginny left it. Anyway, asking would suggest she had some hope that they might end up staying. And she did not. They would leave the hotel tomorrow and continue their trip. Having cheated Meredith of the truth again, Ginny would write to her mother and refuse to do her bidding: *I will return with my sister and she will live with us, and she will have whatever of our father's fortune he wanted her to.* The sisters would have plenty of time to puzzle over the events of the last few days, but the one thing Ginny must not do – she knew this – was to believe there was any chance of the situation changing. She had been comprehensively outplayed by Siobhan in a stupid game whose rackets and balls and field of play Ginny herself had chosen. She wanted to be closer to Adam but in the end had delivered him to another. She would go away from this place and try to learn from what had happened.

'I wondered what you were thinking just then,' said Meredith as they walked back to the hotel together.

'I was thinking about our father,' said Ginny, 'and what a sad and lovely man he was.' Then she asked, 'Meredith, if you liked someone – a man – would you tell him?'

'Is it Adam?'

'No, don't be silly! I just mean – if it happened.'

'Why not tell them?'

'Because they would know they could have me, so they'd find me boring. Maybe they could only like me if they thought I didn't like them.'

Meredith was silent for a moment. 'Ginny, you saved me,' she said finally. 'And even if today is the last day of my life, it was the best day.'

CHAPTER TWELVE

THE LAST NIGHT

Ginny's eyes opened suddenly. There was no dawn light. She could not say what had woken her, other than the uneasy feeling in the pit of her stomach. She found herself remembering Meredith's words. *Something terrible is about to happen.*

She stared at the ceiling, thinking about Dali, and Siobhan, and Adam. About her instinct that in love you must never tell, never declare your hand. Because if you showed your cards you had no way back. As these thoughts ran through her mind, she shifted her left leg towards the other side of the bed and was surprised to find it empty.

Turning, raising herself onto an elbow, she blinked in the dark.

'Meredith?'

She patted the covers to her left.

Switching position, she found her own bedside light would not turn on. She sprawled, stretching her arm towards the lamp on Meredith's side table. Not working either. 'Meredith?' she tried again. She fumbled in a drawer for matches and lit the candle on her bedside table.

It flared indecisively in its copper holder. The covers on her sister's side of the bed were pulled back. She searched the shadowed corners of the room, but the light from the candle was erratic. 'Merry, are you in here?'

Still nothing.

The clock on the wall said just before five. Where could Meredith have gone at this time?

It was hot, and Ginny wore only her undergarments so she wrapped a towel around her waist. Quietly, but with rising panic, Ginny took the candle and made her way to the door of the room. It was dark in the corridor outside. The light from her candle flickered yellow along the walls, picking out scuff marks. With her other hand she clutched the towel to her waist. The floorboards creaked as she stepped.

Ginny was reaching the end of the corridor, and was about to turn left towards the central staircase when she heard footsteps approaching. Her heart raced. She instinctively backed into an alcove, blew out the candle and clutched the towel tighter to her waist.

Unused to the sudden darkness, she could see nothing. The footsteps grew nearer. 'Where are you?' said a voice in the gloom.

She knew it was Adam, but was too embarrassed to reply.

'I can smell the candle,' he said. 'I know someone's there.'

Ginny nervously shifted the candle holder from her right hand to her left. As she did so, her towel slipped.

A match flared in Adam's hand.

'Ginny?'

She offered up the candle.

'Your hand's shaking.' He lit the wick. Together they watched the flame dance in the wax.

'I am looking for my sister,' Ginny whispered. She wanted to pick up the towel to hide herself, but the candlelight only illuminated the top half of her body, so her modesty was preserved.

'Has she gone missing?'

'Yes. I thought she might be creeping about here somewhere.'

The dramatic lighting made her suddenly ask, 'Do you know what it's called when you have very strong light and very strong dark in a painting?'

'No.'

'Meredith told me once, but I've forgotten.' She felt silly asking the question. 'Are you going out to the cliff?'

'Soon. But I have to get up early to lay tables for breakfast so I can dive. It doesn't help that the lights have gone.'

'We're going too,' she whispered. 'We're leaving Cadaqués in the morning.'

'You can't.' He sounded genuinely aggrieved. 'Doesn't your sister want to see Mr Dali again? She was the only one who seemed to – to register with him.'

'Oh, I think Miss Lynch has got her hands on that now.' She said Siobhan's name with distaste, then wished she hadn't made it so obvious.

'You did help a lot with that visit to the artist, Ginny.'

'You're the one who saved the day, Adam. Really.'

The candle guttered and died. They were plunged into darkness again.

'You were so clever, bringing your sister. She's like an art history book.'

'What sort of book? Is she a hardback or paperback?'

'A hardback.'

In the half-light, her eyes widened. He was so gentle, so straight, so true. The words sounded faintly smutty to her, and she wanted suddenly to touch him.

'I can't imagine it will be easy,' she whispered.

'What?'

'Giving your time to Dali. He seems like he must be a perfectionist.'

'How hard can it be to sit or stand for a painting?' He touched her arm and she felt his body, thrillingly, draw closer. 'And guess what, Mr Saunders *will* teach me. Five lessons, he said. To get my dive right. He was quite friendly, considering how much Dali upset him.'

'Well, remember he's a stuntman.'

'So?'

'So his job is to do things that are slightly insane.' He was not touching her any more, but she could feel the warmth of his body.

'He thinks *I'm* the lunatic.' He laughed softly, then caught himself. 'Oh, I didn't mean to mock your—'

'My lunatic? Don't worry. Right now she's in a better mood than I've ever seen her. I just wish I knew where she was.'

She heard Adam shift his position. 'I've noticed how you put yourself out for people, Ginny. Even me. But you never seem to look out for yourself. You're so smart and kind. But you never think about yourself.'

'You're the kind one.'

'Oh no, I'm very selfish. I feel that with – my mother.'

He fell silent in the darkness as if his mention of her had been a mistake.

'Your mother?'

'I can never give her enough time.'

'Where is she?'

'Sick.'

'Sick? In America?'

'Sick here. In Barcelona. They don't really know what it is. She had a virus and it weakened her. Auto-immune, they said. For a while she was in bed, then she got up, but on sticks. We had just come out here with my father's job. I went with her and looked after her in Barcelona. I only did what any son would. But my father said I was getting exhausted. So he took me away. Set me up here, in the hotel, working, near him. He has people caring for her. Professionals. I guess it was right to take me away, but it doesn't stop me feeling guilty.'

'Poor you.'

'Poor her. When you can't find a cause – her doctors are thinking, is it a virus? A cancer they can't find? It's frightening, and so awful for her.'

'And your dad, I guess.'

'But he is away from it, at the naval station here. To be honest with you –' Adam spoke in a whisper so quiet it was almost inaudible – 'he has affairs.'

'Affairs?'

'Maybe he feels guilty. He wanted her out of his mind so he brought me back. He's a hard man to understand.'

'I don't know if I'll like him.'

'You won't have to meet him, don't worry,' said Adam. The finality of his words crushed her.

'Does he come to see you here?'

He coughed, lowered his voice even further. 'He's very – military. He gives orders, my dad. That's what he does. I don't know if Mom was happy for even a single day of their marriage. All the photos I have seen of her as a girl, a young woman, she's smiling and laughing. Then there are pictures of this sad married lady, and now she's sick lying in a bed. That's it. That's a life.'

'Let's avoid that,' Ginny whispered without even thinking.

She could feel him staring at her in the darkened corridor.

'Let me get your towel,' he said.

Ginny sensed that she had knelt down. She felt him scoop up the towel at her feet. 'Adam?' she whispered.

It was silent. She waited for him to stand up, but he did not. She heard his breathing quicken, felt it on the skin of her thighs. On her belly.

She was ready for whatever was coming. She wanted it so badly.

Suddenly the lights came on in the corridor. Adam jumped up. Momentarily blinded, she avoided looking at him. As if waking from a dream she said, 'I'm worried about my sister. I worry about whether she's safe. I'm sorry, I need to see if I can find her.'

'I'm sorry, I'm sorry,' he said hopelessly, and pressed the towel into her hands. She wanted to take one step back and sideways, move towards him and press her breasts to his chest with her hands reaching round and running up his spine, mounting every single vertebra with her fingertips, palms pressing into the muscle of that chiselled back of his – but was immediately so mortified by her desire that she blurted out an indignant goodbye as if he was to blame for what had happened. She drew her eyes from him and started towards the main staircase, feeling his gaze on her back.

She suddenly remembered something her sister had said. *And even if today is the last day of my life.* Alarm fizzed in Ginny's stomach. Had Meredith done something stupid? Taken more of those Bennies, chewed on them, lost it? Might she even have . . . ?

Oh God, no.

Downstairs, Ginny hesitated in the gloom as she tried to work out where to search. Instinctively she followed the narrow corridor that led to the breakfast room. She saw a dim light flickering under the door to the library. Was Meredith in there?

Ginny tiptoed down the corridor, gently pushed open the door and poked her head into the library. Meredith was at a table with a large book open. There was a desk lamp with a flickering bulb, and a burning candle to one side. 'The lights keep going on and off,' Meredith said without looking up.

'What are you doing, Meredith? I was worried. It's a crazy hour.'

Still Meredith did not look up. 'I had to check something.'

'Couldn't it wait until the morning?'

'I'm copying it out.'

Ginny approached. She was relieved to see her sister, but too exhausted to think straight. 'What is that book?'

'A history of the Catholic Church from 1400.'

'What could you possibly want in there – no, on second thoughts, tell me tomorrow. I just wanted to check you were in one piece.'

'I am,' said Meredith, always factual, not seeing the need to apologise, still not looking up. 'I will come up to bed, just not yet. This reference took me more than an hour to find. Half of it is Spanish. It's impossible without a dictionary, but I found one. This is an incredible library but it's a mess.'

Like you, Ginny thought. *Like both of us.*

'Did you know,' said Meredith, 'that Salvador Dali had an older brother? His name was Salvador Dali too! He died before the artist was born. So his mother called the next child Salvador Dali as well. And every week, she took the second Salvador to the grave of the first, and he had to look down at a tombstone with his own name on.'

'What must that do to a person?'

'I don't know.'

'Maybe he has to keep proving he's alive.'

Back in bed and alone, Ginny relived every second of the meeting with Adam. He was having to lay the breakfast tables, he had said. So why was he on the first floor when the restaurant was at ground level, and so was his room?

Siobhan. It could only be. Jealousy surged through her. Adam must have been with Siobhan. She had seduced him already. She was experienced, a grown woman. She thought of the burns lotion. How far had she spread that stuff?

God, thought Ginny as she lay there, she was sounding crazy now. She sounded angry and crazy and mad. Had the encounter with Salvador Dali made all of them mad?

She breathed deeply. Took the warm air of the bedroom deep into her lungs. Felt her pulse calm.

She thought of her towel dropping in the dark, Adam falling to his knees. His face must have been inches from that small rectangle of silk that covered her, inches from the place no man had seen. She imagined the unthinkable – that he had pressed his mouth to the silk then peeled the material back with a finger and used his tongue.

Ginny slipped two fingers past the elastic on her underwear. She opened her legs and led herself, as though leading his tongue, to the most sensitive inch of her body. It was wet already, as she touched herself directly for the first time, until a wave of ecstasy broke across her and she cried out in the empty room.

The next morning Ginny wore a white shirt buttoned up to her throat. She had dressed in clothes which were hardest to pack and she feared she looked absurd as she waited for their taxi. Her dress, a stale tartan, was long and thick – hot in this baking coastal breeze – and she wore her ankle-length brown travel boots and thick socks over black stockings. The hat, impossible to put in her case, was a wedding meringue. She knew she looked like a middle-aged spinster and for once she did not mind, because they were leaving and that was it, that was the end of it.

Standing beside the cases, Meredith waited too. The sisters were in the hotel driveway, bill paid. It had been impossible to avoid Siobhan at breakfast – with her fake 'You're not *leaving?*' as if she actually cared what they did – and although Ginny might have loved to simply disappear from Cadaqués without farewells, she could not bear to go without a last moment with Adam.

He came out onto the driveway from the reception area. For a second Ginny imagined that he had been in her bed before dawn and not just in her mind. Perhaps that explained the embarrassed expression on his face. 'Plans!' he said, with forced good humour. 'The h-hotel will give me time off for Mr Dali. Siobhan has her Bible and knows lots of stuff, so she can answer all his questions. And this afternoon I'll get my first session with Mr Saunders – which is the main thing, if I'm being selfish.'

'You're not,' protested Ginny quietly, just as Siobhan trotted towards them like the difficult half of a married couple.

'Saunders,' she announced, 'is currently jammed under a rather large eiderdown waiting for his toast!'

Adam drew closer to Ginny. 'Well.' He took a deep breath, as if he wanted to move beyond small talk but did not have the words. 'Thank you, Ginny. For everything. What will you do now?'

'We'll take a taxi, then a train to Barcelona.' A second too late, she wondered if the mention of Barcelona would make him think of his mother. 'Do you want us to look in on your—'

'No!' he jumped in. 'You're on holiday. And really, Ginny,' he repeated, 'thank you.'

'For nothing much at all,' said Ginny, smiling

'We haven't done anything yet,' Meredith said. It was a strange thing to say, and Ginny glanced at her. Did she not understand they were leaving?

'I thought you were into this whole p-p-painting business,' Adam said.

'Oh, yes. Yes, I am. We are. Meredith especially. But I think you have it covered.' She hoped she managed not to sound bitter.

'Has she edged you out a little?'

'Who?'

He tipped his head to indicate Siobhan. 'You know who. I think I might have accidentally encouraged her.'

'How?'

'Maybe I flirted, I don't know.'

'Really, Adam.' Businesslike, she stepped away from her sister and lowered her voice. 'This is about Meredith getting better. She wants to leave. She met Dali and that was wonderful for her, but it was enough.'

Meredith caught the end of the sentence.

'We don't have to go.'

Ginny pretended not to hear. But Adam was staring at Meredith. 'See? You can stay.'

'Oh, we've made plans now. We are thinking of Barcelona, then a boat to Italy.'

'Much nicer here,' he said, annoying her. He dropped his voice. 'Didn't the moment with Dali mean a lot to your sister? It was –' Ginny gestured at him to speak more quietly, and he continued in a whisper – 'electrifying, when she identified that painting.'

'Yes, she won't forget that.'

The phrase seemed to lodge with Adam, who repeated it. 'No, she won't forget.' He stared at his feet. Siobhan called his name but he did not look up. 'Can I say something, Ginny?'

'Yes.'

But before he could speak, Siobhan was there, seizing his arm. 'You know, I think I might actually be cut out for this Public Relations stuff, right? The amount of fixing I've done to get all this wired together! I've had calls from London and Dublin today. Words of praise from the top!' She lowered her voice. 'Not entirely sure Mr Saunders will be doing any work with us again, but that's his loss, the pompous oaf.'

'Hey! Don't insult my hero,' Adam protested.

'Sorry, darling.' Ginny flinched as Siobhan put her arm around him. 'Now, the taxi was my only little glitch. Ordered fifteen minutes ago, and apparently they need an hour. But let's see – oh, here comes a car. Come on, Adam. There'll be money for you, my boy!'

Ginny could hardly believe what she'd said, but she kept quiet. The taxi drew up, bright blue with stickers on showing cartoon sea scenes which looked like tourist postcards. All the vehicle's windows were open. The taxi was Ginny and Meredith's of course, but Siobhan barged in front of them and took a place in the back seat. 'Come on, Adam!' she called.

The driver, a little man with skin like an old handbag and a bad limp, hobbled out and popped the boot, reading the name off a scrap of paper:

'HUGHES!' He said it as *yews*.

'That's us, Adam!' said Siobhan.

Ginny frowned. She walked to Meredith and touched her elbow to stop her objecting. Meredith, when she noticed, would be sure to say out loud that this was their cab, not Siobhan's.

The Irish girl must have felt guilty about the taxi, because she turned back and called: 'He looked at me and shouted "You!", didn't he?'

'Goodbye!' called Ginny.

Adam heard her and turned.

'Hey, come on, Adam!' Siobhan called from the back seat of the cab.

He stepped around more decisively, advanced on Ginny,

diverting for a second to Meredith – 'Your art knowledge is amazing, Meredith, and I hope you enjoy your travels with this amazing lady' – and then turned to the younger sister. He swallowed.

'Tell me if you dig my clothes up.'

She smiled. Held up a hand to shield her eyes from the sun. 'Of course I will.'

'I don't mind. I never minded that business.'

'At the start you did.'

'True. Until I met you, I minded. Then I just thought I was lucky. A few old clothes in exchange for—'

'Come on, Adam! Let's not be late! The Spanish man is waiting here, and so am I!'

He tilted his head, ignoring Siobhan. 'Ginny,' he said.

She thought of him diving off the cliff that first day, and wished she was not wearing every single heavy item of clothing that had failed to squeeze into her suitcase. And then she suddenly did not care about any of it.

Adam stared at his shoes and said, 'This counts for n-nothing, I know. But you have stolen my heart.'

'What?' Ginny whispered. This was the last thing she expected to hear.

'I fell in love with you without meaning to. It just happened. I'm sorry I wasted the time we could have had. You are so special, I . . .' He trailed off. 'Lordy, I'm so bad at this. I don't have the words.'

'Adam!' Siobhan shouted. It seemed to jolt him into continuing.

'I love you. You and only you. You, Ginny. Completely l-love you. And I'm not just doing this project to get close to Mr Saunders. I'm doing it to be close to you, and n-now you're leaving. So I feel a fool.'

She dropped the hand shielding her eyes.

'A fool?'

'Yep.'

'But last night I saw you coming from Siobhan's room. So I'm the one who felt a—'

'No. Not from hers. Towards yours. You saw me coming towards yours.'

'My room?' She hardly heard her own voice.

'I wasn't anywhere near Siobhan's. Why would I be?'

Ginny felt so much emotion building inside her she could hear her ears ringing.

'Come *on*, Adam!' Siobhan shouted from the car. Adam turned and moved quickly to the taxi, not looking behind him once.

Meredith pointed. 'That's our taxi. The man said "Hughes", I heard him.'

'Let it go,' Ginny murmured. 'Just let it go.'

The engine fired. Ginny felt like she was drowning in Adam's words. She waved, but neither Siobhan nor Adam looked back. The cab made a cumbersome three-point turn with at least five points in it, then bustled down the drive.

'Don't worry,' Meredith said. 'They won't get far.'

But Ginny was so lost in her thoughts that the words barely registered.

A full hour later the sisters were still at the hotel. They were now dependent on the cab that Siobhan had booked, but there was no sign of it.

The breeze blew warm through the back doors. A radio crackled with news in Spanish, Franco this and Franco that. Ginny remembered Adam's fluency in the language, the way he spoke with Gala. He could easily have translated this bulletin for her. She wanted to cry. She felt her eyes grow heavy with tears she could not shed.

Meredith sat on the sofa near the fireplace, looking intently at her green scrapbook. The hotel called the cab firm again, but the confusion ('They say the cab for Moran-Hughes arrived, and you have left in it' . . . 'No, we are waiting for the cab under the name of Lynch' . . . 'But Miss Lynch has already left') felt like it might go on forever. Ginny eventually established that the car was forty-five minutes away. She thanked the receptionist and, sweating inside her heavy clothes, began to pace the hotel to clear her head.

At the end of the wood-panelled corridor leading from reception lay the reading room. Off to the right was the restaurant and, of course, the library. She stood for a moment and stared at the library door, chewing the inside of her mouth thoughtfully. Then she walked back to the reception area and sat on the sofa beside Meredith. The older woman was using photo-corners on a blank page to stick a sketch into the book.

'You did that yourself?' asked Ginny. Meredith continued with her task. 'The taxi will be another half-hour at least. I'm sorry.'

'It'll give them time, I guess.'

'The others? Oh, they've gone. That's over now. It was an enjoyable part of our trip though, wasn't it?'

'No.'

'It wasn't?'

'I mean it's not over.'

Ginny slid closer to Meredith and gently shut the green scrapbook to get her sister's full attention. 'Tell me, what were you doing in the library last night?'

Meredith turned to Ginny. Her black eyes were suddenly

piercing. There was a certainty as she spoke that the younger sister had never heard before.

'Salvador Dali asked for information on Saint John.'

'Yes, he did,' Ginny agreed.

'And I was reading in the library about Juan de Yepes y Álvarez.'

Ginny frowned. 'Okay.'

'And naturally Siobhan thinks, like all of us, that Dali must have been talking about Saint John from the Bible.'

'Meredith—' Ginny was about to urge her to get to the point, but stopped herself.

'I kept trying to tell everyone. I got shushed by the Irish lady, and you didn't—'

'Okay, okay,' said Ginny. 'Tell me at your own speed.'

'I was awake in bed and I thought of the library. Were some of the books in English, or could I do it with a dictionary?'

'Do what?'

'The book I found about the Catholic Church was long and lots of footnotes were in English, and there were illustrations.'

'Go on.'

'Saint John of the Cross was a man from the 1500s.'

'What?!'

'He was born in Spain in 1542, and that was his name.'

'Juan—'

'Juan de Yepes y Álvarez. His father's relatives were rich silk merchants and his mother was an orphan. Because the father married below his station, he was kicked out by his own family and they lived in poverty, with the father dying when Álvarez was very young. His brother died of hunger soon after.'

Ginny nodded, suddenly gripped by urgency.

'Later he became a priest and he went into retreat with a Carmelite nun. I can't remember her name. She had a lot of

strict rules, like you could never wear shoes. They called themselves Discalced Carmelites.'

'Disc what?'

'Discalced, meaning shoeless. They lived in the desert and prayed
all day. In 1568 he founded a monastery based on the same rules.
That's when he changed his name to John of the Cross.'

'But what has that got to do with Salvador Dali?'

'Well, I also found one more thing,' said Meredith, picking
up her green scrapbook. 'His monastery was in Ávila. One day
he was praying in the loft overlooking the sanctuary. During
his prayers he had a vision of Jesus Christ on the cross, but
seen from above. Here.'

Meredith opened her scrapbook and found the right page first
time. Her sketch was nothing special, and Ginny could see that
her grip on the pencil had been uncertain. All the same, there
was something dramatic about the drawing. It showed the broken
body of Christ hanging from the cross, with the left hand closest
to the point of view, and the perspective defined by the line of
the shoulders, visible from above.

'Did you do this?'

'I copied it from the book you saw me reading. Thousands
of paintings had been created with a view of the cross from the
side and from below, but never from above. I don't know, is
this why Dali is interested?'

Ginny stared at the sketch. She looked at her watch. Looked
outside at the hotel driveway, searching for the taxi.

'John of the Cross was tortured for this sketch,' Meredith
said. 'Another order of priests found it and said it was a blasphemy. They imprisoned him and starved him and he nearly
died. They said the sketch of Jesus from above was "a spiritual
indecency" and he should die for it, because no human being
should ever believe themselves to be above Our Lord.'

Ginny marvelled at just how animated Meredith could be when she was talking about art. And as she marvelled, something clicked. She looked at her sister.

'So Siobhan and Adam are at Dali's house and they have all the wrong answers.'

'Yes, and he will send them away.'

Meredith was matter-of-fact. But Ginny could hear her own panic as she thought it through. 'Siobhan Lynch brings Adam and they get thrown out. And then Siobhan has to stop the contract falling through and – I don't know what she does, but Adam won't get his lessons, and the stuntman will be . . .' She remembered Siobhan's viciousness towards Saunders. 'I don't even want to think about what happens if it all gets cancelled. But it will be my fault.'

'You always blame yourself.'

'But it will be.'

'It won't be your fault. Let the Irish lady look stupid.'

'No, no, no – not with Adam there, he'll be—'

'I did tell you they wouldn't get far.'

'Oh Merry, I wish you'd—'

'*I told you!*' Meredith shouted suddenly, jumping up. A couple passing through reception stopped in shock and looked their way. Meredith slammed her green scrapbook down on the table.

Ginny stood and reached for her sister. 'I'm sorry, Merry. You tried to. We didn't listen. Let's not argue. What do we do now?'

'I don't know,' said Meredith.

Ginny decided for them and rushed to reception, wishing she had even a few words of Spanish. 'Taxi?' she said in an exaggerated voice. 'Soon?'

The receptionist was small, dark-haired, with orange

eyeshadow. She dialled and spoke urgently into the phone, then made a fuss of elaborately replacing the handset in the cradle. 'No,' she said.

Ginny span on a heel. 'We have to get there, don't we? Because if we knew this – if we don't change this, then all I've done is damage. And Mr Saunders will be—'

'Hey!'

At that moment, completely by chance, Russell Saunders had strolled into reception.

'Will be what?'

Ginny looked at him, her mouth moving but no sound coming out.

'You call me, I appear. Right on cue. It's what I do. Will be what?'

'I'm sorry,' said Ginny. 'We have a bit of a crisis here.' Meredith was paying no attention at all, just leafing through her green scrapbook as if her work was done.

Ginny and Saunders stared at each other for a moment.

Then Ginny said, 'Do you have a car?'

She ran and ran. It was that urge inside her again – always there – *to make things right*. Her body bled with sweat. Her skin was soaked. Clothes too. Armpit stains spread across the tweed. Meredith had managed a hundred yards from the hotel and then, halfway down the Carrer Eduard Marquina, began to look dangerously overheated. Two passing Spanish policemen held her elbows for a minute to steady her. She had fished for the crucifixion sketch in her pocket and thrust it at Ginny, who sent her sister back for her own safety. Ginny scrambled alone down the seafront at Cadaqués and felt the stares as she broke into a sprint across the sand. Who was this woman, she could feel them thinking, heaped with tweed and wool, wearing a meringue-shaped hat and big mud-proof boots, racing across the beach in the morning sun?

It had been a mistake to ask for a lift from Saunders. The stuntman was all Californian ease – 'Sure I have a car; a rented Merc 220A, the red beaut back there, convertible' – until he felt someone was taking him for granted, and then he would go up like Vesuvius. No sooner had she explained that there were some problems with the painting schedule and mentioned Dali's name than his veins were jumping in his temples, his pectorals bracing and nostrils flaring like a bull's. She had immediately placated him, apologised, turned and started to run with Meredith.

Ginny was alone now, running in her hot clothes and desperate not to start ditching them.

At the far end of the sand was a path up to the road. By the time she reached the top, Ginny's heart was pumping furiously. She stood by the roadside, her hands on her knees, out of puff.

And then a red car rolled up. A convertible Mercedes with the roof down.

'Rude of me earlier,' called Saunders, leaning across the passenger seat. 'I didn't mean to cuss Dali like that in front of a lady.'

'You did cuss,' said a breathless Ginny, remembering at least two F-words as Saunders had turned the air blue.

'Let the artist be the artist, that's my motto now. After all, this car is part of the deal with him. So I shouldn't begrudge it.'

Ginny was too out of breath to reply. She simply opened the door and flopped into the passenger seat.

'They have seat belts, these new models, but yours doesn't work.' He looked in the driver's-side mirror and indicated. 'Mind me asking, why are you dressed for a Siberian winter?'

'These are all the clothes I couldn't fit in my suitcase,' Ginny gasped.

'Good idea. Running in that gear. Fit.' He pulled back onto the road. 'Glad I have the roof down. You'll cool quickly, don't you worry. Now, where are we going?'

Ginny soon realised she did not know how to reach Dali's house by road. When it became clear a few minutes later that they were lost, Saunders stopped the car.

'I know it's over there,' she said, pointing at the bell above the hermitage of Sant Baldiri. 'But I think we may be out of time.'

Saunders revved the car. 'Honey,' he said, 'when you're in a car with a stuntman, you're never out of time.'

The next five minutes were the most terrifying of Ginny's life. Russell Saunders made the car scream in pain as he revved it on every corner, took it up to seventy-five, careered along a stretch of hillside road with the two right wheels inches from the edge. The speed and wind blinded Ginny, who had never done anything like this before. Saunders seemed constantly to be shouting. 'Is it down there?' he shouted over the din. 'Hey, I can see it I think! Let's fly there!' He negotiated a T-junction by suddenly jamming the handbrake on, which sent the car spinning a full 180 degrees and somehow ended up with the left turn he wanted.

Ginny managed not to scream. Sweat dripped all the way down her back as a cloud of grit and dust thrown up by the car settled on them both. Saunders took off again, but then a dawdling van ahead of them forced him to slow down for a moment.

'You were always safe, young lady,' he said.

'I think the house is around the next bend,' Ginny replied. If she was wrong, it did not matter. She had to get out of the car before she was sick.

'Forgive me if I drop you some way short. I don't want to be any closer to that man's driveway than I need to be.'

'Wait!'

The single word was prompted by the four figures Ginny saw appear around the corner ahead, walking beside the road.

Siobhan, Adam and two young men she did not recognise.

Saunders braked hard. 'Is it okay to leave you here?' She could tell Saunders wanted nothing to do with Dali, even if he was driving a car rented with the artist's money. For the first time she thought his disgust was irrational – more than he could justify by anything that had happened, even the fire – and wondered if there was something behind it which she had not been told about.

But this was not the moment to ask. 'Thank you for the stunning and unforgettable ride,' she told him with a flash of a smile. Then she climbed out of the car and ran towards the four figures.

'Well, thanks a bunch!' barked Siobhan as Ginny came into view. Adam looked unsettled, and Ginny noticed one of his deck shoes had torn around the sole. The other two with them appeared to be local Spanish teenagers.

'I think I might know what's happened,' said Ginny. 'Am I too late?'

'Saint John,' said Adam, shaking his head, staring at his shadow on the road surface.

'But I've got the answer now. I understand what he wanted.' Ginny went to pull Meredith's sketch out of the inside pocket of her thick jacket and realised she had a blank page. She grimaced at Meredith's error. 'It was a different John,' she tried to explain.

'We all know *that*!' cried Siobhan indignantly. 'We got there and Dali was sitting on that veranda of his overlooking the sea.

He had a huge easel, and he was sitting on this stool, astride it, right, his back straight—'

Adam interrupted Siobhan, lost in his thoughts. 'Like a throne. He didn't even look round at us.'

'Had his back to us the whole time, facing the sea, working on the enormous canvas, painting boats I think, with a very long brush, who knows? And then in this silly, theatrical, boasting voice he asked us to tell him about Saint John of the Cross, and I said literally one sentence and we were gone.'

They waited for her to say more.

'All I told Dali was, "Apostle of Jesus, brother of James, author of the Gospel according to Saint John." And that was when he threw us out.'

Ginny repeated, 'Threw you out?'

The taller of the two Spanish boys spoke up, his English better than Ginny expected. 'We work at the – casa? For Mr Dali's – company. He told us to—' He inverted both hands and made his fingers walk side-by-side. The shorter Spanish boy laughed.

'You can stop damn laughing, right, you babblewits,' said Siobhan furiously. She looked at the shorter boy. 'What's your name anyway?'

'He's called Sami,' Adam replied for him. 'He told us earlier.'

Sami was dark-skinned, large around the waist, with sturdy legs and a gap for a missing tooth that only showed when he smiled. He was wearing a train driver's hat that was too small for his head – or perhaps the head was too big for the hat, because the denim shape simply rested on his crown as if someone had discarded it from a passing car. He might have been fourteen, but had the look of someone who was partly adult, partly child. On his nose there was a black freckle as big as a farthing.

Siobhan was incoherent with anger. 'Mr Dali told you to escort us back. So what? What's there to laugh at?' She added, 'These boys said something about Maquis.'

The boys suddenly stopped smiling. Sami pointed to the scenery, there and there and there, making a motion with his arms as if he was holding a rifle and aiming it at the distant hills. 'The Maquis are rebels,' said Adam. 'Against Franco. They're in the area, apparently.'

'Where was Gala?' asked Ginny.

'She came in with these two boys,' Adam said, 'and told us they would take us home for our safety, but probably just to make sure we left. Was that Mr Saunders in the car with you?' He was looking up the road to where the Mercedes had ripped tracks in the gravel as the stuntman sped off.

'Yes,' said Ginny, feeling sad. She guessed Adam's diving lessons would never happen now. They were avoiding looking directly at each other. 'He gave me a lift down here but didn't want to go near Dali's house.'

'It's good to see you anyway,' said Adam quietly, speaking to the tarmac.

'I don't blame the stuntman myself,' said Siobhan. 'The guy was sitting painting, didn't even damn well turn—'

'Okay, okay,' Adam snapped with a rare flash of anger. 'This isn't h-h-helping. We have to decide whether we go back with Ginny's answer or we just leave it.'

They all looked at Siobhan. Ginny fervently hoped she would decide not to come with them, that only she and Adam would return.

'What actually *is* your answer, Ginny?' Siobhan asked. 'Who is Saint John of the Cross?'

Ginny repeated as much as she could remember from Meredith's explanation, but there were gaps, and without the sketch on that scrap of paper she felt she had only half the story. At the end she said, 'Oh, you know, I just don't think I'm confident enough to do this.'

She wanted Siobhan to agree. Ginny would go back to the hotel, collect Meredith and leave this place.

But Siobhan could see no reason not to try. 'Never mind that! One more try, for independent Ireland? Right? We will give it one last shot. If these young men can get us in. Can you?'

Sami shrugged and giggled. 'No.'

The taller one said, 'You mean yes.'

'Which is it?' asked Siobhan.

'Okay, yes,' said Sami, throwing out his arms as if he was completely out of his depth.

'Okay,' said Adam, taking command. He looked furious with Siobhan. 'Let's go back.'

The house was further away than Ginny expected. It took twenty minutes to approach along the dry stone esplanade. When the front door came into view it was open.

'That's strange,' said Adam.

'Maybe thieves have broken in,' Siobhan said. 'Looking for paintings that were worth something, and they left empty-handed.' No one laughed. Ginny glanced at the two Spanish boys, concerned they might have understood the insult. But they were ambling along arm in arm and seemed happy enough.

They arrived at the front door. Ginny and Adam paused. Siobhan shoved her way forwards, gripping the door frame and putting one foot on the lintel. One of the boys tapped her on the shoulder, gesturing for her to move back. The other boy moved inside, banged the red lips door-knocker once, and beckoned the group as if the signal was enough to allow them in. Confidently, the two boys led them towards the upstairs balcony. Ginny herself felt nervous at the prospect of repeating in front of Dali what Meredith had told her about the obscure saint.

Ginny squinted in the bright light from outside as they approached the balcony. Dali had his back to them. He was sitting on a tall wooden stool at a huge canvas, which at first looked as if it was covered only in black paint. Above the canvas was a makeshift parasol which shielded Dali's work from the searing heat. The artist wore a straw hat whose brim was frayed. Long, lank hair protruded from the rim, dancing on his neck in the breeze. The air smelt of the ocean. In Dali's hand was a long paintbrush. The fibres were tipped with a dab of royal blue. His delicate brushstrokes were evident at the bottom of the canvas – thin lines of intermingled blue and white. Clouds? Sea? A series of scratches in the dark paint might have been the beginnings of a boat. Other than that, the entire top three-quarters of the canvas was jet black.

As they moved forward, Ginny's pupils shrank and the light overwhelmed her. They were in direct sun now. Ginny squinted. The two boys parted; Siobhan moved back.

Ginny felt Adam's presence beside her. But she was blind in this light.

She was about to say, unprompted, 'I know who Saint John of the Cross is, Mr Dali,' but before the words were out of her mouth Gala walked onto the balcony.

'Your sister saved you,' she said.

Ginny's eyes adjusted. She saw her sister lean into view beyond the canvas.

Ginny blinked. 'Meredith? How did you get here?'

'The taxi was in the drive when I got back to the hotel.'

'Indeed,' said Dali quietly, never pausing with his paintbrush, never turning. 'Meredith who understands.'

The group was silent. Ginny had no idea what to say. She now saw more clearly – Dali at the canvas and Meredith just beyond, at the edge of the balcony with the sea spread out behind her. Her sister rose from a plastic chair with a sheet of paper in her hand.

Gala strode past them to Meredith.

'She has explained who Saint John of the Cross is, every last detail. She even brought this picture to show us.'

'The picture of Jesus from above,' said Meredith.

'She sketched it herself, did you not?' prompted Gala, but Meredith did not respond.

'My painting will show Jesus on the cross from above,' Dali announced. 'It will be the most sensational, most venerated work of art I have ever produced. And the most real.'

He suddenly swivelled 180 degrees on the stool. He peered at Ginny's outfit. 'You are dressed for the Arctic.'

'The weather was hotter than I expected,' she replied, breathless and unable to tell the full story.

Dali seemed to choke back laughter, and then suddenly became serious. 'Your group has made a series of misjudgements.' He moved his head, looking around the canvas. 'But thanks to this lady, Meredith-who-understands, the project can go ahead. Mr Bannerman, you will pose for my painting. I shall recreate the Christ painted by Saint John of the Cross and it will be . . .'

He tailed off.

Meredith stood behind him, eyes blazing, the sketch in her raised hand. She completed Dali's sentence for him.

'The greatest painting in the world.'

PART THREE

CHAPTER THIRTEEN

The Boy and the Girl

Ginny sat in her new room, feeling her heart race. She and Meredith, having checked out of the hotel in Cadaqués, were now in a *posada*, a much smaller inn close to Port Lligat. This time they had separate rooms.

They would stay till the painting was done. Meredith, who had saved them twice, would go to Dali's with Adam every day. She had gone to bed flushed with excitement at the prospect of watching the great Salvador Dali paint. Ginny could not sleep, and got up again. Thinking of her sister's heart-breaking words earlier: 'I wish my mother could have seen what I am doing. I think she would have been very pleased.'

'How many months will the painting take?' Siobhan had asked Dali.

Both he and Gala had roared with laughter. 'Three days only to complete the background,' said Gala, 'the boats on the shore, some distant figures—'

'And the blackness,' Dali had cut in. 'The darkness behind Our Lord.'

'Three days?' repeated Ginny.

'But to paint Jesus Christ?'

'To paint you, a further ten,' said Dali.

'Me,' said Adam quietly, with a bemused smile.

Siobhan, who had blown her chance to control events, would have to watch it all unfold from a distance. In the mornings Adam would dive with Saunders. Then he and Meredith would spend time with Dali. And Ginny? Now, as she contemplated the covers on her bed – the room was small, the furnishing threadbare – she realised with a shiver that she was far too excited to sleep. Yes, everything had come together as far as the painting was concerned. But it was more than that.

Adam's words to her as they stood waiting for the taxi had hit her with such emotional force. He had said he *loved* her. She would never in a million years have guessed it. But that was what he said. That was his truth. What was hers?

Driven by that thought, she pulled on a bright white blouse and a flowing skirt. A minute later she was leaving the guest-house, noting the tatty doormat as she stepped out, checking she had the key the manager had given her to get back in later. Above her the night sky shone with stars. Her walk was purposeful. She kept glancing at her watch. Past midnight.

Half an hour later she arrived, sweating a little, at the side door of the Hotel Maravillas del Mar. It had not yet been locked. Ginny entered slowly and crept along the dark staff corridor, looking for the green door. Adam's room. When she found it she tried the handle. To her surprise it did not move. Was he still working?

Ginny stood in the corridor, shifting her weight from one foot to the other.

Then the lock clicked and the handle revolved.

The green door opened six inches and she saw Adam, in only his underpants. She stepped forwards and, before he could say anything, pushed her mouth to his. Her momentum carried her into the room, until his retreat was stopped by the frame of the bed behind him.

She took her mouth away from his, holding his face in her

hands, staring into his eyes. He stood motionless. Then, appearing to understand, he raised a finger to his lips and thumbed over his shoulder. There were two beds in the room. Lying under the sheet in the bed directly behind Adam was another young man, head on pillow, apparently asleep.

Adam moved his face against hers, cheek on cheek, until his mouth found her ear. 'The waiters share rooms,' he whispered. 'We have to be quiet.'

'Who is he?' asked Ginny. But as she spoke Adam's right hand swept across her breasts, to her stomach and below. He moved behind her. 'I've never done this before,' he whispered.

She shook her head to mean, *Nor me.*

'I don't know how to.'

'Let's try.'

The room was silent but for the rustle of her clothes against his skin. Adam slowly put his hands inside the white blouse and caressed her. 'Can I?' he asked, but he was already doing it and the movement of her body replied for her. Gently, he felt each rib on the way to her breasts, fingers climbing them like a ladder. When his hands arrived at their destination, stroking the lowest edge of both breasts, she felt weak. She reached her left hand to the wall to support herself and caught the moan that was about to come, too loudly.

'Tell me how to touch you,' he whispered, so quietly she felt the words against her ear like feathers. She did not want to speak for fear of waking Adam's room-mate. Instead she reached inside her blouse and took his hand in hers, moving it upwards and across her naked left breast. No one had ever touched her there before.

She moved his hand in circles across the nipple until it surprised her with its hardness under his palm. He took over the motion and his hand became more forceful. She tried not to cry out. 'Gentle,' she said. Now she moved his hand to the other breast and let him make the circular movement again, taking his other hand and moving it until he had both her breasts cupped in his palms. 'Not too rough,' she whispered, but did not know if he had heard, because his motion was becoming more rhythmic and insistent.

What did lovers do? She felt a hardness pressed into her right buttock, and her hips moved instinctively in circles. She was so desperate for him that she hardly cared what happened next or how embarrassing it would be to show her desire. Would he fit inside her? How could they make love in this tiny room with a person asleep in the second bed? Her breasts felt heavy in his hands, then light and firm as the motion in his arms lifted them and his palms swept the skin. His right hand dropped now, brushing her navel, sliding under her skirt and finding the hair between her legs.

She gasped, broke away and turned.

'Wait, Adam. I want to be in control. I don't feel—'

His hand stayed in place as they faced each other, the end of his finger suddenly finding a spot so sensitive she felt stung. She pulled back and he drew his hand away, then came closer again, folding an arm around her waist and placing his other hand on her rear, pressing his hips to hers. Again they began that instinctive motion, hips moving and sliding against each other. Again his hand probed her, and again she wanted to tell him to stop while not wishing him to.

'Wait.'

He froze. She put her head on his chest and heard his heart racing.

At that moment the figure in the bed behind them shifted.

They both looked, eyes widening. Adam's room-mate lay still again.

'He sleeps so deeply, that guy,' Adam whispered. 'He doesn't wake for anything.'

'I want to touch you,' said Ginny.

She dropped to her knees. Now he had a steadying hand against the wall as she placed her fingers at the line where his underpants pinched the top of his thigh. He gasped as she pressed at the hard flesh below the material. 'Does this hurt you?' she asked in a murmur too quiet for him to hear. Then she shocked herself by pressing her face to his underwear, her mouth feeling his erection through the fabric, soft and hard at the same time. She teased the fabric with her teeth and he gasped again. Now she held him firmly in her left hand and – trying to guess what he wanted, careful not to scratch him with her nails – she touched the flesh below with her finger-tips. She was determined to be in control. She did not know what she was doing, but nor did she wish to be led by him, whether or not he knew what he wanted.

She slid the underpants down his legs. He stumbled out of them, now completely naked as she knelt before him. He turned and leant back against the wall.

Ginny gasped. She had not expected this. His most private part was not modest like him. She moved her cheek against it, backwards and forwards. Adam put an arm across his face, eyes buried in the crook of his elbow as if out of shame. Ginny touched his testicles, almost from curiosity, and as she moved them gently he groaned and so she did it again. Then she wrapped both hands around him and he gasped as she let her grip slowly tighten. She pushed her hand towards his belly, took it back, pushed again. Finally she tried to take him into her mouth.

'Wait, wait,' he said. He sank to his knees and put his nose to hers, talking so quietly she could barely hear. 'I'm about to . . . it will finish if we go too fast.' But she could not remove her hands because there was nowhere else in the world she wanted them to be. She pushed and pulled at him until he made a noise that sounded like she had caused pain. He took her hand and pulled it away.

'Wait, Gin. Come to the bed,' he whispered.

She was staggered at how obvious, how natural it was to let her skirt and underwear fall to the floor on her way across the room. Naked, she turned and sat on the edge of Adam's bed. He sank to his knees and shuffled between her legs, never looking away from her face as his hips gently guided her knees apart. She looked down at her unkempt mound of private hair and, from sudden shyness, covered herself with one hand. He bowed his head. Gently, he kissed her fingers as if suggesting they might move from the place, and they did. His eyes met hers as his mouth moved lower and his tongue probed her. Now it found the place where her skin secretly parted. She gasped and fell back onto the bed.

Never before had Ginny felt so complete as she did in this moment. Her life was so beautiful in this precise second that his flickering tongue seemed almost a part of her. Without thinking she lifted her knees, reached for Adam's head and pulled him deep into that private space. She felt the stubble on his chin scrape the inside of her thigh, and then it stopped, and there was nothing.

'Adam—'

Ginny lifted her head to see his shoulders rise and his tongue now trace its way up her stomach to her breasts. She dared herself to say, 'Go back down there,' but before she could he had fastened his mouth onto her left nipple and a pain shot between her legs. He had entered her, but tentatively. She stung as he moved slowly out again, then back in. She was as tight as the palms of two hands in prayer, and he was so huge now, so full of blood, that she frowned and bit her lip as he used his hand to position himself so that she might open fully for him. Then Adam found the spot and slid instantly deeper. It was agony, yet she wanted more and more of him. Using her stomach muscles, she pulled herself up from the bed and grabbed his buttocks. She gathered him in with such force that they both had to stifle screams.

She placed her hand across his mouth as his eyes rolled up in his head and his face went slack.

Snoring from the other bed reminded them they had not been silent. Adam withdrew from her and moved his head lower again. He used his thumbs to part her, and for a minute he explored her once more with his tongue, moving up and down until she – staring at the ceiling, breath quickening – felt her whole body split open as the ecstasy of their love washed away her pain.

They fell asleep in each other's arms.

It might have been a noise that woke them both at the same moment. They were under the covers in the dark, their foreheads touching.

'Who is the other person in the room?' whispered Ginny.

'Spanish, large, I don't know. He won't have woken, I promise.'

'Spanish, large,' she repeated. 'That's a nice description.'

'Yes, sorry. Sounded like a police report.'

He said something she could not hear.

'I'm a bit embarrassed, really. To do it like that.' She blinked. 'My first time.' As her eyes adjusted she could see the outline of Adam's head on the sheet. Her beautiful boy whom she loved so much. 'I really hope we didn't wake him.'

'It woke me, that's for sure.'

'I worried I might suffocate you.'

'What?'

'Down there.'

'Oh. Now I'm embarrassed.'

'I'm not embarrassed about that.' She loved the power of saying it, the power of having less shame than him.

'But what a way to go,' he said. 'Drowning in your—'

'Hey! You're no good to me dead!'

'Imagine the autopsy.'

She chuckled silently under the covers. He reached upwards and put his palm on her breast.

'Hey, you need a ticket for that,' she whispered.

'Free travel for students.'

Ginny pulled back a little. 'So you know we're staying a bit longer? But in a different hotel. A *posada*.'

'It's small?'

'Tiny. Bad decor. Not fancy like this place, but they were full when we tried to check back in.'

'Where is it?'

'On the road to Port Lligat. To the left of the road there's an – escarpment, would you call it?'

'I don't know. I guess so. Escarpment.'

'With cacti alongside, a great thicket of them.'

'Yuccas, I guess.' She kissed his shoulder. 'It's on the left if you take the road from here. You might remember seeing it. My room is at the top, so quite high up. But it's not very nice. I noticed the windows are rotten. There's not even a pretence at wallpaper.'

'Jeepers.'

'You should get a job there.'

'Really? So I can bring you breakfast in a rotten *posada*?'

'In bed. Yes.'

'Well, at least from there your sister can get to the Dali house, if she's planning to?'

'I think she is more excited about this than about anything that has ever happened to her before in her life.'

'I love you, Ginny.'

'I love you.'

'From tip to toe. Your tiny toes.'

'Are they tiny?'

'I saw them that first day. The clothes day.'

'The clothes! Don't spoil it. I thought you were dead.' Her whispered words were muffled against the pillow.

'If I was, you just raised me from the—'

Before he could finish the sentence, it happened. The covers were ripped from the bed. Even in the darkness Ginny could see who it was.

Siobhan's shirt was open at the front. She wore no bra. But when she saw them both, she froze.

The three of them were motionless for a full second. Adam and Ginny naked, prostrate, interlaced. Siobhan, half clothed above them. She stared at Adam, then Ginny. Then she stepped back, dropping the covers and putting one hand over her mouth. 'Jesus!' she exclaimed.

'Siobhan,' said Ginny, up on her elbows. 'What are you—'

'Siobhan?' repeated Adam. He sat up decisively, reaching for the sheet to hide his body. Ginny also reached for the covers, excruciatingly conscious of her nakedness.

'*You* two?' said Siobhan. She seemed breathless as she pulled her shirt closed and backed away.

Adam was the first to show anger.

'*What are you doing in my room?*' he hissed.

Siobhan fizzed back, 'It doesn't look like it's yours now, does it?' She pivoted on a heel. Then she stopped, as if struck by an afterthought, and turned back towards them. Ginny noticed the short skirt, the lack of shoes.

'Adam darling, I know you said you'd keep the bed warm for me – but I didn't expect you to keep it *that* warm.'

Adam gasped and started to say something but Ginny placed one hand on his arm. 'Let her go.'

Siobhan stalked out and slammed the door. At the other side of the room, Adam's room-mate sat upright. '*Qué diablos está pasando aquí?*'

'*No pasó nada,*' Adam replied, before turning to Ginny. 'What was she *doing* in here?'

'Shouldn't it be me asking that question?' Ginny shot back.

'But I have no idea.'

'Well, I do.' Ginny swung her legs over him and sat on the edge of the bed. 'You don't come into someone's room at four in the morning half naked because you want to borrow a Bible.'

'She must have gone mad,' said Adam, shaking his head.

'Oh, really? Mad?' said Ginny, piercing him with a look. She saw the Spanish youth on the other side of the room still sitting up in bed, eyes popping. 'And *you* can go back to sleep. Show's over for the night.'

'*Buenas noches a ti también,*' he replied.

'He can't understand you,' said Adam.

'He's not the only one,' Ginny snapped back, as she pulled on her skirt and started searching for the rest of her clothes.

'That's not happened before, honestly.'

'Oh, of course, I see,' said Ginny sarcastically. 'But I think quite a lot of tonight has happened before. Goodbye, Adam.'

And she left, walking as fast as possible along the corridor, down the stairs and out of the side door of the hotel – which spring-locked behind her – then down the long path, onto the road and back to the escarpment which led to her hotel. Half an hour of walking, half an hour of tears at the way her life had come together and crumbled in the space of a day.

CHAPTER FOURTEEN

The Red Car

Meredith liked this hotel better. It was cramped and cheap-looking, but when you had spent years in an insane asylum, a rotting window would always be better than a locked one. After a decade feeling her brain buzz like a swarm of hornets about to swoop, she could hardly object to the occasional dawdling housefly in the real world.

She had been down for breakfast already – a warmed bread roll, bitter coffee and jam – and found no trace of her sister. The knock on Ginny's door on the way back to her room had not been answered. She was sure Ginny would not be sleeping. Most likely she had gone for an early walk.

Since the night she'd swallowed the Benzedrine tabs, things had looked a little better. A little brighter. And for that she knew who to thank. Not Ginny. Her sister had simply connected her with Dali. The painter had done the greater thing. Dali had worked the miracle in her. 'You are the greatest artist in the world,' she mouthed now.

Dali had joined Meredith to her late mother in some spiritual way, as if his painting was a veil through which Dorothy's face became faintly visible. Through his brushwork Meredith remembered the mother she had never known. She could feel her mother's love. *Dali paints my mother's love.*

What she liked about this rundown hotel, she realised, was the height. Here she was, like a queen, in the attic room of a building atop a hill that looked left to Port Lligat and right, in the distance, to Cadaqués. There was a skylight above her head, but it seemed to have been painted shut, perhaps by workmen forced to do the job in a rush. Meredith gripped the unsightly steel rod at the upper edge of the window and hung a little of her weight off it, until the frame surrendered with a yelp of split wood. Cool air blew in. She pulled up a wooden chair and stood on it, so now she could see the panorama beyond.

After their first days in Spain, the weather had become more changeable. Today the sky was grey. Meredith scanned the landscape. Fifteen minutes later, still looking out, she saw a red car approaching on the road from Cadaqués. She guessed it was the stuntman's vehicle – from the colour, and from his driving – immediately. The scenery undulated around the tiny red-painted rectangle, which seemed to float like a prop in a puppet show as if worked from below by a child.

Meredith had been wondering how she would get to Dali's. Now she came to the conclusion that the stuntman must be coming to pick her up. However, the car did not continue to approach as she expected. Just when Meredith thought it would accelerate along the main road towards her hotel, it slowed and indicated. Then it shot away to the south, vanishing among the trees. The next time Meredith saw the car it was a red dot, miles away, slowing on the cliff edge further down the coast. If only she had binoculars! She could just about see figures emerging from the car. Maybe one, maybe two. They disappeared. She blinked. The sun came out for a minute and now her eyes, straining, began to water. She hoped Siobhan had not forgotten her. So far as Meredith knew, only she and Adam would be in Dali's house. But Siobhan was supposed to be organising this. Perhaps the car was being driven by Saunders. Was he taking Adam to a cliff to dive?

She saw the young American's face in her mind for a second, and his physique, and she imagined Dali painting him. If it was based on the sketch by Saint John of the Cross it would not be like any of his other surreal paintings. Saint John had sketched his Jesus, blasphemously, from above. She imagined Adam having to sit cross-legged on the floor for hours while the artist somehow traced the line of his shoulders. Or would Adam stand, with Dali slightly higher, on a chair or a ladder, to give himself the necessary view? What would Dali call the painting?

Suddenly Meredith had an idea that shot a thrill through her chest.

Yes, she would tell Dali himself . . .

She wondered if Ginny had an interest in the young American that might go beyond a friendship. Should she not protect Ginny? Was that not her role, as the older sister? On the other hand, what if Adam had feelings for Ginny, and Ginny had not noticed? Could she help by pointing them out? Could Meredith help Ginny understand the risks of love, even though she had never felt it herself? Should she not at least police the situation a little? Meredith knew how misleading feelings could be.

Meredith was adrift. Today was the day for the artist, for her visit, but nobody was coming to collect her. She could walk, but she did not have the confidence and anyway, she did not know what time the artist and his wife were expecting her. Once again she went downstairs to her sister's room, clutching her green scrapbook. Room number five. She knocked and waited. Had she got the room number wrong? There was no response.

She went down to reception, thinking the waitress might serve another cup of coffee if she smiled at her the right way. She turned left into a bright room with metal tables and stools.

The lino was patterned with incongruous green zig-zags and seemed to stick to the undersides of Meredith's shoes. Hanging across a large side window were blinds stuck open at a diagonal, their cords knotted in impossible tangles, the slats allowing too much sun through. A fan in the ceiling had given up turning and Meredith noticed cobwebs clinging to the uppermost edge, where the base touched the plaster. The wall carried a large framed picture of General Franco in army uniform, swaddled in a fur coat that dwarfed him.

In the corner, the one part of the room with proper shade, an older man in a flat cap sat reading a Spanish newspaper. As Meredith sat down and the stool creaked under her weight, he looked up. 'She's coming back, I think,' he said in accented English. Meredith was surprised. She had thought he must be a local. Reluctantly, she glanced in his direction. The face was weathered. Through pebble lenses the eyes peered at her, shrewd and kind. The man folded his newspaper neatly as if readying himself for a conversation. It was not what she wanted. Anxiety always rippled through her in any social situation. She allowed her insides to settle, counting to ten as she had learnt to.

The stranger peered at her. He was old without being elderly. Sixty, she reckoned. Off came the cap. His full grey hair was oiled and tidy. His smile was open, and he was not rushing her to speak, which she appreciated.

'She was just here,' he said. His head dipped as he spoke, like a series of bows. Old-fashioned courtesy, a little overdone.

'My sister was here?' Meredith asked.

'Your sister? Och, sorry for any confusion caused by this old man! No, I mean the waitress. She'll be back, I'm sure. But I should just add a word of warning—'

'I was looking for Ginny.'

'Your sister, is that?'

'Yes. Ginny Moran-Hughes.'

'I'm afraid I don't know her.' The man's accent, she realised, was Scottish. She remembered the drunk, tired, courteous, grumpy, contrary Mr Cairns who had brought her up. The man in front of her had a softer way, but still she wished he would not speak to her when she was unprepared. She slung her hair forward so it drew black shades across her face like curtains.

'I was going to warn—' he tried again, but as he spoke the waitress appeared, a narrow girl with a long and miserable face that tapered so sharply it removed any pretence of a chin. The nose was kinked; at some point it had been broken. Her cheeks were hollow, eyes ringed with dark circles. She looked as if she was still hunting whoever had damaged her face, a mission from which she should not be distracted by trivial orders for breakfast. Meredith had no choice but to emerge from behind her thick black hair and ask for coffee. The waitress stared as if the question was absurd. Looking put out, she left the room.

The man smiled. 'Sorry, I tried to warn you. She doesn't like customers.'

'She seemed upset.'

'Everyone is upset round here,' he said, eyes twinkling. 'They haven't got the hang of tourism yet. That's what war does to you.'

'War?'

'The civil war, when Mr Franco took charge. And then, of course, the Second World War.'

She paused.

'You want a quick history of it? It's one of the reasons I'm here,' he said. Meredith smiled politely, hoping to indicate that she did not. The Scotsman misread her. 'The Spanish civil war began in 1936. Basically the generals denounced the government of the Second Spanish Republic, which was left wing. The generals were led by Franco –' his voice dropped to a murmur, and he passed a napkin across his face to utter the word from behind it – 'a *fascist*. So you have republicans, anarchists, communists, fighting for the government, and the army fighting against it, alongside the Church, nationalists, Falangists. It was over in 1939 when—'

He stopped speaking. The waitress was back in the room. She placed coffee on Meredith's table. As she leant forwards, Meredith noticed her earrings: two yellow canaries, the feathers flecked with grey and brown.

'I thought the same,' the man whispered when she had gone.

'Sorry?'

'How those earrings are the only point of happiness on her face, poor girl. Bright yellow canaries. They do stand out.'

'They are Spanish canaries,' said Meredith, 'because their wings have a little grey and brown in the yellow.'

He raised his eyebrows. There was a long pause.

'I saw you reading the paper, so I thought you must be local,' said Meredith.

'Not even slightly. Glasgow. But I can make out the occasional Spanish word at least. Have you been to Scotland?'

'No.'

'Your sister, maybe?'

'No,' said Meredith blankly. 'At least, I don't think so. We weren't brought up together.' It seemed natural to add this fact, but Meredith wished she had not said the words as soon as they were out of her mouth.

'My name's Tom.' The man made to shake her hand, but she did not immediately offer hers, so he had to stretch. Meredith took his hand loosely and said her name.

'What brings you here?' Tom asked.

'I was ill, so my sister took me touring Europe.'

'She chose this place?'

Meredith did not want to reply, *No, I chose it*, because then he would ask why, and she would have to explain. 'We just happened to come here.'

'Well, young lady, I hope it's all having a beneficial effect on you.'

'It takes a long time if you've been very ill.'

'Oh my Lord. That sounds like a serious illness.'

After a moment she said, 'I had problems with my eyesight.'

That might have been the end of it. But as he picked up the newspaper again and stared out of the window he added, almost to himself: 'Not sure it's going to work out for me here, a bit of a disaster really.'

She looked at him, suddenly interested.

'Oh?'

'Yes, afraid so.' He began reading the paper, and she knew that he was giving her the option of ending the conversation while leaving her wanting more.

'Why is it a disaster?'

'I came to meet a hero of mine.' He put the paper down. 'A painter, actually. You see, I run a little gallery.'

'Is it Mr Dali?' she asked. She enjoyed seeing his intelligent eyes light up. He whipped off his glasses.

'Aye! Why, that's exactly who it is! How did you know?'

Meredith did not want to speak of her encounter with the artist. It was not only that she hated to draw attention to herself. She guarded the connection with the most powerful feeling of jealousy she had ever known. 'Port Lligat is the next village and I know he has a house there,' she said.

'I have money to buy a painting and I absolutely adore what

that man does, but by God, he's not making it easy for me. Getting any sort of viewing from the artist himself is next to impossible.'

'Oh.'

'The whole enterprise seems to be asymptotic.'

An academic, she thought. An expert with his telescopic words. She recalled the doctors in the asylum with their long coats and alien vocabulary. And Dr Scott of the metal orbitoclast and bloodstained apron.

She was sorely tempted to upstage the old man by saying she and her sister had simply walked into the house and found Dali and Gala by their rude-shaped pool. But she held her tongue. She asked politely, 'Where is your gallery?' A car was pulling up outside, so Meredith raised her voice to compete with the noise. 'Is it in Scotland?'

'Yes. I shouldn't have been silly earlier. My name is Dr Tom Honeyman, and it is the Art Galleries of Glasgow which I run, chiefly a place called the Kelvingrove. So it isn't "little" at all. The Kelvingrove is a beautiful place but very fuddy-duddy, and I have been charged with modernising it by a rather –' he coughed and looked around, as if someone might be listening – 'unimaginative group of people who do not know what modernising is. Still, for now they are trusting me! Finally I have persuaded the board to invest in one of Mr Dali's paintings. I thought that was the hard bit. Sadly it was a piece of cake compared to actually getting time with the great man. I am not sure he has an awfully large amount of patience with his – fans.'

'You didn't have an appointment?'

'I thought I did! I went the day before, and the day before that, but no one was in. Last time I went, the house was shut up completely.'

Meredith felt a flutter of nervousness. Had Dali left? *Shut up completely?*

'Possibly he is away in America,' said the Scot with a yawn. 'I just wish I knew what he was painting. I have money! I want to— Oh! Are you okay, young lady?'

Meredith followed his gaze. There in the doorway was Ginny, her face stained with new tears, swaying backwards and forwards.

'Merry.'

'Ginny?'

'Outside.'

'What?'

'They're here to take you to—'

'The red car!' Meredith broke in, desperate to stop her sister saying the artist's name, because then she reckoned the old man would beg her to bring him too. 'Is it really outside?'

Dr Honeyman asked Ginny politely once more, 'Are you all right, young lady? I am guessing you are –' he waited for his brain to give him the name – 'Meredith's sister.'

Ginny looked at him with the blank stare of a hypnotist's subject. But while her eyes were on Honeyman, her words were aimed at Meredith, who was already up from her seat and moving past her. 'You need to go out there now, please. They are waiting. Siobhan won't come in.'

'Who is in the car?'

'Just the two of them, I think. Lynch and – the American.'

The American? That was a strange way for her to speak of Adam, thought Meredith. Why wouldn't she use his name? She smiled politely at the man and continued past her sister who remained in the doorway. 'Are you not coming, Ginny?'

'No. I can't. I just can't. You go, Merry.'

'Not even to say hello?'

More firmly: 'No.'

With her mouth up to Ginny's ear, Meredith hissed: '*Don't tell him.*' The words came out louder than she intended. Ginny looked puzzled.

Meredith glanced significantly at Honeyman. He was gazing benignly out of the window and pretending not to hear.

'*Don't tell him where I'm going.*'

Ginny grimaced. 'Off you go,' she said.

Meredith headed outside. She passed through the passageway that led off the breakfast room. To her left were six windows – large panes of thin glass, the sort you saw in greenhouses; the surfaces grubby, a nightmare to clean. She found herself tracing a line through the dirt with her finger and looking through it to the road and the crowd of hardy yuccas beyond. The shrubs were bunched in dozens, clumped like infantrymen facing battle. This must be the thin-faced waitress's job, she thought, to scrub the windows, and she had never got round to it because she was so angry with the world. The thought made her guiltily remove her finger from the glass. She looked over at the cactus field and it reminded her of Ginny's socks on that first morning – the spikes had torn a hole in both of them and cut her own leg.

Now, at the end of the corridor, Meredith manipulated the loose metal handle of the door to open it. She walked out onto the small forecourt. The *posada* possessed no space for horses or carts, much less motor vehicles, because the building sat up against the road. So the red sports car was fifteen yards away on the road. All Meredith could see was a section of bonnet and two long legs. As she moved towards the car, she saw it was Siobhan, sitting on the front end. The sunroof was folded back. Adam was in the rear seat, stretched out, head lolling, apparently asleep. Siobhan stared daggers as Meredith walked towards her.

'Your little sister not coming out, then?'

'I—'

She cut Meredith off. 'Fine with me if she doesn't. Your boy here has done his diving for the day.' She sounded more and more furious with each sentence, and Meredith was disconcerted by the tone.

'Yes, I saw you drive over to the cliffs.'

'Should have driven over them,' Siobhan snapped.

Adam opened his eyes. 'Siobhan, for God's sake please pack it in, or I'll go straight home.'

Meredith did not know what to say or do. Adam was still reclined on the back seat, face upturned, an arm spread the length of the red leather. But evidently he had not been asleep. He was just shutting out the world. Meredith needed clear signals from people. Having a car turn up to collect her, with the driver plumped angrily on the front bonnet in a foul temper and blocking her way, made her upset and confused.

'Are we going to the artist's home?'

'We are,' said Siobhan. 'I guess your sister must be exhausted.'

Adam sighed in the back seat for some reason.

'Adam is tired too, aren't you, Adam? He's been with Mr Saunders, diving. And taking in some spectacular views.'

'Siobhan . . .' he began wearily.

Having looked forward so much to seeing the artist, to watching the painting take shape, Meredith felt now that she had done something wrong. Siobhan seemed angry with her. Adam looked upset by her arrival. She looked from one to the other and could not understand the fury she felt radiating towards her from the occupants of the car. She began to cry.

Adam was up out of the seat in an instant, vaulting over the closed back door of the car and hugging Meredith. 'Hey. Hey, you. This is just silliness between me and our Irish friend. Don't worry.'

Meredith's shoulders shook.

She felt Adam's head move, as if he was looking past her, back to the hotel. Quietly he asked, 'Have you seen Ginny this morning?'

'Yes,' said Meredith, still in his arms.

'She's okay?'

Meredith did not want to give him the truth, which was that her sister had been crying when she entered the breakfast room ten minutes earlier. But she was never able to lie as easily as other people. Her stumbled reply – 'Yes, um, yes, um, she is fine' – was immediately picked up on by Adam.

He whispered into her ear, 'Give her a hug from me later. Please, Meredith. I'm begging you. Don't forget.'

Siobhan slid guiltily off the car bonnet. Meredith avoided catching her eye. 'Sorry,' she said to the gravel. 'None of this is your fault.' Meredith knew she couldn't read anything reliable in her features. The anger seemed to have gone, but maybe she was just hiding it.

Adam released her and said, 'This young lady has helped you a lot, Siobhan. And her dream is to see Mr Dali paint, isn't it, Meredith?'

'Yes,' replied Meredith.

'And Siobhan, I'm grateful to you for the time with Russell Saunders today. I mean, *really* grateful, because he showed me a tuck and a pike and all sorts of things I was doing wrong. And that's special, and I know he and I will meet again and do more, and I love the fact that you've brought us together . . .'

He tailed off.

'But?' suggested Siobhan.

'But if you want out, if you want to cancel this whole thing, you can just say.'

'I don't.'

'If you are angry with me *for any good reason*, you can just say. Siobhan!' He said her name sharply, as if to ensure her attention did not drift.

'No, I'm not.' She replied almost sullenly.

'I won't ask you to apologise to Meredith, but giving her your death stare when all she's done is help us—'

'I know.'

'It's a little bit unfair on Meredith. I mean—'

'*I know, Adam, I fucking know!*' Siobhan yelled suddenly. There was a long silence.

'Can we go to Mr Dali's house now, please?' Meredith said.

Later that day, Russell Saunders found Ginny in the lounge of the Hotel Maravillas del Mar. 'Hey, buddy,' he said.

'Hey.'

'I thought you'd changed hotels.'

'Yes, I have,' she said. 'But I thought my sister was coming back to this one, so I came to meet her.'

'You okay?'

'Yep,' said Ginny.

'The others not back yet?'

Ginny looked at the clock on the mantelpiece. It was nearly four. 'Haven't seen them.'

Saunders sat down beside her, uninvited, but Ginny did not mind. It was a distraction. And anyway, she was starting to like him. He was a simple soul, honest, open, untroubled by self-doubt. And quick to anger, which she now thought she might be too.

'Is this our routine, then?' he said. 'Madness, if you ask me.

I'm in my room earning money for staring out of the window. I spent the first day eating toast. I don't even like toast.'

'Lucky you,' she replied. 'I'm in my room staring out of the window and I'm not earning anything.'

'No toast?'

She smiled, despite herself. 'Nope.'

'So why get involved in this?'

She went for the easy answer. 'For my sister. But it must be weird for you to be locked away. You're such a famous person, in such a public job.'

'Locked away,' he repeated thoughtfully. 'Yes, I guess I am. But see, a stuntman,' he started, suddenly more animated, turning those muscled shoulders square-on to Ginny and cutting the air with his hand, 'is used to being invisible, to being ignored, to being shut out of the script, left off the credits . . .'

'This must feel like rubbing salt in the wound.'

'Yes! It really does. Now I'm actually being *told* to hide.' He was growing angry. 'Dammit.'

'Can't you take advice on what to do?'

'Oh, sure. My agent is in California. I ring him. It's an expensive call to place, you know? And the line's bad. He's laughing because he thinks I'm telling a joke. He says this guy Dali is a legend, hang with it, because the result will probably be a great painting—'

'Which you had nothing to do with.'

He stopped, nodding. 'I have a conscience. It won't just be a headline: "Stuntman Helps Dali Paint Christ Picture". I'll be interviewed and asked what it was like, and I guess I will have to lie about it.'

'Well, the young American waiter won't give away the secret, I'm sure.'

'You know him? I keep forgetting.'

'A little.' She hated that she was blushing. To make it worse, he noticed.

'You like him a little, maybe?'

'Oh, no, not in that way, not at all.'

'Deny, deny, deny.'

She stared at her hands, saw the fingers twisting around each other. 'There's nothing to deny.'

'I think the Lynch woman has her fingernails into him.'

That hurt. Ginny flinched.

'Anyway,' Saunders said quickly, 'not my business. But let's say the painting gets people talking, which my agent says most of his stuff does, okay, and then your friend Adam—'

'He's not my friend.'

'Okay then, *my* friend Adam is chatting in a saloon bar, a bit drunk, talking to a woman, let's say, as young men do, and to impress her he says, "Hey, that painting everyone's talking about, the Salvador Dali one, it's not the stuntman in it. That person is me." Now you can imagine—'

'He wouldn't do that.'

'What?'

'He wouldn't get drunk and boast like that to a woman.'

'Sweetheart, he's a young man.'

'He just wouldn't.'

'But what I'm saying is, that would paint me as a liar for the rest of my life.' Saunders shook his head, as if trying to shuffle the possible outcomes. 'That said, no one would believe a young guy in a bar, boasting about a painting, would they? Still, I don't like it. But even my agent says, go with it.' His eyes twinkled at her. 'You *do* like him.'

She stood up, offended.

'Sorry,' he said. 'Blame the American in me. I'm a little rough at the edges.'

Ginny looked at her watch. 'I suppose they're still there,' she said, 'or on the way back.' Feeling self-conscious, she walked over to the window.

'I told Siobhan, if she puts a dent in that car, she'll have to paint over it herself. Man, that woman was in a filthy mood this morning. The Irish do a different level of angry, that's for sure.' Ginny's ears pricked up, though she did not turn around. She waited for him to continue. 'Don't know what got into her, cussing all the breakfast waiters out and suchlike. And she looked terrible, like she hadn't slept.'

Ginny waited for him to continue, but he changed tack.

'Now, that American,' said Saunders, 'by contrast – serene. I mean Adam. What a beautiful diver. You know we're both Canadian born? I see a young me when I look at him. But oh my God, I never . . .' He paused, as if unable to say the words: *I never dived like he does.* 'He doesn't know the name of any of the moves he does, but he fires himself into the air and tucks in so perfectly, then arrows down like a . . . like a rocket . . . spilling and sliding in the air like a bead of mercury. And that damned perfect upper frame! I gather we're diving again tomorrow, is that right?'

Ginny barely heard the question. Her eyes had suddenly filled with tears and she knew she must blink them away before turning back to Russell Saunders, or else the stuntman would understand everything.

CHAPTER FIFTEEN

THE YUCCA

That first night, it did not take long for Ginny to realise her mistake. Meredith had returned, not to the Maravillas del Mar, but directly to their *posada* near Port Lligat. Ginny knew what had happened the instant the red car drew up, a full hour after her conversation with Saunders. Only Siobhan and Adam were in the vehicle. She ducked out of view so they would not see her, then fled through a door in the opposite flank of the hotel. Later, back at the inn, she found Meredith. But her sister refused to say anything about the events of the day.

'You saw him paint?'

'Dali and Gala have told me not to say.'

Meredith was staring out of the window, braced against the frame as if she had been exercising. There was power in the poise, a difference about her.

'If you're not enjoying it—'

Meredith span around heavily, her eyes flaming. 'Enjoying it! I was at the side of the *master*.' She made shapes with her hands. 'You know the black he's painting?'

'Black?'

'The background.'

'Oh, sure, yes.'

'But it's not just black! He showed me how many kinds of black there are. Maybe thirty, he said. And he said he would paint a canvas one day that was only black. You would stare and see different worlds. The inside of a body's cell and the outside of a distant galaxy.'

'Right.' To Ginny, it sounded unhinged. There was only one type of black.

'He took so long to make sure the background was right . . . and I found the name for his painting.'

Ginny cocked her head.

'Yes, I was thinking about the painting. The history of Saint John, the way he was killed. The painting should be called *The Blasphemous Christ*. I told Dali's wife.'

'I bet she liked that.'

'Yes. Gala promised to tell the artist. I didn't want to tell him directly. When he is painting I must just sit in silence and watch.'

'Did he paint the American?'

'Adam?' Meredith looked as if she barely remembered him. 'No, they had him in the pool. He is still on the background, remember.'

'The black.'

'And next there's a scene he's composing at the foot of the painting, with boats and . . .'

Ginny lost track of what she was being told. All she wanted Meredith to say was that Adam had mentioned her. But Meredith seemed only to have noticed Dali.

'Was Gala there?'

'Yes. I told you.'

'Did she speak to you?'

'She just said that only Adam and I could come in. We must go downstairs to the studio. If Dali is late, we must not be impatient. When he paints, we must not speak to him. We must just do whatever he asks us to do. She told Siobhan there was no space in the house for her, even though we all knew the underground room is big. Siobhan drove away. We sat in the studio for an hour. Dali arrived. He sent Adam to the pool then told me to watch. I remembered what Gala had said, so I didn't know whether to look while I was watching, if you know what I mean. I didn't talk. Dali said things in Spanish I didn't understand. He only said one thing in English.'

'What?'

'*We must be ready for our Christ when he comes.*'

'That was it?'

'Yes.'

'Christ meaning Adam?'

'Meaning I don't know.'

'*We must be ready for—*'

'Maybe he was talking about all of his paintings. He has done so many surreal paintings, skulls on stilts and dripping eggs and melting clocks, and now the most real painting is the one with Jesus Christ in it. But I don't know, and I don't want to guess, and I shouldn't say any more.'

'I'm staying – we're staying – so you can do this, Merry, and I need to know it's what you want.'

Meredith's dark eyes suddenly flashed with spirit. Her cheeks flushed and she said, enunciating each word slowly: '*I. Am. Loving. It.*'

The phrase left Ginny with nowhere to go. Her sister wanted no more questions. She would have no sense of the pain Ginny felt at being excluded, not just cut out of the adventure at Dali's, but cut away from Adam too.

That night Ginny cried herself to sleep. She was lonelier than she had ever felt in her life.

The letters came, offered to Ginny every day. She could guess the handwriting was Adam's. She did not open them or even take them from the woman downstairs, a cleaner who opened the door for guests and kept their keys. One, two, three . . . when all five letters were offered in a bundle, Ginny finally accepted them. In her room she shoved them under the rug, never to be opened. She knew that opening and reading them would make it worse.

The others had their routine. Ginny guessed at their movements from the regular roar of the Saunders sports car – Adam diving with Saunders in the morning. Siobhan chauffeuring him to the *posada* and picking up Meredith. The red car shooting off to Port Lligat with the sunroof down. Siobhan depositing Meredith and Adam. Meredith returning at six and sometimes after sundown.

Siobhan never entered the *posada*. Meredith said nothing more about her days. She did not need a meal when she returned, so Ginny guessed Gala and Dali were feeding them. Meredith's mind was so literal, her admiration for Salvador Dali so total, that if she had been told not to speak about the project she would say not a single word to anyone. Four days in, Ginny tried to find out more at breakfast. There were half a dozen guests around them, but no one close enough to hear.

'So how is the work going?'

'They didn't want my name,' Meredith replied.

'What name?'

'For the painting.'

'The – what was it?'

'*The Blasphemous Christ*. They didn't like it. His wife called it melodramatic.'

'I'm sorry. Is everything else okay there?'

'You know I mustn't say.' She looked round, then said in a whisper, 'Remember that old man with the hat, Dr Honeyman. He is spying on Salvador. Don't give him any clues.'

Salvador, was it now? Even as Meredith spoke, Honeyman came in. He nodded to the two women and made his way across the sticky lino to take his place at the far end of the room, an uncomfortable corner of metal bench which no one else had chosen. He opened the newspaper and used the top edge of the front page to scratch the stubble under his nose.

'Has he started painting Adam yet?' Ginny whispered.

It was a question too far. Meredith gave no answer.

'Not that I care. So long as you are happy, Merry . . .'

'Dali wants me to stay.'

'At his house? Sleep there?'

'Yes.'

Still no answer. And after that, she no longer saw Meredith at breakfast.

At night, more alone than ever, Ginny found herself imagining Adam back in Siobhan's arms. She hated herself for believing his claims of inexperience. But when she tried to freeze that part of her heart which had surrendered to him, she felt numb. Depression – her father's illness – grew in her like a blackened bud from a rotten plant. She felt it inside her, a physical thing, fibrous, tentacled, tumoural. Soon she started to miss breakfast herself and spend the morning in bed. She had to fight despair. She cried in the mornings. Meredith left a note, more scrawled than written, saying she was now staying at Dali's house and so was Adam. Ginny turned this over, a knot of anxiety forming over the way the letter was left at reception, not dropped off in person, as if Meredith was trying to avoid her; at least there was no mention of Siobhan. But why, without meaning to sound rude, would Dali need Meredith to stay? What could her sister bring to the artist's endeavour, apart from an enthusiasm that was almost childish?

As more days passed Ginny forced herself to walk at lunchtime, once going the whole way to the Hotel Maravillas del Mar and sitting in the drawing room, faintly hoping the stuntman would appear and they could pass the time together, just so she could be less lonely. But he was nowhere to be seen.

The wind whipped up as she trudged back to her hotel. It matched her mood, but even when the sun grew strong again, blanketing the rolling scenery between Port Lligat and Cadaqués with pure white light, she could only feel the raw nub of pain within herself, the dark seed of her family's doom trying to unfold and flower into poison. She blinked it back, this headache that would not be doused in water or softened by aspirin. She thought constantly of her father, whose pain no one properly heard or understood, and who had surely meant to end his life in the Barmston Drain. She thought of the cliffs at Cadaqués. Was that why she had panicked when Adam had jumped on that first day, because it brought back the death of her father?

Properly alone for the first time in her life, trapped in this cheap hotel, she knew she had to fight the torment which had taken her father's life and almost ended Meredith's. She started to run, dressed in a thin blouse, her cotton skirt, white socks and an old pair of plimsolls, slamming the air with her fists as she went. In the blinding daylight she beat back her own darkness.

It was as she was drinking orange juice in the breakfast room at the end of another day, just as the sun began to drop in the sky, that she caught the eye of Dr Honeyman. He introduced himself and she told him she knew his name already.

'Oh, really? Did I suddenly become famous?' There was a kindness and humour about him.

'We met the other day,' Ginny reminded him.

'But you looked a little distressed that morning, I recall.'

'It had been a difficult night.'

'Your sister seems busy? She is rarely here.'

'She has a task she is working on with some friends.' Ginny added, 'But you're right, I haven't seen her here these last few days. She is staying elsewhere to complete her project.'

'Quite a project.' He looked at Ginny for a second with such intelligence in his eyes that she felt he could see right through her. 'What is the project?' he asked.

Ginny was stumped, having to lie. 'Art. Art-related.'

'Art? How funny!' exclaimed Honeyman. 'I am here for art too, but my art isn't going very well.' He stared out of the window, his brow creased. As if quoting someone, he added dreamily, 'It is in the nature of greatness not to be exact.'

Ginny looked around the room. She felt sorry for him and even sorrier for herself. She wanted to tell him everything. She knew Meredith would never forgive her if she did, but she found herself starting to talk. 'My sister is with a friend called Adam Bannerman, and the two of them are currently at the home of the—'

'Oh!'

The cry came from the Scot, interrupting Ginny only a syllable from giving away exactly where Meredith was. Honeyman's yell was followed by a loud crump outside. He jumped in his seat, craned his neck to see better beyond the window. 'They hit the tree!'

A succession of other noises followed the first. The crump became a yawning creak, a tearing of metal. There was the sound of men shouting. A loud hiss. A bang. Silence.

'By God,' said the Scot, turning his body fully to the window of the breakfast room.

Ginny sensed he could see what had made the noise, but when she rushed to the window and looked there was only the road and the tangled greenery opposite.

'It turned over, I think, just there. These damned glasses.' He had pushed them onto his forehead, then back onto his nose, as if they were not working at distance.

'What turned over?'

'The – och, my mind has gone – what are they called? The Guardia Civil. "The Soul of Spain". You know, the police! They crashed in their Land Rover. I just caught it out of the corner of my eye as it happened. Oh God, it's terrible. They took the corner too fast. A wheel lifted, the dust flew up on the road. He must have steered into the skid but it took him off the road into the – oh, that ugly stuff, like cactus. I can't find my words. I know the name, but – come on. Let's see what we can do. Quick, lassie.'

Together they rushed from the breakfast room and out of the hotel, where Honeyman took off his jacket and threw it onto the ground. Long evening shadows grew from the plants. 'I often look at that thicket over there,' Ginny said.

Honeyman mumbled, 'Like a Venus flytrap, with the jaws closed on them.'

Ginny peered. 'You can't even see where the van went.'

'There's a line of smoke, look, from the middle.'

Ginny heard another cry. They both instinctively started towards it, then stopped. On the far side of the road, the rugged bark of a cork tree had been slashed open to reveal the tender cork below. Another younger cork, a sapling, was sliced clean in two. The cries came from beyond them, somewhere in the thick scrub. The scream of one man, the moan of another.

Ginny wrinkled her nose. 'What's that smell?'

'Fuel and smoke,' Honeyman replied. 'That's not a good combination.'

'But we have to help them.' Determined now, she began to march across the road.

'Wait!' Honeyman shouted. 'What if . . .' He caught up with her, breathless. 'Spanish yuccas – those leaves are bastard sharp. You'll never get through them. Let's think for a second. My God,' he cried, 'is no one in this bloody hotel? What is wrong with these people?'

In slow motion their eyes met, as if both of them were coming to the same realisation, but neither could put a name to it. Frowning, Ginny turned back and saw every hotel window was closed. Nobody was visible. The road was unnaturally quiet. She saw the scuff on the surface where the Land Rover had lost traction in the dry dirt and the wheels had slid. Beyond the decapitated cork Ginny surveyed the bunches of yucca, bristling like a chain of bodyguards, their squat trunks armoured like grenades. At the heart of each plant was a whorl of white flowers from which the leaves sprang, tough, broad and razor-edged. The vehicle must suddenly have cut through the plants that closed on the path, as if they would not be taken unawares again. Getting to the injured men would not be easy.

'Okay,' Honeyman said. 'We have to do this together, beat these plants back with sticks.' Ginny found a length of broken cedar, and bent down to drag it from the side of the road. It would be too heavy to swing, so she started stamping on it while holding one end, trying to break it in two. A splinter shot deep into her palm and she barely noticed. She saw Honeyman still combing the ground for a tool, and felt a shiver of frustration that the old man was going more slowly.

A noise behind them made him straighten, hands on hips. On the top floor of the hotel a sash window slammed open.

'Hey! Help!' shouted Ginny to whoever was behind it.

Honeyman frowned.

They watched, frozen to the spot, as a figure moved within the darkness of the upstairs room. The muzzle of a rifle suddenly

emerged from the blank space and flashed. The loud report of
the rifle followed and the two of them jumped for cover.

Ginny and Honeyman were each behind a tree when he
spoke.

'That's why nobody's here,' Honeyman cried. A sputtered
bang and whirr from the crashed vehicle behind them was a
reminder of the chaos the greenery was hiding.

Ginny, trembling, said: 'I don't understand.'

'Guardia Civil. They are hated here.'

That first conversation with Adam came back to her, and she
remembered her joke about not giving guns to men who were
trembling, and the way he became serious in response. And
now she understood why.

'Who is shooting?'

'Someone in the hotel. I have no idea.'

'At us?'

'At them.'

Ginny tried to poke her head out from behind the tree. The
muzzle flashed with a second bullet. She saw the white light at
the end of the barrel, momentary, a ten-cornered cartoon star.
The bullet flew past her, cutting the air.

'No,' the Scot corrected himself. 'At us.'

They waited for minutes, just breathing behind the trees.

'Maquis,' said Honeyman. 'Spanish Maquis.'

'Who?'

'Don't move. They want to stop us helping.'

'There's only one person up there. I saw her a second ago,'
said Ginny, 'but only her face.' It had been thin, like a triangle,
coming to a point in the chin. 'The waitress.'

'From the restaurant? The one with the earrings?'

Before she could tell him not to look, there was a third
gunshot, the muzzle flashing again from the tiny top-floor

window of their hotel. The tree next to Honeyman shivered as the bullet slammed into it with a *thunk* of metal on wood.

Honeyman hissed, 'The Maquis are the resistance, what's left of it, trying to unseat Franco. A van crashing with Guardia Civil inside is a blessing from heaven. You won't find anyone crying about it around here. She wants to stop us helping. You should get away.'

'No.' Ginny was firm. 'We have to help them.' She looked behind her at the crowd of yuccas. Could she crawl into them, using the cork tree between her and the hotel as cover? Surely at some point she would be visible to the waitress. Honeyman was protesting at her foolhardiness but Ginny knew she must do it. Crawl into the greenery. At least try to help. Maybe the only reason she had come to Spain was to save one of the lives of these men she knew must be dying behind her.

She started to back away from the tree on her hands and knees, keeping her head up so she could check the trunk was hiding her movement from the woman with the rifle. Honeyman hissed, 'Let me distract her,' but Ginny hissed '*No!*' at him so loudly he stayed planted behind the tree.

Backing into the plants was harder than she had imagined. They were packed tightly, and their razor-sharp leaves criss-crossed the gaps. Honeyman kept glancing back at her. 'Don't let her see you,' he said urgently.

And then it all changed. From the road came the roar of an engine that could have been a helicopter landing. The red sports car shot past them on the road, U-turned and came back again. This time, just as it approached the hotel, the car braked sharply as the engine screamed and the tyres skidded.

The driver's out of control, Ginny thought. But then she glimpsed Saunders at the wheel and her heart surged because she knew he had not lost control at all; he never would. The effect of the roaring skid was to throw up a fountain of dust and send the back of the car flying into the same foliage that she was now trapped in. The dust hung in the air, and Ginny saw the figure of Russell Saunders do the most unforgettable thing.

In a single movement, he threw his shirt into the cloud of dust he had created. Then, bare from the waist up, the stuntman left the car by the door on the far side. In two strides he had vaulted onto the bonnet. Then he pounced two-footed onto the top edge of the windscreen where the canvas roof met the car's frame. In a single movement, Saunders jumped onto the roof and used the canvas to spring into the air. His jump was superhuman – she saw his legs bicycling as he flew over her head, blocking the setting sun. Somewhere deep into the greenery, Saunders landed. The rifle rang out again, but in the shower of dust the waitress could not aim.

The arrival of Russell Saunders was too late for four of the seven men in the Land Rover. They had been killed outright; one was decapitated when the Land Rover overturned. Of the three who were still alive, two were badly hurt and one barely had a scratch. Saunders lifted the most gravely injured man over his head and, incredibly to Ginny, walked straight out through the bladed yucca leaves, his trousers cut and bloodied, holding the policeman's rifle in his spare hand. She wanted to shout at him to be careful of the gunfire, but looking up she saw that the muzzle had withdrawn, although the top-floor window remained ominously open.

Within ten minutes, more Guardia Civil had arrived: thirty *tricornios* with their distinctive three-cornered patent leather hats. Ginny watched in a daze. Firemen arrived too, laying long wooden ladders across the yuccas to reach the Land Rover, walking across them like tightrope artists.

The Guardia Civil reinforcements and the firemen worked together to lay out the bodies as the sun disappeared. As they were doing this, the Land Rover engine exploded, sending the bonnet flying into the air. The noise of the blast made Ginny's ears ring. She was numb with shock, her arms shaking so much that she had to press them to her sides. Two of the older officers – senior, by the look of their braided silver epaulettes – questioned her and Honeyman together, rifles sweeping left and right, eyeing their surroundings as they spoke. A young policeman whose grasp on English was shaky did the translating.

'They ask, was there gunfire?'

'Yes,' said Honeyman.

'Where from? Who fired?' translated the young officer, a lean man with pupils dilated, the veins jumping in his hands.

Ginny opened her mouth to speak, but Honeyman shifted his stance, catching her attention. She choked back the words. Honeyman gestured vaguely, a full three-quarter turn. 'Somewhere around.' The rifle barrels followed his gesture, to no effect.

The young policeman translated. The older officers stepped closer. 'But where exactly?'

'We don't know,' said Ginny, imagining the immediate response if they mentioned the waitress and the upper window – the police storming the *posada*, smashing the front door, ripping her out of the building by her hair.

Quickly the officers seemed to lose interest in the translated answers, although the young policeman kept asking them as his seniors drifted away. 'What are you come to see in Spain? . . . Why have you been here today when this happen? . . . Did there be more than one gun fired?'

As she listened, Ginny could not stop her body shaking. The evening breeze caressed her forehead, and when she raised a hand to touch the skin, she found it soaked in sweat – and then, moving her fingers through her hair, was alarmed to find it drenched to the roots. She pulled the hand away, wondering if she would see blood. But it was perspiration. Her entire body was covered with it.

A group of officers moved slowly towards Saunders, standing with his hands on his hips, looking like a god. They hugged and thanked him a thousand times. One emotional colleague of the first man to be brought out alive grabbed the stuntman so forcefully his own *tricornio* went flying.

Later Ginny met the stuntman in a bedroom in her hotel. The staff had been pressed by the police to provide their hero with a place to change and clean himself. They did their best to show willing.

'Who did the shooting back there?' he asked, as matter-of-fact as though he was fired on every day. He was sitting on the dressing table stool and she was on the edge of the bed. 'Who was it?'

Ginny clasped and unclasped her hands. She only told him what she had told the police. 'I only heard it, I didn't see.'

'And why shoot?' Saunders asked. 'What was it, some faction?'

She loved the way he used the word 'faction', as if it could explain everything. 'Yes,' she replied gently, 'I think it was a faction.'

'I was in the car. Just driving. Not much else to do. I heard a shot, came racing. Guess I was lucky. Right place and time.'

'We were in the breakfast room. I was sitting there chatting to a gentleman guest. He saw it. The police car crashed.'

'Hit by a bullet, I guess.'

That had not occurred to Ginny. Had the waitress been tipped off about the Land Rover's journey, and sat waiting with the rifle ready? Had it crashed after she fired the first shot? Would they discover a bullet in the head of the driver?

'Don't cry.'

The stuntman's words jolted her back. She saw her tears pooling on the floor.

'What a pair we are,' said Saunders. 'Blood and tears.'

He had not showered yet. He had pulled off his ripped, scarlet-streaked trousers and put on a hotel bathrobe. But as she watched, drops of blood were still falling from his legs to the carpet.

'You were very brave, Mr Saunders,' she said. 'Very brave indeed. I would call you a hero.' Forcing a smile, she went on, 'I don't think I understood how – how dangerous Spain is. I thought Meredith and I could just enjoy the weather, and the rest would leave us alone. But on the very first morning, she got caught by one of those yuccas – the plant that tore your leg there – and I saw her bleed for the first time. And everything that followed . . . has showed me . . .' Now she burst into tears, real choking sobs, and he moved to hug her, but the bedroom stool he had been sitting on tipped as he moved off it and he fell to the floor in a way designed to make her laugh.

'My handkerchief is clean.' He tossed it to Ginny and she dabbed her eyes.

'I was passing,' Saunders said, smiling. 'You can't leave people like that if you're passing. Heroes are people who fight in wars, young lady.'

'But we didn't leave them—'

'Oh! Not meant as any criticism of you and the gentleman. Who was he?'

'Dr Honeyman.' Ginny sniffed, her emotions back under control. The conversation felt normal now. 'He's staying here. We were in the breakfast room.'

'In the evening?'

'They don't have an evening room.'

'Oh, it's *that* kind of joint.' He looked pleased to see her laugh. 'I'm kinda depressed about the Merc. Not sure I can do much with her now. Rear axle broke. The back chassis has collapsed. Both back tyres out and I think the steering column went too.'

'Don't you give Adam his diving lessons every day?' She desperately wanted to ask about what was happening at Dali's house, how Adam was. She felt so cut off from him.

But Saunders was distracted. Looking down, the stuntman had noticed his blood was falling faster – 'Jesus, I'm really bleeding here' – and now reached behind him to the dressing table to pluck himself a single tissue. 'Green carpet plus American blood and English tears equals cleaning problem,' he mumbled, dabbing the stains. 'Tell you what, those guys in the funny hats and those thick cloth uniforms stink. What is that colour? Dark green? Turquoise? Getting hugged by them was kind of an assault on the senses.'

'I thought it was teal.'

'Teal, huh.'

She stared at him. 'I think they can probably be cruel, the police here.'

'Fascist? Probably. Sorry, did you ask me a question?'

It was her cue. 'If the car's out of action, I was wondering how you can pick Adam up from Dali's house to take him diving, that's all. I know Meredith is there now.'

'Oh, he went a little lame,' said Saunders nonchalantly. 'So the diving stopped a few days ago. Boy, was he good. I would say better than I ever was, and I was the Canadian champ—'

The word was cut in two by Ginny's intervention. 'Did you say he went lame?'

'Just a little, so's he couldn't jump.'

'But he's still doing Dali's painting?'

'I think they're staying over, aren't they? Your sister and the young man? Siobhan told me not to worry any more.'

'Yes,' said Ginny vaguely, 'I think they are staying over.'

'With the lunatic. Dali. At that strange house of his by the sea. Siobhan said he's painting Adam on the cross now. That's all I know.'

Something about the way he said it chilled Ginny. She rose from the bed and walked to the window. Above them the moon was full, glowing like a sun. A horse and cart were passing below. A peasant farmer walked alongside the animal carrying a lantern on a stick, occasionally encouraging the horse by grabbing a fistful of its mane or flapping at the head with his straw hat. In the cart were two bulging white hessian sacks which suddenly seemed luminous in the moonlight, their necks tied tight with green twine. Ginny felt panic in her throat. Suddenly she blurted, 'Sorry, I have to go!' and ran out of the room.

CHAPTER SIXTEEN

He Went a Little Lame

Meredith had seen the full moon too, kneeling at the head of her bed. When she lay back down, the buzzing in her head kept on. A current without a fusebox, generated by the passage of blood in her brain. The crackle snarked from the left side of her skull to the right, a polarity she could not exist between. She stretched out her left hand and saw the fingers in front of her as if they were the fingers of another person. In her mind the hand was trembling – yet the one before her was peculiarly steady, so it could not (the logic was unyielding) be hers. She turned her wrist in the light. The moonlight shone off the skin, parched tight like an old woman's. Still the trembling continued. Now she found the shaking hand. It was the right, vibrating like a cello string. She pushed it under her bottom. Still it shook. Clamped below her posterior, the hand threatened to send spasms beyond her wrist and into her forearm. Meredith stared at the ceiling, trying to puzzle out what was happening, what this meant.

She thought back to that afternoon, on the balcony at Dali's house. Had it been more than a week since she had first met the artist? She had lost count of the days. The excitement she felt at being in the painter's home had dulled. She had not been anywhere near Dali himself after the first two days. Hands clasped as if in prayer, Gala had told Meredith that Salvador Dali wished her to fulfil a 'special task'. She had said it with such intensity that Meredith felt there really was no alternative.

In Greek mythology, King Sisyphus was condemned to push an immense boulder up a hill, only for it to roll back down every time he got near the top. It was his punishment for being crafty and self-centred. Meredith's punishment for being trusting and generous was Sisyphean. Two trunks full of newspapers and magazines had arrived from the United States. There were hundreds, maybe even a thousand. But the spread of damp within the trunks while they sat unopened in Spain, combined with the pressure from the heavy iron lids, had compacted the pages into pulp. The trunks had been mailed by a well-wisher in Virginia claiming to have collected every publication which mentioned Dali during his American years.

'We spent Christmas 1940 with Caresse Crosby, have you heard of her?' Gala had chirruped. As if knowing the girl would shake her head, Gala added immediately that Caresse was 'a designer of bras, living near Bowling Green. Do you know where that is, my dear?' Again Meredith started to say no, and again Gala jumped in as if she had known the answer already. 'In Caroline County, Virginia.' She spoke the words while breathing inwards, as if smoking them. 'Anyway. At the time we lived in Monterey and New York. Mostly. From 1940, for eight years.'

For Meredith, the conversation's lateral tilt was baffling. But the question she asked wrong-footed Gala.

'Because of the war, you left Europe?'

Gala opened her mouth and gulped. It was the unspeakable truth, and she must deny it. 'Because of *art*,' she said quietly, the 't' in 'art' as precise as a drumstick on a woodblock, shaking her head and staring at the floor. She had been insulted.

Meredith had set to work, choosing windless hours to extricate each layer of paper from the trunk and spread them flat on the balcony so the sun could dry them and the pages could be separated. If it rained she would bundle them up and take them inside. When the wind blew she would lay pebbles on the piles, scooped from the base of the balcony's iron fence. For hours she scanned the pages, willing them to dry so the print would become clear. Sometimes she was distracted by watching fishing boats drift past on the ocean, at which point Gala would always seem to burst through the balcony doors and call, 'Come, come! No slacking, English girl!' She never used Meredith's name. At lunchtimes, one of the boys in the house would bring simple sandwiches with sour lemonade, but never stayed long and never spoke to her. Once Gala brought a glass of water. When Meredith went looking for Adam in the house one morning, she was turned back by one of Dali's young male friends – these teenagers with little English who seemed to come and go silently, namelessly, moving without schedules or introduction. So long as they did not disturb Meredith on her balcony she would not resent them.

Gala told Meredith, 'You have the very scrupulous brain to do this. None of the others do. He wants them carefully cut out and filed. Just the articles that mention him. Insert each carefully into these envelopes and label them.'

But something was wrong. Meredith had felt it. She was sure that Adam, like her, was staying in the house. But she had not seen him for days. Siobhan had stopped coming in the sports car. She was given an evening meal with the Spanish boys, and there was a bedroom for her. It was sparse, like an unfurnished room from a painting by Van Gogh, hardly the sort of place you would associate with a master surrealist, but for one strange detail: a false door was painted on the wall opposite the bed, with a real key projecting from the keyhole. When Meredith closed the real door at night and settled her weight into the cheap mattress, she felt it crater beneath her.

She worried about Ginny. She had left her sister a note saying that she was overnighting in the house now. When she fretted out loud about whether Ginny had seen it, Gala interjected: 'Don't worry. Your sister will know.' If the words were meant to calm Meredith, they did the opposite.

The job with the damp cuttings sometimes seemed like it might take a month, other times a year. More and more it became like the boulder, always rolling back down. It took a full day to cut out the first mention of Dali, on page fourteen of the *Virginia Quarterly Review*. Just a few lines and a cartoon moustache under the headline SPANISH 'ARTIST' SALVADOR DALI MAKES MADMEN OF US ALL. She opened the enormous box of envelopes provided by Gala. All different sizes, some used, some new. Finding one that was the right fit, she tucked the flap in and wrote the name of the magazine, the headline, and the article date. There was an endlessness about the task which had made her disheartened from the moment she began it. Why could she not just watch the artist at work?

And now her brain was doing . . . oh, it was doing its stuff. Fizzing, crackling. Her head was buzzing, left and right hands alternately shaking, just as they had in the gallery after that first sighting of her father's new family. *Sighting* – what if her blindness came again, here in the home of the painter, the curtains of her mind closing before she ever saw what he was producing down there in the studio? What was that buzz she could hear inside her head? A warning? What had she told Ginny that night of the fire? *Something terrible is about to happen.*

Where was Ginny?

Where was Adam?

Siobhan? Saunders? Where had they all gone?

That night of the full moon Meredith had returned to her bedroom before sunset, and put on the tiny nightshirt Gala had lent her. Her green scrapbook was on the bedside table. But her attempts to sleep this early, and in this state of mind, were doomed. She wanted to be a part of what Salvador Dali was doing. Were they having fun, the artist and the young American? She imagined them joking with each other, drinking coffee. Dali enjoying Adam's company, moving him on to intoxicating drink, the painting abandoned. She could see the delight Dali took in young men, boys even. Adam was broad, bronzed, strapping. Dali would get him to strike poses and laugh. The paintbrush would jab at the air like a sword. Meredith wondered if the painting was only an excuse to have him half naked in the room, then reminded herself it had all been her sister's idea. Lying in bed, she imagined all of them in the downstairs studio, whispering at each other so she could not hear.

On her knees, looking at the moon, she blinked. Tomorrow she would do whatever she could to find the artist, and Adam, and Ginny. To find whomever she could, just to lift her lone-liness. She was suddenly the young child again, stealing bread for her father. She could not bear to think of his death. To imagine him leaving the world without knowing her. She needed to know he had looked back and thought of her.

Tomorrow she would resign. Never mind if it meant enraging Gala and Dali. She did not want to be in the house if she could not be in the studio. Perhaps she would say, 'I did not come here to be your secretary.' She struggled to imagine those brave words coming out of her cowardly mouth. Not even here, in the silence of her bedroom, let alone to another person, let alone to a great artist. But she would try.

Somewhere in the distance she heard the loud report of a firearm.

Then another. And then, after a long pause, another.

Each a single insult to the silence of the night. Her eyes widened. She wondered if somewhere a farmer had a rabbit in his sights, but she could not believe he needed so many shots to destroy it.

Meredith let her head sink into the pillow. Sleep claimed her. And then, some time later, in the middle of a dream about her father, another shot rang out. More like an explosion – louder than the rest. It jerked her from her slumbers. Her eyes flickered open, and she began to listen.

That bullet. It exited the muzzle of a rifle far more powerful than the one the miserable waitress had used in the hotel's upper floor. Earlier, the officers killed in the crash had been covered with sheets taken from the hotel. The injured had been removed. Ginny, back outside in the harsh yellow lights which burnt in the front of the *posada*, stood with the Guardia Civil officers as they smoked and talked about the car accident. The rising panic in her throat would not leave her. She wanted to ask the police for help but could not form the question.

Honeyman had walked up to her, face grim. 'No fun, this.'

'No.'

'Won't be good for my friend the artist.'

Suddenly alert, Ginny shot a glance at him. 'I am having the same thought. It came to me suddenly —'

'He's taken Franco's side. Everyone knows it.'

'Meredith told me that a while back, and I never thought about it until tonight, and now my sister is at Dali's house.'

His glance was sharp, full of understanding. 'Somehow I thought so. This is a wicked night for us all.'

'I fear I have been secretive.'

Honeyman began, 'Look, if Franco —'

The word 'Franco' must have come out of his mouth at the instant the bullet exited the barrel of the gun. Directly opposite them, almost too distant to be seen by the naked eye even in daylight, dilapidated stables were set back a hundred yards on a wild meadow that sloped away behind the hotel. A century ago, travellers using the *posada* would have parked their horses in the outhouse for the night. Under the eaves of the stables, pigeons had nested, gradually wearing holes in the overlapping wooden slats with their comings and goings. It was in one of those gaps that the high-powered rifle flashed, the sparking muzzle like a distant firework in the dark.

Ginny had the strangest sensation – of merest curiosity at how the bullet would feel when it struck her. Her curiosity registered in the millionth of a second between the rifle firing and the bullet impacting. It went straight into the face of the police captain six feet to her left and exploded from the back of his head. For a second he stood there, exactly as he had been, his *tricornio* still in perfect position over the remainder of his head. He appeared – although she must have imagined this – to look for the source of the noise. The only clue that his life was over was the air of boredom that suddenly swept across his face, as if the gunshot could not possibly be an interesting development at this hour. The policeman's shadow — cast from the bright lights of the *posada* — was long. As his body crumpled, the shadow chased it to the ground.

There was pandemonium.

From her bed, now wide awake, Meredith listened. She heard the last rifle shot, louder than the ones before it, but nothing more. Her ears strained. She lay with the back of her head in the pillow, hair splayed out from her head like flames from a black sun.

How long did she lie there, listening? Her body imprisoned her, just as it had on the trolley at the asylum. Now she heard distant shouting in the house. Eventually it moved outside and there was the sound of a car revving. Meredith opened her eyes. Her head had barely changed position on the pillow. She could have been asleep for half an hour or three or five. There was no light beyond the curtains. The bed was uncomfortable. That crater had trapped her in the mattress. More shouting outside – and now a car shifting in gravel, wheels heavy, motor straining. Close to her bedroom window. Someone's foot urgent on the pedal. Meredith pulled up her knees, rolled on her side, turned her shoulders heavily against the sheets and raised herself with her arms. Her face rose gently against the window, her forehead shifting the curtain upwards.

There were shapes in the darkness. Several men and – she peered – was that a woman? Was that *Siobhan*? Surely it could not be her. What would she be doing here, at the artist's home? No sooner had Meredith's eyes adjusted and begun to focus on the long-haired figure in the middle of the group than the person ducked into a car. Not just a car – a police Land Rover. So now the police were here? She saw the three-cornered hats on some of the men. And then another person moved across the front of the group and the door was pulled open for him, and she recognised the unmistakeable silhouette of the artist himself.

She could not believe what she saw. Dali had climbed into the police car and was leaving.

It was past 2 a.m. Meredith was creeping round the house, wearing just her nightdress and a pair of shoes. None of the light switches worked. Shaking with nerves, she expected to be shouted at or sent back to her room. But then she began to realise that it was not only Dali who had gone. There must

have been more than one car. There was no sign of the young
men. She took her green scrapbook for comfort, and entered
the gloomy hallway, then followed the zig-zagging passage that
opened out onto the pool area.

The water sparkled in the moonlight. She noticed a box of
matches on a table and thought about using one to light her
way, but there was enough natural light out here to see by. She
assumed that Adam had abandoned the place along with everybody else. Why would he stay? She wanted to be offended that
he might have left without seeking her out, but perhaps he did
not even know she was here. More than anything, Meredith felt
relieved that everybody had left. She would not have to carry
on sorting through the pulped cuttings on the balcony. Maybe
she could head back to the *posada* and find Ginny. Perhaps this
was the end of the adventure. Perhaps it didn't matter.

She felt anxious. She remembered the gunshots as she looked
up at the stars above her, each dot of light a distant flash from
a gun pointed straight at her. How she wished she could just
feel *normal*. Her anxiety was a physical lump in her stomach.
She imagined a huge dog suddenly jumping out of the pool, as
it might do in a Dali painting, caught mid-air and frozen in a
cloud of droplets, then falling on her and drawing its teeth. In
the darkness the Mae West sofa looked drab, its shocking pink
muted to dull rust. Meredith sat on it, felt her eyes slide shut,
let sleep embrace her.

But only for a minute. Her eyes opened. A thought had
struck her, and she knew she must follow where it led. What
if Dali had left the unfinished painting behind? What if there
was more of it to see, before she left for good?

Meredith stood up and smoothed down her nightshirt. Feeling
a rush of curiosity, she grabbed the box of matches, then walked
towards the hatch that led down to the studio. She wondered

if the painting had perhaps the start of an outline on it. Or would Dali have worked more quickly than that and got his Christ figure down on the canvas already? If that was so, she regretted even more that she had never been allowed to watch, because the chance was now gone.

The hatch to the studio stairs creaked as she opened it. Her stomach heaved with anticipation. Never could she have imagined this: herself, alone in the home of the greatest artist, searching for his latest work.

Holding her green scrapbook under one arm, she struck a match. Light flared against the brickwork as she went down the stairs. She had no idea how to turn the studio lights on or if, like the others in the house, the switches would all be dead. She worried about her balance and gripped the banister on the way down. The light from the match only seemed to cast a huge shadow all around. Her heart pounded. The match went out. She stopped and struck another. Out of nervousness she dropped it when she reached the bottom of the stairs. Fearing fire, she stamped on it.

Another match. And a sudden feeling that there was someone else in the room.

She backed off towards the stairs and thought about racing up them. But somehow the rest of the house felt just as terrifying.

Then, as she struck a fourth match, she saw it.

The painted canvas flickered in the unsteady light. It was ten feet away from her. She made out a yellow shape painted on the black, and saw it was the image of a man. Her heart was pounding now. Surely Dali had not finished his painting already? Instead of trying to move closer, she looked around for one of the spotlights. But she couldn't see one, so she drew closer to the canvas and peered.

The match went out. She only had four left. As she lit one of them, she thought she heard a noise behind her. She turned. Nothing. Just the great black space of the studio, and the staircase in the shadows. She turned back to the canvas and brought the match closer.

It is finished.

Her eyes widened. The canvas was an expanse of black with a shift in perspective that unsettled the eye. Dominating the painting was a huge cross, Christ upon it. But the cross, and the man, were viewed from almost overhead so the head and shoulders loomed out of the top half of the painting, while the feet disappeared to nothing. The cross sank into the black background then reappeared lower down, where the perspective changed. Here the viewpoint was horizontal, a lake and sunset viewed from the shore, boats in the foreground.

She looked and looked, holding the match vertically so the flame ate it more slowly, moving the light up and down the canvas, holding it as close as she could without warming the hardened oil. The crucified Christ was positioned exactly as she had imagined, the view from above the same as the sketch by Saint John of the Cross. But in Dali's painting the Christ was so real that she believed for a second she could reach out and touch him. There were no nails in his hands or feet. The flesh shone yellow, as if picked out by a bright light. For an instant she imagined running her fingertips across the tousled hair and feeling the contours of it in the paint, then down over the shoulder muscles and across the stomach to the point where the body tapered away.

The image of Jesus Christ hanging in space above the world was like a movie, shifting as she looked. In space, then down to earth, the cross bending the dimensions.

'Ow!' Meredith yelped as the match burnt itself into the tip of her thumb and she dropped it. Now there was only a glow on the floor. Obsessed with the danger of fire, which could destroy everything, she ground the glowing match with the ball of her foot. Three matches left. The obvious thing would be to use them to find her way out, but she would not do that. She struck the matches in succession and spent as long as they would allow staring at the painting. She drank in the contrast and colour and depth, the sheer power and beauty and size of it. The cross, the world. It was the greatest painting she had ever seen. But more than that, she could never have imagined she would see a painting like this in the studio of the man who painted it. She did the unforgivable thing as the last match burnt to nothing. As the darkness dropped, she moved her hand towards the painting and led her fingers into the hair of Christ, touching the bumps the oil had made, the grooves left by the master's brush.

The used match smoked. She dropped it on the floor, and with it the empty box. The feeling that she was not alone returned. Her heart almost stopped as she heard the floorboards creak and the ceiling groan. She listened carefully. There was a scratching sound. A mouse?

Darkness enveloped her. But Meredith, of all people, understood darkness. She had been blind for years – this darkness was another form of seeing. She reached forwards and, knowing that when she was working in the gallery she would have reported a visitor for such a thing, she touched the painting again. Now she moved her fingertips all over the image, sliding them with the gentleness of air, feeling the difference on the canvas between the body of Christ and the backdrop. In her mind, the image came together, drawn by her own fingertips.

And then she heard the scratching noise again.

It was not in the studio, she realised. It was upstairs.

Meredith forced herself to breathe steadily. She shuffled slowly to where a splash of moonlight illuminated the top of the staircase. She wanted to turn back and look at the canvas one more time. In the darkness a glance backwards was meaningless. Still she did it and remained frozen to the spot, staring into nothing, until she forced herself to break away and climb the stairs.

At the top she listened again. The scratching started for a few seconds. Then stopped. Then there were two loud bangs, which echoed.

Slowly, Meredith zig-zagged down the passageway which led to the front door. Should she open it and look out? Her insides were jelly already, her legs shaking underneath her. She had the unsettling feeling of being followed.

Quietly, hoping not to be heard by whatever was outside, she pulled the bolts across the inside of the heavy door. It opened, and she gasped.

'Ginny!'

'Meredith!' Ginny stepped forwards and clasped her. 'I didn't know what had happened to you.'

'I can't find the light controls,' Meredith whispered. 'It's just me. The whole place is empty.'

Ginny felt her tears come in waves. 'Meredith, Meredith, Meredith.' She hugged her more tightly, arms wrapped round her sister's solid body. 'Oh God, oh God. What I've seen tonight—'

'What?' asked Meredith, her own voice rising in panic.

Ginny quickly remembered who she was with, remembered her sister's fragility. She breathed deeply and pulled away, searching for Meredith's face in the dark, reaching up with her hands and placing them on her cheeks.

'There was some terrible trouble. With the police and the woman at the *posada*. With us, with the old man from the gallery – and then a policeman got—' She was about to say the word 'shot', and stopped herself.

'Shot,' said Meredith. She blinked at Ginny.

'How do you know that?'

'It woke me. It was loud, even here. I heard it.'

'I'm sorry, Meredith, I'm just struggling with what I've seen. It was chaos. The police rampaging through our little hotel. A firefight, like a Western. Someone trying to escape across the field behind the *posada* and being cut down. And I realised this was all out of control and I needed to come here, to get you. Because it's not safe here. It's really not.' Her words were flowing from her now, without check. 'And Merry, I need to tell you something about – about everything. I need to tell you why I came for you that first day in the asylum. It was so wrong. I feel so wretched about it. I must tell you everything now.'

Had the last sentence so overloaded Meredith she could not process any of it? She looked at Ginny blankly in the gloom and said, only: 'You keep trying to tell me, and I don't want to know.'

'I must tell you. I came to the asylum because my mother told me to. She wants you to sign back the money our father left you. She is worried about the business, she says you can't have any stock.'

Meredith's face was uncomprehending.

'You came to find me because you're my sister.'

Ginny opened her mouth to speak, but no words came.

'Not because of your mother.'

'I came because of her, but we are *here* – you and me, Merry – because we are sisters. I came tonight because we're sisters.

I love you because we're sisters, and I've sent my mother a letter and she is going to have to accept what we tell her.'

'She can have the money,' said Meredith. 'I only want a family.'

Ginny bit her lip, trying not to cry.

'The police were here,' Meredith said suddenly.

Staring at the doorstep, Ginny shook her head. 'Really?'

'I think so. There were cars. One was a police car, maybe two. They took everyone away.'

'Even Dali?'

'Yes.'

'For their protection?'

'I don't know. They took everyone except me,' added Meredith. 'I think they must have forgotten me.'

'Oh, Meredith.'

'I saw it in the dark from my room. Them leaving. All of them. I think I saw Siobhan too. Oh – my head.' She began rubbing her thumbs on her temples.

'What's wrong, darling? Headache?'

'No. Yes. Too much in here.' Meredith physically sagged, her shoulders dropping as she stared at the floor.

'Siobhan?' queried Ginny. 'You saw her?'

'I can't be sure, there was only the moon to light them.'

Ginny stepped across the threshold. 'My darling. I was so worried about you. So Dali just left you here? I think it's political. Dr Honeyman knows all about it. Dali supports General Franco, but it looks like a rebellion is starting, so he is in danger.'

Meredith looked defeated by the detail. 'Oh well. I suppose that's the end of our little story.'

Ginny paused. 'What about Adam? Did Adam leave as well?'

'Yes,' said Meredith, 'I saw him. I'm sure I did.'

Ginny was feeling so sorry for her sister, standing in the

hallway in the dark, that she was almost relieved Meredith had seemed to miss the part-confession that had spilled from her a minute earlier.

'But you got to watch Dali paint,' Ginny said as they moved further into the hall.

'I didn't really. They gave me something else to do. A task.'

'What was it?'

'Cataloguing damp cuttings.'

'Cataloguing damp – how dare they! They took advantage of you.'

'Perhaps they did.' Meredith breathed in, and in the dark Ginny guessed she was on the verge of tears. 'But it's not Mr Dali's fault. He was hard at work. Listen, Ginny –' suddenly Meredith's voice became animated – '*I found what he painted. Really! And I think it's finished. You must come and see it.*'

'What?'

'The painting of the Christ. Downstairs. In the studio. He's done it. But it's dark. I couldn't find the lights.'

Ginny wanted to get out of this place, but she could hear the excitement in her sister's voice. 'Wait, what if the Maquis come when we're down there? There'd be no escape route.'

'That won't happen, will it?' asked Meredith. The uncertainty in her voice called out for Ginny's reassurance, and she gave it.

'All right. Let's look quickly. Then we'll go.'

They hurried to the pool area. Ginny reluctantly descended the studio stairs, aware that her whole body was trembling; she was still shaken by what she had witnessed outside the *posada*. It was pitch black in the basement. 'I am sure the lamps were in that corner,' she whispered. She took her sister's hand and moved further into the darkness, her right arm extended in front of her. 'Somewhere here,' she murmured. Her leg hit something metal. 'God, that hurt!'

'What is it?'

'I think one of them is here by my feet,' said Ginny, reaching down and rubbing her shin in the dark. Her fingers found the metal casing of a spotlight.

'Can you turn it on?'

'Not sure.' Ginny dropped to her haunches. Now her hands groped around the curve of the spotlight metal, the grille in front of the bulb, the cable extending from the back. Carefully she traced the cable to its furthest point and found the wall. The wire fed directly into the plaster. She moved her hands back down the cable and found the main body of the spotlight again.

'I don't think we can turn it on,' said Ginny.

Meredith's voice came suddenly close, as if she had sunk to her knees. 'Wait.'

Ginny and Meredith's hands touched as both took hold of the light casing in the dark. Their fingers simultaneously found it – the slider that would turn on the light. They revolved it and the metal stand ground noisily against the concrete floor. Now they pushed hard on the switch.

The beam of light from the lamp was narrow and focused. It hit the wall to one side of the painting, so the sisters rotated the lamp. Again, the excruciating yowl of metal on concrete.

Suddenly the canvas at the far end of the studio was aglow in the beam.

Neither of them moved.

'The Cross of Saint John,' whispered Ginny, awed.

'The Christ of Saint John of the Cross,' Meredith corrected her.

'The Blasphemous Christ,' said Ginny, using Meredith's title. 'And it's definitely Adam he's painted.' She moved closer to the canvas. 'You can see from the hair and the body. There's mauve in the hair, isn't there? Can you see it? It's absolutely . . .'

They were six feet from it now, and Ginny could not find the word.

'I don't know how to describe it,' Meredith said. 'I couldn't stop looking.'

Ginny placed her hand in front of the painting, the palm flat, as if she was feeling the energy coming off the body. As she did that, there was a noise in the rafters like a trapped pigeon fluttering its wings.

'What was that? Is there something up there?'

'I can't see,' said Meredith.

'God, I'm scared. What was it, a bird?'

'The light. Point the light up there.'

Meredith returned to the lamp and gripped it forcefully and, in the second before it burnt her hand, tipped the light directly upwards. The beam lit the rafters above them.

'Nothing,' said Ginny.

'Wait,' said Meredith. With the light balanced on one corner, she tipped it so the beam moved to the left, to the crossed girders Dali had shown them on that first day.

Adam hung high above them, naked but for a white towel around his waist. His arms were spread left and right across the horizontal girder and held in place with the straps. His head was tipped forward, just like the figure in the painting. His eyes were closed. A large mirror, suspended at an angle above his head, showed exactly the view of Christ that Dali had painted.

As Ginny looked, she saw what was making the noise. Adam had loosened his right foot from the strap around it, and was weakly moving it backwards and forwards.

Ginny would never be completely free of the images of what followed in those panicked minutes, as she and Meredith desperately searched for a way of reaching Adam to help him down.

From above their heads he whispered the word, 'Water.' They stopped and found a sponge by the canvas, rinsed it, soaked it, and pushed it up to him with the blunt end of a long-handled blade they grabbed from the worktop. Adam chewed at the sponge and they realised he was desperately parched.

'We will get you down,' sobbed Ginny.

Meredith, matter-of-fact as ever, asked, 'What is that? And what is the smell?'

Ginny saw, but did not say, that Adam had emptied his bladder and his bowels, and the wood behind his legs was soiled with excrement.

'I was sure he left with the others, I thought I saw him go,' Meredith whispered to herself again and again, not loud enough for Adam to hear.

The stepladder they found was not long enough. But they turned on two more of the lamps and saw Adam gesture, weakly, to a small set of iron rungs drilled into the wall behind him. Ginny climbed up them, but soon realised that unstrapping Adam would be dangerous, in case he could not support his own weight. His feet, she saw, rested on a small step at the end of the longest girder, but his exhausted body seemed to hang against the straps. She noticed that the leather was a dark burgundy. The idea that someone had thought of choosing a colour for this instrument of torture, designed to break a man, filled her with rage.

A figure descended the stairs. Ginny and Meredith froze, Ginny halfway up the rungs, Meredith in the middle of the studio floor. It was only after a few seconds that Ginny realised it was Sami, the smaller of the two boys who had been with Siobhan and Adam when Saunders drove her to the Dali house, the chubby youth with the mark on his nose. The boy looked bleary-eyed, as if waking into a nightmare. 'I am Sami. They – all go –

this – left for me.' He moved the piece of paper in his hand as if to wave it at them, but the gesture did not rise above his waist. 'They left—'

Adam made a gurgling noise. The boy looked up. 'We take him down.'

'*But how?*' screamed Ginny. '*How do we do it?*'

'The – here—'

And then they saw. At the same moment. A rope that hung slack in the shadows behind the cross ran invisibly down the wall. Instantly Ginny began to descend the rungs. Meredith moved too. Sami headed for the rope, pointing.

Ginny realised now that there was a pulley hiding in the shadows above them. The cross could be lifted out of its housing and then lowered. They all three hung on to the rope to move it slowly down. When the lowest point of the iron girder touched the concrete floor, Adam slumped forwards against the straps. Ginny loosened them and Meredith stepped forwards as he fell into her arms. She struggled to stay upright. Ginny ran to her sister and braced her body so they could hold Adam. As they held him, the huge interlocking girders swung towards the painting. The structure sliced the air a foot from the canvas and hit the concrete with a deafening bang. Meredith and Ginny stared at the painting for a moment, and then looked down at Adam, lying on the floor. His eyes were open.

Ginny knew what she had to do. She went back to the artist's worktop and grabbed the long-handled knife. The handle was three feet long, the steel of the blade sharpened on both sides and flecked with oil paint. She held the handle tightly in both fists, her knuckles white, feeling the solid weight of what she was about to do. Then Ginny released her right hand and turned it upwards so she was gripping the implement like a spear. She brought it above her head like a soldier and advanced on the painting.

From the door came a man's voice: 'No!'

Ginny turned, just as she was about to spear the figure of Christ on the canvas. In her mind she had already done it – shafted the body, then taken the blade left across the black paint, and then right to slash through the fishing boats and the shoreline. The wooden handle of the blade projected back over her right shoulder, and her gaze, as she sought the voice behind her, followed the length of the wood as a soldier would line up his target with the barrel of a rifle.

There, halfway down the rickety stairs to the basement and barely visible without the light on him, was Dr Tom Honeyman. His arm was outstretched. His hand level, shaking, the fingers spread, beseeching. 'Please – Ginny – *please*, whatever that man Dali has done, please, no—'

'Why are you here?' She heard the bitterness in her voice.

'You told me almost everything,' he said, 'whether or not you wanted to.'

She ignored him. Stepped forwards, closer to the canvas. Left fist closed tightly at the front of the handle, by the blade. Right fist raised over her shoulder, clenched around the wood. Stab and spear. Her eye caught the blotches of dried oil on the blade—

Then a different sound stopped her.

'Please, Ginny, no.'

It was Adam, his voice quiet, lying on the floor.

He said it again.

'Ginny, no. Don't touch it.'

She said only: 'Adam.' And threw down the blade, went to him and began to cry.

Dr Honeyman rushed over to her and held her. 'My poor

child. Oh, this is terrible. Let us get him help.' He knelt down by the American. 'Adam – that's your name?'

Sami said, without anyone listening to him: 'I did not know this.'

'How could they leave him?' Ginny demanded through her tears.

'Maquis is the answer,' said Honeyman. 'What happened at our hotel was very dangerous for Dali. His allegiances are known. He must have worried they would come for him. We should be careful. They might still come.'

'Maquis,' Sami confirmed, and he made a slicing motion across his throat.

'They bloody crucified him,' whispered Ginny. 'They bloody hung him from a cross, the bastards.' She knelt beside his body. His eyes were closed again and she noticed that his shoulders looked misshapen. 'What's wrong with his shoulders?'

'Dislocated, both of them,' said Honeyman. 'And before you ask, I am medically trained. I don't think he should be moved. Ligament ruptures are a beast to treat.'

From the corner of her eye Ginny saw Meredith approach with something in her hands. The green scrapbook. She had only half turned her head before Meredith arrived at her side.

The older woman took the scrapbook and held it in front of her, open, as if presenting it. Then she grabbed the pages with all the sketches on and tore at them. Everyone stared as Meredith pulled the book apart, ripping the pages and breaking the spine. Sketches and words, bright colours, small print, the precious handiwork of her mother, all confetti as Meredith tore the book apart and tore the pages again and again and let the scraps of paper drift down onto the prone body of the young American.

'Meredith—' Ginny began, but there was no point saying more, and she had seen the unnatural line of Adam's legs. 'His hips don't look right.'

'We'll get to his hip sockets in a moment,' said Honeyman, sleeves rolled up now.

Ginny felt a surge of panic. 'Is he unconscious?'

Adam opened his eyes and blinked, but said nothing.

'We'll get you comfortable,' Ginny told him, but his response was to weakly lift a hand and wave a single finger.

'He doesn't want to be moved,' said Meredith, who was now standing next to Honeyman.

'Let me lie here,' murmured Adam.

Honeyman suddenly froze. 'I'm worried we may not be able to,' he said. 'I think the Maquis will come.'

'What do you mean?' asked Ginny.

'They know this is their chance to take the artist. They loathe him. I'm worried. We shouldn't be here. Quick, find something to cover Adam with.'

Sami said: 'Maquis?'

'You should hide, young man. No – on second thoughts, we need you. Please. Quickly. We must risk it. We are going to have to move Ad—'

Sami did not need to be told twice. He turned suddenly, and ran up the stairs so fast he stumbled at the top and fell onto his knees with a crash, before sprinting off into the darkness of the house.

Ginny looked at Honeyman. 'Are we in danger?'

Meredith was breathing so fast her chest was heaving.

'Merry, wait, we need to think about what we do. Stay calm. Please.' Ginny looked down at Adam, barely conscious. Unable to bear the sight, she squeezed her eyes shut.

'We are in danger, yes, we must leave,' said Honeyman.

Ginny asked, 'We can't get Adam up those stairs ourselves, can we?'

The young American spoke again, the words almost inaudible.

'He is telling us to go and leave him here,' said Meredith.

'That we cannot do, young man.'

'In the corner – is that sheeting? Can we tie that to his feet and pull him?' asked Ginny, pointing away from the light.

Honeyman grabbed the spotlight and turned it to face the corner of the room. Sure enough, there was a pile of white bedsheets spattered with paint that looked like they might have been used as a floor covering while the artist painted. He and Ginny pulled at the sheets while Meredith watched. Gasping at the effort required, Honeyman ripped the largest sheet into three pieces and wrapped it around Adam's chest and under his arms. Then they tipped his body up and slid another sheet underneath it, between him and the concrete.

'We have to drag him,' said Honeyman.

But there came a crash from upstairs, then shouting and a scream.

'Cut the spotlight now!' hissed Ginny.

Honeyman grabbed frantically at the lamps but could not find the switches. Now Meredith leapt to help him and pushed the slider in the casing. The light died.

Ginny stood in the dark, with Adam prone at her feet, the shouting above them getting louder, the light of candles flashing in the space where the hatch to the basement hung open. And then feet appeared at the top of the stairs.

Meredith, Ginny and Honeyman circled Adam as if protecting him. Motionless in the dark, Ginny watched the light flicker at the top of the staircase. She saw boots – one pair, then two. Someone racing past, heavily, then doubling back. Two men were now stationary at the top of the stairs. One bent down so that his upper body and head appeared. He steadied himself against the hatch and seemed to scour the darkness below him.

Ginny sensed all four of them not daring to breathe.

The man at the top of the stairs took three steps, so that now his whole body came into view. He was wearing a black stocking over his head. Ginny felt him peering into the darkness, trying to work out what the basement was hiding.

Then he said, '*Ellos están aquí*,' and withdrew.

Ginny felt Honeyman's mouth against her ear, his breath hot. 'They are here. That's what he said.'

Ginny mouthed, 'Us?' so quietly she did not hear her own word.

Honeyman whispered, 'They will come back.'

There was a crashing upstairs, and another scream.

'Jesus Christ, Lord, save us,' murmured Honeyman.

Ginny's stomach turned over. In the dark she found Meredith's hand.

'They have got Sami.' That was Meredith. They waited, the noises above them stopping for a moment and then starting again. Ginny wondered with horror what they were doing to Sami. She was sure they were wrecking Dali's house in their search for the artist and their frustration that he had escaped them. There was a loud crash, like the noise of a wardrobe falling, and then, suddenly, all the lights on the floor above them were lit.

Now they watched as the bare bulb hanging from the cord in the ceiling high above them came slowly, ominously to life. The filament seemed to spark. Gradually the bulb glowed a pallid yellow. It was enough to illuminate the basement. Ginny reasoned that if the Maquis looked again, they would surely be seen. It was too late to drag Adam out of the studio or leave the house.

'We must try to move Adam,' said Honeyman. 'I wish it were not so. Young man, you must not make a noise. This will hurt.'

'Wait,' said Ginny, thinking furiously. She scoured the vast basement. There was the far corner with the basin and the worktop. There was the painting on its easel, casting a shadow behind it barely wide enough to hide a single person. The second, empty easel stood behind the first. The place had nothing in the way of furniture. There was nowhere they could easily put themselves, unless—

'Could we move Adam under the staircase? Could we all go there?'

They looked down at the young man, his eyes now closed, jaw slack, as if he was peacefully asleep. Bending, Honeyman grabbed the strips of torn sheet which he had placed below Adam's body and silently, skilfully moved one upwards, so it was now behind his head; he moved another lower to give support behind his hips. Honeyman murmured words of hushed reassurance as he worked. To Ginny it was a strange sight – as if the Scot was ministering to the wounded boy, about to bandage him or wash his feet. She was aware of the foul stench and wished she could clean Adam herself. She bent down.

There was a sudden crack in the air above them. The hatch at the top of the stairs slammed shut, the bulb overhead went out and they were in darkness.

'Move him now, quick,' said Honeyman. 'Ginny, you take his shoulders. Move him below the stairs before they come back.'

Ginny sank to her knees and moved around Adam's body to his shoulders. She had a sense of Meredith heaving the sheet to her right, but before his body started to move there was another deafening crash from above. 'What the hell?' cried Honeyman.

The crash was followed by shouting, screaming and gunshots.

Boots thumped on the floor above them. There was the sound of men's voices yelling in Spanish and a noise like scraping on the floor . . . then glass breaking. And then voices shouting again, insistent, coming closer . . .

The hatch opened. Ginny recognised the policeman's outfit as soon as his feet hit the stairs. He moved down them, back ramrod-straight, until his face came into view. On top of his head was the three-cornered hat of the Guardia Civil.

'English?' said the officer.

'Right now I'm happy to be,' said Honeyman.

'It is – now – under control.' The officer pronounced the words singly, deliberately. 'They are – how you say – arrest?'

'Maquis – arrested?' asked Ginny, looking over at Meredith and suddenly alarmed at what she saw in her sister's face.

The officer had drawn his pistol. He waved it at them to indicate that they should approach the stairs, but none of them wanted to leave Adam. 'He is ill. He has been hurt,' said Ginny, pointing.

'You stay,' the officer told her. 'You, and you –' he gestured at Meredith and Honeyman – 'follow me up the stairs. Now, please.'

'You'll be safe, Merry,' said Ginny, 'if you do as the policeman says. Dr Honeyman, please, can you look after—'

Honeyman looked at Meredith. 'Are you feeling yourself, young lady?'

With a gulp of pain, Ginny knew what had happened when she saw Meredith grab Honeyman's guiding arm without turning her face to him. The pair moved awkwardly towards the basement stairs, Meredith reaching out to feel for obstacles. Ginny watched her sister, then turned back to Adam. Her vision tunnelled. She knelt beside him and listened for his breath. She heard the others move up the wooden steps to the open hatch but she did not take her eyes off Adam. His body looked broken and now she wished she had urgently asked the policeman to bring a doctor. His hair was matted. It sprung out from the top of his skull onto the hard floor. She saw the trace of mauve and seemed to feel the sea breeze from that first day, when she had glimpsed him on the clifftop.

'Oh, my Adam, my Adam,' she said. 'I'm so sorry.'

She stroked his arm. His eyes flickered open.

Before either of them could speak, there were three loud gunshots overhead. Ginny saw Adam's eyes widen, and, from the floor above them, heard Dr Honeyman's piercing scream.

CHAPTER SEVENTEEN

ONE YEAR LATER
Glasgow, 1952

Outside it was dark. A gale threw wet leaves against the windows. On the fifth floor the woman brushed past the director's secretary as if she was blown in by the autumn wind itself.

Her coat was exotic, lined with white fur. It shook damp into the air. She might have been royal, or the wife of a shipping magnate, the way she dressed and moved – a blur of height and purpose. There was no acknowledgement, not even a second's politeness for the secretary, a seated woman thirty years older. Looking up to challenge the visitor, the secretary was met with a raised index finger and a stare that would have silenced a classroom.

The woman walked straight to the door marked DIRECTOR and opened it without knocking. At his desk, Dr Tom Honeyman sat as if frozen by a thought. He wore green corduroy trousers and his legs were crossed parallel to the desk.

Seeing her, he stood, just as his phone rang. He answered it. 'It's okay,' he told his secretary. Replacing the receiver, he watched his statuesque visitor take a seat without being offered one. She swept the wet hair back from her shoulders and said her name.

'I am assuming you're the lady,' Honeyman replied, looking at the red hair. She was not what he expected. None of the artists' assistants he knew wore fur, or heels of that length, or dripped with jewellery. But then the artist was Dali, so normal rules did not apply.

'It is, of course, about the painting you have bought,' said Siobhan Lynch.

'I am hoping there are not any further difficulties.'

She took a packet of cigarettes from her handbag, slowly, as if enjoying the power she could feel in the room. Power that emanated from her, as she made him wait while she struck a match.

The cigarette glowed between her lips. She dragged on the tobacco and he drew a breath from the room just as long. Eventually, Siobhan Lynch told Honeyman: 'It will be after Christmas now.'

He took off his glasses, rubbed his face, smiled grimly and stared at the desk.

'I am sorry,' said Siobhan.

'I have paid.'

'An opportunity has – presented itself.'

His head jerked up. 'You don't mean – surely – he wouldn't sell it to a higher bidder? We have the space ready here!'

His anger, after all that had happened, was gathering. Siobhan leant back in the chair and blew a smoke ring towards the ceiling.

'And the reaction!' Honeyman stood suddenly and took three quick paces to the window. 'My God, do you know what they are saying out there about me? Everyone has a view. I had no clue what I was walking into with this. And it's the same view, at bus stops, sandwich shops, in church pews, and not just here in Glasgow but all over Scotland. Even the dogs in the street know the Kelvingrove and its director have lost their collective mind. Everyone seems to believe the purchase an *utter* travesty' – the last syllable in 'utter' was rolled like a bale of hay down a hill – 'aye, a travesty that we would ever fritter this sum on a piece from Spain rather than spend it on a local artist. A student, apparently! I should have bought some student daub with the money!'

'I think you got a good deal. The artist wanted twelve thousand pounds.'

'I was within my rights to say I thought that was too much.'

'So you are paying eight.'

'Oh, don't remind me. Eight thousand, two hundred. The pennies matter around here,' said Tom Honeyman. 'That is regarded as a small fortune, and I am being called a –' he suddenly whipped a newspaper from his desk and flourished the headline – 'look, here – "A Fool and His Money Are Soon Parted". A fool, is it? So please, Miss Lynch, I need to get the Christ here, show them the power of it, so they can see what I see, the complete majesty, the genius of it.'

'However—' she began, but he cut in, his voice inflecting, the tone momentarily stronger than hers.

'However nothing. I have paid over the gallery's money, plus the shipping and insurance charges, nearly five hundred. I did what was asked. On trust. I did it all on trust. Even I, with my love of the artist, cannot justify money spent on a painting we never receive.'

Yet when he turned back, he saw her smiling at him with self-assurance. 'Keep your hair on.' She drew on the cigarette again. 'The painting is yours, Doc, don't worry.'

A silence.

Then, quietly: 'I don't like your tone, Miss Lynch.'

'Apologies,' she said, clearly not meaning it. She paused. 'There is a chance to show the painting. For Dali himself to unveil it. In Spain. Barcelona. So we will do that, before you take ownership of the work. That is all.'

'Barcelona? But it must be unveiled here in Scotland.'

'I'm sorry.'

'But we had such high hopes.'

'I'm sorry. The artist is sorry.'

'I'm sure he is,' said Honeyman, sitting down at his desk again. He reached for his diary, shaking his head. 'May I ask the date of this unveiling?'

'I must kindly advise you not to waste the ink in your diary.'

He looked up sharply. At that moment a huge oak leaf, autumn brown, flew out of the darkness and hit the window to his right with a wet slap. The rain pasted it to the glass. Honeyman glanced and thought he saw in the leaf the shape of a spread hand, the palm flat and fingers wide – like a traffic policeman's holding back a line of traffic. A signal to stop the conversation? But he could not.

'I will come to any official unveiling because the painting is ours.'

'You will not.'

'Must not or will not?'

'Both. You *cannot* come. You *will not* come. Under any circumstances.'

As he stared, Siobhan Lynch continued: 'You have bought the painting. I have told you already that the artist respects that.'

Honeyman felt a threat in the words: *He accepts you are the owner, but he can change his mind.*

'But why?' He knew he sounded pathetic now.

'Dr Honeyman,' said his visitor, 'some facts have come to light in the months since the painting was finished which concern us very much.'

He frowned. She reached into her bag and then, seeming to think twice, removed her hand as if it was not necessary to produce whatever material she had brought.

'At around the time the painting was completed, there were skirmishes with rebels not far from Dali's home.'

'I am well aware of the attack on the Guardia Civil. I was there, where their car crashed, outside the *posada*.'

'Quite. The artist is not a man whose –' she puckered her lips – 'political allegiances have gone unnoticed among the enemies of Franco. So it was a very dangerous moment for him.'

'Mr Dali is known to support General Franco, indeed. That is no secret.' Honeyman chose his words carefully, as if a single mistake could lose him the precious work of art.

'That particular night I facilitated the departure of Mr Dali from his home.'

'I am sure he was very grateful.'

'Rebels – the Maquis – actually entered his house that evening, so yes, he was grateful. And remains so.'

Honeyman hid a shudder that passed down his back. 'Well, I'm glad. But—'

'The Maquis invaded his house. They might have killed him. But he was not there. I had ensured that.' She continued, 'Subsequently the area was flooded with troops and police to restore order. The ringleaders of the terrorist attack were identified. A number were – captured.'

'Captured, hmm.' Honeyman repeated the word in his soft Glaswegian burr, but she heard him.

'I wouldn't want to pass judgement on the operations of General Franco's state security, and I'm not sure you should either.'

Honeyman saw in his mind's eye the flash of a gun muzzle against the back of a man's head.

He remembered the scene that had greeted him at the top of the basement stairs in Dali's house. Four of the Maquis, hooded, lying on the floor on their stomachs. The Spanish police officer shooting the first in front of him. An execution, pure and simple.

In cold blood. The other three screaming and crying. Then Sami, walking towards them as if in a dream, blood pouring from a stomach wound. Reaching out wordlessly and collapsing.

He removed his glasses and stared at the frames.

'Where does this leave us, Miss Lynch?' he asked eventually. 'Sure, there was a ruckus in Port Lligat that night. What of it?'

'After the insurrection by the Maquis, it came to the attention of the artist that there had been an attempt to steal the painting.'

'Surely not.' Tom Honeyman felt a bead of sweat on his forehead.

'We now know that a number of people were given illegal entry to his house by a mentally unwell woman whom the artist and his wife had been trying to help. The group broke into the underground studio.'

Honeyman's breath came quicker.

Siobhan Lynch, her face unreadable, said: 'Don't worry about your *Christ of Saint John*. Thankfully, the intruders did not manage to remove it. But they may have seen things that would embarrass the artist. And it is thus very important, Dr Honeyman, that I ask you a question.'

Outside, the breeze had stilled. Or perhaps Honeyman could no longer hear it over the ringing in his ears.

The clocked ticked on the mantelpiece. Each word Siobhan Lynch spoke next seemed to last a second.

'Were you there?'

Tick, tick, tick.

'Were you there, Dr Honeyman?'

Tick, tick, tick, tick, tick.

'I – no.'

'You were not in the house?'

'I was not.'

'At any point?'

'I was not there.'

She reached for her bag and gripped what appeared to be a square of card inside it, lifting it a touch so just the corner was visible. Then she let it fall back into the bag. The effect was to suggest she had information. Evidence. Surely not a photograph?

'Well,' she said. 'I have been sent to seek that assurance, and I must accept your word. You have denied it three times. I would not dream of questioning you further. You see, we had a description of the incident from one of Mr Dali's young assistants, who saw a group of people invade his studio.'

Honeyman thought: *Sami.* It could only be Sami. So Sami had survived.

'The mental patient had allowed the intruders in,' Siobhan was continuing. 'Her sister would have been one of them. Do you know her sister Ginny?'

'Well, yes, I suppose I could say that I do know Ginny. I did know her, a little, in Port Lligat. I was staying at the same *posada* as her. I would sometimes see her in the mornings.' He must give nothing away. He added, desperate to suggest openness with the facts: 'And the other sister. I don't remember her name—'

'Meredith.'

'Yes, Meredith I remember too.'

'She was unbalanced.'

'I don't know about that. I remember an awkward and somewhat shy girl.' He remembered something else – Meredith clinging to his arm as they moved up the basement stairs, and him, Honeyman, shocked by the tightness of the grip, turning and seeing . . . the unseeing eyes. She had been struck blind!

'An awkward girl with serious mental deficiencies,' Siobhan was saying. 'I think unhinged, probably violent. Mr and Mrs

Dali had allowed her into their home through their good grace but she took advantage.'

'I see.'

Siobhan Lynch suddenly leant forwards, staring directly at Honeyman. This, he thought, was the play. This was what it had been leading up to.

'And what troubles Salvador Dali greatly –' the first use of his full name – 'is that the group who broke into his studio and tried to steal the painting *may have seen something that could damage his reputation.*'

'I see.'

'His reputation –'

'I don't—'

'– which I am responsible for, Dr Honeyman.'

'I don't know what you could mean.'

'Something that could damage his reputation,' she repeated. 'You don't know what I might mean?'

He blinked.

'I have here –' the bag again – 'the witness's account of the group of invaders. The Spanish police have their descriptions. I wondered if I should read them to you, to see if you might know who any of these criminals were.'

The moment hung, as if the air had frozen around them.

'It goes without saying, Dr Honeyman, that the artist could not sell his painting to anyone who had been involved in that escapade.'

'What would they have seen that could be any kind of problem for Mr Dali?' Honeyman asked. He was aware of a tremor in his voice.

'You think they might not have seen anything?'

'I think they might not have seen anything.'

She smiled. What followed sounded like a change of subject,

but he knew it was not. 'The unveiling in Barcelona will be attended by the stuntman Russell Saunders, who was the model for Dali's Christ.'

'Indeed.'

'And when the painting comes to your gallery here, *assuming it does –*'

Those three words cut Honeyman.

'– you will ensure the role of Russell Saunders is not queried in any way, shape or form.'

'I see.'

'You will have seen that the newspapers have already written about his role, because there is a fascination.'

'Yes. I saw.'

'So the descriptive plaque you will place next to the painting in this museum will indicate clearly that Russell Saunders was the model for it. You may talk about how, in his genius, in his spirit of devotion to his art, Salvador Dali suspended Mr Saunders from a gantry in the studio.'

Honeyman stared at her.

She finally removed the square of card from her handbag, and placed it on the desk in front of him. Honeyman looked at the typed letters, staring until they made two sentences.

'This is the wording you want for the gallery's plaque?' he asked.

'Not want. *Require.*'

He read: 'The Hollywood stuntman Russell Saunders was the model for Christ. He was actually strapped to a gantry to help Dali envisage the pull of gravity on the body.'

'Yes.'

'It is outrageous.'

'Why, Dr Honeyman?'

'Because . . .' He surrendered. 'No reason.'

As she stood and brushed down the luxurious coat she had never taken off, her hands smoothing the shine out of the fur, she delivered her final lines to the floor. 'I have no idea whether you are still in contact with those two sisters. But if you are, they ought to know that every police officer in Spain has a picture of them. If they are foolish enough to return to that country, they may find they cannot leave it a second time.'

'Why would anyone want to punish them?' asked Honeyman.

'Oh,' she said casually, 'I wouldn't like to guess. The artist has powerful protectors, so the sisters have enemies. People close to Dali. Perhaps something was said. A word in the right place. From – I couldn't say who.'

She smiled. And he knew what the smile meant.

CHAPTER EIGHTEEN

DESATASCADOR LIQUIDO
Barcelona, 1952

It was the Saturday of the unveiling and there was only one place in the city it could happen. Only one place in the country. Every art critic, every writer, every politician, every Spaniard who had heard about it – from the tramp bedded down on wine-sodden newspapers in the doorway of the Travessera de Gràcia flea market to the powdered upper echelons of the Catalan priesthood – all were in agreement. Salvador Dali must reveal his finished painting inside the Sagrada Família. The Church of the Holy Family.

But while Dali had a finished work of art to show, the church itself was incomplete. 'The architect planned eighteen spires, or towers, we are never sure what they are.' The guide, a short woman who had to bellow to be louder than the traffic, stood, overwrapped in woollen scarves, in front of a small group of elderly Americans. 'He was born exactly one century ago, in 1852. So the centenary of his birth is this year!' She did not get the enthusiastic response she might have expected from the shivering tourists. 'His first public commission was lampposts. Imagine! From bolt-upright, boring streetlamps to this – this church that flowers like alien seed dropped from space.'

Her American group looked up, hard to impress, eyes watery behind their spectacles. Vertical stone ribs made the distant spires look like limbs stripped of flesh. Each spire was dedicated to an apostle – Barnaby, Simon, Judas and Matthew. On high, the pinnacles were mounted with shapes in Murano glass. A bishop's ring, cross, staff, mitre.

Deep below the tourists' feet, the foundations of the cathedral had been laid seventy years before. But since then, the Sagrada Família had come together erratically. Revolutionaries in the civil war set a fire that consumed the architect's studio – a sacrilegious act. The blaze claimed his drawings and priceless miniatures, stored on flammable wooden batons. They vanished in the fire like fragments of a broken dream. Then the Second World War suspended the work completely. 'Of course, the architect himself had already been lost to us. A sudden death in June 1926,' yelled the guide, far too loudly for the subject matter. 'As he walked down there along the Gran Vía de les Corts Catalanes, he was struck by a passing tram and lost consciousness. The tram was number thirty.'

The final line: 'He always wore poor clothes. This was a sad and lonely man. So the hospital thought him a beggar. Even after death, even after he was correctly identified, there was no glory. The church was ignored and building stopped. Not until now do we understand the greatness of Antoni Gaudí.'

'Why now?' asked an American in the group. 'Why not before?'

'Because Gaudí has his champions and advocates at last, making us look again here, at the Nativity Facade' – she pointed upwards at the towers – 'and the monumental imagination of the interior, where stone seems to cascade on our visitors like morning rain. It drips and bends! He made granite melt and bulge! Chief among his admirers, captain of his champions, is the supernatural artist who is to appear inside the Sagrada Família today . . .'

An elderly woman at the front misunderstood, thinking some paranormal event was being promised. '*My God – a ghost?*' she shouted, open-mouthed.

The guide chuckled, explaining to a hum of interest from her audience that the artist was real enough. 'It is Salvador Dali, more than anyone, who has woken Spain from its baffling indifference to Mr Gaudí.'

Next to the Americans was a long line of flower-sellers, bristling with mutual suspicion. A fight had already broken out between two ice-cream vendors. This had been a special week, a week when the entire city, the whole of Spain, was focused on the holy building they had only recently learnt to value.

The pause in construction caused by war had only just ended. New steps had been built to the Nativity Facade, with a ramp alongside, and opened only days ago. Locals were still experimenting with the simple business of climbing the steps, one or two arriving in wheelchairs and using the ramp. As they climbed, they watched the vast arches of the Sagrada Família change shape above their heads, the stone sweating with decorations and appearing to sway. How many more spires would be built? There was talk of twenty in total, talk of another hundred years of work. And now ordinary people had access into the heart of the Sagrada Família itself!

Today, at the top of the steps, positioned on the right by a temporary rail where the first people in the queue had waited overnight, a sign said:

SALVADOR DALI
LA REVELACIÓN
NUEVA PINTURA
'EL CRISTO BLASFEMO'
11AM

The first family in the queue were local, with a sulky teenage boy who was playing up and begging to leave. The parents kept assuring him it would not be long. But it was only nine o'clock and the doors would be shut until ten thirty. Behind the family stood a group of Eastern Europeans. Older, grumpier. Somehow they had been allowed to travel outside the Soviet Bloc. Probably officials, offended by having to stand in line. Next came couples. Three British teenagers, students loudly translating the sign to each other – 'The unveiling of the new painting, *The Blasphemous Christ*' – in the hope that their command of the language would impress two Spanish girls just behind them. Then more couples, more families, more lonely old men and women from the city, more sweethearts and more children . . . dozens, scores, hundreds of people. All shapes and sizes, nationalities, ages. All braced against the cold.

Franco's militia were barely present. The line stretched back down the steps, past the huge site cleared for the building of a crypt and the Passion Facade, past a children's playground and into the east gardens. The Church of the Holy Family towered above them: monstrous, Gothic, distorted, incomplete. The most beautiful building site in the world. And in its shadow, waiting to see Dali's new painting, were more than three thousand people.

By coincidence, the woman had walked down the Gran Vía de les Corts Catalanes. But she did not see the shop she wanted, and she certainly would not have known her brief, accidental connection with the architect hit by the tram. She was seeking a hardware store, with a window full of hacksaws and hammers. The Corts Catalanes was too big a thoroughfare for that kind of outlet, so she turned off the route, her small feet already aching. A backstreet was what she wanted. A shop window that had gone uncleaned in a year, the sign unrepaired, the letters askew despite all the tools inside. She knew what she was looking for.

Her father had worked in such a place. Not here in Barcelona, of course, but back in England, in Hull. So in a manner of speaking, she was searching for the place his working life had started, almost as if she was looking for him. One of the few things she knew about his life before her birth was that he had worked in an ironmonger's. He had spoken about it. In Hull the ironmongeries had become hardware stores. She wondered what they had become in Barcelona. It did not matter. There were only two words she needed today: *desatascador liquido*. She would not forget them.

The sun rose. The cold was unpierced by the light. Cloud had been whipped away like a dust sheet to reveal a carapace of sparkling winter blue above the bell towers. Each stone spire was at an imperfect vertical, looking like a cake decoration stretched and melted in the sun. The bells tolled. Ten. Ten thirty. The queue had lengthened, so at the back visitors had begun to worry they would not get in. They started to push. An argument broke out, and vergers from the Sagrada Família rushed down the line to reassure them. 'There will be space, there will be space, there is space for two and a half thousand.'

'We are more than that!' someone shouted.

As the queue moved, it bunched and narrowed along the side of the Sagrada Família like a caterpillar feeding on a fruit. The visitors towards the back of the queue became anxious again, certain they could not be seated by eleven if the queue moved this slowly. Now there was shoving. A man fell over. When he got up someone hit him with a rolled-up magazine. A woman started yelling in rapid Spanish. The vergers, wheezing in their heavy black robes, had never had to deal with anything like this. Two of them waded in and shouted for calm, which had the opposite effect. Both vergers had their spectacles knocked off. The fattest one fell over, taking an old woman with him, the pair rolling into the grass like two beach balls. The police arrived and arrested someone. They took him to a van, shook him by the collar and released him. The crowd cheered when he rejoined the queue. Suddenly there was humour. The mood relaxed. The line moved.

Siobhan Lynch searched the faces imperiously as she walked up and down the side of the queue, brushing her red hair away from her eyes, angry that the wind was tangling it, angry that she was having to do this. She could see these people would not all be seated by eleven, but Salvador Dali had never been on time for any single thing he had ever done, so why would today be different? The artist had no concept of a special occasion or a big day. To Dali an occasion was special once he arrived. It ceased being special once he left. So every event, every day, every hour, had the same status.

Siobhan knew the inside of the cathedral had been fastidiously prepared, because she was in charge of it. Yet the artist himself was probably still in his hotel bath half a mile away, stretched out under a quilt of expensive foam with only his moustache visible. He would be waiting for her third telephone call of the day, which he would ignore like the first two. Dali would not walk out of the hotel until his audience had been seated for at least half an hour. He would not wish to set off until they had begun to be impatient, and his pace would be leisurely no matter how late he was. She would not call him a bastard under her breath for the thousandth time, because this bastard would make her rich. It was amazing how quickly you could warm to a man who showered you with gold.

Salvador Dali's appearance at the cathedral altar, when it happened, would itself be an outrage. No priest would ever have consented to handing their sacred building over to the worship of this maniac, were it not for the fact that Franco had the Catholic Church firmly in his pocket. Priests had been paid by the state, his state, since the civil war. Siobhan Lynch had come to understand this as the date of the unveiling approached. Far from finding it hard to persuade the church elders to allow their precious cathedral to be debased, she had watched as they fell over themselves to agree. Franco appointed the bishops. The country was declared officially Catholic when the civil war ended, and one priest, Cardinal Gomá, now Primate of Spain, had called for 'divine totalitarianism', meaning total domination of every Spanish institution by the Church. Pleasing the General was as important as pleasing God.

The name of the painting. Now there was another thing. It was to have been *Christ of Saint John of the Cross*, which was as dull as the cataloguing label on a library shelf. Then the crazy sister of that bitch Ginny had suggested a different name, fishing it like a line of spaghetti from the soup of her mental illness. Even Siobhan could see her idea was inspired. Dali's wife had dismissed *The Blasphemous Christ* out of hand without Dali ever hearing the title. But then, in front of Siobhan some months later, Gala suggested the name to Dali as if it were her own idea. He had loved it, cheering and clapping 'my beautiful Gala, my genius' on both shoulders. Then that wizened coot at the Kelvingrove, that tight-arsed Scottish dolt Honeyman who smelt of rain, had told her he could not use the title: 'At the time of the purchase, the painting was called *Christ of Saint John of the Cross*, and so it must stay.' And why? Because Honeyman was getting heat for spending his money on foreign art, and putting the word 'blasphemous' in the title was virtu-ally an invitation to the Scottish churches to join in the uproar. She wondered what they would say when it emerged that, in the painting, no iron nails were visible in the feet and hands of

Dali's Christ, no crown of thorns. These would be further offences to add to the list.

Lynch continued to walk the queue. If that bitch was here . . . no, she would not put it past Ginny to arrive in protest at whatever wrong she felt the artist had done. Siobhan's own conscience was clear. On the night of the shootings she had at first been racked by indecision. Although the violence had taken place at the *posada*, word spread to other hotels in the area before the sun had set. The attack by the Maquis was all the talk at dinner in Siobhan's hotel. The details were sketchy. The heroic leap by Russell Saunders – himself nowhere to be found in the hotel – was already being exaggerated into the equivalent of a Superman-style vault between skyscrapers. Later, in bed, feeling her destiny was in the balance, Siobhan lay awake, willing herself to think. At midnight she rose, quickly gathered all the cash in her possession, and went down to reception where she found a gaggle of guests still jabbering to each other about the gunfire. She had appealed for a Spanish-English speaker. An older tourist from the English home counties agreed to translate for her. Two police officers who were reversing down the hotel driveway were halted by a yelling six-foot-one redhead and the embarrassed-looking, bony woman wearing pince-nez who tried to put Siobhan's flood of words into Spanish. Siobhan told the officers she worked for Dali and, never mind the lateness of the hour, they must take her to the artist's house because Dali was in mortal danger.

When the key phrase was translated – *El está en peligro* – the officers were seized with a sudden sense of mission. Did they realise they could be the heroes who rescued an icon of the Spanish state from the marauding Maquis? They went one better than taking their own vehicle. They commandeered the cars of two other guests they found in reception. The commandeering was not quite at gunpoint, but it was close enough for the guests to realise they had no choice but to drive.

And so it was that the convoy of three vehicles pulled up outside the home of the artist in the early hours. Gala came to the door first, her face caked with an oats-and-honey skin treatment which she had applied before retiring. Perhaps Siobhan had overplayed the danger – 'I think the Maquis are coming!' – to make herself indispensable to the artist and his wife. But she had not anticipated the panic that ensued as Dali, Gala and their cronies packed and prepared to leave. A jittery Gala told her to ensure Adam was pulled down from the cross.

So Siobhan had gone down to the basement. She put the lights on and found Adam strapped to the gantry. Then she berated him, at last able to say her piece to the half-conscious American who barely stirred as she spoke. She told him that he had no right to ignore her, to betray her for that slip of a girl, to make away with her while she, Siobhan, had had to watch the whole thing from a distance. Humiliated! She had been humiliated! She had clearly been in love with him, did he not see that, and did he not understand the importance of respecting that? She told him that the night she had found him in bed with Ginny was the worst of her life, and – well, Adam, 'It really does look like you have made your bed, haven't you?'

One word only came from the American: 'Please . . .'

Then she turned on a heel and flounced off, up the stairs from the basement. Weaving back towards the front door she took a wrong turn and happened to see Sami's room, the chubby boy still sleeping soundly. Evidently he was not important enough to be part of the evacuation. She had left a scratchy note: 'Take the American down from the cross, Sami.' But she could not pretend the handwriting was legible, or that the

English would have been comprehensible to him. It would also not have helped that she left the note, folded into quarters, under a small handbell on the nightstand as Sami snored. She moved the handbell carefully, so the clapper did not touch the rim. Certainly it looked like it could be used as a paperweight. And wasn't a corner of the note visible? Siobhan would always claim, even to herself, that it was an accident, the way the message hid itself.

And yes, by removing the fuses for the overhead lights she thought she had ensured any rescue of the American would have to wait till dawn. By then she would be long gone, her vengeance taken.

When she accompanied Dali and Gala back to the house a month later, she had descended immediately to the studio, realising that she dreaded the sight of a rotted body. Finding the empty cross she was half relieved, half disappointed. She presumed the American had freed himself. She hoped he had suffered.

Siobhan searched the faces in the line as the bells above them tolled eleven fifteen. At the back of the queue she lit a cigarette, then came forwards again, looking for a porcelain-faced girl barely out of her teenage years. Could the older sister also be here? That lump of composted vegetable? Ginny and Meredith together would be easy to spot, the blimp and the stick insect. She remembered throwing back the bedclothes in Adam's room. If Ginny had not gone to his bed like a stinking whore that night, Siobhan would have been there instead. She fantasised about what she could have done with a knife in that room. Sliced Ginny open. Stabbed Adam through the heart so he could feel her pain. The Spanish police were so useless they would probably have called it a joint suicide. Instead she had allowed Adam to be stolen, stolen from right under her nose.

She paused and stared up at the bell towers, which leant into each other like space rockets in a comic book. She decided she should get back into the robing area in the cathedral, where Dali would expect to be welcomed and pampered like a Roman emperor. Yet she could not ignore the gnawing anger at the thought that Ginny might want to be here to ruin his special day.

Siobhan Lynch jogged back up the brand-new steps of the Sagrada Família, hearing her expensive jewellery clink with every step, a reminder of the success she had become.

Russell Saunders sat in the choir loft, looking down on the packed cathedral audience. He wondered if any one of them, glancing up, would know him. Probably not. That was the stuntman's curse. Yakima Canutt should have been famous the world over for his jump under the horses in *Stagecoach*. The man was a genius who invented breakaway stirrups, spring-loaded saddle horns, the snatch-wire rigging used to take a fall off a runaway carriage without breaking your back. But had anyone even heard of Yakima? Did anyone even care about Canutt or Saunders?

Truly, this was the very last occasion he would set eyes on the damned artist. If he was honest, he could not believe he was here now. The Lynch woman had worked it somehow. He had been filming with Widmark in Geneva, tying up final scenes. There was a three-day break in the shoot and he had received a garbled message from Lynch: 'Get in the car, sleep in the back, five hundred miles later you'll be in Barcelona. Four thousand dollars for two days' work. Limo back.' *Four thousand.* Dali spent money like water. Christ, even in Hollywood a bean-counter would have been all over a side deal like this. Someone must have pulled strings to create the break in Geneva and make sure he had no excuse. He had told

Lynch he would be there, but no more than that. Just be there. He would not appear on the stage. He would not stand. Or take applause. Goddammit, if he was asked to acknowledge his part in the painting in any way at all before an audience, he would simply walk out.

The limousine had shown up on time, exhaust puffing smoke into the freezing air, windows tinted. On his arrival in Barcelona, he had been approached by one of Lynch's flunkeys. 'The artist may want to hold you.'

'Hold me? What the hell does that mean?'

Saunders was barely out of the limo, and this Spanish girl was barely out of her teens. His aggression had thrown her, he could see. 'Well, um, perhaps gesture, raise your arm in the air.'

'No.'

'Like a referee holds up a boxer's arm?'

'I won't do that.'

'Or Mr Dali come to you, hug you? Were you not the model for the painting?'

'I was not . . .'

Should he deny it? Seize this moment, his last chance to tell the truth, before he was concreted into the lie? He was profoundly uncomfortable with the deceit. Perhaps it was because his life in movies had been lived as a victim of many similar deceptions. Perhaps it was because he remembered his parents on the farm in Manitoba, digging and scraping, the honesty of their hard lives. His mother was still alive, God bless her beautiful heart. She would certainly see the newspapers. It might even make a front page in the town, local boy made good, all that shit. Mother would ring or write. Guaranteed. Or she would bring it up next time they spoke on the telephone. He imagined her voice, a distant crackle: 'Well done, Russell.' Lying to his own mother. What had he become?

Maybe it was fair that, having never been given credit for what he had done on screen, he was at last taking credit for something he had not done. Except that the loser in all this was Adam Bannerman, the young Canadian he had watched dive from the cliff at Cap de Creus. Saunders had stared in jealous amazement at the boy's Olympian frame as he dived. No wonder the British girl had fallen for him. Adam was a natural athlete. Hey, maybe he could do stunt work himself one day. Start on Muscle Beach like Saunders had, work his way to Hollywood from there. The guy's technique was as close to perfection as he had ever seen. There was nothing he could be taught. Except . . . it was odd, the way they had parted company. Adam arrived one day limping. His right leg had been injured in Dali's studio, he said cryptically. Perhaps Saunders should have asked for more information. None was offered. They agreed to postpone diving lessons until he was better. He would not forget Ginny's startled reaction when he told her – *He went a little lame* – as if she immediately grasped some terrible truth he had missed. Saunders had not seen Adam again.

'I was not . . . comfortable in your limousine,' he told the flummoxed assistant. She looked terribly confused. 'I have a frozen shoulder and an aching back after the journey from Geneva and think I need to be out of the way for this unveiling.'

But the concrete had set. Dali's lie was his lie too. It was truth now. Gene Kelly had never minded coming out with that crap about 'doing my own stunts', but if Russell Saunders was caught lying about this one painting he would be finished. The unfairness made him smart with anger, but he knew his anger never helped. It just made him feel stupid. Powerless.

Chin jutting, Russell Saunders continued to look down at the restless audience from the choir loft.

He would not call them a congregation, because they had

come to worship a man – the flawed and arrogant artist, the Lord of Liars. Dali obviously had little respect for his admirers, for there was no sign of him and it was now almost eleven thirty. Half an hour late! People were still arriving, hurrying to the few available seats far at the back. What had they called that place at the far end? The Baptistry? It looked half a mile away. And this choir stall perched above the cathedral floor – he looked left and right from his elevated position – it must have literally hundreds of seats for the singers. Whoever designed this place was a nutjob who liked a large choir. In the USA, he had read about a new fad called rock 'n' roll. He had even heard an example played on the radio – 'Rocket 88' by Jackie Brenston. Saunders liked it, but the sound was niche and would never reach a mass audience. Only church music and movie stars could fill a space as big as this.

And Dali, of course.

Far below him, slightly to the left, was a huge easel with iron legs. The painting sat on it beneath a black cloth. It seemed to be in some kind of large box. So desperate had he been to avoid credit for modelling Dali's Christ, Saunders had opted for a position above and behind the easel, which he was now regretting. When the work of art was revealed he would like to see it in the same moment as the three thousand pairs of eyes in the audience.

Oh well. He could view it later. The loft was filling with latecomers now, sitting, like him, where they would not be able to see the painting properly. He smiled at the thought that having had first choice of where to sit, he had picked the last-choice seats.

Far below, he saw Siobhan Lynch remove a card saying RESERVADO from a seat in the front pew. She glanced at her watch as she sat down, then looked up at the choir loft. If she recognised Saunders up here, she did not acknowledge him.

A breathless voice beside him said, 'I thought I wouldn't get in. I didn't reckon on all these tourists. Mad rush.'

The words were English, the staccato delivery possibly German. He turned to see a woman younger than her voice, with light make-up and cheap studs in her ears. She wore a leather jacket buttoned up to the neck. 'Isn't this place *insane*?'

'Like a forest made of stone.'

'I like that,' she said. 'So much decoration in here. See, we're above the central nave. There are four aisles along there, and transepts flanked by two aisles. They form a Latin cross. The architect wanted eighteen towers, I think. The tallest a hundred and seventy-five metres. Utterly crazy. If you look at the floor-plan, the top of the Latin cross is there. Near us. This is the edge of the apse. Have you seen him yet?'

Saunders had tuned out the description, but the question jolted him back to attention. 'Seen Mr Dali? Nope.' He looked at his watch. 'Forty-five minutes late is normal for an artist, I guess.'

'That's on the punctual side!' She moved her fingers to the steel buttons at the throat of her jacket and popped them. He took in painted nails and a choker underneath, and for a moment his brain chased the idea that she was attractive and he should find her so. 'I'm an art student. Well, lecturer. But I guess we always remain students, don't we? Hey, we aren't going to see the painting from here.'

'True.'

'Wrong angle. And,' she went on, not even taking a breath, 'I study the post-impressionists, so this man is absolutely at the heart of what the world of art has been doing since the war. But I feel he's lost his way a bit. I mean, since when did a surrealist need a cathedral?'

'It's not a surreal painting, I don't think. It's more like a portrait. A picture of a body.' Russell Saunders felt a tremor of pride. He was holding his own in a conversation about art with a teacher.

'Oh, I see. *The Blasphemous Christ*. Have you got an inside track on it? You've already had a preview?'

'No, I – well—'

'But you're involved somehow? Is that why you sat here? You're part of the show,' she insisted. 'You must be.'

'Well, a small . . . no, not really. Not, um—'

'You know Dali?'

'A little.' He felt caught in the net of his own lie. Would her questions set the tone for the rest of his life: endless congratulations for an achievement that was not his? He tried to find a connection with the artist that would not trigger questions about the painting. 'He set fire to a hotel I was staying in once.'

She laughed, and was about to follow up with another question when the lights dipped. Shadows climbed the walls of the vaulted interior. The stone creatures on the arches seemed to leer, their heads thrown into relief. The audience was suddenly quiet. A whistling started.

Saunders found his upper arm grabbed in the dark. The woman was supposed to be an academic and she was behaving like a hysterical child, he thought. The whistling came from the speaker system. In the gloom the effect was ghoulish. There was a hum and the amplified bump of a microphone being handled. Then silence. A hiss from the speakers. Louder, quieter. The sound of a snake about to strike, or gas escaping.

High up at the back of the cathedral, a spotlight came on, lighting up the huge easel. Russell Saunders stared at the box shape hidden by black cloth. Was the painting enormously heavy, the oil applied to the canvas unusually thick? He wondered who would introduce Dali, and which side of the church he would appear from. The beam of light narrowed, focusing closer on the large box beneath the black cloth.

Suddenly there was a banging sound. It was coming from the box.

The cloth moved suddenly. The easel rocked perilously. The spotlight seemed brighter. There was a crash of glass breaking, and an arm shot out from below the cloth. Saunders leant forwards, trying to see what was happening. The woman beside him whispered, 'Oh my God!'

Another smashing of glass. Fragments tinkling as they hit the stone floor. Now the blanket flew off. It was not the painting that had sat below the black blanket all this time, but the artist himself, bunched up in a large glass box. He had broken through the front of the glass and Saunders could see Salvador Dali now, trying to unbend his right leg and move it down so his foot would touch the floor. But the movement seemed beyond him. The audience, unnaturally quiet for a moment, suddenly started to stamp and cheer with wild encouragement, as if to say to the artist: 'We love this! You can get out of that box, now do it!'

Dali might have been stuck in his glass box were it not for two assistants who ran to help extricate him. One was the young woman who had welcomed Saunders to Barcelona. Each assistant took an arm. One of the artist's wrists had been cut by the glass and was bleeding. By bearing his weight the helpers allowed the artist to slide, almost-but-not-quite gracefully, from his position on the easel. As soon as his feet hit the cathedral floor the assistants rushed off again. Dali milked the applause, but his legs seemed to have cramp, so he was staggering knock-kneed, lurching this way and that, almost falling over. The assistants approached but he waved them away. Now he wrapped a handkerchief around the bloodied wrist. Saunders felt a moment of appreciation for the fellow performer. *God, he must have been curled up like an embryo in that glass case for an hour or more.* He caught a glimpse of Siobhan Lynch's face, pasty white and startled in the reflected light, and knew instantly that Dali had cooked all this up without telling her. The artist tottered on his feet for a second, his legs seeming to buckle. The crowd gasped, then he caught himself. By appearing to be on the edge of collapse, Dali only added to the drama.

Gradually Dali gathered himself as he stood before the audience and waited for the applause to quieten. He stroked his moustache, the ends coming to vertical points that almost touched his cheekbones. He was dressed in pink trousers and a white shirt, frilled at the chest. Even at this distance Saunders could see the shirt was spattered with paint and now had blood on the cuff as well. Dali moved out of the spotlight, kicking his legs as if to get the blood flowing again. Saunders watched as his outline retreated to the back of the apse, becoming barely a shadow in the darkness. He was now directly below the stuntman and his female neighbour. From a space behind the apse an object was pushed out to Dali, sliding across the floor on wheels.

The painting.

Watching from the loft seat, Saunders found his own breath coming quicker. He simply had no idea what would be on the canvas, which was facing away from the audience. As it passed below his section of balcony he caught sight of the painted figure on the cross, but in half-light and for a split second only. Dali swung it round much more forcefully than he needed to.

'It's going over,' said Saunders, but Dali steadied the picture. The spotlight had shifted to the right, away from the remains of the glass box. Slowly now, Dali inched the painting towards the light.

'Damn, I wish we could see it,' said the academic.

'Me too,' said Saunders, completely lost in the moment despite himself.

The painting arrived in the light. There was a sudden gasp from the audience, and a scream. Several shouts of alarm. It took Saunders a moment to realise that it was nothing to do with the painting.

A woman was standing in front of the canvas, illuminated by the spotlight. She was holding above her head a plastic canister with a spray gun attached.

'No!' said the academic.

Saunders said only one word: 'Ginny.'

The academic jumped out of her seat. She shouted over the din at Saunders. '*Desatascador liquido*,' the academic hissed. 'That's what she's holding! Household acid! For cleaning drains! She's going to spray the painting!'

Time froze. Ginny stood in front of the canvas, her arms above her head, the canister held like a trophy. Like a figure in a movie whose projection reel has jammed, the artist's body was halted in a stoop fifteen feet from her, his arm reaching forwards, beseeching, his eyes wide.

She shouted something. '*You or . . . you . . .*' Saunders could not make out all her words above the uproar. '*. . . or you . . .*'

Saunders put his hands over his mouth, willing himself to think, wishing his brain was faster. The church was in chaos now. She would not hear him if he shouted. The lights suddenly came on. The effect was to reduce the searing glare of the single spotlight and illuminate the baying congregation, who were all shouting at Ginny. Some stood and pointed as they shouted, but nobody approached in case it prompted her to spray the painting. From somewhere in the congregation came a shushing noise. It caught as the congregation hushed itself, and there was silence.

Dali remained frozen in a stoop, arm outstretched. Ginny stood with the acid canister poised, two paces from the painting. Saunders caught sight of Siobhan Lynch, her face slated with shock and fury.

Ginny shifted the spray canister in her hand and someone screamed. But then there was a different sound from another part of the cathedral. A male voice, loud and urgent. 'Ginny! Ginny!' There was movement at the end of the church. A man in a wheelchair came into view at the very far end of the aisle. He was carrying what looked like a pile of towels in his lap. One arm was laid across the towels. The other moved the right wheel of the chair, which jumped forwards erratically because its momentum was lopsided. He compensated by shifting the wheel so powerfully that at times the left tyre jumped off the floor.

Ginny's demeanour changed. She lowered the acid canister a few inches as the man in the wheelchair continued to shout. 'Ginny, no!' She turned her shoulder away from the painting a little, while keeping the spray canister pointing at the canvas.

The entire cathedral was silent. The man in the wheelchair moved down the central aisle towards the altar, bursting forwards one moment, stopping and correcting his position the next. Salvador Dali remained locked in his pose, reaching, beseeching. Suddenly there was the sound of a crying baby. 'My God,' said the academic, 'he has a child on his lap.'

And in that moment, Saunders recognised the man in the wheelchair. It was Adam Bannerman. And those were not towels he had draped his left arm over, but a swaddled baby. As the realisation dawned, he saw Ginny drop the acid canister onto the stone floor and run towards the wheelchair. There was an audible murmur of relief from the congregation. They would not see the precious painting destroyed in front of the artist.

Ginny picked up the child from Adam's lap. Saunders saw her mouth the words: 'I'm so sorry.'

She turned towards the altar to repeat the words to Dali, to the painting, to anyone who would listen and understand. But when she turned she saw only the plastic tube she had been holding seconds before. It was now in the hand of Siobhan Lynch, who drew it level with Ginny's head. She squeezed the dispenser on the acid canister and pumped the liquid into her face.

CHAPTER NINETEEN

ADAM
Cadaqués, 1952

He moved the big toe of his right foot. Then the left. Felt the tingle of a nerve straining to connect under the sheet. This was the routine every morning when the sun woke him, the audit of his body under the blanket, the check on what was slowly healing and what would never be right again.

Adam's heart jumped as his eyes opened. He recognised the decor of the hotel he had worked in, felt the plusher stuffing of the guest pillows, and remembered the reason they were here.

Certainly he must accept he might be crippled for life. Perhaps his left arm would always hang. He tried to move it under the bedsheets and felt the limb's dumb heaviness. Then he lifted his head a little and saw Ginny's naked back.

She was standing at the mirror, facing away from him, neck craned slightly. The infant was in her arms. Their son, conceived in a single devastating night, his crown visible over Ginny's shoulder. Six months old, the perfect little body of warmth and need.

The room was cold. He looked at the goosebumps on his lover's back, the small bottom covered by white lace underwear, her waist wider, but still tidy. The events of the previous Saturday came back to Adam like the smack of a hundred-yard golf shot that he knew, as the ball approached, would strike him square in the forehead. At that moment he felt sensation in his right foot. He tried to twist the ankle. The movement was looser than it had been before. The joint was coming free by millimetres. It was progress.

Everything that had happened to Ginny and Adam had been accidental, and yet somehow he saw a thread running through it all, from her original visit to the Hotel Maravillas del Mar to their return now.

'Are you awake?' Ginny asked, as if the question was for the mirror. Her voice was husky.

'Ginny, why won't you tell me?'

'Not this again.'

'Please. So I understand.'

'He's quieter today,' she murmured. Yesterday there had been screaming fits from the child, maybe because of the change of location. 'Hey, Luke, take my breast, little one.' Ginny had wanted her father Rex's middle name for their son. Had the child been a girl, she would have been Faith, after Adam's mother. 'He doesn't like long journeys, I guess.'

Adam wondered why she would not answer.

'I want to travel when you're better,' said Ginny absently. She had said the same thing a dozen times before. 'You know, last year, when Meredith and I arrived at this hotel, I got up one morning in our room and stood in front of a mirror just like this. I was naked. I looked at my whole body and wondered what I was growing into. I felt like I was seeing myself for the first time. A virgin. A complete innocent. And now look at me.'

Adam stared at her reflection in the mirror. He took in the delicate features of her face and remembered again the moment Siobhan had sprayed liquid at her. He had been so certain it was acid. He had even heard the words 'paint stripper' shouted from nearby. Lying there, he relived the agony of his attempt to protect her.

But the liquid was not acid. Not paint stripper, not bleach, not drain cleaner. Not a burning agent of any kind. It was warm water. Ginny had bought the canister, emptied and washed it countless times, then refilled it under a tap. She had wanted only to threaten the painting, not destroy it.

Not so Siobhan Lynch. She had wanted to destroy Ginny. Three thousand people witnessed her attempt to melt the face of her rival. They saw Ginny's lover stumble out of his wheelchair in his desperation to help, reaching for the baby she had taken from his lap. On his knees Adam grabbed the boy and, unable to stay upright, held him aloft as Ginny covered her face with her hands and the fine spray cascaded over the three of them. He had fallen and cracked his head on the stone floor, still holding Luke in the air. The congregation around them had panicked in the pews, shouting and pushing in their efforts to get away.

'Is this okay?' Ginny turned and touched a red mark on the skin below her brow.

'You look stunning. More stunning as a mother. The burn is healing, I promise. It doesn't show.' There must have been a trace of acid in the canister despite all the attempts to rinse it out. 'You won't tell me?' he tried again.

'Let me ask *you* something. Why come to the cathedral, Adam? Why try and stop me?' She squeezed the baby, who broke free of the nipple and gargled the milk. She wiped his lips with her thumb, which she drew across her breast, puckering the skin.

'I knew you must be in the Sagrada Família,' he said. 'I knew you would be where the painting was. There were posters everywhere advertising the event which somehow you failed to mention. As if you wanted me to think you hadn't noticed them! You had been so vague about your plans that morning.

I was happy to let you go in secret if that's what you wanted. But when I thought about it I worried what you might do.'

'You thought I wanted revenge?'

'Tell me. Please, darling. Tell me what you shouted at him, I need to know what you were saying.'

Ginny began to cry. The baby, no longer feeding, joined in.

'Please don't cry. Either of you! It's going to be okay. Honestly, it is.'

'But he destroyed you!' cried Ginny. 'My lover, unable to move. That thing – I can't call it art – that *obscenity* – that absolute *blasphemous piece of shit*.' The words were coming as if she could not control them. She gagged on her own breath, a sob without tears.

After a moment she asked, 'How did you even get to the cathedral with Luke?'

'Don't change the subject.'

'Tell me.'

'I had to stop you. I didn't know if you would see me if I came alone. But our baby – *oofff*.' He shifted his weight in the bed to relieve a stab of pain. 'A mother will always see her own child, feel his presence, even in a crowd of a thousand.'

'I could hardly not see you, coming down the aisle in that place. But how did you—'

'Get there? Me, a useless cripple in a chair? I just shouted for help outside the apartment. Sat in the street shouting. A builder's truck stopped. I told them what I dreaded. They loaded me and Luke into the back.'

'What you dreaded?'

'Yes. I told them, "My wife has gone to the cathedral to kill the artist."'

'Adam, my God!' she gasped. 'How could you think that of me?'

'Well—'

'None of that was true. I'm not even your wife.'

'I'm waiting for your proposal.'

'As if! I'm not allowed to do that.' She shrugged. 'Adam, my beautiful fool, I didn't go to kill Dali. What would I do, choke him with soapy water?'

He laughed for the first time that day. The movement in his lungs hurt his spine.

'Now tell me what you shouted.'

'I shouted, "You or that! You or that!" I wanted to see if Dali would put himself in front of the painting to save it.'

'And take the acid himself?'

'Yes.'

'The artist burning for the art.'

'Turned out he wouldn't even break a fingernail for it,' Ginny said.

'Maybe he was in shock. That's my last sight of him. Like a magician, half crouched, his arms reaching forwards as if he was shooting a spell at you.'

'I just saw a coward. A man facing a tiger. Holding his arms out to stop his face getting bitten. His precious moustache.'

'Ginny. You created a sensation by doing that. You may have scared him, but you made a show for him, with your hair and your eyes wild and your acid—'

'Water—'

'You added sensation to the shock, and Dali loves sensation. Did you see how quickly he left, when that verger charged at Siobhan?'

'He left because he was scared.'

'No. He left because his work was done. You did it for him. I'm not blaming you, but you did.'

Ginny paused, as if what Adam said might be true. She went

back to the one thing she was sure of, a lost person retracing her steps. 'He wouldn't save his own precious painting,' she repeated. 'He hangs you on a cross but he won't even break one fingernail. Why are you defending him, Adam?'

'Perhaps he really does think he is more important than his work.'

'No. *He wouldn't sacrifice himself to save the painting.* Okay? Do you know what that means, Adam? It means it's not worth a life. Not his life, not your life, not anyone's life.' Her voice was getting louder, her anger rising. 'It's a piece of canvas with some oil on it and it isn't even that valuable to the man who painted it. Frozen to the spot! Scared for his precious life. That put the real value on the painting, didn't it? Salvador Dali is human like us all. But he expects others to make the sacrifices.'

'Ginny, I need to tell you something and I need you to listen.' Adam heaved his frame up and round, awkwardly swinging his legs out of the bed. Now he was sitting up, naked, facing a glimpse of the sea through the line of dawn light between the curtain. 'What you don't know, Ginny, is—'

He was interrupted by the phone on the bedside table, half hidden by the tassels of the chintz shade on the lamp beside it. The bell inside the receiver was damaged, so it let out a single *ding-ding-ding* like a wine glass being struck before a speech.

Ginny sighed. She went to pick up the handset, the baby still at her breast. Adam, facing away from her, tried to stand. He used his good leg and lost balance. Tried again, felt a tiny zap of feeling in the left arm that helped him steady himself and gave him hope that he was getting better.

'Hello?' said Ginny into the phone.

Adam was on his feet now. His right leg bore nearly all his weight. The left was not entirely useless. He could feel something, a memory of his physical power and athleticism, old circuitry trying to run a current. Nerve damage, they had said.

Nerve damage.

He looked out to the sea, remembering it all. Remembering how he had flickered into consciousness and acute pain as they pulled him down from Dali's gantry. How he had blinked as Meredith ripped her scrapbook above him and the shreds had drifted onto his face. This puzzling memory had only just returned. For weeks afterwards there would be nothing but a bed. He remembered being horizontal, in traction, immobile, sores across his back and buttocks, blood on the bedsheets from where the sores had burst. He remembered giving up hope of ever walking again.

He remembered agony. Morphine clouding a tube that led into his shoulder, or maybe his neck? And the fury of Zander, his father, spitting tacks about what had happened, initially blaming his son for what he assumed was a teenage prank gone wrong. Eventually Bannerman Sr grasped the seriousness of it all, but was unable to get the police interested. His father began to understand the politics – Dali was Franco's hero, his mascot – so he turned his attention away from getting justice for his son to getting treatment.

Here it got easier, as if the state had only been waiting to be asked. Zander Bannerman offered money to the best doctors. None was accepted. Had the line of specialists who queued to see his son been told it was in the interests of the nation that he recover, that the cause of his injuries never be revealed? Every conversation about the circumstances of Adam's condition was cut short by the Spanish medics. They all used the same mannerism, a single finger pressed tightly to their lips while eyes swivelled from wall to wall as if someone might hear. Adam knew his father had started to wonder if Franco himself had taken an interest in the case. He had pushed the matter with some of his intelligence contacts, but nothing came of it.

Meanwhile, Adam waited for answers to the questions his body was asking. Nerve damage, the doctor said. *I'm sorry. Nerve damage rarely repairs.* He must use the wheelchair. He stayed in Barcelona for treatment, and also because his mother was there. She had eventually recovered from whatever debilitating virus had invaded her body. But becoming stronger only made her determined to end her marriage. Adam admired her, and took strength from her strength. An apartment was made available in curious circumstances. Was the Spanish state behind that, too? Then Ginny came, pregnant with their child. It might have defeated Adam utterly, but instead he reflected on the joy of a new family arriving for him while the old one fractured. His world exploded with possibilities: his lover's return, with child. The two understanding each other at last. Becoming three. Adam would recover for Luke. For Luke and for his lover. They had promised themselves to each other.

He blinked at his view of the sea, moving the fingers of his left hand a little. He half turned to Ginny and his son, feeling his back yowl in pain at the unfamiliar movement.

'Did you hear what I said?' she was asking.

'Sorry,' he said, brought back to the room. 'I was thinking – about everything. And about how you saved me.'

'Destroyed you.'

'This wasn't you.' He meant his body. 'You didn't do this.'

'I love you, Adam, and I can't bear the—'

He cut her short. 'Is he waiting downstairs?'

By the time Ginny had bumped the pram down to reception, Luke was fast asleep under his blanket. She looked at the reception desk and remembered the desperate call for the taxi to Port

Lligat months ago. Then the door marked BIBLIOTECA. She remembered Meredith on the other side, studious by the light of a lamp. *Saint John of the Cross.*

Adam was there already, in an armchair. He had got down the stairs on crutches. He smiled at her without a trace of self-pity, and she gestured that he should not even think of trying to stand. 'Where is he?' he asked, and Ginny shrugged.

'And where is she – Meredith?' she answered, almost to herself.

She went to reception, but got nowhere trying to describe her sister and ask if they had seen her. She looked around, saw the entrance to the restaurant and remembered the fire the artist had started, and how they all had to leave the hotel. She remembered the smoke billowing from the lounge windows, Adam bending over to speak to a distressed elderly lady on the lawn, Meredith sitting on the bench and her warning. *Something terrible is about to happen.*

She left the pram with Adam and went outside. Her eyes settled on a bunch of yuccas on the other side of the hotel driveway which she had never noticed before – now they triggered a memory of the trauma outside the *posada*: the smell of cordite, the sounds of the bullets fired at her and Honeyman from the top window of the hotel. The smell of death. The scramble to the artist's house to find Meredith. And finding Adam.

She could not point to any moment where she could have done something different and changed things, short of never coming to Cadaqués in the first place. Her actions all led into the Sagrada Família and her assault on the painting, which the police had only excused (she now believed) because Siobhan's attack on her was the far more serious crime. An ambulance crew, believing her to have been burnt with acid, refused to let the Guardia Civil take Ginny while she was treated, after which the police appeared to have lost interest. Jesus Christ, what a disaster. She had even broken her baby's father.

Ginny was being tapped on the shoulder.

'Hey,' said Russell Saunders.

She gasped involuntarily. She saw in the stuntman a kindness which had always been there, but had been masked by his bravado and self-confidence. He smiled, eyes twinkling. 'Hey, buddy,' he said, as if she needed reminding who he was.

Ginny followed instinct. Said nothing in reply. Just reached for him and hugged him. Almost fell into his muscled arms. There was nothing impure in the force which drew her frame into his. She just sensed, suddenly, that they had become friends. He had been the one constant in all of this, the truest of all of them, and now that she saw him back at the hotel she realised that she found him adorable. Honest, kind and real.

'Russell,' she said.

'Wow,' he said as he pulled back, still with his hands on her shoulders. 'You meant that.' There were tears in his eyes.

'I meant "Russell", yes.'

'All these months, and finally I get my first name out of you.'

'In friendship.'

'Always in friendship,' he said. 'A stuntman values his few real friends, I can tell you.' She felt moved by his presence, like a child who sees her father in a crowd of strangers. She understood Saunders was still the Hollywood stuntman, still the person who lived and worked alone, whose deepest emotion was expressed through action – jumping from a bridge or between train carriages. His main form of expression was to jut his chin an extra inch further out. She wanted Saunders to say that he liked her, that he understood and valued her, but she knew he could not go that far. He was, she realised, a man both intensely private and intensely proud. She had the sudden urge to tell him how much she valued and admired him, but he might think she was referring to something more than friend-ship. All she knew was that her feelings came from a place of caring deep within her.

'Is he in there?' asked Saunders.

'Have you not been in?'

'I just came up the driveway here.'

'Well, he's waiting to see you.'

'Before we go in,' Saunders said hesitantly, 'how is your sister? I don't imagine any of what happened in Port Lligat can have helped her.'

'No,' said Ginny carefully, 'it really didn't. She became blind, which is part of her condition. It relates to shock. Her body's defence. And this time, it was serious – it was months. She came back to Hull with me and rested. There were some issues we had to resolve with my mother. But we did. We are a family now. It's all she ever wanted. To be a sister. To feel like a daughter. I'm telling you too much.'

'Is she here?'

'Yes, she came. I can't find her at this moment, but yes. She's here in the hotel. She was in the artist's house when –' Ginny did not want to spell it out – 'it all happened.'

Saunders grimaced. 'Poor lady.'

'Well – if she hadn't been there, Adam would be dead.'

Saunders hung his head in hands.

'I'm sorry,' said Ginny. 'I should haven't said that. It's down to me, not you. It was all my stupid idea. Come through and see him.'

When they got back into reception, Adam had left the armchair. Ginny frowned. She saw him before he saw her. He was half hidden by a pillar that split the reception desk in two.

Hidden because, for support, he was leaning his body across the counter. He turned as they approached, uneasily poking at the floor with his left crutch to manoeuvre his body around in a semicircle as he hopped into position with his good leg.

'Sir,' said Adam, his face brightening at the arrival of his hero.

'Young man,' said Saunders seriously. There was no hand to shake, and he patted Adam on the shoulder.

Adam turned to Ginny and, unsteadily, produced an envelope in the hand of his working arm, without removing the forearm from the crutch. 'This is for you from Meredith. I was asking if they'd seen her.'

'For me?' said Ginny. 'It's her writing.' She inspected the envelope but did not open it.

'Can we sit?' asked Saunders. 'You must sit, Adam.'

'I think moving as much as possible is the thing.'

'Man alive.'

'I will get better,' said Adam. 'Did you hear the good news?'

'I would love to hear some good news.'

'We became parents. Luke is over there.' He pointed at the pram, still beside the armchair, a blanket draped over the sleeping infant.

'Well, of course.' Saunders' manner was stiff, formal. But now his face brightened. They moved over to the chair and the pram. 'Tell me in confidence. Are you going to make an honest woman of her?'

'Hope to,' said Adam. 'Just need to be a bit better in myself first.'

'Man,' said Saunders again. 'I mean just – my God.' He straightened, like an actor preparing for the moment his speech is called for. 'I wanted to meet. I asked to meet. It's good of you to meet me. I feel aghast at what happened. I am penitent, a sinner.'

Adam looked genuinely surprised. 'I didn't know you felt like that, sir—'

'Please don't "sir" me. "Sir" is what you call a man of honour.' He was fidgeting with the corner of a straight-backed armchair as he said this, and Saunders unconsciously lowered his voice as he slid into the chair beside the pram. But a movement of his right arm accidentally struck the pram and woke the baby, who started crying. 'Oh, God,' said the stuntman haplessly. 'I'm so sorry. I thought I was a god, but I can't do anything right.' He stood again, shaking his head.

Adam's closest arm was the one which hung, useless. He used his good hand to move the numb arm to his lap, twisted his body with a grimace and used the working limb to rock the pram. It was all done in a moment, but any attempt to pretend his injury and pain were minor would have fooled nobody.

Saunders looked tearful. As if running through a series of bald facts, he stated: 'I am responsible for what happened. I was lounging in a hotel bed when you were taking my place on that cross. I was greedy and selfish. I don't believe I will ever come to terms with what I did. To make it worse, I never told the truth about who was really the model for the painting. I became part of the lie. I became—'

But before he could say anything else, Ginny interrupted him. She had opened the envelope. 'She says she's gone to Cap de Creus!'

Both men stared at her blankly. Then Saunders looked back at Adam. 'I wanted to see you, son, to have time to say this.'

'The note just says, "I'm on the cliff." Why would she have gone there?'

'It's the best view?' suggested Adam.

'That it is,' confirmed Saunders. But Ginny could tell from the tone of their voices that they were as worried as she was.

'I should go.'

'No,' Adam told her. 'Not without me.'

'You *can't* come, Adam.'

'Hey,' said Saunders. 'Let's not say "can't" to this amazing young man.'

'It's nerve damage,' said Ginny.

'Nerve damage never heals,' Adam recited, but shaking his head as if it was a poem he was trying to unlearn.

'I knew a guy in Milwaukee who had nerve damage in his eye, and it corrected itself,' said Saunders, the tone false jollity. 'He started with a squint and ended up as an astronomer.'

'You only need one eye to be an astronomer,' said Adam.

'But the squinty one was the one he used in the telescope, that's the point.' Saunders fell silent, then added: 'Not Milwaukee. Minnesota.' Which just added to the impression that the story was made up.

Ginny said, 'How far is the Cap de Creus? Five miles? I'll go.'

Adam put in forcefully, 'We'll all go.' He started to move, but Saunders stood up, braced himself and took his former student in his arms. Adam's face was pressed into his shoulder, his eyes closed. Saunders lifted him from the chair so gracefully that Adam's frame seemed to float upwards. As he was raised, the younger man's left trouser leg rode up and Ginny saw again how wasted the muscle on the calf was.

The men said nothing as Adam used his crutches to stay upright and Saunders let go.

Ginny was about to say, 'Father and son,' but she found herself so moved she could barely speak. 'Don't you want to carry on talking?'

'I've said some of what I came to say,' Saunders mumbled, 'but not all.'

'You have nothing to apologise for,' Adam told him.

'I'll be sorry for the rest of my life,' said the stuntman.

They took a taxi-van to Cap de Creus. It pootled slowly, leaving a trail of sooty exhaust. Adam's wheelchair was folded and placed in the back. Ginny sat in the front with Luke between her and the driver, the baby lying in his basket near the gearstick. The heater was on too high.

The men were talking quietly in the back and she could not resist listening.

'She rang me, oh my.' That was the stuntman.

'In a bad way?'

'Oh Jesus, yes. Desperate for a placement, something to show she was trusted. She would have licked stamps if I'd asked her to. Frankly, that woman is damned lucky not to be in jail.'

It had to be Siobhan Lynch they were talking about.

'Irony is, it was your lady in the front here who saved her from jail. Putting water in the can. If it had been that – what did it say on the tin? – "describable liquid" . . .'

Ginny mouthed, *desatascador liquido*, two words she would never forget. She kept quiet and strained to hear more about Siobhan.

'You work for the king,' Saunders said, 'he showers you with gold. You fall out of favour, he cuts your head off.'

Adam's response was drowned out by Luke's cry. The baby had woken.

She heard Saunders say, 'Ambition only for herself,' and smiled at the irony of hearing those words from the mouth of a film star as she unlatched the seat belt and cuddled her son. The taxi driver sped up and she said, 'Thank you,' as if he had understood her urgency without needing to be told.

Twenty minutes later they were at Cap de Creus, and Ginny

imagined Adam diving from here with the stuntman while Dali produced his masterwork in Port Lligat. She had only ever seen these black rocks from the distance. The thought of Saunders teaching Adam to dive gave her excruciating pain, because Adam was no longer that person.

She removed his wheelchair from the back of the taxi and, while Saunders unfolded it for Adam, Ginny took Luke in his basket on the front seat. She put her hand over her eyes and looked towards the clifftop. 'I have a strange feeling that Meredith is not here,' she said.

But the other two were not listening. She heard the snap and clank of the different parts of the wheelchair being reassembled. Ginny stared across the rough ground towards the point where the black rocks became air and sky. The hundred-foot drop to the sea was there, five minutes' walk away, but there was no sign of any other human being. Heart starting to pound, she said, 'Wait here, can you?' But it was almost to herself. She moved as fast as she could with the basket in her arms. While she jogged she heard the taxi driver start the engine. She turned. 'No!' she shouted. 'You were supposed to stay and wait!' But there was no chance of the driver hearing her. The taxi-van turned round and left.

Gulping air, Ginny finally reached the clifftop. She stopped and looked around. Behind her, Saunders was pushing Adam in the wheelchair. But the ground was so uneven he was occasionally forced to lift the chair, with Adam in it. Of course he did not lift the chair like any ordinary human being would, with exhausted clumsiness. With power and grace Saunders raised the chair, like Atlas carrying the world.

At the cliff's edge, Ginny set Luke down and covered the upper half of the basket with a layer of muslin cloth to shield him from the weak November sun. He gurgled contentedly beneath it. For

a moment she forgot everything and listened to the sounds her
son was making, which to her were as beautiful as any orchestra.
Then Ginny stepped forwards and carefully peered over the top
of the cliff to the sea far below. She was struck by a sudden
certainty: Meredith had not jumped. It was almost as if her own
lack of panic was proof. So far as was possible, Ginny felt she
knew her sister's mind.

'Meredith!' she called, looking around, and remembered the
first time she had shouted that, on the clifftop at the back of
the hotel, that first day.

By now Saunders had virtually carried Adam the whole way.
'What's up?' he asked.

'Meredith's not here! We needed the cab to get us back. It's
not here she meant.'

But the car was long gone. Too late, Ginny had realised that
for her sister the only cliffs were the ones a mile from the rear
of the hotel, the precipice where they had walked that very first
day. And Ginny knew why Meredith had gone there.

They started back on foot. Saunders pushed and lifted Adam's
chair across the rough terrain until Adam, feeling the older man
weaken, insisted on using his crutches instead. They must have
looked like a strange group as they finally reached the road.

They waited to flag down a car, but none came. They were
rare on these roads. Saunders and Adam moved to one side
while Ginny sat in the shade of a tree and fed Luke.

'I feel I didn't manage to say what I wanted to say, young
man,' Saunders said.

Ginny saw Adam shiver.

'Hey, are you cold? It's not warm, that's for sure.'

'I'm fine,' Adam smiled. He leant against a tree to rest his
working leg. 'You said you were sorry. You didn't even need to.'

'I had no idea on God's earth what had happened to you. Not until I sat in the Sagrada Família, up there in the loft. A thousand seats for a damn choir, but what a place. See, I'd told the artist before – told his little helpers, anyway – that I wouldn't take applause or wave or say how pleased I am with the painting or any crap like that. I wouldn't take credit, because I didn't do it. But what I was never expecting was to see you there, crippled, coming in on a chair.'

'Earlier,' Adam said, 'I started to say something to Ginny and we got interrupted. And I need to say it to you too, Mr Saunders, I think. Hey, Ginny, can we move a little closer?'

The breeze picked up for a moment, then settled.

Ginny patted Luke on the back, holding him with his stomach against her shoulder, the muslin over his head. The baby let out a loud burp and they all laughed.

'Mr Saunders, sir—'

'Russell,' corrected the stuntman.

'Russell,' Adam went on, 'you have apologised to me for putting me in that position with the artist, where I was the figure on his cross. Ginny, darling, you have more or less said the same. You blame yourself for what happened to me, as if it was a terrible thing.'

'It was,' she countered.

Adam moved his good foot into a different position. Adjusted the crutches and looked out across the empty road. The sky was grey, the air cool, and there was now no difference between sun and shade.

'It wasn't,' Adam said firmly.

They both stared at him.

'It wasn't a terrible thing.'

'How can you say that?' said Ginny.

'When I entered the cathedral, I saw Dali smash his way out

of that glass box. But then he brought the painting into view.
You remember how he did that, kind of dragging it on castors
and using his weight against it, almost as if they were dancing?
It was a moment before you appeared, Ginny my darling. But
in that moment I saw the beauty of it, I saw the power, I saw
what it could do.'

Ginny said, 'It's an atrocity.'

'No!' cried Adam. 'It's incredible. It's the most incredible
thing I've ever seen.'

'But it wasn't worth it,' Saunders said, staring at the ground.
'It wasn't a reason to hang you from a damned scaffold – a
gantry.'

'Who do you think hanged me?'

'The artist,' said Ginny.

'Not without me wanting to be up there,' said Adam. 'I
agreed, remember. And I watched from the cross as he painted.'

'But he refused to take you down!' Ginny exclaimed.

Adam replied softly, 'It's not like that. I went up there willingly, and at first I was strong enough. He painted for hours
and hours and hours, days and days. I came down for breaks.
At the start. And then something consumed him—'

'You see?' said Ginny. 'He never thought about you.'

'No!' Adam suddenly shouted. 'Listen, Ginny. Please listen,
because I don't want to have to say this again and again for the
rest of our lives and not have you hear me. I saw the painting
come together inch by perfect inch. I saw the way the artist
was completely consumed by painting it. I saw the beauty of
it. It was powerful – so powerful – I can't – I can't even explain
it. And I, Adam Bannerman, who had nothing to say for myself
up until that moment in my life, who was just a waiter in a bad
shirt with nothing to recommend himself . . . I *wanted* to be
the person at the centre of that painting. I *wanted* to see myself

on that damned cross when it was finished. Even though I felt my body break up there. I felt this –' he gestured with his working arm – 'all of this happening on that wretched gantry. I did not want to come down. I would have died up there if that is what the artist had wanted.'

'Died?' repeated Ginny.

'Jesus Christ,' said the stuntman.

CHAPTER TWENTY

THE CLIFF

A passing Land Rover picked them up. Ginny panicked when she saw the green vehicle bumping down the road towards them. She assumed at first that it was a police car and wanted no more attention from the Guardia Civil after what had happened at the Sagrada Família. The spare tyre was loose on the rusted vehicle bonnet, and as Saunders waved and the van braked, it shivered on its spindle like a record starting. Before the Land Rover had stopped, the door was open and music from the dashboard radio came out.

'Olavi Virta!' shouted the driver.

'Well, hello back!' Saunders called enthusiastically, although the three had been deep in thought since Adam's revelation.

The young American murmured, 'He's the singer, I think, Olavi Virta,' but only to Ginny, who managed a smile. The tune was familiar, and as they shot back towards Cadaqués, Ginny realised she had learnt a Spanish word: '*Quizás, Quizás, Quizás*' must be 'Perhaps, Perhaps, Perhaps'. The man at the wheel of the Land Rover was dressed in torn corduroy trousers and a white vest with oil stains. His face was lined with folds of old skin, and he drove with a smile that locked his three-inch underbite in place under his beard. His dialect was impossible for Adam to understand, so they managed only to communicate the name of their hotel in Cadaqués and thank him for stopping.

As they drove, Ginny pondered. If Adam had willingly put

himself on that cross, should she not be angry at him instead of the artist? By that stage she had been pregnant. She would have to bring up a child with a broken father who could not even accept that the damage to his body was a cause for regret. Surely the artist was responsible for leaving him on the cross? No, no, that had been Siobhan, Ginny was certain. Siobhan and Ginny herself had been responsible. So why exactly *was* she angry with the artist? Dali was like vapour in her mind. As soon as she reached out to throttle him, his image evaporated and all that was left was the moustache. She was certain she would never set eyes on him again. He would be forever frozen by the cathedral altar, arms stretching towards his precious painting, eyes bulging with shock, face haggard. Reaching out but not moving forward.

The sky had brightened a little when, two hours after the taxi-van first dropped them at Cap de Creus, the Land Rover finally trundled down the gravel track that ran alongside the hotel in Cadaqués and came to a halt. The driver had caught on that nobody understood him, so he had eventually stopped talking. Out came Ginny first, with Luke, who was sniffing back tears. Then Saunders emerged at the other side of the Land Rover, also silent, gently lifting Adam with his hands at the younger man's armpits. He leant Adam against the vehicle. As Saunders shook his legs to uncrease his trousers, the driver pulled forwards and Adam tumbled to the ground.

'*Hey!*' the stuntman yelled.

'Hey, it's fine, really,' said Adam, his patience a wonder, dusting gravel off his elbow and reaching for Saunders' proffered hand. The driver had jumped out of the front seat with the crutches and was apologising in another torrent of words. He unbuttoned the canopy at the back of the Land Rover. Ducking underneath, he wrestled the folded wheelchair out. Ginny watched. She felt the tears come. It was not only the way Adam did not resent his injuries. It was that he seemed to think they had been a price worth paying. As if their life as a family was worth so much less.

Saunders saw her tears. 'I have an errand,' he said. It was clearly an excuse to get away.

'No, stay with us, Russell. Let's find Meredith together.' She was holding back the sobs.

The Land Rover backed up. Adam was on his crutches and Saunders carried the folded wheelchair. Ginny was still carrying Luke in his basket.

'We're like a defeated army,' Saunders said.

They began to walk towards the hotel garden. At the end of it, where the lawn became flowerbed and gravel, they took the path to the left. The same route Adam and Ginny had gone the day they first met. They stayed clear of the canopy of trees and took the path towards the top of the cliff. After a mile they came to her. Meredith was sitting on the ground, facing the sea, alone.

As they drew closer to her, the sun broke out from behind the clouds. The air was cool. There was no breeze. The sea below the cliff was calm.

Ginny did not want to shock Meredith, so she simply said, quietly: 'Darling sis.'

'You were so long,' Meredith replied without turning.

Saunders and Adam hung back as Ginny walked towards her sister. She was conscious of a sweet smell in the air, and thought of lilies. There was a pile of clothes on the ground beside Meredith. Ginny did not need to look closely to see what they were. She turned to Adam. 'These are yours.'

'What – what are they?'

She handed over the pile. The length of blue cord that had

been his belt, the underpants, the vest, shorts, socks and red sports shoes, all discoloured by the soil.

'My clever sister has actually dug your clothes up.'

'You're j-joking.' He began to laugh. Ginny laughed too, shaking so much she had to place Luke's basket carefully on the ground.

'I'm liking this moment,' Saunders said, 'even if I don't understand it.'

Ever literal, Meredith rose, taking this as a cue to explain. 'A long time ago, Ginny saw Adam had taken his clothes off—'

'*All* of them,' said Ginny.

'Yes, all of them, and he dived naked off the cliff, and then Ginny fell off the cliff too.'

The four of them were standing, facing each other.

'How did I not know about this? The famous freefall cliff demonstration by you, Ginny,' the stuntman laughed.

The sun hid behind a handkerchief of cloud again. Ginny said, 'I fell about six feet.'

She felt their mood lifting as a group. Adam had the greatest stuntman in his life. Her lover would get better. Didn't even nerve damage heal? And, for years to come, thought Ginny, Russell Saunders would be a true friend.

The stuntman reached out his hand to Meredith. 'You look in good shape. Strange smell round here, like a skunk went off.'

Ginny wondered if the past year had been kinder to Meredith than she, the younger sister who had watched her throughout, had ever expected. Her moods were still erratic. She could bubble with laughter, her eyes shining with humour and appreciation as they were now. And then she could be morose for days. Sometimes she needed just to sit at her bedroom window. Stress was still dangerous.

When they had returned from Spain, Ginny confronted her

mother in Hull. The letter she had sent ahead of them never arrived, so the conversation began with a series of crossed wires. But Ginny was clear as it went on. The part of Rex's legacy which was left to Meredith would remain Meredith's, she told Nancy. It had been a terrible mistake to seek her out with a hidden agenda – to take her abroad with the undeclared intention of trying to convince her to waive an inheritance she did not even know was hers. So yes, if Meredith wished to cash in her share of the family fortune and cast it across a roulette table, pay dressmakers for a different outfit every day or just spend every penny helping the poor, then she could. And, Ginny told her mother, she should be allowed to do it with their blessing, because surely Rex would have given his?

Nancy had exploded. Ginny expected her mother to be combustible when the subject came up – she had kept Meredith out of the way while the fireworks went off. 'Who even *is* this woman?' had been the worst of it, to which Ginny had softly replied: 'Your late husband's lost daughter.'

She appealed to her mother with the simple truth, 'I can promise you, Mama, that all Meredith wants is love and to belong. And I might remind you that she has no sight.'

Then Nancy did the one thing Ginny had not foreseen: she started to cry. Suddenly Ginny knew it would be all right. She needed her mother not just to accept the difficult fact of the legacy but actively to bless Meredith's presence, to fall in love with this strange misshapen girl just as she had done. Meredith would not recover her sight unless she felt at ease in their house.

'She was not blind when you left England.'

'The story of what happened in Spain is too long for me to tell it now. I will just say, Meredith was a victim of some viciousness out there. We all were, in different ways.'

'I shouldn't cry.'

'It is beautiful to see your compassion, Mama.'

'There is something Meredith must know . . .'

Ginny asked what it was.

'Your father's will bore a sealed memorandum. There was no name upon it. I have opened it. I found only Meredith's name, and three words. "For your dreams", it said. Do they have special meaning?'

'I don't know,' said Ginny, 'but she must see the memorandum herself.' And then Ginny had told her mother everything that had happened to them in Spain. And Meredith was able to rest, and her sight slowly returned. She took a quiet job in a library where she spent all day with her beloved books. 'One day you will work in a gallery again, dear Merry,' said Ginny once, but the thought seemed too difficult for Meredith. As for the money, when Ginny told her more about it – the telling like a second confession, even harder than the first – Meredith seemed baffled by the trouble it had caused. She would not draw on any assets so long as she was in the family home, she said. Only Meredith could say that without it sounding like a mild form of blackmail.

So now they stood there, the four of them, on the top of the cliff where it had all begun. Ginny remembered seeing Adam naked through the greenery. Her heart leapt as she understood fully, in that moment, how much she loved him and how she would do anything, anything in her power, for him and for their son.

And it occurred to her that there were five of them, not four. Not hearing the conversation around her, she picked up Luke's basket. The five of them.

Meredith was holding something in her hand and showing the others.

Saunders jokingly took the two objects and swung them in the air in front of his face.

'Where did you find them, Meredith?'

'Buried,' she said. 'Near your clothes, Adam. I had to do a lot of digging. There was a lot under the ground.'

Ginny felt a chill pass across her shoulders as she focused on the objects.

'What sort of bird is that, anyway?' Saunders asked. 'Splotches of yellow, and a dark back?'

'Canary,' said Ginny.

'I thought they were all yellow.'

'It's a Spanish canary. They have the dark feathers too.'

'Oh,' said Saunders, talking almost to himself. 'Hence the Canary Islands.'

'I've seen these canary earrings before,' said Meredith.

His attention clearly flagging, Saunders said something to Adam that Ginny did not hear. They both laughed. Ginny's eyes were clouding with tears. She touched her sister's arm. 'How long were you digging?'

'Everyone was asleep when I went out.'

'When was that?'

'Hours ago.'

'What else did you find?'

Meredith could not speak.

'What did you find, apart from Adam's clothes?'

'Others,' was all she said.

'Can you show me?'

They walked away from Saunders and Adam, who were still talking. Ginny looked back at them. She caught only one phrase – 'As sorry for what happened as I can ever be, or will ever be' – and guessed this was another apology from the stuntman, because it was delivered with great tenderness and ended with the two men hugging again, Adam desperately unsteady and with one arm still hanging. As the young man leant on his crutch, Saunders unfolded Adam's wheelchair. He steadied it as Adam lowered himself gingerly onto the canvas seat. Then Saunders moved round the back of the chair, took the handles and began to push Adam slowly forwards for a better view of the sea.

Ginny followed Meredith. The sweet smell that she thought might have been flowers became more sickly. Sickening, even. They headed for the forest floor where they had buried Adam's clothes the previous summer. Ginny soon saw the results of Meredith's labour. Over a wide area the soil had been turned. Meredith had not dug a single crater but several individual holes, perhaps no more than a yard square. Each had a mound of fresh soil piled up beside it.

'Where did you find Adam's stuff?' asked Ginny.

'That one.' Meredith pointed. Ginny looked over at the empty hole and remembered their tears and panic that day, and their foolishness, believing the boy was dead.

'The smell is terrible here. Where did you find the earrings?'

'There.' Meredith pointed at a shallower hole, some fifteen feet to the right.

By now Ginny was gagging and reaching for a handkerchief to press to her face. 'Can you tell me what else you found? Did you find the waitress?'

'Waitress?'

'The one who fired on the police. The earrings were hers, she was Maquis.'

Meredith did not seem to have made the connection with the *posada* waitress who fired on the police, but then she had not been with Ginny and Honeyman when it happened, and the events had been lost in the chaos at Dali's house. Ginny pictured the long, sour, chinless face. The look of anger that greeted every order of coffee. She remembered the muzzle-flash at the upstairs window and knew, with absolute certainty, that if this woman's earrings were here, then her body was too, and she would not be alone. She wondered about the Maquis who had invaded Dali's home. At least one had been shot on the spot.

'I don't know if I found the waitress. I found others, I think.' Meredith's eyes were black, the pupils dilated.

'This is where the Maquis end up,' said Ginny, on the verge of tears. 'This is where it ends, with a view of the sea.' She gripped the Moses basket, looked down at Luke. Now she understood something that had eluded her on every day of their visit, and every day since. She could not use her innocence as a shield against truth. She could not ignore the reality of what happened here. This was a place where the sun shone, but the shadows were darker than night.

Franco executed his enemies. In the year since she had first returned from Cadaqués, she had been told that many times. One Sunday, leaving their church in Hull, she had spoken of the beauty of Spain to the priest as he stood in the doorway shaking her hand. The eastern coast of Catalonia, she told the vicar, was one of the most perfect places in the world.

The man had tipped his head quizzically, their hands freezing in the air, mid-shake. 'Janine, I am quite sure you don't mean that.'

'I felt it was perfect.'

'But Franco is a beast. It is a heaven run by the devil. He kills his enemies. Murders them.' The vicar's nostrils flared. He seemed genuinely angry. She left him, shocked and upset by her own naivety.

'Hey!' Saunders was at the edge of the canopy. The sun caught him, just for a second, and Ginny felt again that powerful rush of caring friendship for the older man.

It was Meredith, behind Ginny, who responded. 'We're here.' As if Saunders could not see them.

'Come back to the clifftop, you're going to love this.'

'What's happened?' Ginny was already moving forward, with Luke in her arms.

'Adam got out of his chair. I think he wanted to try those old clothes on, the ones you found for him.'

'They're dirty,' said Meredith, and Ginny thought she would like to wash them a hundred times before Adam wore them, because of what she had just seen in the ground. She held Luke under his bottom and felt the warmth of a nappy that needed changing as she broke into a jog to keep up with the stuntman.

'His leg,' Saunders said breathlessly, 'the damaged one, he's getting some movement back in it, I swear.'

'Really?' asked Ginny, excited.

Meredith wheezed, still too large to move quickly, struggling to keep up. Their feet found the gravel path back to the clifftop.

And then Ginny saw him.

'Stop,' she said suddenly. They all came to a halt.

'What's he doing?' asked Saunders.

'Darling! *No!*' shouted Ginny.

Adam was on the edge of the cliff, naked apart from his underpants. He did not react to Ginny's cry. Or to the obscenity from Saunders which followed. Or to Meredith's scream. He simply turned towards the sea, raised his right arm into the air, and launched himself from the top of the cliff towards the expanse of water below.

EPILOGUE

When the alarm was raised today and I raced to the Dali room, I was not sure what to expect, but I admit I sensed it might involve the old lady. What I saw was horrifying.

She had mounted the painting. Her feet were on the lowest bar of the picture frame. Thank God the wood supported the lady's weight or the whole thing might have come down. When I came in, her arms were spread so her wrinkled and scrawny digits gripped the sides of the picture. This meant her face was buried in the middle of the canvas. The thing was that her position was the very same as Christ's in the painting, almost as if she was trying to embrace him or pass through the canvas and make contact with him. I should point out that I am not spiritual. I immediately shouted to my staff, DO NOT TOUCH HER, DO NOT PULL HER OFF, because I feared her clothes might stick themselves to the canvas and rip it apart as she came back down. For all I knew she might have glued herself to the paint or used hooks.

Two members of staff were crying with shock, not including Tyra Gayle although she had sunk to her knees.

It was an extremely disturbing situation. I quickly appraised that the lady must have found a footstool normally used by cleaners. She would have slid it into position below the painting. She then stepped onto the stool which allowed her to place one foot on the picture frame. Then she must have grabbed each side of the frame by stretching her arms left and right, kicked the stool away and moved her other foot onto the frame.

As I approached the old woman from the side I could see she was weeping.

At this point I said to myself, this is the greatest painting in the world and if it is destroyed it will be a tragedy for many generations. I must act to save the canvas from any more damage.

I called for calm and for all other visitors to be removed, and told Tyra to radio for the gallery to be closed immediately. Then I used Leadership Skills to try to begin a conversation with the old woman. She was squeezing her eyes shut and crying, and it looked like she was in a panic too, because she was shaking.

At this point I feared that the lady's salt tears could interfere with the oils in the painting. I gave Scottie and Morrison (security staff #4 and #17) the order to gently remove the lady by carefully lifting her jacket at the back. That way we could see if she was stuck or hooked into the canvas. It was at this point I saw that her right shoe had penetrated the lowest edge of the painting. I noticed that she had tiny feet and I admit I shouted, 'Jesus Christ' when I saw the shoe.

We all stopped what we were doing immediately. The old woman was still half attached to the painting. It was at this moment that she started screaming.

The rest of today's events are a matter of public record because of the arrival of the emergency services, at which point I stepped back, and latterly accepted suspension pending this inquiry. I contend and argue that the gallery staff did all they could to protect the painting both before and after the attack. However, if there is responsibility to be assigned for a lapse, I should be personally accountable and not junior staff, especially not Ms Gayle, who I believe has been off work herself with stress because of wrongful feelings of responsibility. I have no further defence for my actions other than what I have set out in this statement today.

Mr Craig F. Maskell, security guard (senior)
Kelvingrove Art Gallery and Museum

Maskell wished he had worn his tie with his uniform. A tie would make him look more official. But the tie said 'Kelvingrove' and that was not appropriate. This was not the gallery. This was the hospital.

He was searching for AA4 but was not sure how to find it. Was AA4 a whole floor or a zone within a floor? The hospital had directions on the walkways, walls and ceilings, colour codes with letters and numbers, arrows and circles underfoot, but they bamboozled him. Out of sheer stubborn pride he was reluctant to retrace his steps to reception. So he turned left and right, and span on a heel with such efficiency he found himself thinking a random thought about dance steps. Well, a person living alone could fall prey to all kinds of silly private indulgences.

The hospital corridors were full of light from unusually intense sunshine that bathed the city today. The rays poured in through the long procession of lead-lined windows above him. Embarrassingly, Maskell's uniform confused several hospital visitors, who approached to ask where this or that ward was. He did not have the honesty to tell them he didn't know. Instead he directed people left and right, guessing as he went along. He never told them he was lost himself.

Eventually Craig Maskell arrived at the reception desk of zone AA4 and found the sign above it was marked GERONTOLOGY. There was no nurse at the desk, which was a stroke of luck, because he did not know the name of the lady he was looking for. He only knew one thing: Glasgow Royal Infirmary, AA4.

He found the ward and walked through it. There were two men and eight women, all so aged that their flesh hung off their faces. Their mouths drooped slack, showing rude gaps for teeth. Heads lolled on stacks of pillows, eyes closed or unseeing. *Please God*, he thought, *never let me get like this.*

Maskell did not recognise the lady among these people.

About to give up, Maskell noticed a door ajar at the end of the ward. His view of what was inside was blocked by what he saw, as he approached, was the back of a man wearing a tweed jacket.

Maskell knocked. The tweed moved, forwards and a little to the side. It was a gentleman perhaps a few years younger than him, tall and well groomed, the jacket a perfect fit around his chest and waist. He now saw the figure in the bed.

It was her. The woman.

Craig Maskell's immediate thought, as he entered the private room, was that she looked better than every other patient on the ward. Although she was thin, her face still had shape and character. Her eyes opened a little wider when he entered. He turned to the man, suddenly forgetting what it was he had intended to say.

'Ah. We were expecting a nurse,' said the man without rancour, dropping a mobile phone into his jacket pocket. 'We have been put in this room, and I thought it was a better place for her, because it's private. But I think she may be being ignored a little. I need to ask about her medications.'

'That's not me, sadly, sir,' said Craig Maskell. He reached out his right hand and said his name.

The man fixed him with intelligent eyes. As they shook, he responded: 'I'm Luke Bannerman.'

'Is she your mother?' asked Maskell, his curiosity intense now.

The other man regarded him politely before responding. Maskell was jealous, in that instant, of the shape of his body, of his extra height, of the way his waist did not sag over his belt and there was no spare fold of skin around his neck or under his jaw. The fellow's hair was full, too, unlike his own; his mop of brown was turning only slowly to grey. He would like to have a friend like this, thought the security guard sadly. But he knew he never would have a friend like this because he was just a grunt, just a paunch in middle age who stopped the exhibits in a gallery being damaged, and if he had had one job it was to protect the Dali, and he had not even managed to stop an OAP from mounting the painting and riding it like a twenty-five-year-old.

'I feel I should ask who you are,' said Luke Bannerman, smiling, 'before I answer that. Data protection and so on.'

'I am a security guard at the Kelvingrove,' said Maskell, and as soon as he heard the sentence come from his mouth, far blunter than he meant it to sound, he silently cursed. Luke Bannerman's smile immediately vanished. He looked at Maskell's uniform as if it all suddenly made sense.

'No, please,' Maskell said, 'it's not what you think.'

'I can't have you guys invading this place and bullying her! I know what she did was wrong, but there's all kinds of—'

He stopped. Both men turned. In the bed, the old woman was signalling with her left hand and saying something.

'Auntie Meredith, sorry, I didn't mean to raise my voice like that.' Bannerman moved round the bed and pulled up a chair.

Meredith. Maskell had not known her name. Standing at the end of the bed, looking down at the old woman and her middle-aged nephew, he wished he had not come.

'Auntie,' Bannerman said, 'Ola will be here soon, and the boys. They want to see you.'

Her voice would not come the first time, and the words emerged as a croak. Then, with effort, she pushed up her chin. 'Am I in trouble?' She sounded like a child.

Slowly, Luke turned to Maskell. He stared at the security guard as if wanting him to answer the question. 'Is she?'

'Can I be honest?' asked Craig Maskell.

'I don't know,' said Luke Bannerman, but there was no edge. 'Don't get yourself into difficulty, Mr Maskell. And please don't worry her. Just say whatever you can to help. Pull up a chair. She won't mind me telling you, she is not a very well lady. Are you, dear Auntie?'

'I am sorry to hear that,' said Maskell. 'I did suspect it.'

'If you can talk off the record and reassure her, it would help. I'm going to trust you.'

Maskell slid a chair to the side of the bed. As he sat, he spoke only to Meredith. 'I don't know you, madam. I certainly don't want my presence today to worry you. I wore the uniform, to be honest, only so I could get here without being stopped on my way to the ward. There's been an inquiry at the Kelvingrove. The police let the gallery know that you had been hospitalised, which is how I knew where to find you. They have interviewed me. They are looking for advice on whether to prosecute. I was concerned. I happen to know—'

He was reaching for a piece of paper in his pocket, but Luke Bannerman interrupted. 'Why would she be prosecuted? It's 2001, for heaven's sake. Eh, Auntie? You've had such a long life.' He turned to Maskell again. 'She was born in 1915. She went through the Second World War. She has spent most of her life with terrible mental health problems.' Once again he turned to Meredith. 'I am so sorry to speak about you so openly here, Auntie, but it's important I share this.' She nodded as if it was a formality she had to go through. He lowered his voice. Still he did not show anger, only urgency. 'The poor lady. Never married, no children, undiagnosed schizophrenia and BPD, you know, bipolar. The full English. So she gets consumed by things. "When sorrows come, they come not single spies, but in battalions." And she's had the battalions. I want you to see that. There was no malice in Auntie that day. A jury wouldn't convict her. She just got obsessed with that painting and she was off her medication, and she saw something in the news that triggered her – oh, I don't even know what it was.' At that, Maskell saw the old woman withdraw her left hand from below the bedsheet. Luke carried on. 'She slips sometimes. I'm in London, we didn't know what was happening until the incident. Which we are *truly* sorry for, as a family.'

Again, Meredith moved her left hand. Now it hovered above the bedsheet.

'Is she pointing?'

Luke looked. 'What is it, Auntie?'

Meredith indicated the floor below the far side of her bed. 'My handbag.'

'I'll get it,' said her nephew. As he moved around the bed, he said: 'She has a bit of a thing about that painting.' He lifted the handbag and placed it gently in front of Meredith, who sat up and started sorting quickly through the contents.

Luke Bannerman lowered his voice. 'She got it into her head that my father is in that painting. When she gets an idea, you can't shake it.'

Maskell could not take his eyes off the old woman's hand,

which now came out of the handbag and began beckoning. 'I think she wants to speak,' Luke said.

'I met Salvador Dali,' the old lady said. 'He painted Luke's father.'

'This again,' murmured Luke.

'It was your father in the painting, Luke, not the stuntman. I'm not being silly.'

'Of course, Auntie, I understand.'

'Madam,' Maskell said, 'I came to say I am going to do everything I can to make sure the police don't become involved. We just need a letter saying you won't come to the gallery again. If I could just get you to sign this.' He produced the piece of paper he had brought with him. Luke took it from Maskell. He thumbed towards the door to indicate that the two men should talk out of earshot.

As they stood just inside the doorway he whispered, 'Look. I appreciate this. It might set her mind at rest. But other family members are on their way. I don't want this all to be about the gallery today. Can I think about it? Bloody hell, the gallery security people should have done better.'

'That was me,' said Maskell hopelessly. He glanced back into the room, seeing Meredith now fishing items out of her handbag and making a small pile on her bed.

Luke apologised with his hands. 'The painting wasn't damaged, was it?'

Here Craig had to lie. So far the gallery had admitted publicly only that there was minimal damage. The artwork was being withdrawn from display temporarily for routine checks. But it most definitely had been damaged. The canvas had been torn around the lowest edge, where Dali had painted the fishermen's boats. The tip of the old lady's right shoe had penetrated just above the frame. Her thumbs had indented the fabric on either side with what restorers called a 'stretch bruise'. It was true that the central part of the painting had been spared despite the old lady's full-body contact with it. But restoration work on the canvas and frame would still take at least eighteen months.

However, all this worked in the old lady's favour. The gallery did not want a court case, because evidence of the precise nature of the damage would be aired in public if there was one. They might not be able to maintain the pretence that very little repair work was needed, but at least they could try. And Maskell would not make things worse by telling the truth now.

'So if it wasn't damaged, what's the charge?' asked Bannerman.

'It would just help if she signed the letter,' Maskell insisted.

'She has terrible delusions and psychoses if she stops her meds,' Bannerman said. 'This story about my father came up out of nowhere. I think she might have been in Spain in the fifties. I don't know. She gets confused. I just wish we'd known she was going into the gallery daily. That's a sign, repetitive behaviour.' He glanced into the room. 'She shouldn't be on this ward. Physically, she's well. But they have to get her back on her medications and stabilise her blood counts before we get her home. I don't know why I'm telling you all this. I guess I'm hoping you can plead her case with the gallery.' He took the piece of paper from Maskell. 'Yes, I will most definitely ensure this is signed. I feel –' he paused, checked Maskell's face – 'yes, I know I can trust you.'

'Is your mother still alive?'

'She's younger. Yes. She lives in Hull. She's on her way up now with my siblings to see Auntie – she's always been devoted to her.'

A thought was forming in Maskell's brain. He was remembering a particular instant before the attack on the painting. The tour with Tyra Gayle. Meeting Stella. And behind them,

Meredith trying to prise the gallery label from the wall. What did the label say?

Bannerman was looking at his mobile. 'I can't get this damn thing to beep when a text comes in. I think they're here.'

Maskell made to leave, suddenly self-conscious. Luke Bannerman unintentionally blocked his way, opening the door and saying to whoever was approaching: 'I only just saw the message!'

Suddenly the room was crowded. Craig Maskell had to endure himself being described as the person who had found Meredith, the generous soul now trying to help her. He was introduced to at least ten people, including Luke's brother, Luke's teenage children and his brother's wife. One of the teens was a goth. Another had come with a boyfriend, or so it seemed. There were two tiny babies, whom he guessed might even be twins. 'I hope it's visiting time,' someone said as they all made a fuss of the old lady in the bed.

Sunlight broke into the room and suddenly Meredith looked all her years and more, her skin drawn and papery. The contents of her handbag were still spread across the bed cover. Maskell noticed for the first time the battery of drugs on the bedside table. He was being asked about the gallery, about the incident, the painting, and Luke was politely requesting that the visitors not discuss it too loudly because it might upset his aunt.

'Does she live up here?' Maskell asked Luke's wife.

'She moved to Glasgow a while back, into some sheltered living. Perhaps we shouldn't have let her, but she wants to live her life, you know?'

The whole family seemed aware of Meredith's mental disorder, the trauma-associated blindness which had once afflicted her, the long stays in hospital in the fifties and sixties, and then the period of stability made possible through electro-convulsive therapy and new medications, which allowed Meredith to have a good career in a public library and take a degree in art history.

'Where's Mum?' asked Bannerman at one point.

'Ola's in the car park with her.'

Craig Maskell saw Luke's wife had left the room. He warmed to this family. They had made trips from all over the country – London, Hull, Cornwall – to be here with a lady who was no one's mother herself. Like Meredith, Maskell had never married, but he did not have a reserve army of loving relatives like this. For a second he imagined he was part of a family this large, this loving. Even the youngsters seemed cultivated and kind. He wondered what Meredith's sister would be like.

He stared out of the window, five floors above the car park, as the conversation went on around him. Below, he saw Luke's wife emerge from a temporary exit and assumed the car she was walking towards was driven by Meredith's sister. Luke appeared at Maskell's shoulder as he watched. 'There's always a problem with ticket machines with Mum. Will you stay and meet her? I hope you know how much we all appreciate what you've done.'

'What's your mother's name?'

'Janine. Everyone calls her Ginny.'

Maskell said no more. He was watching the car far below, thinking from the outline it was an Audi of some kind, certainly not a new one. An old woman stepped out of the vehicle. She had thrown her arms wide, as if explaining something to Ola. 'Oh dear,' sighed Luke good-humouredly. He pulled out the pocket phone which looked small in his hand and prodded at the buttons. Maskell did not have one of these new devices, and he was still bowled over that a person in a high-rise hospital room could just ring his wife in the car park below. 'What's happening down there?' Luke asked into the mobile, listening to the response. 'Oh, it's probably still in the machine. She did this before. Have a look, or do you want me to come down?'

Maskell watched as, five floors below them, Ola relayed the message to Ginny. The older lady bent down to the car window and said something into it. The passenger door flew open and a man stepped out.

'Dad to the rescue,' said Bannerman.

The man jogged with lopsided speed back to the ticket machine. He must have found the ticket, because he waved it above him and jogged back to the two women in seconds, moving between the parked cars.

'Paralympian, back in the day,' said Luke with a proud smile.

'I should leave now,' said Maskell, feeling awkward.

'At least meet my mum,' said Luke. 'She will want to thank you. Hey, Susan, where are you going? Susan is my little sister,' he explained.

'See Grandma and Pa,' said Susan in a baby voice, holding two infants in her arms, 'aren't we?'

From the bed, Meredith said: 'Is Ginny here?' She seemed brighter. She used her elbows to raise herself. Relatives pushed pillows behind her.

The goth teenager said, far more politely than Maskell would have expected: 'Here, Great-Auntie Meredith, let me tidy your handbag up, it's all spilled.'

Meredith said: 'Is she coming?' Her voice actually had laughter in it. 'Show her this!' And she lifted a folded piece of paper from the bed cover before her young relative removed it. Despite peering, Maskell could not see what it was.

He watched Susan and the children emerge in the car park. The Audi was parked. Luke's mother took one child, his father another.

'They make a lovely couple, don't they,' Luke said.

'The babies?'

'Well, of course! But I was thinking of my parents. They've been together a long time, my mum and dad, since 1951. Fifty years this year.'

'Your dad looks lively.'

'He has the most positive, generous spirit of any man I've ever met. The kids love him. His stories. He used to dive competitively, despite being disabled.'

At Luke's shoulder a teenage girl appeared. 'Tell him the hair story, Dad.'

'Hair story?' Luke repeated.

'The beetroot.'

'He used to rub it in his hair because of saltwater damage, or sun, or something.'

'That's not much of a story, you just destroyed it,' giggled Luke's daughter. She walked away.

'You know,' he said quietly to Maskell, 'I have no idea where this idea of Meredith's about the painting would have come from. It's sad, to see the way mental illness works. And the worst thing is that you end up humouring the fantasy. So we say, "Yes, of course he was the model for Dali's Christ."'

'The model for it was actually a movie guy,' said Maskell neutrally. 'The name will come to me.' In that instant, a phrase from the gallery label appeared in his mind with blinding clarity: *He was actually strapped to a gantry to help Dali envisage the pull of gravity on the body.*

Luke's phone vibrated. 'This is a modern marriage,' he said. 'We ring each other from car parks instead of actually meeting. Hello, darling.' He listened. '*What?* Both of them? I'm looking now. Oh God, I see!' Again, he listened. 'Okay, take your time.'

The room had thinned out a little because a number of the relatives had gone downstairs to greet the newcomers. 'This shouldn't be funny,' Luke said, 'but it is. Dad takes Susan's twins and they vomit on him.'

'Och, no! Stereo vomit.'

'Double trouble. Technicolor.'

The party was making its way back into the hospital now. The first to arrive in the room were Ola and Ginny, with the younger relatives bringing up the rear. Meredith smiled and reached out her arms from the bed, the folded piece of paper still in her hand. The two sisters hugged.

Craig watched, envious. If only he had had a sister or a brother.

Luke introduced him to his mother. She might be in her seventies, thought Craig, but she had the most beautiful face and kind eyes. 'Craig is from the gallery,' Luke explained. 'He's trying to help us.'

Her head tilted. 'I am so sorry for what happened. I've read so much about it. I was dreading that the painting was damaged, but they are saying it wasn't?'

'Well – fortunately, that's right.'

'Craig had some advice to help us,' said Luke.

'I feel so sorry for the gentleman who's been sent home,' said Ginny. 'I saw it in the papers.'

'That'll be me,' said the security guard.

'Oh! My big mouth.'

'You weren't to know, madam – oh, look, I think your sister wants to show you something.'

Ginny turned. 'Merry, darling, what is it?'

Meredith was on her side in the bed now, up on an elbow, reaching forward with the folded piece of paper in her hand. She passed it to Ginny wordlessly. Four or five separate conversations were going on in the room, but Craig Maskell stayed focused on the interaction between the two sisters.

Slim, wearing a narrow fleece under a brown leather jacket,

Ginny sat in the narrow space at the edge of her sister's bed. Maskell noticed with what kindness the younger woman bent her head towards her sister as she unfolded the paper. Ginny wore thick glasses. Her blond bob showed grey at the roots – but with that long, unlined neck the lady was still youthful even though she must be long past sixty. And Maskell could see she was upset. 'Oh, oh,' Ginny said several times as she looked at the paper. 'Oh dear. When was this?' She had clearly found the answer in the document. 'Ah, now I understand all this. I'm sorry, Merry. We shouldn't have left you to deal with this on your own.'

Maskell was desperate to see what was on the paper, but the single sheet was tucked between the two sisters. Meredith was staring up at her sister's face with a look that was almost beseeching. Ginny just kept shaking her head. She handed the piece of paper back to her sister. Luke had approached Maskell silently and startled him when he spoke. 'Hey, my best friend is an employment lawyer and he will represent you if you've got trouble at the gallery,' said Luke. 'We will fight this.'

This helped put Maskell's mind more at ease, but still something gnawed at him. The image of Meredith pulling at the label on the wall beside the painting. What did it mean? Where had her fantasy come from? What was on the piece of paper Ginny was now holding with such focus?

And beetroot.

Beetroot.

'Where is Dad?' Luke asked Ginny.

'Probably looking for a shirt, after what the twins did.'

'Come on, Mr Maskell,' Luke said. 'I'll show you downstairs. I am sure we've used up enough of your time. Auntie, can you say goodbye to Mr Maskell?' They walked up to her bedside.

He realised he did not want to leave. He moved closer to Meredith as Luke guided him to the door.

'Just to give you my good wishes,' he said stiffly to the woman in the bed. 'I think you and I both have special feelings for that painting. I won't trouble you further.'

This prompted Luke to speak, as if he had nearly forgotten the purpose of Maskell's visit. 'Well, look, we certainly do trust you, Mr Maskell. Meredith, the gentleman has given me a letter for you to sign. To reassure the gallery. I'm going to suggest you should. I think we have a man of honour here.'

Meredith moved her body in the bed, reaching for the sheet of paper Maskell had given Luke. Maskell took out his pen – and Meredith, lacking a free hand, instinctively passed the folded paper she was holding to the security guard.

She spread the letter on her lap. Pulling a pair of glasses from the bedside table, Meredith marked it with her signature – barely a squiggle, the pen hardly pressing the page.

Then she fixed Maskell with her gaze. 'The artist made him a cripple. But it was not Russell's fault, not at all.' Her sentences had blinding clarity.

'Russell?' said Maskell.

Luke whispered, 'We just have to humour this, I'm afraid.'

But Meredith was saying, 'See,' pointing at the folded sheet now in Maskell's hands, which he took as permission to open it and look.

Luke murmured kindly, 'I think it's time for you to sleep.'

Maskell saw he was holding a faxed news article. An obituary. The headline was: RUSSELL M. SAUNDERS, STUNTMAN IN MOVIES, IS DEAD AT 82. The date was 17 June 2001, and at the top of the page it said *New York Times*.

'I got it sent to the library.'

'Where she works,' said Luke, unnecessarily, now almost pulling on Maskell's upper arm to get him to come.

'The day before,' Maskell remarked softly. 'The day before

you started visiting us. Now I understand, perhaps. The model. I know the name, of course. The man on the gantry. The man in the painting.'

Meredith's eyes suddenly widened and she reached out. 'No! That was my sister's husband. They broke him for that painting.' She added again, 'It wasn't Russell's fault.'

Maskell frowned. Luke laughed. Ginny moved past them, towards Meredith. 'Ssshh, my darling. Adam has had a wonderful life. And he is still having it! He became a father of three beautiful children, your nephews. And we don't need to mind any more about it.'

'But Russell,' said Meredith.

Ginny repeated: 'But Russell.'

'Did he?'

'Did he what?'

'Have a wonderful life too?'

'I honestly believe he did.'

Ginny was clearly not expecting anyone to hear that last exchange. But when she glanced up and saw the security guard looking over his shoulder at the two sisters, she blanched in surprise.

Maskell felt the room swim. He followed Luke to the door, only half aware of members of the family saying goodbye to him and thanking him for his help. 'Let's see if we can find Dad,' said Luke.

They exited the ward full of geriatric patients and passed down a long corridor with a stairwell at the end. Maskell still felt dizzy. 'You okay, Dad?' Luke called.

'One at a time,' replied a voice tinged with an American accent from the bottom of the stairs.

'He finds the stairs a little tricky,' Luke told Maskell. 'He's seventy now, you know.'

'I'll give you seventy of the best if you say my age again,' said the voice.

'You need a shirt, Dad,' said Luke. 'You can't wander a hospital topless.'

'I've been told there'll be one in Meredith's ward,' came the cheerful voice. 'You don't want to see the state of the shirt I took off. The twins absolutely covered it.'

Luke moved aside so Maskell could look down the stairwell to see who he was addressing.

The head of the figure below was bowed. The arms stretched left and right to the banisters. The body was naked from the waist up, the torso packed with muscle. He recognised every sinew. He recognised the shape of the shoulders and the head. He knew the line of the chest and the ridges in the hands. He saw, or thought he saw, the hint of the purple in the hair.

He saw in that moment the Christ of Saint John of the Cross.

Craig Maskell's blood ran cold. As he blinked, he felt his lips shape the words: *I believe that you are the Christ, the Son of the Living God.*

Then he said goodbye, shaking the old man's hand on his way past, and headed out into the afternoon.

Russell M. Saunders, Stuntman in Movies, Is Dead at 82

By DOUGLAS MARTIN

Russell M. Saunders, whose daring stunts as more than 100 movies overshadowed even his acrobatic antics in Santa Monica's fabled Muscle Beach, died on May 29 at a nursing home in West Los Angeles. He was 82.

Doubling for actors like Alan Ladd, Gene Kelly, Red Buttons and Jack Benny, Mr. Saunders literally threw himself onto the profession of appearing to risk his life, sometimes bringing that appearance perilously close to reality.

Once when doubling for Richard Widmark, he jumped off a 50-foot cliff and broke his arm so badly on a rock in the water that he could never fully straighten it again. His partners in subsequent acrobatic acts had to learn to perform with one crooked arm to preserve the all-important symmetry.

He did Ladd's famous tight scene in "Shane" in 1953, jumped off a 60-foot bridge for Robert Cummings as "Saboteur" in 1942, and was the agile figure leaping from rooftop to rooftop at the 1948 version of "The Three Musketeers." That ended with his catching a waving flag that

An acrobat who performed at Muscle Beach and in more than 100 films.

ripped, then swinging on its shreds onto an open window.

Fay Alexander, the great circus acrobat who himself doubled for Tony Curtis and Dave Day in circus moves, said that performance was the greatest move stunt he ever saw. Mr. Alexander, who died last year, called Mr. Saunders "without a doubt the best all-around acrobat I've ever known."

He certainly had the right look. Salvador Dali used the perfectly proportioned acrobat as a model for his painting "The Christ of St. John," making him what fellow stuntmen delighted in calling the ultimate double.

Indeed, other stuntmen, many of whom learned their skills from him, praised Mr. Saunders's often breath-

taking skills. Brayton Yerkes called him flamboyant, and "the best all-around stuntman I've known."

Another stuntman, Gary Morgan, lauded Mr. Saunders's ability to emulate an actor's precise mannerisms, down to the peculiarities of his walk. Mr. Morgan, who learned the tricks of the trade from Mr. Saunders, remembered him working on several movies at the same time on the MGM lot: diving through a window for one picture immediately doing a fight scene in another and then racing off to do acrobatics for Gene Kelly.

"He sometimes got four checks in a day," marveled Mr. Morgan, who got his first job through Mr. Saunders and whom own most recent stunt work was for the coming film "Rush Hour II."

Mr. Morgan pointed out that stuntmen used to face far greater dangers than they do today, when they can use supporting wires that can be digitally removed from the film.

Russell Maurice Saunders was born on a farm outside Winnipeg, Manitoba, on May 21, 1918. One youngest of eight children. His father was a farmer and railroad worker

His only immediate survivors are two sisters, Eden Hall of Penticton, British Columbia, and Dove Sanders of Newport Beach, Calif.

His future was foreshadowed when, as a very young boy, he jumped off the barn, cradling two chickens, sure that they would enable him to fly. An older sister who worked as a cashier at the local movie house let him in free. He hung around circuses.

He went to a summer camp specializing in acrobatics and began to develop skills that propelled him to Canadian championships in diving and gymnastics. He tried to enlist in the Canadian Air Force, but was rejected because he was color-blind.

He then moved to California, where one of her sisters was living. He thought he might go to college, but got only as far as making friends with the diving coaches at the University of Southern California. The University of California at Los Angeles, who helped him find jobs in water shows, one of which starred Bing Crosby.

During World War II, he volunteered to serve in the United States Army as a paratrooper, but was later assigned to an Armed Force Aquacade in England.

Soon after his arrival in California, he heard of Muscle Beach, then a platform just south of the pier in Santa Monica, where the great acrobats came to practice and show off their skills. The same home of body builders like Jack La Lanne, another admirer.

Mr. Saunders refused to lift weights. "He said he'd rather lift girls than weights," Mr. Morgan said.

Among his achievements on Muscle Beach was unremarking over 14 people who were standing side by side and bending over.

He also became so well known as a generous teacher who never charged for his considerable expertise that some called the beach Russell Beach, Mr. Saunders said

Even after the platform that defined Muscle Beach was torn down in 1959 because the city thought of moral censory crowds, he continued to

Russell M. Saunders performing at a resort near Palm Springs, Calif., in 1948. "He said he'd rather lift girls than weights," a friend recalled.

take his own equipment, including trampolines and teeterboards, to the beach to teach children. He called his trainees Muscle Beach Acrobats.

"This has to be the only place in the world where someone can just walk up and receive free gymnastic instruction from pros," he said at an interview with The Los Angeles Times in 1986.

Mr. Morgan and Mr. Saunders

was offered chances to move up in the movie business, including as offer to direct. But he never accepted a directing job, though he was often confined with Russell Saunders, a well-known assistant director, who died in 1987.

"Russ was like a big kid," Mr. Morgan said. "He didn't want to interfere with anything that would interfere with him having fun"

Bernard Strehler, 76; Studied the Causes of Aging

By WOLFGANG SAXON

Dr. Bernard Louis Strehler, a biochemist and gerontologist who investigated and described the physical causes of aging, died on May 13 at a nursing home in Agoura, Calif. He was 76.

The cause was a stroke, said the University of Southern California, where Dr. Strehler taught from 1967 to 1980.

He made his mark as a biogerontologist with the publication of "Time, Cells and Aging" in 1962

Dr. Strehler began his career by studying photosynthesis and bioluminescence. As a graduate student at Oak Ridge National Laboratory in Tennessee, he helped solve the puzzle of what makes fireflies glow

He needed thousands of living specimens in the laboratory, so he paid children to catch fireflies for a quarter per hundred. By extracting from them a known substance, luciferin, he traced the process by which the insects produced it.

Dr. Strehler and a fellow researcher, William Arnold, established in 1951 that all green plants are bioluminescent as a result of the first steps in photosynthesis. That finding prompted the University of Chicago to recruit him as an assistant professor of biochemistry.

In 1956, he joined the National Institutes of Health, where he was in charge of cellular research at the institutes' gerontology center at Baltimore. He was appointed a professor of biology at the University of Southern California in 1967. He organized and directed the university's Andrus Gerontology Center.

Born in Johnstown, Pa., he was a 1947 cell biology graduate of Johns Hopkins University, where he received a doctorate on the subject three years later.

Hot wife, Theodora, died three years ago. His survivors include two daughters, Jan and Patricia, and a son, Bernard.

"My view of aging is those things that go wrong when cells lose their ability to divide," Dr. Strehler said in a 1981 interview. "If we could replace our cells as rapidly as they deteriorate, we could probably live very long, if not indefinitely."

The New York Times   For home delivery call 1-800-NYTIMES

ACKNOWLEDGEMENTS

I wouldn't have been able to write a word of this without Hannah, Kerr and Rachel. You'll see the dedication at the front of the book to Rachel, my wife; Kerr MacRae is my book agent, a great guy who brilliantly turned his book-loving circle of friends in Kent into a formidable Salvador Dali focus group which helped me no end. Hannah is my editor at Hodder who brings a new meaning to multitasking and whose understanding of my fascination with the Dali painting was something I was so touched by.

Also at Hodder: Emma Knight and Helen Flood, and Lucy Hale who was among the first to read my manuscript. Not forgetting Alasdair Oliver and Erika Koljonen. Thank you.

Also at home: Martha and Anna. I love you girls. You are always streets ahead.